BONAIRE BLONDE

BONAIRE BLONDE

A TAMPA BAY TROPICS THRILLER

GEORGE L. FLEMING

ST. PETERSBURG PRESS

Published by St. Petersburg Press

St. Petersburg, FL

www.stpetersburgpress.com

Design and composition by St. Petersburg Press

Cover design by St. Petersburg Press and Isa Crosta

Paperback ISBN: 978-1-964239-22-4

eBook ISBN: 978-1-964239-23-1

First Edition

❀ Created with Vellum

LINDA'S DISCO DEDICATION

I'll always treasure the night of January 31, 1976, when we danced like Travolta and Donna Summer beneath The Courthouse Disco's groovy mirror ball in Clearwater, Florida.

Yes, we danced as if this were our last dance, our last chance, for true romance.

We kissed for the first time. Your lips were like pink satin pillows. You tasted of an exotic nectar more fitting for Zeus than for this mortal upstart.

We fell in love for the last time.

I love you now and forever, my Wild Irish Rose.

Forword

I am humbled and honored to have been asked by my dear friend
George L. Fleming to write the foreword to his latest novel, *Bonaire
Blonde.* I had the pleasure of reading every chapter before St. Pete Press
editor Amy Cianci took command of the manuscript. I hope that that
fact, and our occasional discussions and disagreements about the book,
qualify me to write the foreword and to introduce you to this wonderful
novel.

An origin tale filled with murder, mayhem and romance, *Bonaire
Blonde* tells the story of Jake Dupree and Reed O'Hara's meeting for the
first time in 2014. There also is a separate, present-day storyline that
trades chapters with the origin narrative, where the couple attempts to
solve the murder of a troubled young woman in present day Tampa Bay.

I first met George in an ancient salsa club in Cartagena, Columbia.
It was deadly dark inside the club and raining los gatos y los perros
outside that evening. I sensed it might be safer in the perilous streets of
the five-century-old Barrio Viejo than inside this seedy dance hall.

George was cleaning a .357 Magnum handgun with a war-torn rag
when my femme fatale Jackie and I sat down across from him.

"Hello, pilgrim," George said to me.

I knew right then George and I would become the best of friends. I smiled and slid my Browning 9mm pistol across the table to him. He slowly pushed his Magnum across the table to me.

"Mine's bigger," he growled.

We then got into animated discussions about world events, politics and favorite writers.

George and I discovered a mutual interest in writing. It was the start of a beautiful friendship.

I feel as if I've gotten to know the main characters in *Bonaire Blonde*, Reed O'Hara and Jake Dupree. I met them first in book one of George's Tampa Bay Tropics Thriller series, *Bad Habits*.

I also met Ravel, another recurring character. Please keep it to yourself, gentle reader, but I developed a crush on her that has grown with each novel.

George followed *Bad Habits* with *Don Coyote*, then *Nevermore*, with *Bonaire Blonde* being the fourth novel in the series. He has more on the way, but I'm not at liberty to discuss them. All right, fine: rumor has it, from a reliable though sometimes mercurial source, that George's next novel will be *Everything's Jake*. You didn't hear that from me.

Each of these first four novels has cleverly hidden "Easter eggs," direct references and wispy allusions woven into the fabric of the story, some of which I picked up on immediately, others I know I missed entirely. This is one of many qualities in his novels we can enjoy, while being engaged in the story itself.

And now for your reading pleasure, here's *Bonaire Blonde: A Tampa Bay Tropics Thriller*.

Randy Sexton, author of *Reachable Moments*

In fact, she wanted to run away ninety miles north to Florida . . .
home to the panhandle dubbed ""LA" or "Lower Alabama,"
an unabashedly phallic capitol building among
Tallahassee's Seven Hills of Rome,
casinos, bingo! and pink flamingos,
the Big Mousetrap in burnt orange Orlando,
the tropical paradise of Gulf Coast's Tampa Bay,
moonshots over Cape Canaveral,
the Golden Triangle of antiqued
Mt. Dora, Eustis & Umatilla,
the sun-soaked lunatic asylum AKA Miami,
the string of pearls that is
the Conch Republic of
the enigmatic
Florida
Keys.

Chapter 1

Tampa, Florida · 2022

"Brando rode a Triumph!" were Cuban dancer Alicia Serrano's last words before three rounds from a Smith & Wesson 500 Magnum revolver tore into her body front and center.

Despite her wrong-side-up horseshoe of a life, Alicia didn't anticipate her being murdered at four a.m. on Lois Avenue in Tampa. In fact, she was close to resolving a dangerous case of divided loyalties. Alas, she was only *close* to tossing a ringer, and "close" doesn't get you a big-ring Cohiba cigar.

A twenty-one-year-old expatriate from Santiago de Cuba, Alicia was a popular performer at Namaste nightclub in West Tampa. Hispanics flocked to Namaste to savor the Latina's sensual, authentic dance performances. Anglos especially were taken with Alicia's exquisite renditions of salsa, rumba, soca & mambo dancing.

"Nunca dejes de aprender, nunca dejes de ser la mejor," Alicia chanted before every performance. "Never stop learning, never stop being the best."

Ever since she was a young girl, she devoted herself to dancing. Her time in the studio and at school was a fifty/thirty split, with the remaining twenty percent devoted to eating, bathing and sleeping at home.

As a teen, Alicia had no interest in boys and booze and bonfire beach parties.

For her, dance was her only religion.

"And I'm never gonna lose it," she often told her parents.

But life's distractions and temptations have a nasty way of interrupting dreams, sacred, profane or slouching in purgatory.

Trouble started for Alicia when she first swung a leg over her ancient, intermittently reliable, German MZ 5M125 motorcycle with a four-valve, single-cylinder engine. A motorcycle was an affordable way to get around Santiago. However, the MZ broke down too often, and she knew nada about motorcycle mechanics.

By coincidence or by plan, she befriended a thirty-year-old woman who was a motorcycle gearhead. Obsessed with hip-hop diva Queen Latifah, the woman demanded she be addressed as "Reina LaTina" in Spanish, or "Queen LaTina" in English. Alicia would learn later that calling her "Tina" was a guaranteed express-lane beat down.

Alicia and Queen LaTina became fast and furious friends.

What little free time Alicia had was spent at her friend's garage watching the older, more mechanically inclined, woman take apart a motorcycle, then carefully & confidently put it back together, as if she were constructing in a glass bottle Hemingway's fishing boat *The Pilar*.

Queen LaTina, in turn, visited Alicia's dance studio to observe the now eighteen-year-old's dance routines.

Like a lit tapered candle whose flame fluttered perilously, this all-too-brief time in Alicia's young life was a period where things were more than all right for her.

The flame blew out on a sunny Saturday in Santiago de Cuba when Queen LaTina took an imperious tone with Alicia.

"Mi querida, you're so busy with the dancing, and you're progressing so very well," Queen LaTina exclaimed.

Humph, here it comes, Alicia thought.

"But I want you to join my BarraCubas Motorcycle Club. I am club president, the only one who chooses recruits. I choose you."

"Aren't the BarraCubas a biker gang?" Alicia asked. "And all women, sí?"

"We prefer 'club,' y claro, si no hay los pitos o los carajos o las bananas, no hay las problemas."

Alicia completely agreed with Queen LaTina: boys and their pet penises were nothing but trouble.

She bit her lower lip, then said, "Aren't the BarraCubas criminals?"

"Of course we are, proud of it," Queen LaTina answered. "We take from the rich and give to the poor, who happens to be *us*, our club, our families, our friends. Only way to survive on the Island of the Beard."

"I don't know if I could do that," Alicia said.

Her friend smiled menacingly, then lasered dark brown eyes at Alicia.

"This isn't an invitation, idiota pequena. Your choice: join or die. Don't be like that foolish girl who turned us down last month. You want to talk with Camila, go find her at Santa Iphigenia Cemetery."

Alicia chose to dance another day.

After the mandatory beat-in, where she earned a black eye, two forearm hematomas and sore buttocks for her troubles, Alicia joined the BarraCubas.

Queen LaTina promptly took away Alicia's MZ motorcycle. In its place, she gave Alicia a Baby Harley Super 10.

Having finished her primary education, Alicia focused solely on dancing. She transformed herself into a focused, disciplined and physically powerful young woman, which was exactly what the BarraCubas sought in her.

For the next three years, on every Saturday evening, Alicia posed as an attractive, yet affordable, sex worker to European and Scandinavian tourists, including poseur London EastEnders, Euro-pinching Parisians, bawdy Bauhaus Berliners and young Swedes who couldn't fjord uber upscale sex workers back home in Stockholm.

She rarely had sex with her dates. She never allowed the marks to kiss her on the mouth. She expected them to buy her dinner and provide her with a small gift. When the talk came up of going to a hotel motel holiday sin, she usually said no, no, no. Instead, she maneuvered the marks to a Plaza de Marte or a Plaza de Dolores alleyway, claiming she preferred sex standing up while enjoying the night air.

Alicia and two other BarraCubas then pounced on these men,

ordering them to disrobe at knifepoint. The men gave up cash, jewelry and passports.

As foreign sex tourists engaging in illegal activity with Cuban sex workers, the victims didn't seek out assistance from law enforcement.

Alicia always received her cut of the gelt from plaza take-downs.

In three years, she amassed enough savings to leave Cuba, which was her plan all along.

Don't see how Florida can get any crazier than Cuba, Alicia foolishly thought.

Her plan was simple: journey to Tampa Bay, then jump-start her career as a professional dancer.

Queen LaTina reluctantly gave Alicia permission to leave Cuba. Reluctantly, because the beautiful young woman was the most sedulous earner on the Santiago plazas.

"I have one requirement before you abandon us," Queen LaTina said, as she rubbed her temples and ran her hands through long raven-black hair. "You must agree, Alicia, to join the BarraCubas' Tampa chapter."

Alicia was crushed.

"Why, why, can't I be free of Cuba and free of the BarraCubas? Why can't I just dance?"

"What, you think you could escape Cuba *and* the BarraCubas? There's no room for negotiation. Join the Tampa sisters or we'll hunt you down, break your ankles and slice your face. You'll never dance again, because everyone will laugh at your Noriega pineapple face. Even those titty bars in Tampa, they won't want you. What's it gonna be?"

Tears tumbled down Alicia's cheeks.

"Will there be another beat-in?" she asked.

"Claro, pobrecita. Tampa will want to see if you're tough enough."

Within two weeks of arriving in Tampa, a politically asylumed Alicia found a small apartment in West Tampa and employment as a performer at Namaste, a nightclub owned jointly by Tampa attorney Reed O'Hara and her husband Jake Dupree.

Because Namaste employees were banned from openly associating with criminal enterprises, the BarraCubas ordered Alicia to manage Chicas Cheveres, the biker gang's profitable escort service.

Armed with bookkeeping skills she acquired by way of scant business courses available at school in Santiago, coupled with knowing she didn't have to sell her body, Alicia welcomed the chance to manage Cheveres.

She maintained complete anonymity, since the service had no brick-and-mortar storefront, relied upon internet advertising and employed a digital network of smartphones, tablets and laptops.

She kept her association with the BarraCubas as secret as the location of Jimmy Hoffa's grave site.

Alicia's plan worked.

Until it didn't.

Chapter 2

Bonaire

Southern Caribbean · 2014

"At least Rick and Ilsa will always have Paris," Jake Dupree said wistfully to Reed O'Hara. Newly acquainted solitary travelers were discussing loyalty, trust and love through the rom-noir looking glass of *Casablanca*.

Former Army Ranger and CIA black-op field agent, Jake left nothing to chance. As an advanced marksman sniper, expecting good fortune to come his way was a foolhardy game to play.

With matters of love, as well, he refused to leave promising romance to the mercy of fickle chance.

It wasn't a coincidence, consequently, Jake came upon Reed on a gorgeous sunny afternoon sitting by herself in the Bonaire Blond Brewery in Kralendijk, capitol of Bonaire.

Jake recently left the Central Intelligence Agency after performing two-dozen assignments where he served as judge, jury and executioner of thoroughly bad people wishing to harm the United States. Was he protecting the U.S. Constitution by decapitating a hard target with a single .50 caliber round from a Barrett M82 sniper's rifle? Jake reassured himself, yes, his kills were righteous, that unchecked evil was a pox on good people. He saw himself as an antidote to this malevolence.

But with each kill, he grew less certain of his essential goodness.

Recent nights, deep dreadful doubt awakened him with a *swoosh*! *blam*! of the guillotine blade faithfully performing its duty.

To deal with his post-traumatic stress disorder, Jake traveled to the ABC Islands, former Dutch colonies, now sovereign nations, of Aruba, Bonaire and Curaçao. He was attracted to the southern Caribbean islands' temperate climate soothed by constant trade winds. For him, A-B-C was as easy as 1-2-3 in getting peace and quiet this far south in the Caribbean, as Bonaire was only fifty-miles north of the Venezuelan coast.

Quite unexpectedly, Jake first came across Reed kite surfing off the windward coast of Curaçao. He just finished a rave swim, where he encountered emperor angelfish, harlequin sweetlips and a shiver of big-eyed Cuban dog sharks. He felt a special kinship with the sharks.

He wore orange board shorts and Oakley sunglasses. He slung a black backpack over his left shoulder. His well-defined pecs and abs glistened with perspiration.

Jake was a good two-hundred feet away from Reed shredding waves with unchecked abandon on her blue and white kite surfboard. Despite the distance, he noticed her sculpted quads and glutes flexed when she snared air. The source of her graceful athleticism, he saw from his vantage point on the beach, was her streamlined five-foot-tall body ripped core to shore with sinewy muscles well-defined.

Can't be an ounce of fat on that woman, Jake considered.

He almost applauded when Reed, wearing a white rash guard and deep purple board shorts, bent backwards on the board, while holding tight to the kite, then dipped her blonde hair into the glittering turquoise water.

She appeared as a gorgeous mermaid on holiday.

There's a strange magic to this woman, but gonna move on down the beach, before I creep her out, Jake decided.

Now, one might accuse Jake of tracking Reed, since he signed up for the same group ride as Reed's with the extraordinary Paso Fino horses on nearby Aruba.

One also would be wrong.

Jake made a reservation for the Paso Fino group ride a month in advance of journeying to the ABC Islands. In fact, the Paso Finos incentivized him to have an active vacation in the islands, as he didn't want to lounge the entire time in a hammock, while eating ceviche and drinking virgin pina coladas. Programmed into his DNA was the belief that inactivity leads to slothfulness, followed by carelessness, qualities that were not part of his calculus for survival.

He dutifully researched Paso Finos, discovering Columbus brought the horses to the Caribbean in 1493. He also learned a Paso Fino's inimitable rhythmic & synchronized front-to-rear gate produced smooth balanced strides. Paso Fino's classic brio made the horse ideal for saddle riding.

For Jake, a Paso Fino represented fourteen hands of seventh-heaven bliss on horseback.

To be fair, he was a capable rider. Not once did a horse throw him or roll him while crossing a creek. While riding a horse, be it in the Gila-monstered Sonoran Desert, the red clay roads & cotton fields & pine forests of Georgia or the rainforest high up in Jamaica's Blue Mountains, he embraced Foghat's mellow mantra, *"Slooow ride, take it eeeasy."*

Was it pure luck Jake and Reed were part of the same group ride in Aruba? Was fate at work on this paradisal island in the southern Caribbean?

Alas, there was no cosmic influence, no interference from ancient Greek, Norse or Mayan gods, no Elizabethan star-crossed lovers' alchemy at work.

That's because Reed spotted Jake two days earlier ambling across the pontoon Queen Emma Bridge in Willemstad on Curaçao.

She found the man's wavy brown hair, muscular build, impressive height and confident air quite appealing.

He'll get bonus points for no wedding ring ... or ring tan line, she thought.

Consequently, Reed took a shot in the dark this obviously athletic man would ride the world-famous Paso Finos on Aruba. She learned El Paseo Ranch Aruba had the highest ratings and best reviews on the island. After slipping fifty Aruban Florin to an El Paseo wrangler, she discovered the tall, handsome man was Jake Dupree, who signed up weeks ago for the next day's ride at daybreak.

The following morning at El Paseo Ranch, guides assisted nervous riders in the corral. Reed already was saddled up, allowing her time to study Jake, who appeared relaxed & confident as he climbed on a Paso Fino.

Jake caught Reed spy glassing him. He gave her a sly wink. She was less than impressed.

Rather forward of Mr. Jake Dupree, Reed thought. But now it's time to see if this man can ride.

Twenty riders in all, the group formed five rows of four riders each as this Caribbean calvary line clip-clopped in sync on an asphalt street leading to a windward beach framed by rubbly rock formations fringed with coconut palms, sea grapes and wind-sculpted fofoti trees.

Once the group reached the beach, the guides turned loose horse and rider to gallop along the shoreline. With ocean spray keeping them cool, Paso Finos seemed thrilled to sprint wildly across the beach.

At the start of the equine breakout, Reed charged to the front. After all, her life motto was, "Lead, follow or get the *fuck* out of my way." Every aspect of her time on earth was a competition to be first, to be dominant, to be the big kahuna in all things at work or play.

But innate competitiveness caused her to forget the mission: determine if Jake ride can ride decently and if he has an *in*decently nice derriere.

First his buns, then his brains, best way to size up a guy, Reed said to herself.

She allowed several riders to jockey past her. Jake lagged near the back, but he eventually passed Reed. With her rear-view of Jake riding his Paso Fino, she observed his firm yet gentle control of the horse, not at all resorting to punitive sidekicks or rein whipping.

She also took note of Jake's posterior.

Man fills out those Levi's nicely, Reed decided.

A woman rider galloping alongside Reed spotted her admiring Jake's backside. The woman gave Reed an enthusiastic nod. Reed smiled, then winked.

No novice at reconnaissance, Jake knew Reed was checking him out, an odd experience for him, as he was more accustomed to scoping his prey, holding his breath, then triggering life out of his target. One shot. Confirm kill. Slip away. Exfil. Mission completed.

Understandably, he wasn't certain he enjoyed being this woman's prey during the group ride.

Since turnabout was fair play in matters of romance, Jake maneuvered his way behind Reed to study her riding form as well. Despite getting covered in saltwater spray and wet sand kicked up by Reed's Paso Fino, he still could admire her silken riding style and classic form, befitting of a gymnast or a tae kwon do martial artist.

With each four-step gallop, Reed's blonde hair and her Paso Fino's black mane undulated in perfect unison, creating in Jake's eyes a slow-motion portrait of power and sensuality joined at the hip.

Have I ever encountered a more alluring woman? Jake asked himself.

Though they exchanged slight nods after the ride, Jake and Reed didn't speak with one another. They went separate ways, like two boxers having learned much at the weigh-in, but weren't ready to enter the ring to engage in passionate combat.

Consequently, when Jake saw Reed stroll into Bonaire Blond Brewery the day after the Paso Finos ride, he decided to make the opening move.

Chapter 3

Alicia Serrano, Namaste performer and biker gang banger, was acutely aware of the BarraCubas Motorcycle Club's ferocious pride in its Cuban heritage. Fortunately for the high profile and wealthy BMC Tampa chapter, there was no scarcity of eligible Cuban female recruits in Tampa Bay.

It helped Tampa shared a storied history with Cuba.

There was the rise in the late 1800's of the Cuban cigar-making industry in Ybor City, a community mostly of Cuban, Spanish and Italian immigrants that Tampa incorporated over a century ago.

Tampa also was launching point for thousands of U.S. troops, including Teddy Roosevelt and his Rough Riders, to steam out of Tampa Bay, head due south in the Gulf of Mexico and liberate Cuba from Spanish control in 1898.

Havana and Tampa, two tropical cities inextricably linked by baristas and bolita, Batista and the Beard, bootleggers and bomb throwers, a true bitch's brew for the ages.

Occasionally, Alicia noted, the BarraCubas allowed in a Guatemalan or a Mexican or a Venezuelan, long as the woman demonstrated useful nefarious skills. The waifish Ecuadorian Catalina showed great promise as an expert cat burglar. She scaled all nineteen floors of the Hotel

Floridan Palace Hotel in downtown Tampa, only to die from the mandatory beat-in.

"I told Eden to take it easy on poor little Catalina," chapter president Paz Iberra told Alicia. "But that Eden wouldn't listen. I think she tried to beat the Ecuadorian out of Catalina, and Eden did *too* good a job, sadly."

It was to their great advantage for the BarraCubas to groom their public image. Insisting on being recognized as 'BarraCubas Motorcycle Club,' not as a motorcycle gang, the Cubans maintained their spit-and-polish image throughout Tampa Bay.

They made substantial contributions, *never* anonymously, to Planned Parenthood of Southwest and Central Florida, the METRO LGBTQ+ Welcome Center in St. Petersburg, the Katie Jones Centre for Wayward Women and the Habitat ReStore of Pinellas County.

Once a month, the BarraCubas held a fiesta libre in Curtis Hixon Park on the Hillsborough River across from the exotic minarets and late nineteenth-century architecture of the University of Tampa. The gang provided all comers with cafe con leche, pressed Cuban sandwiches, 1905 Salads, paella and arroz blanco con frijoles negros, known locally as "Los Moros y Los Christianos," from famed Columbia Restaurant in Ybor City.

And no, the BarraCubas never distributed frozen turkeys on Thanksgiving, a New Jack City tradition that would only mar their public image.

Costing them a fortune, the BarraCubas formed their own pirate krewe to participate in the annual Gasparilla Pirate Festival, which included a wildly popular parade down Bayshore Boulevard, as well as an "invasion" by Tampa Bay's upper crust One-Percenters dressed as bead-tossing pirates. Most krewes got sodden, then snarky, from grogging mojitos and Jose Marti-nis all day and into the night. But Paz wouldn't allow BarraCubas to imbibe, thereby preserving their freshly starched prim & proper profile.

Taking a page from Al Capone's playbook, where Capone and the Chicago Outfit lived in the grandiose Lexington Hotel in 1928, Paz and select BarraCubas lived on the top floor of the refurbished Floridan Hotel in downtown Tampa. Keeping the top floor all to themselves required the gang to pay triple the rack rate. They kept their motorcycles in the hotel parking garage, but never grandstanded when they pulled into or out of the garage, though Paz enjoyed surprising people when she drove out of the hotel in her Phantom Black Audi A8.

The BarraCubas rarely wore insignia patches, where the upper crescent or rocker read "BarraCubas MC," the lower crescent "Tampa, Florida" and in the center, a barracuda head flashing its ripper teeth. Club patches usually were stitched or fastened on the back of denim or black leather jackets.

Sometimes, the BarraCubas wore WWII vintage leather aviator helmets with goggles, sheepskin-lined leather bomber jackets, leather pattern gloves with silk inserts and leather escape boots, all a tribute to WWII pilot & all-around badass Shirley Slade, member of the Women's Airforce Service Pilots, or WASP, during World War II.

When the BarraCubas went to the Floridan's Sapphire Lounge or to its Crystal Dining Room, which boasted immense crystal chandeliers and hand-painted cherubs, the women wore full make-up and maxi-tiered Bardot dresses, with their gorgeous Latina black hair straight pinned.

Paz preferred brightly colored silk blouses with tulip skirts. Every once in a while, she wore her favorite outfit: a sheer black corset top with netted detailing, a black *fireworks!* emblazoned long oversized jacket she let slip off her shoulders and wide-legged, high-waisted black trousers.

"Every woman has a good side and a bad side," she lectured the gang. "We must always show our *best* side."

Alicia mostly avoided the Floridan Hotel, though she was glad to manage the Chicas Cheveres escort service, where she steadfastly built a big black book of rich, gullible clients. Her network of female escorts, which expanded exponentially with the dramatic increase in customers, was drawn entirely from BarraCubas rejects.

"Waste not, want nada," Paz said of re-purposing rejects.

While Chicas Cheveres was a profitable venture, the biker gang generated most of its cash flow from illegal drug sales, extortion and burglaries.

Police weren't much of a threat. The gang avoided investigations and arrests by bribing Sheriff's deputies and police officers, who quietly sent word through the Great Blue Vine to not bother the motorcycle gang. In addition, BarraCubas embedded attractive, computer savvy operatives in law enforcement dispatch centers, IT departments and administrative offices, allowing BMC to regularly get the heads up on imminent police raids. Should a biker get arrested, the gang retained three of Tampa Bay's finest criminal defense lawyers, all complete assholes as well as vicious courtroom rottweilers, who never missed a single legal maneuver or the slightest procedural error on law enforcement's part.

"Please, you can rest easy, mi guapa," Paz said to Alicia. "Under my leadership, not one of us has spent any real time in jail, much less in prison."

Alicia, in fact, was instrumental in the BarraCubas landing their finest catch from the legal system: a circuit court probate judge who settled disputes over wills and estates. Turns out, Judge Ian Testate had a profoundly illegal taste for private-school boys, a pervy passion he kept secret from his wife and children and from fellow judges. Only Judge Testate's bailiff, Aristotle Nostradamus Shannon, was aware of His Honor's sick hobby. The same bailiff was on the BarraCubas' payroll.

Alicia arranged for an eighteen-year-old female escort to shape-shift her long black hair into a Peaky Blinders haircut, then dress as a male Hillel Academy freshman, complete with conservative white dress shirt, khaki chinos, sockless penny loafers and a kippah atop the head of the young lad named "Noam."

The judge agreed with Alicia: the prudent approach to satisfying his needs was to hire a barely legal female escort posing as an innocent schoolboy. That approach was preferable to bagging an actual male minor of good breeding, a true endangered species for upscale pedophiles such as Judge Testate.

"To paraphrase Hamlet, my dear, the play's the thing wherein I'll catch my dainty darling," His Honor testified loftily to Alicia.

"Okeee, whatever floats your pirate boat, long as you make a ten-thousand-dollar *cash* contribution to our Cuba Libre campaign. And don't even think about taking a tax deduction."

"You're not a 501(c)(3), huh?" Testate whined.

"Nope."

"Then of course I will follow your instructions, as to payment for my lovely lad, 'Noam in the Moaning.'"

So fuckin' gross, Alicia thought. Nothing more disgusting than a bald, bladder-busted old fart of a *pederass* mo-fo.

Game. Set. Match.

It was a *Bad Times at the El Royale* moment for Judge Testate. The BarraCubas filmed the entire encounter between Testate and Noam through a two-way mirror at the sadsack daddyshack Norma Jean's Motel on Hillsborough Avenue in East Tampa. The dingy by-the-hour dive was BMC owned.

"My ass sure as shit hurts, but at least we nailed that disgusting toad," Noam said to Alicia, who rewarded Noam with an extra grand.

The next day after his assignation at Norma Jean's, Testate discovered a small package on the seat of the high-backed leather executive chair in his courthouse chambers. Inside the package was a video disc marked in blackest Sharpie, TRIUMPH OF THE WILLS: THE MOHEL'S CUT.

Bowels-from-hell horrified over his night court porn Hollywood (Florida) premiere, Judge Testate agreed to scout other fellow judges with similar, even *vaguely* similar, perverted pastimes, whom the Barra-Cubas could bend to their will at a healthy profit.

"Won't be long, Señora Presidenta, before we have a criminal judge in our pocket," Alicia announced proudly.

Paz squinted her anthracite eyes and smiled warmly at Alicia.

The Prez lounged this afternoon in rose-red silk pajamas & pink puffy slippers. The first three buttons to her pajama top were undone. Her café crema breasts were on rapturous display. Though entirely asexual, Alicia found Paz's breasts breathtakingly beautiful.

"You keep going like this, Alicia, you'll be part of my inner circle," Paz predicted.

Alicia basked in Paz's praise, though it wouldn't be long before her spirit chilled and died.

That's because a certain Tampa narcotics detective was about to take Alicia down a wascally wabbit hole from which there would be no escape.

CHAPTER 4

BONAIRE

SOUTHERN CARIBBEAN · 2014

REED SAT ALONE DRINKING a bottle of Heineken at a small table in Bonaire Blond Brewery. She meant for the three unoccupied high-backed chairs at her table to connote drawbridges up at Castle O'Hara. She chose to be alone. She was happy with her choice. For now, all was calm and quiet in her world.

The pub was more Euro than Carib: plump comfortable chairs of brown leather worn smooth as tumbled jasper nestled into reading nooks; a cinnamon-cherry finished ladder bookcase that lent saucy romance novels, potboiler adventures and pulp fictions in Dutch and in English, as well as boardgames such as *Risk* and *Monopoly*, all meant to keep bar patrons drinking beer and noshing grilled & fried pub grub keelhauled toward fleshy fish, squiggly cephalopods, crazy conch & mad shrimp gone Mothra.

Plaster walls were the color of sunflowers and adorned with framed photos of native divi divi trees, prickly pear cactus and majestic monarch butterflies flirting among surreal purple bracts of bougainvillea vines.

There were six tables of varying sturdiness. Each had four wobbly double-jointed chairs that somehow fended off gravity, at least for now.

Eight tall bar stools, six of them occupied, nuzzled up to a worn brass foot railing at the pub's long dark oak bar.

The bartender, who also was the pub owner, insisted on playing Baroque music over the sound system. While Baroque was her personal favorite, she counted on the monody combination of solo voice and basso continuo of Claudio Monteverdi, Gregorio Allegri and Jean-Baptiste Lully to quiet raucous patrons.

Today, Antonio "The Red Priest" Vivaldi's *Gloria*, replete with choral annunciation, contemplative "Et in Terra Pax" in B minor and a jaunty duet for women's voices, offered celestial inspiration to enhance & elevate the patrons' beer suds buzzes.

Like I always say, if it *ain't* Baroque, then fix it, Jake thought.

Standing at the bar by himself while nursing a highball of coconut water with crushed ice, Jake admired Reed's barely there canary yellow sun dress highlighting her full breasts, deep tan and trim figure. He was particularly smitten with her petite feet protected from the pub's sandy stone floor by Coach thong sandals.

Damn, if it isn't Grace Kelly in *To Catch a Thief*, he exclaimed to himself.

It was time.

It was time for Jake to approach Reed.

In some strange metaphysical manner, he sensed his life was about to change dramatically, he hoped in a positive way.

He set his drink on the bar, thought better of it, then picked it back up.

Hollywood highball prop in hand, he strolled over to Reed's table.

What're the chances I'm a dead man walking, he mused.

"Hello there," Jake said.

His manner was too studied. He vibed a nasally Kevin Costner, rather than a smooth single-malt Scottish brogued Sean Connery.

Jake teetered over the abyss of eternal rejection.

Would Reed extend a helping hand?

Nope, nope & no.

She wouldn't shepherd hook the teetering man.

Using the manicured forefinger of her right hand, Reed played with condensation dripping down the shaft of her Heineken bottle. Stroke down. Stroke up. Flick the droplets. Lather, rinse, repeat.

She looked up at the tall man and smiled at him.

"Hello, Jake Dupree, I was starting to think I needed to make the first move."

"Yeah well, sitting around ..."

"Or in your case, standing around," Reed noted.

"*Standing* around and wishing something good to happen is pointless. Act boldly, get equally bold results. Agree?"

"Yes, I agree with both points."

"Touché knowing my name. I really do apologize for my tentativeness. Afraid I'm rather rusty with matters of this sort."

"Away at prison, were you?" Reed deadpanned to the man in need of a lifeline.

"It seemed like prison, but no, just too involved with my career to chat with beautiful women such as yourself."

"Ah, our man in the gray flannel suit endlessly enduring the Pear of Anguish?"

"Ouch! More like the rack of lamb led by mint jelly to the slaughter."

"Not too bad, but I would have gone with the Chappy Chopper."

"You seem acquainted with dungeon hijinks," Jake said. "Hobby or career?"

"Now that's a Knee Splitter! Nope, I went on a London Dungeon Tour last year. Fascinated by the Tower of London's torture chamber. Creepy good stuff. Besides, I respect a professional's devotion to her craft, no matter how ghoulish the endeavor."

Jake smirked.

"Trying to scare me off with the crazy-lady-in-the-sexy-sundress routine, aren't you?"

"Is it working?" Reed wondered playfully.

"Not in the least."

"Good, because you're kinda cute in a big galoot sort of way."

"I prefer lummox, since it's more British East Anglian and I used to drive a mint green car called an Anglia. Reliable, sporty, in a no-sex-please-I'm-English kind of way."

"Hmm," Reed pondered archly. "Then big lummox it is, and you're lucky I'm Irish American, what with your tweaking the Brits' nips."

"Always glad to have the luck of the Oirish on my side, though I'm French American."

Reed smiled at Jake.

Her eyes, the color of blue agate quartz, verily shimmered.

"Eh bien, monsieur, set your little croissant down in one of these chairs."

"Merci beaucoup."

Big Lummox sat down with as delicate a *harumph*! as he could muster. The chair creaked perilously. Fortunately, it held the muscular 200-pound man, cute croissant derriere and all.

"You know, this may be just the right moment," Jake proffered.

"The right moment to do the wrong thing?" Reed asked.

"Ah, the great Charlie Chaplain, he certainly knew a thing or two about doing the wrong thing at the right time, didn't he?" Jake answered with a question.

"Endnoting my Little Tramp allusion doesn't answer my question. But you've piqued my interest. Tell me all about this right moment."

Reed leaned forward. She rested her elbows on the table. She lowered her arms. Palms up. Castle O'Hara drawbridge opened. Slightly. Cautiously.

"It's the right moment for what probably will be only time I get to use it," Jake said.

"Go ahead, Fisher King, wet your line in my pond," Reed responded.

Jake gulped. Cleared his throat. Performance anxiety set in quickly.

"Of all the gin joints in all the towns in all the world, you walk into mine," he declared.

"Bogart's Rick Blaine, *Casablanca*. One of my favs, strictly for the film's noir elements, of course."

"Of course, but I admire the love story in *Casablanca*," Jake added.

"Seems to me Rick and Ilsa's love affair didn't work out so well," Reed said.

"At least Rick and Ilsa will always have Paris."

A romantic, Reed noted to herself. Should be fun seeing if opposites really do attract.

"There's that, isn't it?" she replied.

"I also hope I'll never use that line again."

Palms down. Drawbridge raised. Hard stop messaged.

"Slow up there, friend. Only certainty here is that we've met. I'm O'Hara, Reed O'Hara, by the way. Today, we're simply feeling each other out, kay? No more premature projaculations, all right?"

Jake nodded affirmatively.

"Men, we rush into waters where wiser angelfish fear to tread," he said. "So can I ask you an important question?"

Reed polished off her Heineken.

"I'll answer right up front: yes, it hurt a little."

"Hey, wait a minute, what hurt a little?"

"When I fell from heaven."

Jake laughed like a murder of crows.

"Thanks, I'm glad you were only winged."

"Cute. Now ask me your question. I promise no more interruptions."

Jake saw Reed cross her fingers on her right hand.

"I noticed you're quite the athlete, Reed, I saw you grabbing air on your kite surfboard the other day."

"That was *you* on the beach studying my form on the board."

"Guilty as charged. Did I make you uncomfortable?"

"Not at all, but you were smart to keep your distance," she said.

"Glad I didn't overstep my bounds. Now, to my question. Since you're obviously athletic and brave, which circus act would you perform, taming tigers under the Big Top while wielding a whip and wearing a rouge sang jumpsuit, or donning a gold-sequined leotard and being shot high up in the air out of a giant cannon?"

Reed chuckled.

"'Dear *Penthouse Forum*, today I met a total hottie wearing a blood-red jumpsuit with tall black boots and a big whip, and underneath, she wore a gold-sequined leotard. I think I'm in lust and really want to, ya know, help her out of that circus outfit. Any advice? Sincerely, Throb Bone Jones.'"

Jake snort laughed.

"Impressive, your wide range of reading. Would *Paris Review, Mad Magazine* and *Penthouse,* about cover it?"

"Yes, but I get *Penthouse* only for the photos."

"Well played. Which circus act will it be, then?"

Reed's delicate facial features ... musical notes for eyebrows, transcendtally blue eyes, a straight small symmetrical nose and lips like pink satin pillows ... formed an inquisitive frown.

It was an indication she took seriously Jake's question.

"I object to how circus animals are treated. Ethically, morally, spiritually, I couldn't participate in tiger taming. But there's a personal reason as well. You see, I grew up in a neighborhood where this elderly fellow owned a tiger cub named Sphinx."

"Uh oh, don't like where this is heading," Jake said.

"Or *beheading.*"

"What?" he asked.

"Screwing with you. I got to play with Sphinx a few times. Like a kitten on steroids. I quickly figured out this fluffy fur ball could chomp my hand off with one snap of his powerful jaws."

"Did Sphinx ever attack you?"

Reed stood up and stepped back from the table.

"Look at me, dear boy, all of my extremities appear intact," Reed said as she showcase-waved her left hand, starting at her legs, rising to her waist, finishing at her chest.

Like what you see, bub? Reed inquired to herself.

My god, she's gorgeous, Jake thought.

"You look well put together," Jake answered throatily. "Where do you keep your angel wings?"

Reed grinned almost lasciviously.

"Oh, I left them upstairs in my home."

She sat back down.

"Of course, Sphinx never bit me. But he got bigger and bigger. Eventually, my father forbade me from playing with him."

"Why do I suspect there isn't a happy ending to this cat tale?" he asked.

Reed giggled. She put her hand over her mouth, as if she were embarrassed over laughing at his question.

"I'll go out on a limb by predicting this story hasn't a happy ending," Jake predicted. "But keep in mind I get kinda squeamish at the mere mention of blood."

"Yes, my plus-size pearl clutcher, there will be blood. So where was I? Oh yes. One day I heard sirens a *wai-wai-wailing* all through my neighborhood. Don't know why, but the sun up in the sky told me Sphinx was involved. Ran to the old guy's house. My sister Debbie raced me for who got there first."

Jake leaned forward, resting on his crossed arms.

"Then what happened?"

"Oh, I beat my sister to the house, I always win," Reed answered smugly.

"No, I mean, aw screw it. What'd you discover when you two arrived, first you, then Debbie, to the elderly gentleman's home?" Jake asked.

"There was a lit-up prowler and ambulance parked out front. A policeman ran out of the house. He instructed the paramedics to wait outside."

"Oh no."

"Oh yes. The officer sprinted to his cruiser and pulled out of its trunk a strange-looking rifle."

"A tranquilizer rifle?"

"How'd you know that?"

"I've used them before," Jake said casually.

"Okay. Well. Turns out, Sphinx tore off the old guy's right arm, then ran out of the house with the bloody arm in his mouth. He sprinted down the street toward the Carlouel Yacht Club."

"Did the police catch Sphinx?"

"Yes, but only after he disrupted a tennis tournament at the yacht club. Sphinx and the bloody arm got all tangled up in a tennis net, so the cop hit him with a dart and the cub went to sleep."

"What about the one-armed man?"

"From *The Fugitive*?"

"No, you know who I meant!"

"Old guy? Yeah, they couldn't re-attach the arm. Sphinx gnawed off too much of it."

"You're enjoying this, aren't you?" Jake wondered.

"God yes. There's a streak of American Gothic running through me. You've been warned."

"Thanks for the heads up, but that makes me like you even more," Jake replied. "I take it the gentleman survived the attack."

"Just barely. I snuck inside the house. Never seen so much blood, except when I saw a farmhand up in West Virginia get his wedding ring caught on the glide wheel to a buzzsaw and got his hand deli-sliced real nice."

"You, Reed O'Hara, are one clever and enchanting storyteller," Jake said, "Please, one gruesome tale at a time, all right?"

"You make me blush over your generous compliment, Monsieur, though I will save that story of bloody bucolic life in West Virginia for another time."

"Thanks. Why did Sphinx attack his master? And what was the man's name?"

"Can't remember his name, so let's call him OG, all right?"

"For 'old guy'?"

Reed giggled.

"No, you goof, for 'Original Gangsta'!"

"Really?"

She put her right hand in Jake's left hand. It was the first time the two lonesome travelers touched.

"OG made a serious mistake of feeding whole chickens and slabs of round steak to Sphinx," Reed said.

"Raw?"

"Raw. I guess Sphinx pooped everywhere until he got used to raw meat. Not to be coy about it, but the big cat loved jumping over the backyard wall to invade the neighbor's koi pond. OG and the neighbor never talked again."

"So much for domesticating the big cat."

"Exactly. The morning of the kitty cat attack, OG slept in and neglected to feed his fast-growing tiger cub. It was noon. Sphinx still hadn't eaten. The teen tiger beat a path into OG's bedroom, then proceeded to rip off the man's arm as easily as pulling a wing off a roasted turkey."

"What happened to Sphinx?"

"He got sent off to a big cat sanctuary somewhere in Oklahoma, I think."

"And Original Gangster?"

"It's '*gangsta*'! He had to wear a prosthetic arm with a chrome claw. Scared the living crap out of neighborhood kids when he dressed up as Captain Hook and had a stuffed Tick-Tock the Croc on the front porch for Halloween. We didn't go near the place."

"That's a sad, tragic, hilarious story wrapped in Goth cloth and decorated with a black gauze bow."

"Very good, Jake. Are we starting to loosen you up?"

"Yes indeed, but are you using the 'royal we'?"

"No, I'm not. It's the 'we' of you and me."

"Sounds promising."

"Does, doesn't it? Oh, almost forgot to mention it didn't work out so well for OG."

"How's that?" Jake asked.

"While replacing a breaker panel in his garage one day, he got his claw stuck in live wires. Electrocuted himself. Neighbors found him sprawled out dead on the garage floor. His toupee was still smoking. Claw was stuck in the breaker panel, spritzing sparks all over OG, may he rest in peace. True story."

Jake smiled.

"Made that up, didn't you?"

"Jake Dupree, I'm verily shocked that you think I would do such a thing."

Chapter 5

Tampa, Florida · 2022

Ernie Friekorps blitzkrieged into Alicia Serrano's life like a Panzerkampfwagen bypassing the Maginot Line to roll directly into the City of Lights.

"Look, *A-lee-see-ya*, I happen to have a good working relationship with the Bavarians. You know, those crazy neo-Nazi head splitters on motorcycles we all love and admire. Role models for society, yup, that's what they are."

Friekorps approached Alicia at 3:30 a.m. in the near-empty Namaste parking lot. He flashed his gold shield. He made certain she saw his holstered Beretta.

"What the hell you want with me, Detective? I'm just a dancer trying to make a living in this tough-ass world."

Friekorps' loud laugh caught the attention of Namaste Security Chief Andre, who stood with muscular arms folded at the nightclub's lighted front entrance. His six-foot-five-inch, two-hundred-fifty-pound frame cast a giant shadow in the direction of Alicia and Friekorps. Neither Fritz Lang nor Alred Hitchcock could have lit the scene any better.

"Is there a problem, Miss Alicia?" Andre asked in a deep booming voice. "That gentleman bothering you?"

"Kami-sama mama, it's Black Godzilla!" Friekorps exclaimed.

Alicia whispered *hush* to the detective.

"No hay una problema, Andre. Just talking with an old boyfriend. No worries, okay?"

Andre unfolded his arms.

"All right then. You have my number if you need any help."

He walked to his race red F-250, climbed into the truck, then drove away into the chiaroscuro Tampa Bay night, which was hot, hazy and ready to rain at any moment.

Alicia couldn't stop gawking at Friekorps' face, a pastiche of disheveled tawny hair, a complexion pocked beyond the pale, patchwork whisker stubble and a nose broken at least twice, but more likely three times.

He flashed a sinister smile at her.

"You're not going to need Big Papa's help. You see, we're going to be best of friends, beastie besties, BFW's ... whateva fuck you wanna call it. But first, stow that crap about you being only a dancer. If the Barra-Cubas heard that, they might could get their dainty dyke feelings hurt."

Alicia's eyes glowered like an angry chupacabra.

"Pendejo, they're not all lesbians, I mean ... whatever."

"Both your little feet just pas de deuxed into flamingo poo, sweetheart. Only a dancer, huh?"

With her leather jacket slung over her Harley, Alicia decided to play the river card. A security lamp backlit her. She leaned sexily against her bike. After a long night of performing at Namaste, her body gave off an erotic musky scent. In the cool night air, she felt her large dark nipples, centered on Champagne-glass-size breasts, protrude through her white midriff blouse. Her derriere rested on the bike's black leather saddle. Her palms-down, straightened arms propped her up. Her long legs were crossed at the ankles.

Alicia *dared* Friekorps not to stare at the inviting V in the crotch point of her Levi's jeans.

Friekorps gutter-uttered, "Beautiful, baby ... excuse me while I whip this out."

He took out his phone to click several photographs of Alicia, starting with close-ups on her feet, then her legs, midriff, breasts and face, finishing the forced photoshoot with proscenium views of her full body.

Each *click*! of the camera felt as if a nail gun pierced Alicia, because she understood its significance.

"I have to say, I've worked with better chicas, but not many. Talk about some good wanking material, if & when I ever get back to my deluxe apartment in the sky. Now listen, should you not agree to be my CI..."

"CI, papi?" Alicia asked.

"Confidential Informer, you twitclit. As I was saying, and don't interrupt me again, if you won't be my CI, I'll put these photographs on Instagram, tell everybody you're my new girl. Only got a thousand followers, but it's a select crowd who'll get my continental drift, know what I mean?"

"You wouldn't, no lo creo."

"You bet I would, Ed Wood."

"I'd get killed," Alicia protested.

"Play stupid games, win stupid prizes. Way it goes."

Alicia was crestfallen, utterly defeated.

"Why me?"

"Because you got talent for keeping shit from people. Left hand of Namaste got no idea about the right hand of the BarraCubas, correct-o-mundo, chicklet? Ima only axing you to tell me wassup with the biker women, then I'll pass it on to the Ba-Ba-Bavarians, Barbara Ann."

Alicia cried, as her body appeared to turn in on itself.

"How long?" she asked.

"I don't know, maybe a few weeks. We'll see how it goes. Give me good enough intel, you know, stuff that'll get Bavarians all Oktoberfes-terin', and I'll be done wid chew."

Alicia was silent as a cemetery at the devil's hour.

Friekorps casually picked his teeth with a plastic corner point of a nicotine gum wrapper.

"Así, todo esta de acuerdo, Alicia?" he asked, as he kept a pickin' and a grinnin'.

"You speak Spanish?" she exclaimed with stygian eyes wide open.

"Claro, Jean Harlow. You know well as I do, this town iza babblin' bouillabaisse of ring-a-ding-dong lingos. My line of work, it's good to patois among zee furreners. So don't get 'Ay mi madre' and 'Ay tu madre' mixed up when you talk to me, sí?"

"Sí."

"Bien. I texted you my digits. Let me know how tomorrow's meeting of the Re-Pressed Cuban Sammies goes down. Don't make me call you, Choo Choo Mama."

Friekorps didn't bother to say goodbye. He scampered like an arthritic possum to his restored '66 peacock blue Bronco. The V8 engine roared awake as Friekorps banana peeled out of the Namaste parking lot.

Alicia sat motionless. She resembled a miniature motorcyclist poised atop a second-place racing trophy.

How the hell am I going to get out of this jam? she thought. Why can't people just let me dance?

In the following weeks, Alicia performed frequently, though it was mostly tap dancing around Namaste, the BarraCubas and the tarnished gold shield of Ernie Friekorps.

Informing on the BarraCubas was as horrible for her as she expected. Though it sickened her, Alicia eavesdropped enough to provide Friekorps a nearly complete picture, a sort of jigsaw puzzle missing but a few pieces, of the BarraCubas' retail drug network that included South Tampa, Ybor City and West Tampa, territories Bavarians hadn't yet tapped, yet very much desired.

Sitting in the living room of Paz's grand suite at the Floridan Hotel, Alicia sipped a café con leche from a large white porcelain mug. She pretended not to listen to Paz talk strategy with Eden, her sociopathic left-handed right-hand woman.

"We're making good money right now, my thrilla killa, but we must keep expanding," Paz said to Eden. "That includes those Bavarian bone-heads' territory."

In public, Alicia noticed Paz was poised, elegant and well-spoken. Always diplomatic. Nary an obscene word or coarse expression uttered by Paz among the local Hohenzollern. Within the cool dark private confines of her hotel suite, sitting with women she trusted, she was her true self, the former Havana sex worker who acquired serious cred de la calle when she slashed a Dutch tourist's throat for trying to sodomize her, zonder toestemming, on the Malecon Esplanade.

"Stupido, stupido, stupido! Why you think my asshole's there just for the taking, huh?" Paz yelled at the man, who sat up against the seawall and gurgled incoherently through his tulips. Crashing waves baptized the dying Dutchman with sea spray as he bled out. His last words were unintelligible, though they most likely had something to do with Paz meeting up with him in Hieronymus Bosch's trippy medieval hell.

Paz removed his passport, diamond-stud earring, gold chain-link necklace, white gold wedding band, Gucci leather belt with a brass snake buckle, a surprisingly cheap Velcro wallet and his Valentino Garavani crochet sandals.

"Maricon, these shoes, they're for the women. Just about my size, too! Gracias, pobrecito."

Paz knew dead men don't say, "De nada."

She wiped his blood from her abalone-handle switchblade onto the pant leg of the dirty dead Dutchman. She headed into the starry black night in search of another customer.

Holding a mango slice harpooned on the tip of her infamous abalone-handle switchblade, as she relaxed in a comfy chartreuse chintz armchair in the hotel suite, Paz said to Eden and Alicia, "Eurotrash prick treated me like a back door whore."

Alicia remained silent.

Eden spoke up.

"He got what he deserved, baby," she answered in a soothing, sultry voice.

Eden fingered a necklace around her neck. It was the same gold chain-link necklace previously owned by Double Dutch the Sodomizer. She wore the necklace to show everyone she was Paz's partner in all things BarraCubas, public and private.

A short curvy physically powerful stone-cold killer from Camaguey, Cuba, Eden loved how the gold chain glittered against her Black skin.

"You think I was justified killing that piece of shit?" Paz asked.

"Absolutely, these Anglos, they treat us like animales," Eden replied. "Mi jefa, how we gonna mess up those Bavarians?"

Paz stabbed an orange papaya slice hiding under lime green honeydew chunks in a Waterford bowl resting on a rosewood side table.

"We're gonna hit 'em where it hurts the most. In the next few weeks, we take over their territories in Brandon and Plant City to the East, then Riverview, Gibsonton and Apollo Beach in South County."

"Take over by force?" Eden asked eagerly.

"We'll be pretty in pink at first, sell our superior product at a lower price, gentle sell of course, no elbowing their distributors, all cool manners and hot empanadas, querida."

"If that doesn't work?" Eden practically panted.

Eden sat on the very edge of the matching sofa. Her breathing grew heavier. Perhaps she was fantasizing over squeezing the life out of a Bavarian. Or two. Or three. Very slowly. Miles Davis style.

Alicia watched Paz rise from the armchair and walk over to the large picture window that framed Tampa's gleaming downtown skyline of mirrors.

"Did ya know this hotel was once Florida's tallest skyscraper? Paz asked. "The Sapphire Room downstairs, it was called the 'Surefire Room' during World War II, 'cause soldiers training in Tampa could always get sumpin'-sumpin' in that bar."

"That's cool and all, Paz, but you didn't answer my question," Eden snarked impatiently.

"Do not press me, una gordita negra," Paz warned.

She tapped her retracted switchblade on her right hip.

"Lo siento, mi gran jefa," Eden said in a little girl voice.

The Shirley Temple schtick worked.

"No worries, my Eden," Paz said silkily. "Bavarian butt boys wanna play tough, I'll make them regret it."

"Excellent, just tell me where and when, baby, I already know how," Eden growled.

Paz winked at Eden, then panned over to Alicia perched on a sofa.

"Tiny dancer, you haven't said a word. Wassup?"

Alicia smiled dreamily, as she unfolded her dancer legs from underneath her.

Eden stole a glance at Alicia's stunning legs shimmering from shea butter lotion.

"Soaking it all in, is all, Paz," Alicia said casually. "I know when to speak up and when to shut up."

Paz reached over to squeeze Alicia's thigh.

"That's my smart little goody two shoes," Paz proffered.

Then she said to Eden, "You could learn from Alicia."

Eden squinted deep brown eyes at Paz and Alicia.

"You both take a piss on that."

Thanks, Paz, thanks so much, don't need Eden all up in my grill, Alicia thought. Not now, not ever.

She left the Floridan to make her obligatory visit to Friekorps' apartment.

Alicia was cross wired over the deceit, betrayal and paranoia intertwining within her. She anesthetized herself by pounding back shots of Herradura tequila and smoking blunts, hollowed-out cigars filled with cannabis.

She especially was distraught over Friekorps demanding the name of BarraCubas' major drug supplier.

"Baby girl, I don't give a crap about the chronic and the black rock," the detective told Alicia. "Just need to know who's the hero and snow wholesaler, his shit so good, Bavarians could step on it three, four times and still keep customers happy."

Alicia took a *deeeep* toke from her blunt, followed by a tequila shot. She didn't bother with salt or lime this time, or for the other six shots she'd previously slammed.

Detective and CI lounged on a battered pink panteaze pleather sofa in Friekorps' apartment.

Friekorps diddled a line of cocaine on the battered coffee table, then snorted with glusto. Alicia provided him the cocaine free of charge, meaning she now was informing on *and* stealing from her club.

"Papi, I can't tell you who's our heroin and cocaine connection," Alicia pleaded. "If I did, Paz would figure it out and kill me right quick."

Friekorps blew snot into his hands, then wiped them on his black jeans.

"Talcum powder," he muttered.

"What about talcum powder?"

"BarraCubas cut the coke with talcum powder. Causes cancer, doesn't it?"

"I don't know, papi. Did you hear what I said?"

"I heard you all right," Friekorps said, as he sat up on the sofa. "You're gonna tell me his name, chica, or Ima gonna slap the brown offa you."

"Papi ... "

Whack! went Friekorps' right hand across Alicia's small delicate face.

"Go ahead, call me papi again," he said menacingly. "Now who's the supplier?"

"I can't!"

Whack! right. *Whack!* left. *Whack!* right. *Whack!* left, each slap harder than the one previous.

Alicia's face was as red as a barfly's eyes in a Sunday morning mugshot. Blood streamed from both of her nostrils. She curled into a fetal position on the sofa. She covered her face with her hands.

Friekorps jumped up and stood over her. He was prepared to slap her as many times as were necessary.

"No, no, Ernie, no mas. I'll tell you who he is, okay?" Alicia plead.

I'll be good, Daddy, I will, just don't hit me no more, I'll be a good girl, like you always want, concussed Alicia thought deliriously.

The detective smiled at his CI. She was an emotionally broken young woman, lost in space with a gruesome *Forbidden Planet* id monster glooming over her.

Alicia divulged the name of the BarraCubas' wholesale heroin and cocaine connection.

"Sonuvabitch! I know that guy! He's in charge of security at Port of Tampa. Amazing, from the banana boats directly to the BarraCubas. This oughta get me a tall stack of Benjamins from the Bavarians. Thank you, sweet pea. Pure dream sickle, that's what you are."

Claiming she had the flu, Alicia took a week off from performing at Namaste. She couldn't let Reed O'Hara see her bruised, swollen face. She knew full well Reed didn't tolerate abuse of women of any sort.

This can't go on, Alicia declared to herself. I gotta talk to that scumbag Friekorps.

Surprisingly, scumbag Frieskorp readily agreed to meet Alicia for lunch at the Vietnamese restaurant Pho Quyen, located in an East Tampa community monikered "Suitcase City," called that due to its transient, economically stressed & depressed multi-cultural residents struggling to survive, much less thrive.

Sitting with Friekorps in a booth with beet-red plastic seat covers, Alicia noticed he had combed his hair, shaved and trimmed his eyebrows & nose hair.

He wore a bowling shirt festooned with bright red roses.

Like putting lipstick on a pig, Alicia thought, and I don't trust it at all.

Friekorps greedily ate two spring rolls, quaffed most of his iced coffee, then attacked a large steaming bowl of pho, rice flour noodle soup simmered in beef bone broth, accompanied by thinly sliced beef, bean sprouts, fresh basil, mint leaves, scallions, lime slices and chiles.

Alicia also had a bowl of pho, though she didn't touch it. Instead, she drummed like Gene Krupa on a double espresso. Instead of drumsticks, she used cheap wooden chopsticks on the Formica tabletop.

Friekorps eschewed chopsticks, preferring a fork for snow shoveling rice noodles into his gaping maw.

The man wouldn't stop making loud slurping sounds as he engorged himself on pho.

"Stop that tapping shit, chica, I'm trying to eat here, and you're a rata tap tap tappin' like a College Hill crackhead."

"Sorry, Ernie. I'm such a wreck being your inside girl. I gotta get out of this sitch, like pronto, Tonto."

Friekorps inhaled more noodles, then packed in beef slices with bean sprouts pilot fishing the beef.

"'Pronto Tonto,' uh? Good to see ya sorbin' some that all-American p-p-p-pop culture. Opened some doors for me, I wanna to tell you. For instance, know how I learned good manners? Watching TV like on a cheap-ass portable television set when I was a kid growing up in *Baldimore*."

A noodle fell from his mouth while he talked. It landed on the table. While under the internationally agreed upon five-second rule, he tined the errant noodle and returned it to his mouth.

"Waste not, what not, baby, know what I mean?"

They made for the oddest of odd couples, the pale lanky Friekorps, with Icelandic white blond hair, cruel blue eyes and blotchy complexion, sitting across from Alicia, her dark hair cut twee style with thick eye-framing bangs, her eyes a Nefertiti deep brown, her complexion a sensual café crema.

Friekorps polished off his iced coffee.

"I could drink these Viet Minh coffees all day. So like these guys. Kick our butts in 'Nam, outhustle us stateside, go and get their sprouts in Stanford and Harvard, then have the audacity to make the best damn coffee in the world. Jeez Louise, can't a white man ever catch a break? I guess we at least got these noodle shops."

Please, dear God, don't let 'em say it, Alicia thought.

"Know what I mean?" Ernie Friekorps uttered.

Ernest Goes to Jail ... I wish, Alicia groused silently.

"I took off a whole week from Namaste. Reed O'Hara still noticed the handprints on my face. She didn't say much. This time. And the BarraCubas, ay mi madre, they been giving me the hoodoo eye lately. Especially Eden. Only matter of time, baby, only matter of time."

Friekorps held up his glass to the Vietnamese server as a signal he wanted another iced coffee, then casually threw ice from the glass into Alicia's face.

She was shocked into an icy silence.

"I'm your baby, huh? Stop tryin' to cuddle hustle me, Serrano. Won't getcha' nowhere."

The server brought Friekorps another iced coffee, then handed a bar towel to Alicia.

"Thank you," she said to the woman, who gave her a gentle nod as she smiled oh so subtly.

The detective reached over and took Alicia's pho from her.

"Hey, you ain't gonna eat it, I will," he declared.

He jammed a clownish clump of noodles into his mouth. For a moment or two, noodles dangled from his mouth, making it appear there was a nest of baby albino serpents wiggling out of his mouth. With guillotine efficiency, he teeth-cleaved the snake noodles, some of which wiggled back into Pho Out Pond.

Beyond gross, Alicia shuddered to herself.

"So why do you wanna to break up our little arrangement?" Friekorps said in a hushed voice. "You're making a buttload of money, while keeping me happy with your intel, and let me mention, I never took dollar one of'n you, and I know you make serious scratch at Namaste."

"I can't take this pressure, Detective. I'm going to explode, if I don't get killed first."

Friekorps belched loudly.

"Nobody's getting killed, aight? Are you serious about breaking up with me?"

"I couldn't be more serious."

Friekorps placed his left index finger vertically across his lips and tucked his thumb under his chin. Just as he was trained to do in the police academy, he scanned the dining room. There were only three other people eating.

He studied the servers as they talked amongst themselves.

"Vietnamese ever remind you of Germans? No matter what they're sayin, and it could be a fuckin love sonnet, they always be sounding angry as shit. Just like the Germans."

Clearly annoyed with his sidestepping her concerns, Alicia said indifferently, "I guess you're right, haven't ever noticed that."

Friekorps flashed his car salesman's streamers-balloons-inflated tube dancers-zero down-low monthly payments-free tank of (regular) gas smile.

"All right, my lil' sombrero, Ima gonna lose money on this, but here's my very best deal: pay me an early exit fee of five-thousand U.S. and you can take a hike in three weeks. No strings attached to my little Cubana dancer. No hasta luego, only vaya con Dios. What the heck, I'll throw in rust proofing and floor mats. No hidden fees, no taxes, no dealer prep. What say you?"

Guy's crazy, Alicia said to herself.

See that look in your eyes, Friekorps thought. Yeah, loco en la cabeza I am, makes me even more dangerous, it do and does, indiddly do.

"That's a fantastic deal, Ernie! If you really mean it, I accept!"

"Keep it down, Serrano. Don't get all giggly girl on me, aight? Way I see it, the Bavarians will move on the BarraCubas real soon. Won't need you anymore. All you gotta do for the next three weeks is feed me righteous intel and keep it on the DL with the biker chicks and Reed O'Hara. Easy peasy, nice and sleazy. Think you can handle that, girlfriend?"

Alicia smiled angelically. "I can do that. Absolutely."

"Good, now let's get the hell out of this greasy chopstick. Wait five minutes, pay the bill, then vamoose your caboose."

Friekorps belched and broke wind simultaneously.

"Anh ay that kinh tom," the server said to a co-worker, who shook her head in disgust at Friekorps.

He rose from the table without saying goodbye, then ambled out of Pho Quyen all cocky like a winner of a two-dollar scratch-off lottery card.

CHAPTER 6

BONAIRE

SOUTHERN CARIBBEAN · 2014

REED AND JAKE continued chatting up one another at the Bonaire Blond Brewery.

"I take it, Reed, you'd prefer being shot out of a cannon, as opposed to taming a tiger in a steel cage?"

Reed instantly lit up.

"You bet Jake. But not by default. See, when I was a kid, I wanted to run away to the circus, be shot out of a cannon, fly a hundred-fifty feet in the air, maybe do a somersault, then land safe 'n sound in the rope net."

"That's fantastic. Really and truly. So, may I suggest your next beer?"

"Maybe I don't want another beer."

"But if you *were* to have another beer, consider a Bonaire Blond pale ale. Combines a hint of lime with aloe vera that grows all over the island. No enhancements. Brewed right here. Fresh as fresh can be."

"Do you like this beer?"

"Me? Nah, never touch the stuff. Have enough albatrosses around my neck. Why brine 'em in beer?"

"How is it you know about Bonaire Blond beer?"

"Read the poster on the wall behind you."

Reed put her small hand on Jake's bear paw of a hand.

Feels like low current running through me, Jake said to himself. And there's that strange magic again.

"You, sir, are a scamp, and a clever one at that. I think I'm going to like you."

With her hand still resting on his, Jake air-kissed Reed's hand, Euro style. She didn't flinch or pull away. Instead, she smiled softly at Jake, who answered with an embarrassed grin, as he ran his left hand through his curly brown hair.

Talk about aw-shucks charming, Reed observed. He's Will Rogers with a nice ass.

Jake stared into Reed's eyes.

"Is it too early for a kiss?"

Reed's face flushed. Slightly.

"Don't you heed Oscar Wildes's warning that 'A kiss may ruin a life'?"

"Seems worth the risk. Besides, 'The sunlight claps the earth, and the moonbeams kiss the sea: what are all these kissings worth if thou kiss not me?'"

Reed laughed in a playful manner.

"Goodness, Shelley's your wingman?"

"Well, no. Yeah. Maybe. I don't know."

"Hmm. You go from shy to bold then back to shy. Must admit, you're far sweeter and far more erudite than most of the other men I've met."

"Thanks, Reed," he aw-shucked.

"You're welcome. Now. Let me answer your question. It's way too early for a kiss, old sport. Try to think of it this way, the best part of a first kiss is in its smoldering anticipation."

"Am I to infer there'll be a first kiss?"

"No. Yes. Maybe. I don't know."

"Hah! There is a chance. Excellent. How about I buy you a Bonaire Blond?"

"Nope. If I'm going to get a little tipsy, I'll buy my own beer, at least this round anyway. I'll try the Bonaire Blond and get you ... what are you drinking there?"

"Coconut water with ice. You put it in a blender. Pour into a high-ball glass. Add a lime. Miniature pink umbrella, optional."

Out came Reed's Mona Lisa smile.

"Is that all, Jake? No crystal chalice? No calfskin coaster?"

He shaded her a grin.

"Bar doesn't have crystal anything, and they ran out of calfskin coasters. Cruisers swiped 'em. Must make do with a regular glass and, I can't believe I'm saying this, a damp pulp coaster."

"Buck up, Buckaroo Banzai. Know which paper was used to print *Black Mask* and *Dime Detective* magazines? Pulp. That's right. Some of our best hardboiled detective stories were printed on cheap pulp paper. It's how we came up with 'pulp fiction.' If pulp were good enough for Dashiell Hammett and Raymond Chandler, a pulp coaster ought to suit you, don't you think?"

"I agree. Enthusiastically. Look at the fantastic company I would keep: Hammett, Chandler and O'Hara. Hey, sounds like a West Coast law firm, doesn't it?"

"Or East Coast," Reed said.

"How so?" Jake asked.

"Never mind. All right, time to get some drinks."

Reed rose from her chair and, as she stepped behind Jake, gave his shoulder a light pat.

Head spins every time she touches me, Jake noted.

He admired Reed's graceful walk to the bar, calling to mind a grand white swan gliding across a great pond at the grandest of Irish estates.

Several thirsty tourists, most likely from a cruise ship docked at nearby Kralenjik Cruise Port, strolled into the pub and joined the scrum at the bar. Consequently, Jake lost sight of the beautiful swan making her way through the crowd.

She returned in under ten minutes.

"I thought I was in the Tokyo metro over there." she said jocularly. "Miss me, Jake?"

"Better believe it."

"I would've gotten back sooner, but I was waylaid by a little twerp hitting on me."

Jake frowned.

"Was it that guy over there at the end of the bar?" he asked.

Jake referred to a sunburned elderly man, short as Hercule Poirot and thin as Nick Charles. His white Panama hat sported a black band announcing in bold block letters, 'Just Went Over Viagra Falls.' The man wore an aloha shirt festooned with pink flamingos, white Bermuda shorts, over-the-calf white socks and white wide-toe-box, arch-supported Zeba sneakers.

"Pretty easy to spot, isn't he?" Reed said.

"Yeah, he stands out even in this crowd. His outfit's about as loud as Foghorn Leghorn. *I say, I say, I say,* did Mr. Pink Flamingo create any problems for you?"

Uh oh, don't like where this is heading, Reed thought. Need to nip it, in the bud.

"Nothing I couldn't handle myself, Jake. He asked me where I'm from, I said Tampa. He said he's from St. Petersburg. He asked if he could cross the 'Howard Frankenstein' to meet me at Marriott Channel-side for a 'drinky poo' in May. On the first Monday of May. At midday."

"What was your response?" Jake asked gruffly.

"Well, Detective Surly, I first praised the preciseness of his overture, then I told him to go away."

"How did he respond?"

"Mr. Pink Flamingo said he expected me to brush him off, and that he learned the value of preciseness during 'Dubya Dubya Two,' when he was a Screaming Eagle and part of the Normandy Invasion on June 6, 1944."

"Oh really? He said that, huh? I'll be right back."

Jake got up and marched to the crowded bar.

Damn, I was starting to like this guy, Reed thought.

Jake stood next to the bar stool upon which Mr. Pink Flamingo was holding court.

Jake placed his hand on the man's boney shoulder, then spoke to him.

Mr. Pink Flamingo eased off the barstool. He stood facing Jake.

Looks like Kat Williams and Shaquille O'Neal staring each other down, or up, depending, Reed thought.

The older man spoke to Jake for nearly two minutes. Jake nodded affirmatively a couple times. When he was done, Mr. Pink Flamingo stepped back and saluted Jake exactly as he was taught in 1941 at Keesler Field in Biloxi, Mississippi. Impressed with the old man, Jake promptly returned a standard-issue salute. Both men back-wacked hugged. Before Jake walked away, he handed the bartender some cash, while pointing at Mr. Pink Flamingo. The bartender nodded that she understood.

As he walked back to Reed, he heard the old man yell, "Hooah!"

Jake stopped, turned, then roared back, "Hooah!"

"Sorry about that, Chief," Jake said as he sat back down with Reed.

"Don't you get smart with me, young man. What did you two talk about? Perhaps old flames extinguished, others still simmering?"

Why in hell did I say that? Reed wondered.

"More like old war stories. Turns out, he really was a Screaming Eagle in the 82nd Airborne in 1944. Gave me enough details, damn precise details, to convince me he's the real deal."

"Why did you salute one another?"

"I was an Army Ranger awhile back."

"Hmm. And the hug?"

"Sign of brotherhood."

"The 'hooah'?"

"Heard, understood, acknowledged, hooah!"

"Bought him drinks, didn't you?"

"Small way to honor an old warrior who laid down his sword and shield a long time ago."

"Have you laid down your sword and shield, Jake?"

She cast her question in a firm, yet gentle manner.

"Yes, yes, I have, Reed. Recently, in fact. I must say, though, laying down those memories is a much taller order altogether."

They grew silent.

A single tear welled up in Jake's left eye.

Reed held his hand.

"Jake, my question wasn't meant to upset you. I came off being insensitive toward your military experience, maybe even flippant. Sometimes I crack wise about subjects I may not fully understand. I am truly sorry."

Jake's chiseled facial features loosened some, as he carefully squeezed Reed's hand. He smiled tentatively.

"No need to apologize, Reed. I didn't think you were flippant. I'm freshly mustered out of government service. I've only begun squaring away how I feel about my actions. All were performed in the service of our country. That's all I can say about it for now. If we become good enough friends, I might share more, all right?"

"I think we're on our way to becoming delightful friends, Mr. Dupree. Whenever you wish to talk, I will listen. That's a promise spoken and fortified with this delicious pale ale."

Reed kissed the index and middle fingers of her left hand, leaned toward Jake, then tapped the two fingers on the tip of his nose.

"Don't worry, that's not our first kiss," Reed said reassuringly to him. "*That* will be much more spectacular ... I promise to make your toes curl, *dahling*."

Jake was momentarily speechless, then said, "I can't wait, but I will."

"Thank you."

Reed finished her beer. She set down the empty glass with a resounding *thunk!* on the wooden table.

She giggled.

"Yeah, maybe I'll hold off on my fifth beer."

"Sounds like a plan. I'd love to know more about you, but what if I first tell you about myself?"

He's controlling the narrative, Reed thought. Don't like it, but I'll go along, for now.

"Fair enough. First, though, tell me your full name. Date of birth, social security number, blood type, all optional. At some point, I'll need to get a swab."

Well played, Jake said to himself. Yanked the story reins right away from me.

"Let's see now, can't divulge my DOB or SSN. Blood type? O Negative, making me a universal donor. I was featured as 'Mr. Speedo' in last year's American Red Cross blood-drive calendar. Big money maker for ARC, *really* big. And my full name? It's Jacob Jordan Dupree."

Reed's smile shone brighter than Aruba's California Lighthouse.

"A good and fine name."

Jake smiled as well.

"Thanks, but I'm starting to blush, because all I wore in the calendar photoshoot was a pair of Speedo swim goggles and a very em-bare-assed smile," Jake replied.

"Blush away. I remain agoggled that you were a beefcake calendar boy. *Sooooo,* what kind of work do you do? And what are the chances I can get a copy of that calendar?"

"Officially, I'm on a permanent reserve list, because you never completely leave this line of work. Unofficially, I see myself as a free man ready to take on the world, on my terms and on my say-so. The ARC calendar? I have only a few copies. I'll sell ya one for ten bucks or a carton of filter-less Chesterfields, which is what my grandfather smoked until he died from stomach cancer."

"I'll have to pass on your generous offer, since I got Mr. Speedo right here in the flesh," Reed responded. "Are you still in the military?"

"I was in the Army for one hitch. Joined up right out of high school. After the Army, I got recruited for civilian government work."

"I see, and what did you do in the Army?" Reed asked.

"I grew up in Carthage, which is way north in Upstate New York. Did a lot of deer hunting in the Adirondacks. Used a compound bow and sometimes a lever-action Marlin 336C rifle. Army recognized right off I was a good shot and a decent tracker. Qualified for the Rangers. Became a squad advanced marksman. My handle was 'Watermelon Man' but keep that between us."

"Why 'Watermelon Man'?"

"I could reduce a cannonball watermelon to a seedy pink mist using a Barrett M82 at a maximum effective range of 1,969 yards."

"A Barrett? Don't send a boy, right?"

Reed surprised Jake.

"You're familiar with the Barrett?"

Reed crossed her arms and leaned back, readying herself for an adult discussion on weaponry.

"Some. I know the Barrett pierces brick, concrete and Kevlar. One round from the rifle into a truck's engine block disables it. Best long-distance sniper rifle in the world."

Jake pretended to wipe perspiration from his brow.

"Whoa! I'm really impressed. How do you know so much about the rifle?"

"Been a gun enthusiast all the way back to when I was a runt hunting squirrels in West Virginia's Blue Ridge Mountains. I used a slide-action Winchester .22 rifle. Had a beautiful twenty-four-inch blue steel barrel. What I would give to have that rifle today."

Reed uncrossed her arms. She rested both forearms on the table.

My God, she's gorgeous, Jake observed.

Reed continued her discourse.

"I also own a Glock and a Sig Sauer, oh, and a .38 Colt Special that's more antique than service revolver. I practice once a week at a shooting range out in East Hillsborough County. Most of the men and woman who hang there are veterans, some of them Vietnam vets. After shooting practice, I usually sit with them, while they talk shop and swap war stories. I just listen. That's how I learned about the Barrett M82."

"You're pro-Second Amendment, then?"

"Yes, I am, matter of fact."

Suddenly, mayhem ensued at the bar.

Using an index finger while grasping a glass of beer in the same hand, an angry man, likely a local, poked Mr. Pink Flamingo in his bony chest. Each time the man poked, he splashed beer onto old MPF. The local was several years younger, a good fifty-pounds heavier and a half-foot taller than the old man who came from the sea. Like a crazed cocka-too, the man screeched a Caribbean patois that flustered Mr. Pink Flamingo's feathers.

Two barflies, nested comfortably on bar stools, quickly moved away from the approaching Birds of Paradise Showdown in the Caribbean. The two patrons comprised a middle-aged couple of plus-size dimen-sions, whose plan was to open, then close, the Dutch pub.

Both dedicated beer drinkers expected blood spilt over the imbroglio a fermenting in the brewery. The two got off their stools and stepped back three feet, because neither wanted blood spattered on brand new matching t-shirts promoting Conch Fu Dine In/Take Kwan Out Sea Food Shack.

The bartender, a short stocky attractive woman with long auburn hair, did nothing to intercede. She simply rang the happy-hour bell, signaling the official start of two-four-one Bonaire Blond drafts.

The barfly couple moved surprisingly fast in grabbing their pints and returning to a ringside view of the growing melee.

Sweat trickled down the local man's chubby onyx face as he poke-provoked the now beer-drenched Mr. Pink Flamingo. The instigator's aim was to goad the old goat into pushing back, thereby casting MPF as the instigator.

This wasn't going well for the aged warrior.

Reed watched the drama unfold, then said to Jake, "Looks as if it's my turn."

"Can you handle the situation?" Jake asked politely.

Reed *pfttt!*

"Hell yes, I can handle it. Way I look at it, want a decent omelet, ya gotta crack a few skulls."

Chapter 7

TAMPA, FLORIDA · 2022

FOR WHAT WOULD BE her last time, Alicia Serrano climbed on her BarraCubas-gifted Harley Davidson Low Rider and roared out of the Namaste parking lot.

Lightheaded from Detective Friekorps releasing her from informing, Alicia felt added joy over her fine night of performing at Namaste.

The nightclub was packed in like a New Mount Zion Missionary Baptist Church service featuring an appearance by the Reverend Al Green. Many of the guests came specifically to watch Alicia perform. They invested in her promise made the week before to ditch her blues and re-energize her sensually exuberant stage persona.

She kept her promise by enthusiastically performing a spicy mélange of salsa, rumba and soca.

DJ Koala, talented and beautiful West African who wore her signature white silk track suit, played an extended re-mix of Miami Sound Machine's "Rhythm is Gonna Get You."

Alicia's caramel skin glistened in the stage lights only minutes into her performance.

She wore a deep blue split dress with tiered tassels and Dolce & Gabbana pink satin pumps. Her dress shimmered in rhinestones, sequins and crystals. When Alicia shook her hips, three tassel tiers swirled like comets against a nightscape of flickering stars.

The audience was hypnotized by her dress.

The audience also was hypnotized by her petite breasts, narrow waist, robust derriere and long legs sculpted as if from Emperador marble.

An obviously inebriated man stood shakily to call out to Alicia, "Your rhythm's got me, all right, I'm one happy gringo, mamacita!"

Security Chief Andre made a move toward the man. Alicia waved him off. She gave a slight nod to the liquor-sodden, yet likely harmless, Anglo.

The man's wife yanked on his billowing black suit coat that was an "X" too many for her fellow.

"I'm miserable enough here, then you go acting the fool, and 'sides, that's a brownie you're flirting with, shame on you, why can't we go to Dixie Darlings down in Riverview?" the woman said in one impressive dragon's breath.

The man *harumpfed!* into his chair.

He'd been chastised by his wife, with the nightclub watching. He was tired. He wished only to evaporate into his circus tent of a suit, leaving but a pair of pointed black shoes peeking out.

"Doris, dear, this is where it happened. I still can't believe it. Have you no sense of history? Raven met her match here. This is Deep South sacred ground, tragic sacred ground. May we never again witness such an ignoble fall from grace."

The dragon roared.

"I *do* have a sense of history, ya pinhead, but this place reminds me of Vicksburg or Atlanta, goddamn to hell those bastards Grant and Sherman, and the same goes for Reed O'Hara."

"Now, Doris, don't get all verklempt on me. Supposed to have fun, while paying our respects."

"Don't use Yid around me, buster, I'll get upset if'n I'm of a mind to, praise the soul of Robert E. Lee, who most art in pure white Heaven, and sweet Jesus, you look like a damn mortician in that suit, stop going to the Salvation Army for your clothes, c'mon, let's get out of here, *right now.*"

He lowered his head, sighed deeply, then nodded to Doris. He was defeated. Once more.

The couple rose from the table and made for the exit, with Doris leading the way, as per edict from Doris, of course. Then the man turned to wave goodbye to Alicia. She blew him a kiss. He grinned like a schoolboy gazing with prepubescent fervor upon forbidden treasure of a big-bosomed bearded lady in a traveling carny.

Lordy, don't let Doris hear me thinking this, but brown-skinned women, they ain't so bad, he conceded.

Alicia climaxed her stage performance by dancing to the conga drum pounding *rat-tat-tat-tat!* in Gloria Estefan's "Turn the Beat Around."

The performer didn't miss a beat as her hips kept pace with the song's withering pace. When Havanna-born Estefan scatted with her band, Alicia conjured hot tropical moves evoking an erotic cachet of mariposa blooms, Cuban sazon and her own serpentine body electric.

After she finished, people rushed forward, placing hundred-dollar bills in a Degas-blue ceramic bowl at the foot of the stage. She received a standing ovation.

Reed and Jake stood at the bar at the back of the room. They raised their glasses to Alicia, who appeared unbound & reborn, with new-found freedom coursing through her body.

This is what normal feels like, she thought. Could get used to it.

No one took notice of Doris and her husband leaving.

No one other than Reed and Jake.

"You know, Megan told me about that pair of matching asshats," Reed said. "Apparently, they're loyal members of our Confederatess Raven Doyle's occult of personality."

Jake's square jaw framed a broad smile.

"What?" Reed asked him defensively.

"'Occult of personality,' love it, babe."

Reed gifted him her Katzenjammer Kids smile.

"Why thank you, my love."

"Bien sur."

Jake sipped from a highball glass of coconut water over ice and rimmed with raw sugar and a lime slice. He preferred the drink flash-blended into a slushie, but blenders weren't allowed at Namaste.

"Something tells me you've already had Ravel check out those Dixie dimwits," Reed said, as she slipped two fingers into Jake's drink, extracted two ice cubes, popped 'em in her mouth, then crushed the crystalline cubes with tiger-chomp ferocity.

"You are correct, Madame," Jake said, indifferent to Reed, in a manner of speaking, once again taking Jake's lunch money while giving him an undressed 'bony sammich.

I'm a giver, after all, Jake thought.

Snack-size Ravel wore two hats on behalf of Reed and Jake.

Officially, she was assistant manager at Namaste, handling the night-club's finances, with Jake titled general manager.

Increasingly, though, as Jake became more involved with O'Hara & Dupree Private Enquiry Agency, Ravel took on greater responsibilities in managing Namaste.

Occasionally, she assisted Reed and Jake in their investigations, but Reed leaned heavily toward overprotecting Ravel.

A talented hacker, there were few systems she couldn't breach, be they government, corporate or civilian. Her office at Namaste was bunkered with computer monitors, a laptop and an impressive HPE ProLiant DL 360 Gen10 rack server.

Sitting in her lumbar-supported Carib green leather executive chair, Ravel could operate Namaste, hack through a firewall virtually anywhere in the world, watch *Sponge Bob* and FaceTime with Reed about what Jake planned for their late-night dinner.

Swiss Ravel was a recalcitrant nomad. She had her own bedroom in Reed and Jake's downtown Tampa penthouse. Sometimes she crashed at her office on a luxurious Harper & Bright futon sofa bed. Failing those two options, she slept over at her girlfriend Sierra's condo, if the pair weren't arguing.

Ravel was cocooning in her Namaste lair when Jake called her about the couple.

"Be happy to check 'em out, Jakester. Give me ten minutes."

Ravel needed only six.

"What'd you learn from Ravel?" Reed asked Jake.

"She got into the FBI's facial recognition program. Sure enough, there they were. You're spot on about their being part of Raven Doyle's white supremacists' network. They're big-time donors to Raven's schemes as well as to her legal defense fund."

"And their names?"

Jake gave Reed their full names.

"Thank you, my husband. Goodness, whatever would we do without our Ravel?"

"Lead a much less informed life." Jake answered. "Do you ever get tempted by Ravel?"

Reed sat her glass of iced pomegranate juice on the bar. Yes, the juice was iced. But she preferred everything's Jake.

She thought of the time, after having rescued Ravel from Russian mobster Victor Petrov, she allowed Ravel to kiss her and to touch her breasts. Reed was surprised by how much she enjoyed the experience.

"Yes, Ravel's brilliant, beautiful and far more unrestrained than I," Reed answered. "It's nothing I can't keep in check, love."

Jake lifted his glass in salute to his wife, ignoring that most of the ice in the glass had gone AWOL.

"What do you think about Alicia?' Jake asked. "Is she our griffin rising from the ashes?"

Just then, Alicia positively beamed when she collected her gratuities. As she left the stage to return to the dressing room, Andre held aside the black curtain covering the doorway. Performer and bodyguard nodded to one another.

"You're right about her being a phoenix, Jake. Don't trust it, though. I catch tells in people's facial expressions. And Alicia, she has the look of a person relieved to get out of a serious jam probably of her own making."

Reed gulped down her juice, good manners and decorum be damned to Templar Malta.

Thirsty is as thirsty does, she thought. Think I'll have a chat with our Alicia tomorrow evening.

Alicia spent over an hour talking to fellow performers in the dressing room. She got so involved with the cornucopia of complaints, gossip and shop talk, she almost forgot to change. Slipping out of her dance dress, she felt flattered by the Swedish performer Sierra admiring her svelte, naked body. She winked at Sierra, who then pursed her full lips at the Cuban beauty.

Oh, you naughty girl, Alicia thought. Better not let Ravel catch you hittin' on me.

Alicia put on a white cotton shirt, not bothering with a bra, followed by Levi's jeans, black engineer boots and a black leather jacket. There was a series of snap-fastener sockets on the back of the jacket. Resembling a connect-the-dots puzzle, the sockets made curvy-wurvy patterns on the jacket.

Alicia knew their purpose. On the rare occasion she rode with the BarraCubas, she'd snap in the club's colors or patches, with the upper crescent reading "BarraCubas MC," the lower crescent reading "Tampa, Florida" and a grinning barracuda head grinning centered between the crescents and projected against an outline of Cuba.

Jake inquired about the empty sockets on the back of her jacket.

"Should I be concerned, Alicia?" he asked tentatively.

"No worries, Señor Jake. I found my jacket in a thrift store in Ybor. Cost me three bucks. People there, they thought it was pleather. It's not, it's real leather. What a steal, sí?"

No direct eye contact, too many details, he surmised. No way a biker would donate his club jacket, but am I pitching too fine here?

"I'll let it go, Alicia. Please don't make me regret it."

She gave Jake a wink and a smile.

After getting the skinny from fellow performers, Alicia left the dressing area and walked into the main room.

Sehar was performing onstage traditional Indian dance routines, accompanied by genre-shattering sitar play of Anoushka Shankar, daughter of sitar master Ravi Shankar.

Alicia sat down at a table reserved exclusively for Namaste performers, off limits in all ways & means to guests.

Chef Glen was kind enough to keep his kitchen open so that she might partake of a Tortilla de Alicia, an omelet made with caramelized onions, sharpiest cheddar, fiery salsa picante, chopped chorizo, sour cream and avocado.

The chef himself brought the plated omelet to her.

"You are to eat every bit of your namesake tortilla, young lady," Chef Glen mandated jovially.

Alicia clapped with joy.

"Gracias, mi guapo," she said

Chef smiled, "De nada, Señorita Lambada."

So damn cute, she thought. Won't be telling him Lambada's Brazilian, not Cuban.

Sated by conversation and food, Alicia was the last performer to leave Namaste.

Grooving south on Lois Avenue, she met little traffic as she headed to the on-ramp to Interstate 275.

The cloudless night sky shimmered with an astro light show conducted by La Luna waxing poetic till dawn.

Alicia was relaxed. She was content. She earned two-thousand dollars in gratuities. Double the nightly tips in recent weeks. Before she climbed on her Harley and left Namaste, she slid twenty Benjamins into her biker's billfold.

Sixties Detroit soul played on her ear buds.

Alicia joined Marvin Gaye and Tammi Terrell in singing "Ain't No Mountain High Enough":

'Cause baby, there ain't no mountain high enough
Ain't not valley low enough, ain't no river wide enough
To keep me from getting to you, baby

She was too exhilarated to notice double entendre foreshadowing in those lyrics.

As she approached the lighted intersection, where she'd take a left and get onto Interstate 275, Alicia noticed another motorcyclist had rolled to a stop.

He was waiting for the traffic light to turn a go-go-green.

She rolled up to the rider's portside. She nodded to him. He responded with a thumbs up.

He conjured an image of the Pale Rider late-night riding, enjoying empty streets and freedom to roam.

Then Alicia whiplashed an about face: the rider dressed exactly as Marlon Brando portraying biker gang leader Johnny Strabler in 1953's *The Wild One*, which was Alicia's favorite film. She watched it at least a dozen times in Cuba, where the film's dialogue was dubbed in Spanish. When she heard the original Anglo soundtrack for the first time in Tampa, she gushed over Brando's soft pansexual lisp.

The man's attention to detail astounded Alicia. Just as Brando did in *The Wild One*, the biker wore an iconic Schott Perfecto black leather jacket over a simple ringer t-shirt, Buscarlet black leather gloves, Levi's 501 jeans and Chippewa engineer boots. Instead of a helmet, he sported a Johnny Cap, a tan canvas motorcycle cap with a gold stretch metal band and black leather front bill.

The biker covered his face with a neck gaiter, the only item not part of Brando's original outfit.

Metal-framed aviator sunglasses shuttered his eyes.

Piece de resistance was a replica of the silver second-place trophy, stolen by Johnny's Black Rebel Motorcycle Club. The man strapped the trophy on the front of his bike, just as Johnny did in *The Wild One*.

Despite the traffic light turning green, both riders stayed put. They stared at one another.

Alicia decided to test the man's familiarity with *The Wild One*.

Above the deep gurgle of idling motorcycle engines, she called out, "What're you rebelling against?"

The man howled like Wolfman Jack, then shot back, "Whaddya got?"

Alicia let out a "Ha!" She saluted her approval.

Then she experienced a 120-volt shock to her system. She was so fixated on his outfit, she only just realized the man rode a Fat Bob 114 Harley Davidson, not the 650cc Triumph Thunderhead that was Brando's personal motorcycle and the bike he rode in *The Wild One*.

Damn it, his Harley ruins everything, Alicia fumed to herself.

"Mira, amigo," she said.

"Yeah, wassup?" he answered.

"Brando rode a Triumph!"

Pulling down the neck gaiter, the man grinned ghoulishly. He took off his aviator sunglasses. He continued to stare. Alicia thought his eyes were blacker than the Seven Deadly sins.

"I know, *Senorita Alicia Serrano*, but I wouldn't be caught dead riding a piece of shit Triumph."

Alicia's survival instincts kicked in.

She put her bike in gear.

She attempted to speed away.

She was too late.

With fast-twitch agility of a pond gator scarfing up a Muscovy duck, the Brando bandito whipped out a Smith & Wesson 9mm revolver and fired three rounds into the tiny dancer, one round in her face, another in her throat and a third round in her chest.

Alicia flailed like a netted silver-hair bat. She fell on the asphalt. Her Harley collapsed with her. The young woman's life force evaporated as quickly as spilt water in 127-degree Death Valley. Her deoxygenated maroon blood pooled into a beatific halo around her small head.

Her eyes and mouth remained open.

Her face expressed disappointment rather than terror.

In a few seconds, Alicia Serrano's life was extinguished.

No more dreams.

No more goals.

No more beautiful dancing.

Lamenta blemente se fue para siempre.

Yes, gone foreva and eva.

The shooter placed his revolver in a shoulder holster. He kickstood his motorcycle. He paused to admire his handiwork. He got off his bike. He walked over to Alicia's body. The killer extracted the cash from her bi-fold and stuffed the bills into his jeans pocket.

He wasn't done.

The man took from his jacket BarraCubas club patches. Pushing her body on its side, he snapped in the upper and lower crescents, followed by the club emblem in the center.

The shooter drank from a Mexican silver flask. He poured some of its amber contents on the asphalt next to Alicia's body.

The killer got back on his motorcycle. With a green turn arrow, he took the on-ramp to Interstate 275 with all deliberate speed.

As Mick Jagger sang in "Gimme Shelter," "War, children, it's just a shot away, it's just a shot away."

CHAPTER 8

———

BONAIRE

SOUTHERN CARIBBEAN · 2014

BEFORE REED LEFT to rescue Mr. Pink Flamingo in the Bonaire Blond Brewery, Jake asked her, "Suspect the old guy might've caused this cluster cluck?"

"Yes, he has quite a mouth on him. I wonder, when you join AARP, do you turn in your filters in exchange for a recycled canvas grocery bag?"

Jake laughed.

"I think so. But we need to make a move here. Can you handle the guy picking on our Screaming Eagle?"

"No problem. Palooka's a bully who probably couldn't fight his way out of a Chuck E. Cheese ball crawl."

"A what?" Jake asked.

"Think of it as a mosh pit for tykes," Reed answered.

"Got it."

"I'll deal with the bully. All those brawls with my brother in West-by-God-Virginia taught me how to make little boys cry."

Jake said with a mock grimace, "I'll keep that in mind."

Jake watched Reed march over to the bar. She barged between the palooka and the frightened old man, frightened because he knew he was *waaay* over matched.

64

Reed first spoke with Mr. Pink Flamingo. She wagged her index finger at him, as if he were a misbehaving child. He listened intently to her. Twice he nodded in agreement.

Once she finished her lecture, Reed gave him a peck on his right cheek, took hold of his shoulders, turned him around, then pointed him to the door.

Reed gave him a pat on the rump to send him on his way. He left. No fanfare. No braggadocio. Just an old warrior retreating with his dignity left mostly intact for another day.

All this time, the bully watched the small fearless woman ruining his playtime with tourons. He felt cheated, what with the old guy walking away with nary a scratch or bruise.

A foot shorter than the bully, and barely half as wide, Reed craned her head skyward and spoke in Angry Bird to Mister Jerk Chicken. Her face reddened. Her eyes resembled a pair of crystalline blue lightning storms.

At first, the man cowered from Reed's verbal assault. Then he recovered. Still clutching the empty beer glass, he used the same hand to poke her left breast, a criminal act meant to intimidate her.

In her peripheral vision she saw Jake rise from the chair. She shook her head at him without breaking eye contact with the bully. Jake sat back down.

In a flash, Reed slapped away the man's poker hand, causing the beer glass to fly a straight trajectory toward the bartender, who caught the glass and set it aside in one motion, all the while drawing a draft from the Bonaire Blond beer tap.

For a few seconds, everyone in the pub, including Reed and MJC, marveled at the bartender's manual dexterity.

Bartender shrugged indifference toward her feat.

After Reed and the bartender nodded to one another, Reed stomped on the bully's left foot with her right heel.

She shattered the man's foot bones, specifically the phalanges, tarsals and cuneiforms, producing the snap, crackle, pop of a woodfire roasting marshmallows for making S'mores.

The man screeched in pain. He hopped on one leg like Big Bird on a lost weekend bender at the Beverly Hills Hotel.

"You want some s'more, big boy?" Reed yelled at him.

His response was a sweeping right cross aimed at Reed's head. She ducked. She shifted to her left. He punched air.

The crowd turned on him.

"Fat boy Ronald better lay off McDonald's," a woman called out sarcastically.

"You not pregnant, Ronald, you only *look* like you pregnant," another woman said.

Ronald tried to ignore the insults.

He groped toward Reed. She was waiting for him. She kneaded his doughy belly with her right knee, pounding his gut four times rapida-mente. She was aware her dress billowed a la Marilyn Monroe straddling a subway vent in *The Seven Year Itch*. Reed didn't care her muscular buttocks covered in demure white panties were on display. She was having too much fun to worry over propriety.

"Swiggity swooty, damn what a booty!" a male bar patron yelled

"Million-dolla checks don't bounce off that ass!" another said.

"Pardon me, miss, but do you work out?" a third patron asked.

Even Jake laughed at that one. Reed as well.

Time to end this massacree, she thought.

Reed finished him off with a not-an-ounce-of-fat-hundred-pound-backed left uppercut to the man's jaw. He tumbled like a burlap bag filled with a lovely bunch of coconuts.

"Shit, so much for dignity in defeat, right?" an old man commentated.

The bartender took charge.

"All right, it's over. We need to clean up before the police show up in those silly-ass uniforms. I need two of you to take this idiot to his home."

The crowd stayed silent as paid seat fillers at a pervy uncle's funeral.

"That's how this is going down, eh?" the bartender grumped. "Fine, first two of you picks up Ronald gets to drink free rest of the night."

The rotund barflies got pushed aside by two quicker & younger men, who helped Ronald to his feet.

Ronald continued to cry like a Jamaica Brahman newborn calf.

The bartender threw a bar towel in his face udderly covered in sweat & tears.

"Enough of that wailin', Ronald. It isn't manly. And you best stop messin' with tourists. Bad for you, bad for my business. Besides, there's no shame in getting your fat ass handed to you by the likes of this Bonaire blonde hottie."

Ronald muttered, "Okay, all right."

The two volunteers rushed Ronald out of the pub. They were in a thirsty hurry to get battered bully boy home.

Bartender set a plastic pitcher of ice water on the countertop next to Reed.

"Here, mijn liefje, put your hand in the ice water, it'll help with the swelling," she said soothingly to Reed.

Also keeps this beauty near me for a while longer, she hoped.

Bartender stared at Reed as she twirled her long, elegant fingers in the ice water. Reed plucked two ice cubes from the pitcher and popped them in her mouth.

Patrons attempted to get in drink orders. The bartender ignored them. Completely.

Oh hell, what's the harm in asking, she decided.

"Any chance, mi lady?"

Reed smiled.

"You're a most handsome woman, and believe me, I'm tempted. But sorry, I play straight poker at the table and in the bedroom. Most of the time. Thanks for taking care of me, though. What's your name?"

Bartender pouted slightly.

"I'm Sanne."

"I'm Reed."

"Pleasure. Just my luck, your being hetero and all. And you're welcome. You gotta ice that hand after every fight, remember that."

Reed leaned across the bar and gave Sanne a full-on kiss. Sanne closed her eyes and lost herself in this wonderful moment of pleasure, or as the Dutch would put it, heerlijk moment van genot.

"Made this Dutch broad's day, thanks, Reed," Sanne said breathlessly, while staring into Reed's eyes.

"It was my pleasure, Sanne," Reed responded breathily as well.

Reed casually walked back to the table, then said to Jake, "Sorry about that, now where were we?"

He let five seconds tick-tock-o'clock before he spoke.

"Do you have any idea how excruciating it was for me to *not* pound that punk after he jabbed you in the chest?"

Reed smiled.

"More accurately, Pokemon got me in the left boob, a direct hit I'll feel for a while, but it's no biggie."

"Are you going to answer my question?"

"Oh, I'm sorry, I thought you were being rhetorical. Well, all right, sit back and relax, because I've got a couple points to make. You barely know me, so you couldn't be certain I'd take him. Whattaya' know, Jake Dupree, the Fresh Poppin' Doughboy went down in the first round. Granted, you aren't aware I'm a black belt in tae kwon do. Still undefeated after fifteen official matches and, um, six *unofficial* bouts."

Reed paused to finish off her beer.

"I've always liked to fight. I never back down. I've got the stitches to show for it. It's sort of an O'Hara family tradition. Longer I'm around you, the better you'll appreciate I'm a woman of my word. If I say I can handle a situation, I can. Finally, I sense you probably need to keep your nose clean during your retirement years from the CIA, so I was happy to step into the fray."

"Wait, Reed, I never said I was in the CIA."

"Didn't have to, figured it out all by my lonesome. You're obviously a former Army Ranger sniper who went straight into the CIA. What did you do for the Company? Make origami butterflies, write haiku and perform the chanoyu tea ceremony? No. At least *this* little grasshopper doesn't think so. You were an operative, an asset shaded back to black. When you first approached my table, I noticed no one paid any attention to you. You hid in plain sight, just as you were trained. Getting into a brawl only raises your profile."

Jake exhaled, then lowered his head.

"You're right, about the brawl thing," he admitted.

"I've got an idea something wonderful is developing here at this table, Jake. At a terrific rate. My head is practically spinning."

"Yeah, I'm a little dizzy dean myself," Jake said.

"If we're going to let this thing between us grow, trusting one another is imperative. Trust is more important than love. Agree?"

Jake smiled broadly at Reed.

"I agree totally, Ms. O'Hara."

"All right then, Mr. Dupree. You now may kiss me ... if you like."

CHAPTER 9

TAMPA, FLORIDA · 2022

"Toast the bitch, Beatrice."

Noir pulp master Ross MacDonald once described dawn as a gray shaking hangover.

More like goddamn fright-night terror plus one refusing to leave my party, Reed thought. So I'll cry if I wanna.

She was alone in bed in the master suite of their apartment in downtown Tampa. She was naked, except for a pair of Tropical Lifesavers striped footies. As was her habit, she pulled the white eider-down duvet over her head to ostrichsize herself from the world.

She drifted off to sleep. She was eleven again. She was back on the family farm in West Virginia, exploring an old hollow, or "holler" WVA speak.

Reed instantly transfixed on eerie sounds emanating from a forest of sugar maple, yellow birch and black cherry trees standing broad & erect like arboreal sentinels on both sides of the holler.

Might be black bears or nightjars or flying monkeys, she theorized. Now why'd I think of flying monkeys?

Awake or dreaming, Reed didn't frighten easily. Besides, she felt comforted by the Winchester pump-action .22 rifle slung over her right shoulder. She wore a Thin Mint green Girl Scout uniform, complete

70

with sash covered in merit badges, deep blue Civil Air Patrol helmet and red rubber rain boots.

No hiding in plain sight for her.

She spotted a large black hole high up the east side of the holler. In a flash, a shiny brass monocular materialized in her left hand. She eyed the black hole through the looking glass darkly.

Not a bear cave, might be an abandoned coal mine shaft, she noted. Let's check it out, shall we?

The monocular vaporized. Reed still had her rifle as she ascended the mountainside. Woods were as quiet as lunch with Harpo Marx at Tommy's World Famous Hamburger in Hollywood.

She slipped on a wet moss-covered rock, resulting in an impressive gash to her right knee. She took off her sash. She wrapped it tightly around her wounded knee. She squeezed the makeshift tourniquet enough to stop the bleeding, making her proud of her gold advanced first-aid merit badge that featured not one, but two, embroidered Band-Aids.

Somehow, Reed was inspired to recite aloud the Girl Scout pledge: "On my honor, I will try to serve God and my country, to help people at all times, to live by the Girl Scout Law and to solemnly, sincerely and truly declare and affirm that I will tell the truth, the whole truth and nothing but the truth, so help me God. Play ball! *Wait, what*?"

In a snap, Reed stood on the first-base side of the Riverfront Stadium infield. She stared into an empty Cincinnati Reds dugout. Flying monkeys swirled ominously above her. Pete Rose and Ty Cobb sat together behind home plate. They filed each other's steel spikes on their cleats.

Cobb was heard to say, "Ain't nothing pink tea about baseball."

Rose grunted in agreeably.

Without transition, Reed appeared in front of a black hole, which turned out to be an old mine shaft.

Dad, he'll whip me for sure, but I gotta look inside, she decided.

She chambered a round in her rifle. She stepped gingerly into the mine shaft.

Bats aplenty fluttered, while *squea-squea-squeaking* in the tar pitch darkness. Bats didn't bother Reed, though she was aware that if bats laid eggs in her hair, she'd go insane, possibly even become a New York Yankees fan. She tapped her Civil Air Patrol helmet to make certain her long blonde hair was safe from bat eggings. She was glad for her red rubber rain boots, as she repeatedly stepped in malorderous bat guano.

With each step forward, the light from the mineshaft's entrance dimmed like the fading generator light on a vermillion '70 VW Beetle.

Let there be light, she exclaimed.

Reed pulled a candle and a box of matches from a pocket in her uniform.

Not sure how they got there, but ain't no way I'm complaining, she thought.

The lit white wax candle illuminated the tunnel before her.

She remembered coal miners used heavy sledgehammers, pick axes and steel wedges to burrow horizontally into the mountain.

Once the tough-as-rawhide miners found a coal seam, they dug down to find the anthracite mother lode.

Those vertical tunnels made abandoned coal mine shafts incredibly dangerous to explore.

Sometimes children disappeared inside them.

Probably should go only twenty feet or so, she decided.

She reminded herself Ben Dover got lost in a mine shaft. Poor little guy wasn't right in the head. Reed still felt bad blaming him for the case of Tang she and her siblings ate on a lazy hazy Sunday afternoon. She conceded that at least they got out of a whooping by their father.

A hot breath rushed out of the dark recesses of the mine shaft. Reed's candle blew out. She couldn't find the matches.

Not good, not good at all, she thought.

Suddenly a voice emanated from the bowels of this dark black hell.

"Reed, I need to speak with you," the voice uttered menacingly.

"Who the *hell* is that?" she asked.

"Do you hear me, Reed?"

She put her hands on her hips and planted her feet like Wyatt Earp's huckleberry Doc Holliday.

"You don't scare me at all. Just who are you? What do you want?"

Reed realized seconds spent in silent darkness felt more like minutes.

"I never ate your dang Tang. And you know what else? I'm *special*, I ain't a 'tard, like your father called me."

Reed had never been so shocked, except maybe when she flew out of the O'Hara station wagon and rolled down the mountainside as the family made its way to Easter service. She was shocked, that is, because she survived her *coming 'round the mountain when she comes* en plein air tumble.

"Ben? Ben Dover? Is that you?"

More silence. More hot air hit Reed's face.

"God, Reed, even trapped in my friend's lair, you're still a smartass. It's *Benjamin* Dover."

"Sorry, Benjamin, but what do you mean by your friend's lair?"

She heard a maniacal laugh.

Then she saw a pair of molten red eyes the size of Arcoroc ruby saucers.

An immense form shuffled toward Reed.

"Allow me to introduce you to my best friend, a dragon who kept me safe all this time," Benjamin said.

The dragon roared six feet of flames.

"There's no place like home, there's no place like home," Reed chanted as she tapped the heels of her red rubber rain boots.

"Toast the bitch, Beatrice," Benjamin ordered.

Reed had dropped her Winchester. She fell to her knees to feel around for the rifle. She found only pieces of it.

It was fortunate she knelt, because the great yellow & red flame that shot out of Beatrice's fanged maw would've burnt Reed to a deep-fried crispiness had she been upright.

As it were, only the very top of her Civil Air Patrol helmet was singed.

Yeah, it's a nightmare, all right, she thought. Time to end this guilt trip down memory lane.

Still under the covers, Reed barely made out a soft tap tapping on the bedroom door.

"Can I come in, babe?"

It was Jake.

Reed threw off the duvet, then sat up. She saw she was naked, except for her rainbow striped footies.

"Bad dream again?" Jake muffled through the door.

Reed slid her tan muscular legs over to the left side of the king bed. Her feet dangled a few inches above the Macassar ebony hardwood floor. She hopped off the bed, with her full breasts jiggling. She took a running start and slid on her footies across the floor to the bedroom door.

She opened the door.

"Yes, another nightmare and yes, you may come in. I need to make love to you. Get out of those duds, stud, and into bed ... holy crap!"

A Tampa Police Department uniformed officer stood in the living room and had a full view of her nude body. The officer gazed at Reed, then abruptly turned his back to her.

"Good morning Ms. O'Hara. Sorry for the intrusion, but I have to say, you rock those socks," the officer said.

Husband and wife laughed.

"Thanks for the compliment, officer. I'll treasure this moment. Really. Now let me close this door, so I can put on some clothes."

Jake and the officer responded in unison, "Yes, ma'am."

After tossing her footies in the general direction of her walk-in closet, Reed paused to admire her svelte body in a full-length mirror.

Jake Dupree, you're one lucky man, she concluded.

She slipped into matching black bra and panties, Levi's skinny jeans and a midnight navy silk blouse. She slid into Gucci slides, then walked into their spa bathroom, where she washed up and brushed her bobbed hair the color of Oro Vino Spumante.

Time to face the world, and those two lummoxes, she thought.

Reed marched confidently into the living room. Jake and the officer sat at the dining table. They drank coffee. They weren't smiling. Strangely enough, Jake didn't put on music. Usually, he began his day with Bach or Bob Marley or the Black Keys.

Jake and the officer looked up as Reed approached.

"Don't make me ask who died, guys," Reed said less than half in jest.

Jake stood up, as did the officer.

"Please have a seat, Reed, we need to talk," Jake said.

He held her chair as his wife sat down.

"Reed, this is Officer Terry Rowland of the Tampa Police Department. Terry and I go back a few years. He plays a mean game of tennis, when he's sobered up."

Rowland laughed, then grew somber again.

"Pleased to meet you, Officer Rowland. To what do we owe your entirely too early Sunday morning presence?"

Shit, she's pissed, Jake observed.

"Ma'am, I wish I could've met you in less revealing circumstances, but it's a real pleasure to make your acquaintance."

Reed slapped her hand on the table.

"God damn it, I'm not some hothouse flower who can't handle bad news. Officer, tell me what's going on."

The officer looked at Jake.

Reed sighed, "You don't need permission from Jake to speak with me, Terry."

Rowland cleared his throat.

"Yes, ma'am. At approximately four a.m. today, Ms. Alicia Serrano was found dead from an apparent homicide. She had been shot three times, probably at close range. Our crime scene unit is still there at the intersection of Lois Avenue and Cypress. It appears Ms. Serrano intended to take the on-ramp to Interstate 275. Her motorcycle remains at the scene. Her bifold wallet was empty of cash."

Reed stood up with such ferocity, her buffalo leather chair somersaulted into twin bookcases in the dining room.

"Are you fucking telling me Alicia was killed for just a little bit of money!"

"No, Reed, it was a hit, not an especially professional hit, but a hit nevertheless," Jake interjected.

She walked over to the large picture window and cried with her back to the two men.

As Officer Rowland got up to leave, he noticed a bedroom door slightly ajar. A deep purple eye stared at him. The little dragon of the mighty Matterhorn smoldered in sulfurous anger.

Chapter 10

Bonaire

Southern Caribbean · 2014

The Kiss.

It was sensual.

It was grown-up romantic.

"All right then, Mr. Dupree, you may now kiss me … if you like," Reed said with coquettish bravura.

Amid a gathering storm of drunken pub patrons at Bonaire Blond Brewery, Reed and Jake leaned toward one another to kiss for the first time.

It was a sweet full-on buss lasting nearly a minute.

Jake kept his right hand on Reed's left shoulder. She held his face with her right hand. She delicately stroked his jaw line with a to-die-for manicured index finger.

For a moment, Jake stared into Reed's crystal blue persuasion eyes that'd melt Tommy James and all his Shondells.

Jake started to pull back. Reed placed her hand behind his neck, then darted the tip of her tiny pink tongue between his lips.

They both sat back to catch their breath.

What I'd give to be that guy with Reed, pub owner Sanne thought.

She clanged the brass bell bolted into the bar countertop.

"Listen up! A free Bonaire Blond draft to any of you who saw what looked to me like a first kiss. Congratulations, you two!"

Sanne waved to Reed, who returned her wave.

Locals and cruisers rushed to the bar, all claiming they saw The Kiss. Sanne couldn't pour drafts fast enough. Even patrons smoking on the back patio crushed out their cigarettes and rushed inside for free beer.

"Wait just a minute, Mike, are you saying you witnessed The Kiss *through a concrete wall*?" Sanne asked an elderly local.

"Indirectly I did, Sanne," he answered. "Felt a twittering in my Maypole that musta come from the spirit in the sky, I do testify."

"Spirit in the sky, huh?" she asked skeptically.

"You betcha, when I die and they lay me to rest, goin' up to the spirit in the sky, amen and amen, 'cause I got a friend in Jesus."

A nearby patron spit-taked his pale ale and misted Manichean Mike.

"God damn, Mike, you owe an apology to Norm Greenbaum for butchering his song," the man said.

Mike wiped beer mist off his face, then licked his fingers.

"Haven't any idea what yer talking about," he said disdainfully. "Sanne, do I get my free beer or what?"

"What," the man answered for Mike.

"Hush, Pieter," Sanne interjected. "Yes, Mike, you get a free beer."

She slid a red Solo cup of ale to Mike.

"Gotta pay for the next one, though," Sanne said.

Mike nodded reluctantly.

"Put the old fart's next few beers on my tab," Pieter said.

Mike bowed to Pieter, then walked off singing, "I got a friend in Jesus and in Pieter DeVries, they're a gonna lift me up to that spirit in the sky."

Reed and Jake held hands in silence until she said, "I warned you, if we kiss, it changes everything."

"For the better?" Jake said hopefully.

"We'll see, won't we? All I know for sure is I'm on fire right now."

Jake held her hand and kissed it.

"Then let me be your last first kiss," he requested.

Reed stared at him.

"I won't give you that right now. We've just met. We know so little about one another. But I'll keep an open mind on the subject."

Jake smiled.

"Seems as if you pinned me down as far as my career choices." he said.

"Lucky guesses all. I have no problems with your career choices. You served our country faithfully. Your sacrifices are immeasurable. I'm honored to know you."

Jake cleared his throat, then said, "Thank you, Reed, no one has ever said that to me."

"You're welcome, and I mean every damn word," she said. "I've been around enough psychos to know you're not one."

"Thanks. So how about you tell me about what you do back in Tampa Bay."

"All right, but first you have to get me another Bonaire Blond."

"You got it," he exclaimed.

Jake practically leapt from his chair and power walked to the bar. He wove his way through the crowd, not bumping into anyone and apologizing for even the slightest brush by.

An attractive middle-aged brunette placed a hand on his shoulder. She attempted to engage him in conversation. Jake smiled. He took her hand off him. He wagged a finger at her, then pointed to Reed, who finger fluttered a wave to her. The woman sulked off.

Jake returned with a Bonaire Blond draft in one hand and his ice coco crush in the other.

"Excuse me, Miss, but haven't I seen you someplace before?" he inquired.

Reed took her beer from Jake, then said to him, "Yes, that's why I don't go there anymore, and thanks for the cerveza."

"Ah, you're being flippant because you think I'm a lousy kisser?" Jake asked.

"God no, you're a wonderful kisser. Flippery flippancy, acerbic retorts, cruel putdowns, manipulative compliments, an occasional slap: that's my personal arsenal for defending myself back home in Tampa Bay."

She sipped from her beer.

"Sorry, Jake, but sometimes this stuff slips out of me for no apparent reason, and not only when I've been drinking."

"Why do you have to defend yourself in Tampa Bay?" he asked.

"Because I'm an attorney, a female attorney with blonde hair and a nice body. Not a month goes by where I don't get Tail Hooked, in some fashion. Also, many male lawyers don't take me seriously. But some do, when they can get beyond my being a woman and appreciate my quality work. All of them know, however, I won't tolerate any bullshit from them."

"Pretty rough being a female attorney, I guess?"

"It can be. Allow me, kind sir, to illustrate. And this occurred *before* I started practicing the law. During an interview with a Tampa law firm, a senior partner who resembled Bartleby the Scrivener asked me what kind of birth control I use."

Jake exclaimed, "*What?*"

"True story."

"How'd you answer him?"

"Have to say, I enjoyed my comeback. I told him I use Don't Kid Yourself extra-large condoms, an intrauterine IUD and Handy Man Gel. See, you apply the gel to a guy's junk, couple minutes later, nutmeg-burning sensation ensues, et voilà, guy isn't interested in sex anymore, perfect birth control."

"Well played, Reed."

She drank pale ale.

"Thank you, thank you. I told the nervy old perve I'd just discovered another form of birth control. He asked what discovery that might be, foolish boy that he was. I told him his face, of course!'"

Jake laughed.

"Brutal, simply brutal. What did he say to you?" he asked.

"Let's see, I think I can remember his exact quote: 'Miss O'Hara, you are a nasty, dirty woman. I need to go make water. Be gone before I return.'"

"You got in the last word, I hope."

"Yes, I said, 'Going to make water, old sport? I can take a nice nap and be out of here long before you get back.' Never did get an offer from that firm."

"What's the name of your law firm in Tampa?"

"Let's just say it's an established firm that's silk stocking from knobby knees to hammer toes."

"What kind of law do you practice?"

Reed drank heartily from her glass of beer.

"I mostly do defense work for Big Tobacco," she said sans enthusiasm.

"Enjoy it?"

"Loathe it. I've worked too hard to shill for these heartless corporate bastards. If you think about it, Big Tobacco is just a white-collar drug cartel, although I readily acknowledge even these clients deserve proper legal counsel."

"What're you going to do? I can't see the sense in spending your career defending those assholes."

Reed lifted her V-shaped chin.

"My plan is to save as much of my earnings as I can, while allowing for an occasional trip to the Caribbean, where sometimes you meet the most attractive people."

"Why thank you, Reed," Jake said.

"Silly boy, I wasn't talking about you. I was talking about Sanne."

Reed looked up, caught Sanne's attention and gave her a wink. Sanne parlayed faux shock, then parachuted a smoochie-smooch to Reed.

"Should you be leading Sanne on?" Jake asked reproachfully.

Reed squinted at Jake.

"Who says I'm leading her on?"

"Fair enough," he said. "How about we return to your plan."

Reed polished off her beer.

"Where was I? Right, I've avoided buying a house and taking on a brutal mortgage. I drive an Accord, not a Benz or a Beamer. I dress professionally, but when it comes to suits and shirts and shoes, I never *ever* pay full price. And I don't need to buy underwear because I go commando."

"Seriously?" Jake asked.

"No, you ninny. Yoost a yoke, mang."

"Hmm, how buzzed are you?"

"Breaker breaker, Smoky's on my tail. Really though, I'm bumble bee buzzing just right, aight?"

"Absolutely."

"Thank you for your support. You see, I've learned how Big Tobacco operates: delay, delay, delay, until the plaintiff gives up or dies. I've learned all the tricks. Ashamed to say, I employed them myself all too often. It's okay, though, because in a few years, I'll hang out my own shingle.

Reed paused to finish her beer.

"I'll practice personal injury law. Sure, PI work can be slimy as hell. But it's the last area of the law where the power*less* sometimes gets justice from the power*ful*."

Jake reached out to hold Reed's hand.

"That's truly remarkable, Reed. You're running with the Devil long enough to learn how to defeat him and his minions. Brilliant, really."

"Merci, but it's hard for me to accept compliments gracefully. Okay, I must go make water, shall we say. On my way back, I'll get myself one more beer and you one of those cuckoo for loconuts drinks. Sanne will remember how to make it in the manner to which you're accustomed. When I return, I want to hear every hot little detail about your love life."

"Then you'll tell me about *your* love life?" Jake asked.

"We'll see, won't we," Reed answered.

CHAPTER 11

TAMPA, FLORIDA · 2022

FOR REED AND JAKE, this sunrise felt more like a blood orange sunset.

Alicia was gone. Murdered in the dead of the night.

Reed laid her head on Jake's shoulder, as they reclined on the living room sofa in their penthouse apartment.

Jake held Reed. They listened to the Johann Pachelbel's *Canon in D Major*.

"Sweetheart, do you remember what you once called old Johann?" Jake asked.

"Appreciate your trying to distract me, but no, I really don't," Reed sniffle voiced.

"Yo, Paco Bell," he said.

She laughed and cried at the same time.

She mumbled, "Now I finally get it ... like when rain comes down on a sunny day."

Reed disappeared into the great hulk of her husband's body. She knew running from pain this extreme was like trying to ditch her shadow. But after sufficient grieving, Reed expected to unleash her bad-ass self.

Soon come, as Jamaicans say, soon come, only she meant it.

Reed sat up. Jake followed.

She straightened her tear-stained silk blouse. She ran her hands through her hair. She wiped tears from her now-bloodshot eyes with a facial tissue.

Least I didn't put on mascara, she equivocated. Rocky Racoon eyes, *such* a fuckin' good look.

"Tell me again, except with more detail, about how you found out about Alicia," she asked.

Jake stretched his back. While completing a Cartegena assignment, Jake was struck in the back by his assigned target wielding an aluminum softball bat. Fortunately, the target had a nasty hook in his swing, thereby preventing a direct hit on the government-issued hitman's vertebrae.

Still hurt like a sonuva rhubarb pie, Jake whined to himself.

He sat back and exhaled loudly.

Can't recall a worse Sunday, he thought.

"Terry called me about five a.m. I was drinking a cup of English Breakfast tea at a Waffle House."

Reed smiled.

"I never thought I'd witness your conjoining 'English Breakfast Tea' with 'Waffle House.' What's this world coming to?"

"My love, I am a man of the people, a common man among fellow commoners, an avatar of Jeffersonian democracy."

Reed shook her head.

"Keep it up, I'll light a match. How about you get back to your report, and I stop interrupting. Deal?"

Jake nodded yes.

"Terry was part of the crew who caught the case. When he recognized the victim, he called me. Pretty ballsy of him, but I damn well appreciate it."

"What'd you do then?" Reed asked.

"I left Waffle House in a hurry. I drove down to the intersection of Lois and Cypress. There were a half-dozen Crown Vics and Chevy Caprices all lit up around the crime scene. Ambulance, coroner's station wagon and CSI van, all parked nearby. Officer at traffic control stopped me. I flashed him my P.I. license. I lied by telling the rook that Homicide asked me to come by. I got waved through."

Jake rose from the sofa. He walked briskly into their kitchen boasting of enameled lava countertops, Viking stainless steel appliances and solid cherry wood cabinets.

Having nice shit doesn't keep away loons, goons and derpy dragoons, he reminded himself.

He called out, "Gonna fix us some java. I'll talk while I work."

"Roger that, Brockmire."

"Reed O'Hara, that's uncalled for. Do I talk as if I were announcing a baseball game while we're having sex?"

"Sort of, but it's major league stuff."

"Keep it up, Reed, and I'll make your coffee so weak, only Bartleby would enjoy it."

"Bartleby, you remembered!" she exclaimed in a hoarse sleepy voice.

"I remember everything about you," Jake answered.

He poured boiling water into a Bodum nested with seven scoops of freshly ground Lavazza dark roast.

"Let it sit for four minutes, right?" Reed asked, wanting Jake to appreciate she could make a proper cup of coffee with a Bodum, should the prohibitively unlikely need arise.

"Yes, my love," he said.

Jake leaned against the island in the kitchen. He checked his Breitling Chronomat 44, an over-the-top birthday gift from Reed, to pinpoint exactly when to plunge the aromatic grounds to Bodum ground-zero.

Goddamn Timex takes a lickin' and keeps on tickin', old John Cameron Swayze used to claim, he thought. And what's a Timex cost, maybe forty bucks?

Jake continued his narrative.

"Harvard Kirby was detective in charge of the crime scene. He's an okay guy. Haven't yet had any run-ins with him. Harvard knows of you, Reed, of your P.I. investigations and the pro bono legal work you do for financially strapped women. He said you helped his niece. You, my dear, are the reason I was allowed inside the taped-off crime scene. That, and the fact that Terry told Harvard I knew Alicia."

Jake carefully pushed down the plunger, glass cylindering five cups of bad-to-the-bone-tomahawk coffee.

"Alicia's body resembled a Matisse sculpture asleep on the asphalt," Jake said.

"Get upset when you when you saw Alicia's body?" Reed asked.

"A little, probably because it was Alicia. Never experienced that emotion in my previous line of work, except for the time Sergio got killed. Those twenty-five kills of mine were human beings I turned into corpses. Got so, I felt like the Charon carrying the dead across the river Styx."

Reed smiled.

"Anyone else said that to me, I'd tell them to stop taking the piss. But you, warrior poet, I totally get it. I've decided you've nary a hint of pretentiousness."

"Thank you, love."

Jake poured two cups of coffee, putting cream and sugar in his cup, cream only in Reed's. He carried both cups of steaming coffee into the living room. He handed Reed her cup, then sat down next to his wife.

"Once I got over the shock, I began studying Alicia. She'd been hit in the face, throat and chest."

Reed put a hand to her face, then uttered, "Jesus Christ."

Jake took hold of her hand.

"Babe, is this too much for you?"

She shook her head.

"No, I want to hear it all."

"Okay. There were no empty shell casings around the body. We have either a shooter who picks up after himself, or someone using a high-powered revolver."

".357 Magnum?" Reed asked.

"Maybe, but three close-up rounds from that cannon wouldn't have left Alicia intact. My guess is it was a 9mm revolver."

"Didn't know they made 9mm revolvers."

"Smith & Wesson makes a good one ... reliable, well balanced, lethal beyond description."

Jake sipped his coffee, then continued his discourse.

"Alicia was shot up close. Three slugs exited her body. TPD hopes to find those slugs embedded somewhere nearby."

Reed finished her coffee.

"If they do, can they get a match with the weapon used?"

"Most likely. If the slugs are intact. Are you ready to hear something strange?"

"Yes."

"Alicia was wearing BarraCubas colors on the back of her black leather jacket."

"That's what those fasteners were for!" Reed said. "That never came to me, how about you?"

"How about I get us another cupa?"

"How about you answer my question first."

He rubbed his eyes.

"What're you, boss of my life?"

"Maybe."

"Fine, whatever. I was somewhat certain what Alicia was up to with her jacket. Not for nothing, but I know several bikers. From actual biker gangs. Dudes not to be messed with. Unless it's necessary. I learned about a motorcycle club's colors or patches. I noticed how Alicia could snap in an upper crescent, a lower crescent and a club emblem in the center on the back of the jacket."

"Why didn't you say something to me?" Reed said accusatorially.

Jake snorted derisively.

"I don't have to tell you everything, Reed. I really don't. Sometimes I take my own initiative. Without asking your permission, I decided to confront Alicia by myself."

Reed slid away from her husband.

"Hmm, and how exactly did that work out?" she asked.

Jake picked up his coffee cup to throw it against a wall.

He caught himself in mid-windup.

"You know you just balked, batter advances to first base," Reed said.

Jake smiled. Reluctantly.

"Balk nothing, ump. I thought only horses sleep standing up."

For the second time that morning, husband and wife laughed together.

"Seriously, babe. I fucked it up every which way with Alicia," Jake said.

"Hey, we both need to ease up on the f-bombs. Before you know it, we'll be pink-mist shag carpet f-bombing most of Tampa Bay, Mr. Watermelon Man."

Jake winked at her.

"Think you're pretty clever, don't you?"

"Of course I'm clever, *effen* happy to say," Reed answered.

"Good. I confronted Alicia about that jacket. She didn't act as if I ambushed her. She said she wasn't a member of a biker gang. She got the jacket cheap. She hadn't any idea why fasteners were on the back of her jacket."

Señor Jake said to Señora Reed, "She looked me right in the eyes, she didn't blink, she didn't appear to have dry mouth."

Why did I just lie to Reed? he wondered.

"You've made a couple comments about how beautiful she is, did her looks fool you?" Reed inquired.

"Absolutely not."

"Why did she fool you, then?"

"Please, Reed, she was a superb liar, that's how she got me."

"You gave her a pass," Reed said almost disdainfully. "Nice, well done."

This time, Jake split-finger fastballed the coffee cup against a Fernando Botero portrait of an exaggeratedly ripe Mona Lisa.

"Message received, *fucker*," Reed said with wicked-hardcore sulfuric acidity in her voice.

Suddenly Ravel called out from her bedroom, "Jesus Christ, will you two assholes shut the fuck up!"

CHAPTER 12

BONAIRE

SOUTHERN CARIBBEAN · 2015

"I GET IT ABOUT COMPLIMENTS, Reed. Don't trust 'em, right? Reminds me when I had a girlfriend awhile back in Arizona. Got pretty serious. Her name's Zorica."

Bonaire Blond Brewery got busier and louder by the half-hour.

Vivaldi would've sprung forth bloody apoplectic had he witnessed bar patron revelry drowning out *The Four Seasons,* the finest, most enduring, composition of the Baroque period.

Sanne placated the Red Priest simply by raising the volume, allowing gale-force winded "Winter" to give locals a taste of hibernal Jack Frostiness, stile Italiano.

Reed had to raise her voice to respond all too eagerly, "All right then, Jake, lez hear about zee amazing Zorica of zee Zonoran Dezert."

Jake chuckled over Reed's playful zest for alliteration.

"Zorica is from Zerbia . . . I mean, Serbia. No surprise, she's beautiful, arrogant and a Balkan blast to be around. She still bartends in Tucson, home to the Arizona Wildcats and the biggest bunch of desert ratnecks you've ever seen. Droves of guys from the university and the Sonoran Desert, they'd walk into her bar, get stinking, tell her what a hottie she was, then try to kiss her. Bartending spoiled Zorica's taste for compliments."

"Nice, real nice," Reed said with searing sarcasm. "I think the only drunk guy I enjoy being around is Nick Charles."

"Ah, from *The Thin Man* novels.

"Yes, sir! Nick and Nora Charles and their wire fox terrier Astra!" Reed exclaimed. "I *love* jazzing with you about books and movies ... you know, you might be the most handsome pointy headed nerdo I've ever encountered."

"Pointy head nerdo, huh? I think of myself as more of a Hurdy Gurdy Man."

Reed laughed far too loudly for Vivaldi's lurking re-atomized presence.

"Hurdy gurdy, hurdy gurdy, hurdy gurdy gurdy, he sang," Reed recited.

Jake joined in with his new friend.

"Here comes the Roly Poly Man, he's singing songs of love," he baritoned to Reed. "And hey, how much of this is your beer talking, young lady, because flattery will not get you out of this here racing-with-my-heart traffic ticket ... license, registration, proof of insurance, and please, ma'am, no jive that you can't drive fifty-five."

"Whatever, Dudley Do-Right. Don't know how many times I've talked my way out of a speeding ticket."

"A few, Nell Fenwick?"

"A bit more than a few times. Always remember, Dudster, you never go wrong showing cleavage to get out a ticket."

"I knew it! Women really do that, don't they? I'll keep that in mind next time I get pulled over. I'll flash the policewoman a peek of my perky pecs."

Reed giggled like a teenager trippin' & dippin' the light fantastic at the 2001 "Hanging by a Moment" Senior Prom at Clearwater High School.

"And you're not even drinking," she exclaimed. "Does your silliness come au naturel?"

"Yes, I believe it does," Jake said.

"Thought so. Now tell me more about *Zorica*.

"First, I need to hit the head," Jake said, slightly embarrassed.

He rose from the table. He headed straight to the gents' room.

"Stay alive no matter what occurs, I will find you!" Reed called out to Jake.

He stopped, turned and asked her, "How is it everybody in *The Last of the Mohicans* had such great looking hair? Were there frontier salons back then?"

"Yes! A chain of log-cabin salons called 'Majestic Manes'," Reed answered.

Jake laughed, bowed to Reed, then once more made his way to the restroom.

"You're a funny lady, you know that?" a stranger uttered to Reed.

An obese middle-aged man, perhaps a Double Diamond cruiser, loomed over Reed's table.

His outfit was vintage touron. He wore a too-tight orange t-shirt outlining his DD-cup man teats while exposing part of his large pimpled belly. He complimented said orange t-shirt with a pair of blue plaid Bermuda shorts.

He held in his right hand a large margarita collaring an upside-down bottle of Corona beer, known in the Caribbean as a Corona-Rita.

He wore salt-water stained Birks. No nail tech in the entire world could resuscitate his yellowed, split and ingrown toenails poseuring as Smaug's claws.

A large gold Saint Acerinus medal dangled from a gold chain stretched too snugly around a neck swaddled in pink bulbous jowls.

Reed telescoped the man's outfit.

"Let me guess, University of Florida, class of 1901?" she proffered derisively.

When the man laughed, his entire gross tonnage got jiggy with it.

"Excellent, Earth establishing contact with *Yer*anus," the fat-uous man uttered.

Reed studied the remaining beer in her glass.

Yup, too much beer to waste, she thought. Keeps it up, Frisch's Big Boy's gonna need a St. John Lucci medal, right quick.

"It's *U*ranus, not Ur*anus*, Captain Jerk."

"Well done, Missy. Say, mind if I sit down?"

"Don't mind at all, long as it's in another bar," Missy replied.

"That's a good 'un, all rightly. I'll just stand then, okee dokee?"

"Do as you like. Hope your knees hold up."

This time, he did not laugh.

"What the hell's that supposed to mean, huh?" he demanded of Reed.

Jake came out of the bathroom. He saw the fast-organizing squall.

Guy's a moron, he concluded. But no way I'm getting involved, not this time.

Jake hung back and watched.

"Buddy, you have your entire life to be a prick," Reed told the man. "Why not take today off?"

"Wass' up, butta cup, don't you like me?" he asked disingenuously.

Reed gave the man an Italian noblewoman Lisa del Giocondo smile.

"I'd tell you how I really feel about you, but I wasn't born with enough middle fingers," she deadpanned to the man.

Fatman's face flushed with anger.

"Why I oughta teach you a lesson in good manners, ya little bitch."

A deus ex machina voice suddenly announced, "No you won't, Stanley."

The voice belonged to a tall thin attractive woman having gracefully arrived in her early fifties. She concealed an alluring figure in elegant linen folds of a matching white top and slacks.

The woman held a frozen drink.

Stanley said to the woman, "Olivia, you never let me have any fun."

Olivia arrived at Reed's table at the same time as Jake, who stared at her drink.

"Pardon me, ma'am, but is that ..."

"The cat that chewed your new shoes?" Reed wondered aloud.

Silver-haired Olivia smiled like Ava Gardner and spoke like Hedy Lamarr.

"Yes, it is, per se. I saw what you were drinking and asked Sanne to fix me one exactly to your specifications."

"How do you like it?" Jake asked.

She sipped her drink.

"Refreshing, not too sweet, perfect for a hot sunny day in Bonaire. Needs a sugar cane swizzle stick or a pineapple wedge, maybe both. By the way, your drink has been named Sanne's Coco Loco. Just thought you should know."

Reed interjected, "Trademark infringement, your Honor, move for treble damages and thirty days in the humble pie hole!"

Olivia raised her eyebrows at Jake.

"Does your lovely lady friend like to alliterate when she's drunk?" Olivia inquired.

Reed gave Olivia the squirrely eyeball.

"Like my momma always said," she interjected. "'Better to alliterate than to make an assonance out of yourself.'"

Jake could barely muffuletta his laughter.

"This is my friend Reed, Olivia. She's had a couple beers, but don't let that fool you. She's a regular Dorthy Parker, buzzed or not."

Olivia asked, "Has your friend over imbibed, Mister ..."

"Gittes, Jake Gittes."

Reed giggled, then made sad forlorn sounds from an imaginary King Silver Flair trumpet.

Jake smiled at Reed, then said to Olivia, "Reed has had a couple beers, but don't read too much into that."

Reed piped in, "Why you wanna know about Jakey and me, Miss Olive Oil?"

Insulting little shit, Olivia thought.

"Let's just go with 'Olivia' for now, Rude," she bit back.

"You said 'Rude,' I'm Reed."

"My apologies, *Rube*. Truly."

"Don't worry 'bout a ting," Reed answered. "Every little ting gonna be all right."

"Yeah, whatever." Olivia said. "Now, Jake, was that really the first kiss, or do I have to pay for my free beer?"

"That *was* our first kiss. It was like Jay Gatsby finally getting to kiss Daisy Buchanan."

Olivia looked at Reed, who remained seated at the table, studying her empty beer glass with a tragic Zelda Sayre stare.

"What the big palooka said," Reed commented to Olivia.

Having faded into the yellow plaster wall, Stanley moaned, "O, I want to leave, I don't feel quite right."

He sat down at their table without asking permission from Reed.

"Can we get outta here please, Olivia? I'm weak, weary and woozy."

She stared at him with a withering gaze.

"Don't forget 'whiny,'" Olivia said. "We can go, but I want you to realize your big mouth just got us into another fine mess, Stanley."

Stanley belched loudly, then said, "Yes, dear."

Olivia said to Jake and Reed, "Alas, parting is such sweet sorrow, but we must repair to our cruise ship, the *Brilliance of the Seas*. In just two sea days, we'll be in Havana."

Reed gave the couple a queen's wave, then said, "Toodles." "Pleasure meeting y'all," Jake said.

"I enjoyed meeting such a romantic couple," Olivia said in a haughty voice. "Oh, one last thing, Mr. Gitts."

"It's *Gittes*, but what's on your mind?"

"Forget it, Jake, it's Chinatown."

He heard her. He didn't respond.

Olivia and Stanley walked briskly out of the pub.

Jake sat back down at the table.

He stared at the open doorway of the pub.

"Are you buying Stanley and Olivia's schtick, Jake?"

"No I don't, but you're not as buzzed as you appear," Jake answered.

"I'm buzzed, but not bombed. By acting all drunky like, Olivea paid me no mind atoll. She knows as well as I, it's almost impossible communicating with a drunk, which allowed me to check 'em out thoroughly. Right off, I saw there was something wonky about them."

"Bravo, that was a big Golden Globes award-winning performance."

Reed sat back and patted closed her dress' plunging decolletage.

"You were peeking at my breasts, weren't you? 'Big golden globes,' I mean for goodness's sake, Jake."

He chuckled.

"All right, guilty as charged. As an all-American male, am I *not* supposed to admire your physical attributes?"

"You can admire my attributes all you like, as long as you're a gentleman. Only don't make stupid puns about my breasts or any other body parts. It's unbecoming."

"I understand. Mea culpa. Geesh! Wonder if I'll ever get one by you."

"As the old clover hitch said, 'I'm a frayed knot'!"

"Score one for Reed O'Hara, and do you think you came out ahead with our friend Stanley?" Jake asked.

"Sure, but it wasn't a real competition. Too damn easy. Like he was asking me to abuse him, to start a tussling."

Jake asked, "What do you make of that?"

"I'm not sure. Give me a novel, a short story or a poem, I'll analyze the hell out of it. My boyfriend at Florida was an English major named Leonard. It was fun explaining how utterly wrong he was about Hemingway's 'Hills Like White Elephants' or 'A Clean Well-Lighted Place.' Yeah, Leo the Faint Farted was one lazy English major who insisted on taking the escalator up Kilimanjaro."

"All good stuff, Reed, but what's your point?"

"I'm not adept at analyzing live-action human behavior. Are you?"

"I was trained to do just that. Also helped I have a natural aptitude for seeing under the surface of most situations."

"So how are you at literary analysis?"

"Pretty much suck eggs. I really wish we knew each other in high school. Where were you when I went up against *The Love Song of J. Alfred Prufrock*?"

"Probably taking non-Euclidian geometry while eating a peach most daringly."

"You know I think this may be the beginning of a beautiful friendship."

"I agree, but only if I get to play Bogie," Reed said.

Jake smiled.

"Sure, why not," he conceded. "All right, in the mood for a little Q&A regarding our new friends? I might convince you that you're as good with human psychology as you are with deconstructing Hemingway."

"Let's do this," Reed answered.

"First question: if you agree Stanley and Olivia seemed like a comedy act, whom do they remind you of?" Jake asked.

"Burns and Allen?"

"Not close," he said.

"Stella and Meara?"

"No, but don't worry about gender," Jake assured Reed.

"I don't know, Abbott and Costello?" she asked.

"You're close. C'mon, you can do this."

"Stanley and Olivia, Olivia and Stanley. Jesus Christ, I've got it!"

"Yes?" Jake asked.

"Stan Laurel and Oliver Hardy. Laurel and Hardy! And it was right there foxtrottin' in front of me."

"Excellent. Now, what do you think of these two birds posing as slapstick royalty?"

"They knew we'd get it, that they were acting on a stage and we were an audience of two," Reed said.

"Yes, exactly, it was a set-up, as much for their personal kicks as for anything else," Jake said. "Damn, we make a good team!"

"Whoa, slow your Paso Fino there, pahdner. We've only just started this cattle drive. We haven't even crossed Red River yet, okay? Now it's your turn, Jake, what do you make of Olivia and Stanley?"

"Olivia's a most capable individual. Smart. Not her first rodeo. The alpha. Likes playing with her prey. And Stanley? He shouldn't be discounted as a threat just because he's a loudmouthed fat ass."

"I'm getting creeped out now," Reed said. "What are these people up to, and don't say, 'This is complicated stuff, little lady.'"

"I'll give it to you straight. Laurel and Hardy might be top-level operatives. I've heard about a couple just like them. They'd snuff anyone for the right price, long as they could get in a free round of golf at some snazzy country club. Ask yourself, why would they target an attorney from Tampa vacationing in Bonaire?"

"They wouldn't."

"Indeed, but I'm relieved they're not coming at you. Yeah, I'm the target."

"Because of your work with, you know?" Reed asked.

"Pretty safe bet. Somebody is looking for a little payback by employing this wet-works team. I don't know, Reed, I think I should take off. I don't want to endanger you any further."

"Are you armed?" she asked.

"Yeah, first thing I did when I arrived, bought a Browning 9mm and two boxes of cartridges."

"Then you best get me a sidearm. Browning. Sig. Glock. Doesn't matter. Get hollow points. Chummy chub boy might be difficult to take down with standard-issue rounds."

"Jesus, Mary and Joseph, are you kidding me about all of this?"

"No, I'm not. Use your noodle, Jake. Think you can run off to Venezuela and they *won't* take me hostage? These guys will appeal to your sense of a knight errant rescuing a damsel in distress. Very Phillip Marlowe, right?"

Jake lost his smile. Darkness enveloped his face.

"Back in the day, and I hate saying this, I would've let you die. That's how much of a cold-blooded bastard I was. I *never* let feelings sway me when I was on the job."

"But?" Reed interjected.

"Everything's changed. I can't let any harm come your way."

"So don't leave," Reed said.

"Do you really want us to stay together?" he said.

"I'm not at all happy my vacation got screwed up and my life is in danger. Wasn't in my itinerary. But I'm a Mountaineer who welcomes a fight, fair or unfair. Looks as if you might get to see what a bitchin' badass I can be. I'm an expert shot. I've a black belt in tae kwon do. I'm pissed somebody wants to hurt my guy."

"Your guy, really?"

"Um huh. You became my guy when we kissed. Are we in agreement that we'll team up and outsmart Laurel and Hardy 2.0?"

"Yes. Might we seal the deal with another kiss?"

"Absolutely."

Reed and Jake shared a wet sloe gin kizz.

Sanne rang the brass bell.

"Aw, look at the love birds!"

Someone called out, "Free beer again?"

Sanne laughed boisterously.

"Oh, hell no, but if I get another kiss from Reed, verdomme ja, free drafts for everyone!"

CHAPTER 13

"POSED NAKED FOR A MAGAZINE YESTERDAY," Ravel told Reed and Jake.

Standing in her bedroom doorway, she proudly showcased her almond-shaped violet eyes, bobbed black hair, fulsome pearly breasts and mounds of Venus.

Yes. Ravel was naked. Again.

As usual, Reed & Jake paid her no mind.

As usual, Ravel was disappointed, since Reed barely looked at her.

"Course the newsstand owner would've preferred cash," she *ba-da-boomed!* with perfect delivery.

Jake and Reed didn't respond. They were preoccupied with an argument of epic proportions, a veritable Cecil B. DeMille technicolor production casting a dozen emotions, including anger, recrimination, rage and inevitable ad hominem.

Ravel's bare breasts revealed extraordinary scars seared across her chest. Russian mobster Victor Petrov inflicted the scars. He kidnapped her on a late night in the Namaste nightclub parking lot. Petrov's plan was to use Ravel as a bargaining chip for his takeover most hostile of Namaste.

Reed eventually rescued Ravel, though the Swiss beauty was

sentenced to a lifetime with no parole from physical and mental disfigurement. She suffered occasional *tsk, tsk, tsking* from the few people allowed to see her scars. However, she never pitied herself. Nor would she allow others to patronize her into feeling vandalized and hideous. No. The scars were her declaration of independence from conventional notions of beauty.

"Heard the one about the postal carrier encountering a naked woman in an open doorway?" she asked.

Reed cracked ever so slightly.

"No, I haven't, Ravel."

"Yeah, he was shocked the woman knew where he lived."

Reed and Jake erupted in laughter.

Mission accomplished: Ravel popped the hot airngry balloon.

"Ravel, please put on a robe, then come out and talk with us," Reed said. Ravel *pftt*! then said, "Hey, I'm here all week. Don't forget to tit your servers."

With that, Ravel closed her bedroom door. She dug through a sacred burial mound of clean and not-so-clean laundry, until she found the blue terry cloth robe Reed and Jake gave her for Christmas. She accepted only modest gifts from them now, since she herself earned enough now to purchase her own luxury items, such as a red Porsche Boxter or an Hublot Tutti Frutti stainless steel watch.

She put on the robe, cinched it loosely around her waist and walked out into the living room.

Ravel sat in a vintage Ralph Lauren leather writer's chair, into which she almost disappeared.

"Anyone ever tell you that you're a runt, Ravel?" Jake asked grumpily.

"Anyone ever tell you that you're a cunt, Jake?"

"Ravel!" Reed shouted.

"What? He started it! And I refuse to take shit off jolly green avocado head over there."

Jake stared menacingly at Ravel.

"What, you want a piece of me, Dupree?" she asked.

"I do not, tapa pequeña."

Reed clapped her hands.

"Jesus Christ, enough of this bullshit, you two. First, Jake, 'tapa pequeña' is redundant. Second, if we don't keep it copacetic, every-thing'll come apart at the seams. Guarantee it, y'all, the center won't hold."

Reed understood Jake and Ravel were archrivals contending for her attention and affection.

She gave each of them considerable leeway, but this exchange went too far.

Ravel spoke first.

"Jake, you know I don't enjoy being reminded I'm tiny. I mean, want to throw down with me, call me a fucking runt or Keebler Elf or Tinker Bell. However, and I can't believe I'm saying this, I apologize, no, I'm sorry, for laying into you, while we're all dealing with this awful tragedy."

My God, Ravel's maturing, Reed thought.

Jake pinched his nose.

"I'm sorry as well, Ravel. Having a hard time keeping my shit together right now. I was an asshole for lashing out at you."

"Thanks, ya big lugnut."

"Wiley rival," Jake fired back.

Ravel's smile was as bright as lit magnesium strips.

"Why, Jakester, first time you ever called me your rival. Over whom are we jousting, hmm?"

"You know," Jake said sulkily.

"Yes, well, let's get back to the matter at hand," Reed said, after clearing her throat.

Jake and Ravel nodded yes.

"First, we need to get organized, get on the same page," Reed shudder uttered.

Then she broke down.

Jake placed a hand on her shoulder.

"Babe, I have some experience with this stuff. In a little while, I'll head down to the medical examiner's office to identify Alicia."

Reed seemed relieved Jake was stepping forward with the M.E., though she wasn't unfamiliar with dead bodies.

When she was ten, her grandfather was laid to rest in an open coffin for three days in the family parlor in West Virginia. She and her sister Debbie flannel-gowned down the first night to poke the body, making sure gramps crossed over to the great beyond.

Then there was that incident in Bonaire eight years ago, of course.

"Does that mean you'll see Alicia's cadaver?" eager-beaver Ravel asked.

Jake snorted softly, "No, I'll just look at a photograph of her. Apparently, the county medical examiner thinks it more humane than having someone see the deceased on a gurney."

Reed jumped in before Ravel could make another ghoulish remark.

"I'll go, Jake. It's not a problem," she said.

"No, no, I'll go. Said I would, and I will," he replied.

Look at that, Jake's growing a pair, Ravel thought.

"All right, I guess," Reed answered sullenly.

Jake picked up her negative vibe.

"Tell you what, Reed, please consider having you and Ravel contact Alicia's family in Cuba, then make funeral arrangements here if we can't send Alicia's body back to Cuba. Would you be okay doing that?"

"Yes, I suppose," she answered.

"Good. Thank you, love."

"Before we start making phone calls or sending out emails, Reed, you need to know something about Alicia," Ravel said.

"What's that?"

"She told me she had a terrible relationship with her father."

"How bad?" Reed asked.

"Very. No shit. She said most every Saturday night, from when she was about ten until she was thirteen or so, el padre got drunk, beat her, begged for forgiveness, then ran her a scalding hot bath to sear the sins off of her, especially down there."

Jake kept silent.

Reed said only, "Fuck me."

"Yeah. Explains why she hated men, all of them," Ravel said as she shot a purple laser light at Jake.

"My God," he said. "The sins of the father visited upon the children."

Ravel smiled condescendingly

"Not exactly what Exodus and Numbers had in mind, but you're close enough."

"Impressive, Ravel," Jake said.

"Hey, I get inspiration from reading the Bible, only it's not what you think. I leave fairy tales to the billions of morons out there. Why, just the other day I came across Luke 12:2. It captured exactly how I approach hacking. Captured it *perfectly*."

"Nothing is concealed that will not be revealed," Jake said.

"Bet your sweet ass, Jakester. Whomever wrote the Bible had a damn good understanding of human nature. Past centuries haven't proven them wrong."

"Let's bring this back to Alicia," Reed interjected. "I take it, Ravel, the father won't be receptive to our sending home Alicia's body."

"Doubt it. Guys like that generally want their perversion to be treated as ancient history. He doesn't want to be reminded. Alicia told me daddy-o was happy that she was leaving Cuba, but he expected her to send money to him."

Reed frowned.

"We owe it to Alicia to try to contact her family. They blow us off, we'll give her a proper funeral here."

"Good plan," Jake announced pomp and circumstance.

He's making his move, Ravel surmised.

"Thank you, Jake, thank you so much," Reed commented sarcastically.

"What, Reed?" he asked.

"I get the feeling you want to take charge, and you know I usually run the show," she answered.

"Yeah? Perhaps this time you don't need to play puppet master."

Reed was shocked.

"What's going on, Jake? Why are you being cruel?"

Ooo, that's a good 'un, girl, Ravel thought.

"I'm not being cruel, Reed," Jake fired back. "I'm being frank, candid, transparent, you pick one."

"I pick angry. You've demonstrated nothing but anger toward me and toward Ravel, what in *hell* is going on?"

Jake again pinched his nose.

What's next, he's gonna mine for gold in them thar nostrils? Ravel asked herself.

"I am full of rage right now, okay? I shouldn't take it out on you two. I know that. If I'd been tougher, maybe I could've saved Alicia. When she was around me, I sensed she wanted to talk, wanted to get something off her chest. Did I encourage her to open up? No, I didn't. I thought I was too damn important to play summer camp counselor."

"You're being rough on yourself, Jake," Reed allowed.

"Let me finish. How about the leather jacket? Huh? So obviously a biker's jacket. Bold move on Alicia's part to wear it around Namaste. But what the hell, I let her skate. Both of you know I can get my head turned by Hispanic women. I'm certain Alicia sensed that, and I allowed her to work her mojo on me."

"Is that all?" Reed asked with steel filings in her voice.

"One more thing, then I'm done. Reed, you've shown me how to be a human being again. How to love without reservation. How to *feel*. But I've lost my edge. I'm not living among the normals. I *am* a normal. That's why I screwed up so badly with Alicia. Do you get it? Do you?"

Ravel interceded.

"I get it all right, you jerk. Reed helped you become a decent human bean. She domesticated a feral predator. Now you're blaming her for *losing your edge?* Whatever the hell that means. It's Reed's fault Alicia's dead? God damn, you're an asshole."

"Ravel, that's not what I meant," Jake protested.

"It's the message you sent," Ravel ricocheted. "And another thing, Jake Dupree, you get around some Cuban cooch and you can't think straight, fuck it all, how old are you, twelve?"

"Ravel, please," Jake said.

"No, no! Don't talk to me. Talk to your wife!"

He slid across on the sofa toward Reed, but she held him at arm's length.

"Let's stay out of each other's personal space for now," Reed said.

Jake slid back across the sofa.

Sit *there*, boy, sit *there*, yeah, such a good boy, Ravel thought. Oh my, I'm a wicked, wicked fish called Wanda.

"Reed, I don't blame you for Alicia's death. That's not what I meant. My point got lost in all this other bullshit. My hunter's instinct got blunted. I lost my edge. That's why I failed Alicia. It had very little to do with getting my head turned."

Silence enveloped Reed, Jake and Ravel.

"Anyone else feel that chill in the air?" Ravel asked.

Reed wouldn't play.

"It's the AC kicking on," she said.

"Or is it, my pretty?" Ravel replied.

Reed's laugh was as delicate as a hummingbird indulging in a pink powder puff bloom.

It was laughter, nonetheless.

"What exactly did you mean by 'all this other bullshit'?" she asked Jake.

He put his face in his hands. He exhaled.

Oughta be worth the price of admission here, Ravel surmised.

"I meant, my beautiful wife, there's nothing wrong with my going it alone sometimes."

"Are we talking about wankin' or investigatin'?" Ravel interjected.

"Ravel, stop it," Reed said, using icy words carved by a Zwilling Pro serrated knife. "You're not helping at all."

"Oh, I'm sorry, Reed, you obviously misunderstood that I'm here to help, I'm not," Ravel said.

Reed glared at her, who returned the glare with raised eyebrows and an impish smile.

Cute little shit, Reed thought.

She turned away from Ravel. She looked at Jake.

"We have to make some decisions together, Jake, in order to be a unified team."

Right on, Newt Knute, win one for the Gimper, Ravel chortled silently.

"Up 'til now, I haven't deviated, we work together with you leading the way," Jake said.

"Up until now?" Reed inquired.

Rah, rah, rah, it's a Bolivian coup d'état, Ravel thought.

"I'm taking the lead in finding Alicia's killer. I'm better suited for this kind of investigation, since the biker gang underworld is involved. I have contacts that you don't. I've spent time in that shitty world. You haven't. You want to help me, great. Otherwise, stay out of my way."

"Go ahead, my husband, take on this investigation," she said. "Try not to fuck it up."

"I'll do my best not to, my *wife*. Do you want to help me out?"

"Today? Not on your life. Maybe tomorrow. Today, I'm gonna hang with Ravel in her bedroom and get started on funeral arrangements for Alicia. No boys allowed."

Jake shook his head.

"Now who's the twelve-year-old? But hey, do what you want. I'm heading over to the coroner's, have a sit-down with the Bavarians, then go to Namaste for the evening."

Reed was incensed.

"Sounds as if you're going to be a busy lad. I hope you get some leads. But don't go and join a biker gang out of spite. I'm warning you, if you do join the Bavarians, I'll *never* ride bitch."

Reed turned away from Jake. She walked arm-in-arm with Ravel, who thrust out a serpentine tongue at Jake.

Such sweet victory, Ravel thought. And there'll be even sweeter things to come.

Reed shut the bedroom door.

Jake heard her lock it.

He slammed the drawbridge-size front door on his way out, causing a reproduction of Renoir's *Dance in the Country* to unhinge from the wall and crash to the floor.

Somehow, Magritte's *The Lovers* remained well hung on the wall.

CHAPTER 14

BONAIRE, SOUTHERN CARIBBEAN · 2014

ONE DAY, the couple's authorized biographer, who most assuredly will
be a savvy & sophisticated individual who values truth over fact, will cite
this rare instance where Jake walked ahead of Reed as they left Bonaire
Blond Brewery.

He stopped at the pub's open doorway. Reed almost bumped into
him from behind. First, he looked back to check for anyone following
them. Next, he scanned the sidewalk crowded with partying tourists and
locals throwing the party.

"All everclear," he announced. "In the mood for a walk?"

As Reed stood next to Jake, she realized he was about a foot taller
than she.

No biggie, she thought. I may be short, but I stand tall in the hearts
of men, including this palooka, this lummox, this gorgeous man who
rides tall in the saddle.

"Sure, I'll go for a walk. Need to clear my head. It's not every day I
pound *back* a few brews, then pound *on* a guy in a bar fight. Just
wondering, is this walk more about the journey than the destination?"

Jake held her hand as they walked.

"Probably both. Nothing like strolling under a skyful of stars with a
beautiful, charming and intelligent woman. But I thought we'd walk to

the Blue Garden. Maybe a mile's walk. Has some of the best Brazilian food I've ever eaten."

"Sounds excellent," Reed exclaimed. "Been to Brazil?"

"Yes."

"Business or pleasure?"

Jake chuckled, "What do you think?"

"Business."

"Nope. Strictly pleasure."

"Complete bullshit, isn't it?"

"Probably."

Reed noticed Jake surreptitiously scoping their surroundings.

"Everything okay?" she inquired.

"Yeah, I think so. You know, I'm starting to figure out Olivia and Stanley."

"How so?" Reed asked.

They continued strolling down Kaya Grandi, Kralendijk's main street. Enough daylight remained for them to enjoy pink, blue, yellow and green pastels enlivening bars, restaurants, dive centers and souvenir shops lining both sides of Kaya Grandi.

"Remember when Olivia said they had to leave to board their cruise ship?" Jake asked.

"Um uh, she said their next port of call was Havana, Cuba."

"Reed, what's wrong with that remark?"

"I'm not sure."

"Are you familiar with cruising?" he asked.

"Not really, but I do plan to cruise. Seems wonderful sailing on the open seas aboard those incredible ships."

"Cruise lines like Carnival and Royal Caribbean, you'll often see their ships in the ABC Islands," Jake lectured.

"I'm listening," Reed said.

"President Obama might allow Americans to cruise to Cuba, probably in an attempt to lower tensions with the largest island in the Caribbean."

"Kind of a détente, then?" she asked.

"Yes, but the *Brilliance of the Seas,* right now, isn't allowed to dock in Havana Port."

"What's your point?"

The driver of a small white jitney bus beeped his horn one-two-three-times at Jake and Reed. She stopped in her tracks. Jake waved casually to the driver.

"What the hell was that, Jake? I thought I did something wrong."

Jake laughed heartily.

"That's how folks in the Caribbean say hello to one another. Not waving or beeping back is considered an insult. By the way, that driver was the fellow who sold me my sidearm."

"Speaking of which ..."

"Yup, strapping right now."

Reed giggled.

"What?" Jake inquired.

"Oh, nothing."

"Reed, let's hear it."

"Fine. I felt your back. I thought you had a vestigial tail. Glad to know it's your Browning."

"Think you're funny, don't you?" Jake asked.

Reed tilted back her head and laughed.

"Oh, I *know* I'm fucking funny, Mr. Dupree. What were we talking about?"

"The cruise ban on Cuba that includes *Brilliance of the Seas*."

"Holy guacamole, Olivia was lying about cruising to Havana!"

It was a scene straight out of Hitchcock's *Notorious*.

Reed and Jake stood cloaked in shadows. Out of reach of show-and-tell streetlights. The kabana palms on each side of Kayi Gandi were still and silent as Buckingham Palace's Royal Guard. Traffic was lessening. There were fewer pedestrians.

Reed and Jake faced one another in the darkness.

"Reed, Olivia expected us to figure out she was lying. Now I get it with the Havana reference. It's payback for some work I did there about four years back."

Reed held Jake's hand.

"Work as in *that* kind of work?"

He gently squeezed her hand.

"I'm afraid so. Let's keep walking, okay? Don't want to be stationary targets."

Reed detoured speedily to an overflowing trash receptacle. She vomited most of her Bonaire Blond pale ale, and probably the Heinekens as well. She spit twice. She wiped her mouth once with the back of her hand.

"You all right, Reed?"

"Yes, I am. Look, I knew I liked you an awful lot. Had no idea I might end up taking a bullet for you. I mean, who woulda thunk it?"

Jake gathered her in his arms, then said, "I will not let anyone harm you, I promise."

Reed hugged him back, then replied, "I promise not to let any harm come to you, guaranteed."

Chapter 15

TAMPA, FLORIDA · 2022

JAKE DIDN'T EXPECT to spend the better part of his morning at the morgue.

First, he introduced himself to Dr. Arland Hutchinson, C.M.E., then he completed a stack of forms thick as a mortgage application, followed by his identifying Alicia Serrano from an official photograph: head and bare shoulders only, white sheet covering her from chest to feet, her long dark hair brushed by someone on staff, her expression of epic disappointment etched frozen on her face.

Little could be done with Alicia's ghastly wounds from that powerful 9mm revolver. This is what *I* used to do to people, Jake thought.

He spent the lion's share of his time at the morgue speaking with Dr. Hutchinson in an office absent of windows or wall hangings, and offering only two rickety chairs, three tissue cubes arranged on an abused coffee table and lined white plastic buckets bookending the table. A Dell Optiplex Micro Business Desktop PC sat atop Hutchinson's desk. An ancient Brookhaven cherry veneer swivel chair, with one slat missing in the chairback, docked alongside a desk begging for decommission.

109

Dr. Hutchison sat with Jake in the spartan sitting area. He noticed Jake eyeballing his desk.

"Odd, isn't it? That costly sophisticated desktop poised somewhat precariously on a cheap chrome and particle board desk that survived the last thirty years, paired with a chair I picked up for a prayer at Habitat for Humanity.

The doctor absentmindedly picked his nose.

"You see, Mr. Dupree, I want the public to appreciate that, while I demand the very best in technology, I don't give two tins of Shinola for overpriced office trappings. I want people to see where our limited funds go and *don't* go."

Jake nodded his approval.

Two tins of Shinola, huh? Jake thought.

"I get it, Doctor. In my previous line of work, I requisitioned and received the best equipment. Everything else didn't matter much."

"If I may ask, what was that line of work?" the M.E. said.

"Pest control, mostly."

Dr. Hutchinson laughed.

"An exterminator, eh?"

The doctor was tall, thin and fit for a man in the fourth quarter of his sixties. His broad friendly smile framed white teeth that would've made Veronica Lake or Cheshire Cat envious. His eyes were the color of fresh-spun blue cotton candy.

Dr. Hutchinson explained to Jake that he was a medical examiner deeply committed to his work. Among his most important missions was to reconcile the dead with the living, no matter where it took him. He couldn't be bribed. He couldn't be coerced by powers above him to shade an autopsy with a suspicious, case-closing storyline.

"Army, Mr. Dupree?"

"Yes."

"Thought so. You're not wonky enough for the Air Force, too stable for the Navy, too intelligent for the jarheads."

"I guess that's a fair assessment, though I have to say, outside of the Rangers, the Marine Corp's the finest fighting unit in the world," Jake said.

"I did two tours with the Corps in Vietnam," Dr. Hutchinson said proudly. "Might have turned it into a career, if Agent Orange hadn't exfoliated my balls, a la Jake Barnes."

The sun may also rise, but it sure as fuck goes down, too, Jake thought.

He extended his large hand to the medical examiner.

"Thank you for your service, Doctor."

"And thank you for yours, Mr. Dupree."

Veterans shook hands.

"How long were you enlisted, and what did you do in the Army?" the doctor asked.

"Did one hitch as a Ranger designated marksmen. I was assigned to take out long-range high value targets, thereby extending the tactical reach of my squad."

"A very clinical job description. You were a hunter, then?"

"In a manner of speaking, yes."

"Do any hunting after the Rangers?"

The doctor couched "hunting" with air quotes.

"Can't talk about it, Doctor. You know that."

"Indeed, I do. Worth a try, though. I couldn't help noticing, Mr. Dupree, how you scanned every millimeter of this office while we've been chatting. Old habits die hard, don't they?"

"Some do, some don't, the really bad habits tend to linger," Jake said.

"Vague and tight lipped about your previous life in the, shall we say, 'unofficial' heart of darkness. I respect that. But please, ask me those questions you're mulling over in that fine mind of yours."

Jake nodded.

"I get the tissue boxes on the coffee table, but why two trash cans? I mean, I doubt people would use enough tissues to warrant *two* trash cans."

Dr. Hutchinson chuckled condescendingly.

"We prefer to describe the trash cans as emesis stations. You'd be surprised, or perhaps you wouldn't, how many poor souls vomit at the sight of the departed, even of one in a photograph. Why, just the other day a young beautiful woman arrived here with the top of her cranium cleaved off by a metal sun visor in her BMW, *ahem,* first responders reported to me. We wrapped the top of her head in gauze. Alas, her dear mother still spewed forth uncontrollable emesis upon seeing the photograph. She was so upset, she could barely speak.

Dr. Hutchinson paused to readjust himself in his chair.

"I had to insist she stare at the photograph until she verbally identified her daughter. Took a while, I should say. Fortunately, the mother expelled much of the vomit into the emesis station. I've gotten adept at grabbing a 'trash can' in the nick of time. Also, certain facial expressions predict when there'll be an eruption. In retrospect, I probably should've put a bonnet on the daughter's head."

Jake paused before speaking.

"You told that story with a modicum of enthusiasm, Doctor."

Dr. Hutchinson smiled, again bearing those perfect teeth white like banned ivory.

"No more enthusiastically than when you swap war stories with your Ranger buddies over a backyard fire pit in some cookie-cutter suburb that evokes all the charm of Elmer's glue drying."

Fella has more sand in him than I thought, Jake noted.

The doctor studied Jake's striking blue eyes.

I've far more sand than you ever could imagine, young man, Dr. Hutchinson thought.

"I take it this spongy mat under our feet is for people who don't make it to the barf buckets," Jake said.

"Please, *emesis stations*. After all, this facility isn't the Delta Tau Chi fraternity house," Dr. Hutchinson admonished.

Man has burned "emesis" into my subconscious, Jake lamented privately.

"Sorry, Doctor, sometimes I tilt toward the coarser side of good manners."

Spoken by an autodidact rube, Dr. Hutchinson thought. I'm guessin' New York State's North Country, alas, he can run, but he can't hide, from his baser nature, though who can?

"No worries, Mr. Dupree. Your rough edges are part of your charm."

"The floor covering, Neoprene?"

"Oh goodness no. Even if we could afford Neoprene, I wouldn't purchase it. Much too expensive. No, plain old run-of-the-mill poly-chloroprene works fine. It absorbs much less emesis, urine, blood and other bodily fluids, than does standard textile rugs, at a price consider-ably lower than that of Neoprene. I have polychloroprene set down in areas where it helps when we're on our feet all day, or all night. My one fit of lavishness was to floor my office with polychloroprene. *My* feet need all the help they can get."

Guy's a talker, but damn if I don't enjoy listening to him, Jake conceded.

"Why are there no windows in your office? Seems as if you work in a claustrophobic bunker. And there are no framed diplomas, no photos of family or of bucket-list trips. No artwork, no impressionists, no pointillists, no abstract expressionists, not even dogs playing poker."

"Cassius Marcellus Coolidge," Dr. Hutchinson said.

"Beg your pardon?"

"Coolidge painted eighteen versions of poker-playing doggos, dating all the way back to 1894," the doctor said.

"Are you an aficionado of those paintings?"

"Hardly, Mr. Dupree. Though I do enjoy Cassius' irreverence and subterfuge. For instance, he modeled dogs after Caravaggio, Georges de La Tour and Paul Cezanne. No, I have an abiding passion for Whistler, James Abbott McNeil Whistler, to be more precise."

"Whistler, of *Whistler's Mother* fame?"

Such a blunt instrument, not certain he's worthy of my attention, Dr. Hutchinson thought.

"You mean *Arrangement in Gray and Black No. 1*. A perfectly dreadful painting. Only after several years of trial and error at the easel did Whistler turn away from moral allusions, sentimentality and narra-tive content to embrace art for art's sake, by emphasizing tonal qualities and composition. Make a pilgrimage to the National Gallery of Art in D.C., you'll see for yourself Whistler's evolution."

Jake smiled mischievously.

"Toto, I don't think we're in a Kansas City dogs-playing-poker parlor anymore," he said.

Dr. Hutchinson let out a sonic boom of a laugh that, had there been artwork hung on the walls, the frames would've ripped free of their moorings.

Boy's showing promise, finally, the doctor silently assessed.

"You are too kind and too clever, Mr. Dupree. No, I couldn't bear to have Whistler's paintings, especially the *Nocturnes*, around me at work. Too distracting. But my home, that's another story."

"Go on, Doctor, you have my attention," Jake urged.

Really must see the Bavarians, but I can't pull myself away from poker-playing dogs, barf buckets and Whistler's mama, oh my, Jake thought.

"I commissioned expertly hand-painted reproductions of Whistler's *Nocturne Sun* and *Nocturne – Blue and Silver*. Brilliant compositions. Whistler used thinned gray paint for the background, then delicately flicked white oil paint to suggest lights, shoreline and ships. Gorgeous. Eerie. Ethereal. Ominous, even. Rather like Monet gone mad noir. I also commissioned a reproduction of *Arrangement in Gray: Portrait of the Painter*, which I placed between the two *Nocturnes*. I hung the paintings on a wall fronting the table at home where I play solitaire and chess on the computer."

"Impressive, Doctor. And why aren't there any wall hangings of any sort? Seems bleak and sterile in here."

Dr. Hutchinson smiled, this time benevolently.

"I've no need to ballyhoo my education. I have no family. I never take a vacation. Succinct enough for you?"

"Perfectly. I appreciate your enduring my questions. I'm getting a picture of a man dedicated to important work."

"Thank you, Mr. Dupree, but I bet dollars to donuts you're puzzled about the absence of windows?"

"I am."

"Perhaps this is your first visit to a morgue, though I doubt that. No morgue or coroner's office ever has windows, which is especially important for us, since we're surrounded by apartment complexes and single-family homes. Need I say more?"

"Not at all, Doctor," Jake answered.

Dr. Hutchinson's face became as gray as dusk.

"I admit that when I walk outside, I see the world that produces these corpses, which were fellow human beings fraught with flaws, yet possessing dreams, desires and a will to succeed beyond merely surviving. All of it taken away in a flash by that environ beyond these walls. Why would I want a window to see out at that sordid outside world? I have reminders enough of its dirty deeds in our many morgue freezer cabinets."

And some of those dirty deeds were done dirt cheap, Jake reminded himself.

"Doctor, I've done more than my share of filling morgue cabinets. I'm not uncomfortable with death. I've simply been unfeeling about it. But I treasured Alicia Serrano. Now she's gone. It's the first time in many years that I've experienced heartache."

"You remind me of the Irish warrior poet Finn McCool, in that you haven't allowed your assassin's mind to crush all the humanity out of you. That brightens my day, because I was certain your type was extinct."

"Not extinct, just an endangered species. But, Doctor, I never told you I was an assassin."

Dr. Hutchinson squinted his pale blue eyes.

"You didn't have to tell me, Mr. Dupree. I can see it in your eyes. In your facial expressions. In your mannerisms. You strive to come off as a regular Joe Schmo. You probably fool many people. I know it's your cover, one you've honed and nearly perfected. You remind me of that Jim Thompson novel, hmm, what is that title, ah yes, *The Killer Inside Me*."

"You're not far off," Jake said.

Dr. Hutchinson smiled warmly.

"Fascinating, isn't it, two people so involved with death having a perfectly civilized conversation on that very topic."

"I admit this is a kind of therapy for me, Doctor."

"For me as well, Mr. Dupree. I cannot forget D.H. Lawrence's remark, 'The essential American soul is hard, isolate, stoic and ...'"

"A killer," Jake said.

They sat in silence, then Dr. Hutchinson spoke.

"Even though my patients have the patience of Job, I must return to my work. Something tells me, however, you've one last item to discuss with me."

Jake cleared his throat.

"Will you perform an autopsy on Alicia?" he asked.

Dr. Hutchinson chuckled.

"Of course I will, Mr. Dupree. You know that. What you're wondering is whether I'll share the results of her autopsy with you."

"Will you?" he asked.

"Yes. On one condition."

"Name it."

"You're a private investigator. A very good one. So I've heard at least. I'm certain you'll devote all your energies to finding Ms. Serrano's murderer."

"Better believe I will."

"If you promise to cooperate with the Tampa Police Department by not stepping on their investigation, I'll share Ms. Serrano's autopsy results with you."

"Doctor, you have my word that I'll play nice with TPD."

Jake and Dr. Hutchinson once more shook hands.

"All right, I must shoo you out of here, Mr. Dupree, but not before I share a morgue joke with you. Think of it as a parting gift from your friendly neighborhood Chief Medical Examiner. I find humor works better than a couple tabs of sucrose and calcium carbonate."

Just can't say Tums, can he, Jake noted.

"Let's hear it."

"Why does the medical examiner enjoy his work so much?"

"I don't know."

"He doesn't have to wait until he gets home to crack open a cold one."

Jake smiled, then laughed.

As he was about to leave, Dr. Hutchinson placed the bony claw of a hand on Jake's left shoulder.

"I will give Ms. Serrano my full attention. You can count on that."

CHAPTER 16

BONAIRE

SOUTHERN CARIBBEAN · 2014

"FEELS like I'm in a womb with a view," Reed said.

Reed and Jake entered the Blue Garden Brazilian Restaurant with only forty-five minutes remaining before closing time.

At Jake's request, the manager sat the couple at a table in the back of the restaurant, well away from the front entrance, kitchen service door and the restrooms.

"You catch on quickly, Reed. The key is respecting your suspicions. Approach life that way, you'll be safe in your world and in mine."

Reed laughed softly.

"Jake, do you think you're paranoid or is everybody out to get you?"

"Definitely both."

They studied the menu.

"I have no idea what I'm looking at, I'm hungry and my head feels like it's trapped in the Large Hadron Collider," Reed said.

"Hold on," Jake said.

He scanned the open-air dining room, which featured royal blue walls and columns, oak floors, a bar done in soft blues and softer browns, a dozen wooden tables with brown wicker chairs, sea turtle paintings on the far wall and ornate chandeliers & white French doors.

He spotted a server. He waved him to their table. The two men

117

spoke in Portuguese. The server saluted Jake, then quickly made for the bar.

The server returned with a cocktail, two bottles of Perrier and a small glass bottle of aspirin. He set down a Perrier, the cocktail and the aspirin bottle in front of Reed. He placed the second Perrier to Jake's right.

The server voila'd.

Jake nodded approval.

"What have we here, Mr. Dupree?" Reed asked.

"First, acetaminophen for your headache. Of course, take two tablets with your Perrier. This pain reliever is chock full o' caffeine. You'll percolate right up."

Reed popped two acetaminophen tablets in her mouth, then drank some of the sparkling water.

Nice, getting perky with it already, she thought.

"And this drink in front of me, kind sir?"

Jake took a healthy pull from his Perrier.

"That, mi lady, is a passion fruit and pineapple caipirinha made with Leblon Cachaca."

Reed approached the cocktail warily.

"Looks sneaky dangerous," she said.

"Not at all. Cachaca is the distilled pride and joy of Brazil. Supposed to have the same woody flavor as tequila, but nowhere near the kick. So I've heard, anyway. Made from fermented sugarcane. Some people think it's Brazilian rum. It isn't. Rum is made from molasses and sugarcane byproducts. Cachaca? Made strictly from whole sugarcane, giving it a purer taste. Again, so I've heard."

Reed's facial expression suggested a Leo da Vinci playfulness.

"Tell me something, Jake, if and when we get around to making love, are you going to talk the entire time?"

Jake's surprised facial expression suggested Stratigos' portrait of Salvador Dali.

"Not if you gag me, I won't," he replied.

"That may or may not happen, but it'd be further down our road to perdition."

"Fair enough. Please try your adult beverage. It'll settle your tummy."

Reed took a dainty sip of her caipirinha.

"Goodness, that's amazing!"

She took another sip.

"Incredible. Really."

This time, she took a much healthier sip.

"I *do* feel better. Guess old F. Scott was right: 'Alcohol is the rose-colored glasses of life.'"

"Yeah, but I wonder if Zelda said that first," he asked.

Reed drank more of her cocktail.

"Wouldn't doubt it, Jake. She was every bit the writer her husband was. In fact, F. Scott lifted passages from Zelda's journal, then folded them into his writing. I re-visit her novel once a year."

"*Save Me the Waltz?*"

"No, *The Great Gatsby.*"

Jake snort laughed.

"How about another chupacabra?" Reed asked.

"Of course, but we also need to order, they're getting ready to close down the kitchen," Jake said.

Crikey, drink has a wicked wallaby kick to it, Reed thought.

Jake brought over the server, who was no older than sixteen, then told him in Portuguese what they wanted to eat. The young man didn't bother to write down the order. He saluted once more and sped off to the kitchen.

In under two minutes, he brought Reed her second "chupacabra."

Reed flapper-girl sipped it.

"This goat sucker is better than the first," she declared.

She needs to slow down, can't have my partner in crime getting ploughed, Jake noted to himself.

"Hope you don't mind, but I ordered for the two of us," he said.

"No worries at all. I place myself in your hands. Just don't squish me. Squeeze me? Sure. Squish me? No, no and nope."

"I won't. Promise. Like to know what we're having to eat?"

Reed drank more of her cocktail.

"Sure, but first answer me this: how'd you come by speaking Portuguese?"

Jake got serious.

"Part of an assignment in Brazil required language immersion in Portuguese, including a couple Brazilian dialects. Spent six weeks on the island of Fernando de Noronha, which is part of an archipelago of islands about 350 klicks off Brazil's northeast coast."

"Klicks?"

"Sorry, kilometers. It was a fat life for a few weeks. Learned Brazilian Portuguese taught by a funny-as-hell local field agent from the mainland. His being a cross-dresser didn't bother me at all. He claimed he dressed like a woman only when he was 'undercovers.' Guy like to crack me up. Weather? Incredible. Food? Amazing. And I got in rave swims twice a day."

Pity the fool who banks on Jake being pithy, Reed thought.

"So how did that assignment play out for you?" she asked.

Swear to God, she's batting her big blues at me, Jake noticed.

"No, no and nope, Ms. Nosy Rosie."

"Worth a try, right? I mean, once I kissed you, I thought Dutch dykes would break *wiiide* open about your past."

"Dutch dykes, huh?"

"What, it's simpler to say than steel-reinforced flood gates located in the Netherlands, a lesson in simplicity you could use."

"Not happening. But I'm getting pings in my head that you might be a honey trap."

"Honey trap? Not sure if I like the sound of that. What the hell is it?"

"An operational term for a female spy using her sexuality to gather intelligence from a value target," Jake said.

Reed frowned.

"I think you just pissed me off."

"I'm sorry, Reed. The more you get to know me, the better you'll realize I sometimes can be a first-class oaf. But I won't hide behind the old chestnut that I was only kidding. Try to understand I'm still fresh from leaving the organization. I remain a thoroughly indoctrinated, well-trained, highly effective black operative. It's not easy shucking off that identity. I apologize for being suspicious of you."

Reed smiled pleasantly at Jake.

"I don't expect you to be an altar boy or an Eagle Scout or a stormin' Mormon from Norman, Oaklahoma. You've some sharp edges to your personality. But damn it, Jake Dupree, I'm falling for you, and I'm not sure how to handle it. I'm navigating in terra incognito. My love sextant is spinning like a red & black roulette wheel."

Jake reached over to hold her hand.

"How about I tell you what's for dinner tonight?"

Reed smiled and sniffled at the same time.

"Speaking of non-sequiturs, time flies like an arrow, but fruit flies like bananas," she said.

"Ba-da-boom!" Jake exclaimed.

"Jake, what will we sup on at this beautiful restaurant?"

She finished her cocktail.

"We're going to start with grilled scallops skewers and pao de queijo, which is Brazilian cheese bread. It's made with yucca flour."

"Sounds promising. And then?"

"Your entrée will be grilled lionfish, which I think you'll appreciate because lionfish are detrimental to coral reefs. Want to know why?"

"I think so, but first order me another chupacabra."

"Yes, ma'am, one chupacabra coming right up."

He gestured to their server and put in a request for another caipirinha for Reed.

"Where was I? Ah yes, the destructive lionfish. They eat herbivores that eat algae from coral reefs. Sans herbivores, algae growth gets out of control, harming, and sometimes killing, the living coral reefs."

The server brought Reed her third cocktail. She noticed the young man admiring her. She gave him a playful wink. The embarrassed server practically ran away.

"Jake, let me leave the tip for that little cutie."

"Roger that."

Reed admired her cocktail, then took a sip.

"Now we're cooking with gas!"

"I actually prefer cooking with gas," Jake said. "Better heat distribution."

Reed rolled her eyes.

"I have so much work to do with you, you know that?"

"Unlike Van Gogh, I'm all ears as how you'll first deconstruct me, then rebuild me into a hipper, cooler dude," Jake opined.

"Wisecrack's not bad, bubba," Reed evaluated. "Anyhow, I thought lionfish have poisonous spikey things. Is this a variation of the Japanese puffer-fish bravery test?"

"Not at all. Needle-sharp spines and venom glands in the lionfish's fins are carefully removed before fileting. There's nothing to worry about. The filets are flaky and buttery. The only test for you is whether you trust me. Will you give lionfish a go? If not for yourself, then for the coral reefs?"

Reed again drank from her caipirinha.

Trust first, then love, she reminded herself.

"All right, I'll try lionfish, but enough with the Nat Geo guilt trips!" she exclaimed.

"Yes, of course. I also ordered mukeka di pirka which is calamari, tiger shrimp and lionfish cooked in a tomato sauce and topped with coconut cheese. *So* good, *so* good, *so* good."

Jake appeared pleased with himself.

"Okay, Neil Diamonique, what's for dessert?" Reed asked.

"Saved the best for last. We're going to share choco noir pizza. It's a pizza crust filled with dark chocolate and topped with mango sorbet & red berries."

Reed grinned like a Girl Scout field-tripping to Willy Wonka's chocolate factory.

And this time, I'm not pairing with that awful Veruca Salt, she promised herself.

"Let's have dessert first!" Reed cried out, all Oompa Loompa like.

"No way, we'll prolong gratification by enjoying the first and second courses before dessert. Think of it as making love. Appetizer is the foreplay, right? Main course, that's the real fun sex part. Dessert, the climax. Would you skip foreplay and sex to go straight to orgasm?"

Reed wiggled her eyebrows Groucho Marx style.

"Say the secret woyd and win a hundred dollas," she said, ashing an imaginary Cuban Belinda cigar.

"You bet your life it's 'orgasm'!" Jake said excitedly.

Time to kiss this man, Reed thought.

She grabbed the back of Jake's neck. She pulled him toward her. Like an inland taipan tasting the air, she twirled and darted her tongue around his welcoming lips.

The young server arrived maybe ten seconds after they clinched. He cleared his throat to get them to their respective corners.

They did.

Jake and Reed tried not to appear embarrassed.

They failed.

The server set down the grilled scallops' skewers and a basket of pao de queijo, then vanished as fast as a gambler's stack of chips at the island's Divi Flamingo Casino.

They didn't say a word, as they set upon the spicy sea scallops and warm cheese bread.

Reed daintily used a brown cloth napkin to pat her full lips, whose natural coral pink hue even Pat McGrath Labs couldn't reproduce.

"That was delicious, Jake. I could make that my dinner."

"Glad you enjoyed the appetizer. It's time for the main course."

On cue, the server brought steaming plates of seafood to their table. He set before Reed her grilled lionfish, Jake the mukeka di pirka.

Without hesitation, the server raced to the bar, where Reed's next caipirinha rested on the bar counter, awaiting delivery to the petite blonde who grew more effervescent with each cocktail.

When the server set the drink to Reed's right, she said to Jake, "Are you trying to get me toasted?"

Jake flashed his best Errol Flynn grin & tonic.

"Toasty, not toasted," he answered.

Reed sipped from her cocktail, then set upon her lionfish.

"This is incredible," she said.

"Restaurant takes great pride in its lionfish preparation," Jake proffered.

She waited for Jake to drink from his Perrier before saying, "And here I thought I was going to have sex with you tonight, but not after that pawthetic pun."

Jake choked, then coughed, on the bubbly bougie mineral water.

"How about if I pun nevermore?" he asked. "Would you change your mind about that other thing?"

"I'll think about it," Reed said with zero commitment.

The couple focused on their entrees. The clink of flatware upon stoneware was the only sound emanating from their table.

Reed drank more of her cocktail.

Jake finished his third bottle of Perrier.

"Now that we've cleansed our palates, let's have dessert, okay?"

Reed smiled.

"Why do I think our young man is standing behind me right now with the choco noir pizza?"

"Because he is," Jake admitted.

He nodded to the server, who placed the dessert between the couple, along with two spoons and paper napkins.

Reed tried choco noir pizza.

"My goodness, that may be better than sex," she said.

"I hope not," Jake countered.

Reed chuckled, while she spooned chocolate and mango sorbet.

"Here, open up, Jake."

"Geesh, I thought I've been opening up all day long."

"Smartass!"

Reed slid a spoonful of choco noir pizza into his mouth, though she saved just enough to dabble dark chocolate on the tip of his Gallic nose.

They both laughed.

Reed finished her cocktail.

"Jake, that was a lovely meal. And I've had a wonderful day getting to know you. For the record, you're an excellent kisser."

"As are you, Reed."

"Thank you, but I think it's time to say good night and grab a taxi, no, a jitney, back to my hotel."

"Are you at all tempted to stay with me tonight?"

"You're a bold one, I'll give you that. I'm tempted. You're a special man and I'm rather attracted to you."

"As am I to you."

Reed paused for a few seconds, then paused for a few seconds more.

"No, we'll go our separate ways tonight. I'm staying at Harbour Village. How about we have breakfast there in the morning, then snorkel? We can shoo away those lionfish."

"That sounds great! Breakfast at 0800 hours?"

"Eight a.m.? Silly boy. Make it ten a.m."

"Bravo zulu. Meet you in the lobby?"

"Bravo zoot suit! See you then, Jake Dupree."

They lingered over the final kiss of the night.

Across the street, two figures hid behind a tall natural fence of datu cactus. One figure sat on a collapsible lawn chair. The other was on both knees, peering at Jake and Reed through a Kowa TSN 99 Prominar monocular.

It was Olivia and Stanley.

"Can't tell if the lovebirds are shackin' up tonight," Stanley said, as he avoided sharp cactus thorns while scoping Jake & Reed.

Olivia popped another piece of four-milligram nicotine gum in her mouth.

"What I would give for a Dunhill Blue right now. I seriously doubt that woman is your everyday slutso. Nah, they'll part company. But who cares? I'm enjoying this leisurely pace. All in good time, sweetguns, all in good time."

"Yes, my love," Stanley answered.

CHAPTER 17

TAMPA, FLORIDA · 2022

"C'MON, Reed, I want to give you one of those French tickle kisses."

Ravel was at it once more.

She saw her opening when Reed released the Kraken on Jake for insisting that *he* led Alicia Serrano's murder investigation. Ravel angled Reed was vulnerable, her defenses down, what with the couple going their separate ways, him storming out of the apartment, Reed retreating to the relatively safe confines of Ravel's bedroom.

No better time to seduce a woman than when she's pissed at her man, Ravel surmised.

The women sat cross-legged, facing each other on the unmade king-size bed. Their knees touched slightly.

Ravel reached across and cupped Reed's face with her small delicate hand.

Her skin's so soft, so warm, Ravel thought.

Reed gently pushed away Ravel's hand.

"There'll be none of what Sehar calls 'paddlecakes' until we've made a good faith effort in locating Alicia's family in Cuba."

Oh my, Miss Prim Properly, there's no fooling around *before* our work is done, Ravel chortled privately.

Le crap, she caught my faux pas, Reed thought.

Ravel opened her blue terry cloth robe just enough to reveal her snow-white breasts and deep red nipples, as well as the scars across her chest.

Reed ignored her ploy.

Ravel reluctantly closed her robe.

Reed nodded approval.

Her electric blues locked in with Ravel's violently violet eyes.

Pointing at the laptop resting on Ravel's lap, Reed asked, "Any progress locating Alicia's family?"

"Struck out initially. Family's difficult to locate. Don't think they're well off. Probably nowhere on the grid."

Reed smiled.

"Made you more determined to find them, didn't it?"

Ravel returned the smile.

"Yeah, kind of annoyed hitting that goddamn wall. So, instead of bull-rushing *through* the wall, I went *around* it."

"How so?" Reed asked.

"I sniggle wiggled into the Direccion de Inteligencia, the rough equivalent in Cuba of the CIA and the FBI combined."

"And?"

"Agency spies on virtually every citizen. There's only eleven-million Cubans, but that's still an impressive surveillance effort. Ruskies taught them well. In all fairness, Cuba's intelligence network probably is superior to the United States'. Only, Langley, and Jake for that matter, would never admit it."

Reed frowned.

"Ravel, cut Jake some slack. Sometimes he's a first-class asshat, but he's never a homer."

Ravel grinned wickedly.

"Not even a Homer Simpson?"

"Hardly. Besides, if he were Homer Simpson, that'd make me Marge, and who would you be?"

"Lisa! Yes!"

"Nope, Bart Simpson."

"Ay caramba!"

"Enough of this foolishness. Find out anything about Alicia's family via Hermano Grande de Cuba?”

“I did,” Ravel answered.

“Well?”

“Don’t have a cow, man. I was gonna get to it. Eventually.”

“Are you stalling to keep me in your bedroom longer?”

“Yeah, but it’s also really shitty news about the Serrano family.”

“How bad?”

“Horribly bad.”

Reed straightened her back. She squared her shoulders.

“Let’s have it, Ravel.”

Ravel sighed.

“First of all, I put this data through my translation app twice, just to be certain.”

“Go on, please.”

Ravel sighed once more.

“Alicia’s family imploded. The mother caught the father molesting Alicia’s younger sister who’s only twelve! Out of some fit of righteous momma batshit crazy, Mom strangled Dad with an electrical cord still connected to a toaster. Police photos show father dearest dead as a dildo in his Lazy Boy. Dude was naked, wearing nothing but a blue death grimace and a four-slice Toastmaster wang dang dangling ‘round his neck.”

“What happened to mother and daughter?”

For the third time, Ravel sighed. Deeply. Painfully.

“Momma’s in Prison de Mujeres Occidente in Havana. For the rest of her life. Unless they deport her to the United States. Little sister is a ward of the state. Reminds me of when Norma Jean Mortensen got shipped off to an orphanage after her mother was institutionalized.”

“We saw what happened to Marilyn, didn’t we?” Reed asked.

“Yeah.”

“Is it safe to assume we won’t be transporting Alicia’s body back to Cuba?”

“Safe as an all-chica weekender at Liberace’s Vegas mansion,” Ravel answered.

“Clever simile, a little dusty and rusty,” Reed said. “I think we ought to wait for Jake to come home before we finalize Alicia's funeral arrangements."

"Assuming he's coming back. He might've returned to the Company or signed up with those Bavarian cream puffs or joined the French Foreign Legion. You know, never to be seen again, never ever."

Reed laughed.

"A little wish fulfilment going on there?"

"Yes, of course!" Ravel admitted.

Reed held Ravel's hands.

"Do you really think I would leave Jake for you or for anyone else?"

Ravel squeezed Reed's hands.

"I do not. But our work's done for the day. Might we explore? Just a bit?"

"Depends on what you have in mind," Reed said, not in an entirely unfriendly tone.

Ravel tried not to appear too eager.

"Only this. You've never touched my scars. Would you now?"

Reed gazed into her eyes.

"Ravel, I'd be honored to touch your scars."

Ravel opened her robe. She breathed heavily. She was equal parts bold, vulnerable and frightened.

Reed slid over to Ravel's left side, then held her face with both hands.

"Sweetie, you are one beautiful woman," Reed said in a throaty whisper.

She and Ravel kissed. Lightly. Delicately. No French tickling.

Reed pushed Ravel's robe off her shoulders.

With eyes closed, Reed glided two fingertips along narrow ridges of scar tissue on Ravel's chest. She encountered braille borne of horror and pain. She fingertip read Ravel's story of brutality, bravery and an unconquerable will to survive.

Ravel closed her eyes as well. She tilted back her head. A single large tear rolled down her cheek.

"I never thought this day would come," she said with *hush-now-don't-you-cry* joy.

Reed's fingertips went back and forth across Ravel's scars, imagining in her mind's eye the savagery her dear friend endured.

When she touched one of Ravel's breasts, Ravel drew away from her. Reed understood.

Reed opened her eyes. She closed Ravel's robe. She tapped the tip of Ravel's nose.

The two women smiled lovingly at each other.

"Thank you, Reed, I love you so much," Ravel said in a whisper.

Reed wiped away Ravel's tears.

"I love you as well."

The women hugged.

Reed looked around.

"Do you *ever* pick up your bedroom?"

"How would you know if I did?"

"Touché," Reed acknowledged.

"Can we snuggle for a while before the big lug comes back?" Ravel asked.

Reed laughed.

" I thought Jake wasn't returning?"

"Oh, he'll come back. Guarantee it. He loves you even more than I do."

Reed jumped off the bed.

"Here's my best offer. We'll make the bed together, then we'll snuggle for twenty minutes with the bedroom door open."

"Hope I can remember how to make a bed," Ravel said.

She remembered.

In no time, the women stretched out on the fluffy white duvet. Ravel placed her head on Reed's shoulder and snuggled with her. Reed kept her left arm around Ravel.

"Remember, no paddlecakes," Reed warned.

"Yes, ma'am."

The only ensuing sound was their pacific breathing in unison.

For a few minutes, the world outside, with its brutes and bumpkins and buttheads, was silenced.

For now.

Chapter 18

Bonaire

Southern Caribbean · 2014

"Reed, got any problem with my wearing a Speedo today?"

"You've got the body for one, but what color and cut?" she asked.

"Modest cut, dark blue. It's no banana hammock, I assure you."

"Acceptable. Proper manscaping?"

"Jesus, getting kind of personal, aren't you?" Jake opined.

Reed already acquired a taste for making Jake quake, quiver and shake.

Man brings up a Speedo this early in the day, Ima gonna have my fun, she thought.

"Stop being such a chick and answer the question," she said.

"Yes, I'm properly manscaped," Jake gave up begrudgingly.

"Full Brazilian, I hope?"

"What!" Jake yelped.

Reed giggled.

"Just messing with you, Jake. Wipe your brow and chill. I don't have a problem with your wearing a Speedo. I do have a problem when men with ginormous bellies wear bathing suits best left to fitter men."

"Would you wear one?" he inquired pointedly.

"I have worn a Speedo. Nothing more. Only in Jamaica."

The two travelers met at ten a.m. in the lobby of Harbour Village

Beach Resort, a small five-star Bonaire hotel featuring a sixty-four-slip marina and a secluded beachfront enclave. The lobby reflected the resort's tastefully laid back, welcoming vibe, what with its crème café and sea foam color scheme, as well as its traditional Carib mahogany furniture and landscape-seascape artwork painted by local artists.

Jake hugged Reed.

He looked around.

"I love it. Could sit in one of those overstuffed lounge chairs long enough to finish *Infinite Jest,* I kid you not."

"Oh goody, I thought you'd like it. Over my budget, but totally worth it. How about we breakfast before snorkeling? We can take a resort boat out to the reef. I've scheduled a couple's massage for when we get back. Thoughts?"

"I'm blown away. I like not doing the planning. Feels liberating. Good for me to let go of control, sometimes. A couple's massage? Will that certify us as a couple?"

"I'd like to think so."

Reed got on the balls of her feet to kiss Jake.

"First kiss of the day, you two?" a matronly desk clerk called out.

Reed gave her an embarrassed smile.

"Yes, ma'am, and they'll only get better, I promise," she replied.

"Such a beautiful couple," the woman said. "I wish you a romantic day together."

"Thank you," Jake replied.

As soon as they left, the desk clerk made a call with her personal phone from behind the front desk.

"Hello, yes, it's Cherish. They're together. Off to breakfast, then going on a snorkel excursion. What? Yes, my brother will captain the skiff."

Cherish spotted a family approaching the lobby.

"They're getting a couple's massage later this afternoon. What? In the spa of course. We don't do massages on the beach, my gracious. You want what? No way. Too risky. Be satisfied with dee pretty little boat ride."

A family, most likely a quartet of Cheeseheads, entered the lobby and approached the front desk.

"Welcome to Harbour Village, my new friends," the clerk said, then spoke into phone, "Madame, we will send down a fresh set of bath towels immediately."

Reed and Jake strolled on a path lined with coconut palms shimmering in the freshening breeze. Jake held her hand. They smiled at one another.

"What, no golf cart?"

"Not at this resort, Jake."

"Ah well, can't have it all, can we?"

"Only if you're patient. After all, you lose patience, you lose the battle."

Jake chuckled.

"Really, Reed, going Gandhi this early in the day?"

"Seems as if we've read the same books and seen the same films. Might musical differences, but that's okay by me. We could be a match made in Hollywood *and* from the *Harvard Classics*."

"Definitely classic Hollywood, most certainly the *Harvard Classics*."

"You've read the Five-Foot Shelf of Books?" Reed asked.

Might seal the deal with this guy, Reed thought.

"Yes, I have. My parents gave me the collection when they figured I wasn't interested in college. Started reading the *Harvard Classics* at sixteen."

"Why didn't you want to go to college?" Reed wondered.

"Been self-taught ever since I was a kid. I learned to do many things by watching and doing. And I got a great education in high school. Didn't see a real need for college. I wanted to get out in the world, do what George Bailey couldn't do, have a wonderful life traveling and exploring."

Reed kissed him on the cheek.

"Don't know how you do it, but you're excellent at combining the soft and hard sell."

He blushed slightly.

"All about proper training I guess," he said.

"From your parents?" she asked.

"No, from the Company."

"Ah yes, of course. That whole suave James Bond thing, right?"

Jake frowned.

"Hardly," he said in a huff.

"Stop being so touchy. I meant that as a compliment. Look at you, frowning like a Pussy Galore."

"Remember when Bond asked Pussy what it'd take for her to see things his way?"

"I do," Reed replied. "Pussy said, 'A lot more than you've got.'"

"Ouch, all right, you win, I'm done sulking," Jake announced.

"Excellent. Let's go grab a table. I'm starving. And I haven't had my cappuccino. *Danger*, Will Robinson."

They climbed the stairs to La Balandra Restaurant, an open-air pavilion looking out over white-quartz-sand beach and turquoise water. Reed commandeered a table affording an unobstructed view of the Caribbean Sea. The only music was the hypnotic crashing of waves on the beach.

Jake held Reed's chair for her.

"Thank you, kind sir. I suspect good manners are all we have left to stave off zombies and Morlocks.'"

He sat down.

"Just good manners?"

"Fully loaded Browning 9mm semi-automatic with a spare clip comes in handy as well."

Jake made a strange face.

"Are you all right?" Reed inquired of him.

"Yes, just experiencing a little stiffness right now."

Reed feigned embarrassment.

"You scamp, kilting me softly with a George Lazenby. And I didn't realize until now that my talk of handguns and full ammo clips and cartridges ready to fire would result in your pitching a tent in your kilt."

"Reed!"

"Turnabout is fair play, buddy. I mean, it was just too perfect."

"Yes, perfectly bawdy."

"What was George Carlin's punchline when he said men are from Earth and women are from Earth, too?"

"What?"

"*Deal with it.*"

"Yes, ma'am."

"Now let's look at this menu, shall we?"

Jake placed the breakfast menu face down.

"You're familiar with this restaurant. How about you order for the both of us, long as it includes a giant cappuccino."

"Of course. Any food allergies?" Reed inquired.

"No."

"Shellfish?"

"No."

"Peanuts?"

"Nope."

"Durian?"

Jake laughed.

"Not allergic to the world's stinkiest fruit," he said. "Just disgusted by it."

"Durian is delicious, if you pinch your nose while eating it," Reed lectured. "Fruit inside is the consistency of cheesecake."

"Julia Child, you can't even bring durian aboard a plane, but I promise to try it with you one day," Jake declared.

"Good on you. Our being open-minded bodes well for this budding 'thing' we got going on, agree?"

"Agree."

"All right, Mr. Dupree, we'll start with cappuccinos and a tropical fruit plate. No worries, durian's not on the menu. Avocado toast for me. They put a poached egg atop smashed avocado on wheat toast. Yummy yummy. For you, we need something more substantial. Ah yes, smoked salmon on a bagel with red onion, tomatoes, capers and cream cheese."

"Did you get that?" Jake asked.

"What?" Reed answered, puzzled by his question.

"Not you, look over your left shoulder."

When she did, Reed saw a young server standing behind her and smiling.

"Yes, for the gentleman and his lady, I have your breakfast order committed to the memory," the young server said proudly.

He walked away at a deliberate pace.

"Stealthy little server dude," Reed said.

"Actually, he's not that stealthy," Jake replied with a pinch of pomposity.

"How do you figure?" Reed asked.

"He clopped his shoes on the wood floor to signal he was coming up behind you," he said. "Ready for another quick lesson in observing your surroundings, while still enjoying yourself?"

"I guess so. But I need my cappuccino."

"Then we'll wait."

"Won't have to wait long, Jake, our server is coming up behind you."

"Yes, I know."

The server set down two large cappuccinos, then centered on the table a tropical fruit plate bedazzled with vibrantly colorful fresh papaya, mango, cherimoya, carambola, passion fruit, sugar apple and sapodilla.

Reed and Jake sipped their cappuccinos.

She said, "*Muuuch* better."

She forked a slice of papaya and popped it in her mouth. Carambola, cherimoya and mango soon followed. She wiped her mouth with a white cloth napkin.

"There. All better. Now I'm ready for a lesson from 'Dr. P for Paranoia.'"

"Hey, if you're not going to take this seriously, I won't say anything."

"Fine. Don't say anything."

"What? Really? I was speaking in jest."

"Yeah, you're *infinitely jest* a big pouty baby."

"Screwing with me again, aren't you?"

Reed gave him a classic Foxy Brown crooked smile that was alluring, confident, stand-offish, bad ass.

"I *know* that smile. And you *are*, too," he said.

"What would that be, hmm?"

"Just like Foxy Brown, you're the meanest chick in town," Jake said.

"Oh bravo, gallery applause and paparazzi camera flashes and all that. Remember the *Foxy Brown* movie poster, 'She's brown sugar and spice, but if you don't treat her nice'..."

"She'll put you on ice!" Jake warned.

"You continue to amaze me, Jake. I will listen attentively now to your discourse on joyful paranoia."

Jake ate the last piece of passion fruit, but not before Reed gave him an approving nod.

Such good manners, such gorgeous blue eyes, delightful, simply delightful, she remarked to herself.

"There's no reason you can't have fun while keeping an eye on your surroundings," Jake said. "Look carefully yet casually, you probably will catch tells from the poker faces around you."

"I think I understand."

"Let's try it out before the server brings the rest of our breakfast."

"All right."

"Sip your cappuccino and turn your head slightly. Scan the restaurant. Check out the people."

She did as Jake asked.

"What did you see, Reed?"

"There are three couples sitting at separate, side-by-side tables. They're all putting on the feed bag, big time."

"Go on please," Jake said.

"Don't know how they did this, but they're perfectly arranged. I determined the Latvian couple is in the center, the Estonians to the right, the Lithuanians to the Latvians' left. Nothing like geographically correct table settings. Impressed, Baltic Bob?"

Jake quietly clapped.

"That's amazing, really. You are so full of ..."

"Jake, easy now."

"The most sophisticated and hilarious bolshoi I've ever heard."

"Why thank you, sir."

Jake paused.

"Is it possible to fall in love with only a person's mind?"

"Sure, but I come with a killer booty to boot, so count your lucky stars," Reed said, all coquette of the walk. "You know, I had a guy fall in love with me to gain access to my feet."

"Yes, I've noticed those petite feet replete with wonderment," Jake said.

The smile-happy server delivered avocado toast and smoked salmon on a bagel.

"Let's eat, then you can continue your lesson on happy peppy paranoia," Reed suggested.

Jake chuckled.

"As you wish, mi lady."

With only a couple of bites left of her avocado toast, Reed spoke up.

"You haven't told me much about Zorica, your long-lost love."

Jake raised his left index finger requesting patience from Reed as he chewed a large bite of his smoked salmon bagel. A caper fell off the bagel. It rolled across the table. It headed straight for the floor. A nearby cat waited to pounce. Jake caught the caper midair.

"Nice reflexes," Reed said. "That's what I call another cat caper foiled."

"Yeah, I figured Bonaire resorts don't like us to feed the cats."

"Tell me more about Zorica," Reed asked, having tired of kitties and capers and her own little cat feet.

"You really want to know? What about the lesson in observation?"

"First Zorica, then on the lesson."

Jake wiped his mouth with a cloth napkin.

"I've been in love twice. The first time almost cost me my job. Believe me, you do not want to get retired by the Company if you screw up."

"Why not?"

"Instead of a gold Rolex, you get your feet set in a bucket of wet cement, then you're unceremoniously dumped at sea. They call the cement bucket a dunkin' donut."

"Wow. Tough-ass employer."

"Tell me about it. My first genuine romance was with an Irish operative named Lou. We both got assigned to Paris for a joint op."

Reed arched her lovely eyebrows.

"No, Lou is a *woman*, a fiery blue-eyed blonde, a scone over five-feet tall and as Dublin-down satirical as Jonathan Swift himself," Jake said proudly.

Reed's eyes sparkle danced an Irish jig.

"Does Lou remind you of anyone?"

"Reed O'Hara, of course," Jake answered.

"And do Lou and I remind you of your mother?"

"You mean before Mom passed away from pancreatic cancer?" Jake asked solemnly.

Reed inhaled sharply. She brought a hand to her mouth.

"Jake, I'm so sorry. How could I be so inconsiderate? Can you forgive me?"

"Sure, why not, Mom is alive and well in Upstate New York with Dad. *Gotcha*, Reed."

"Jake! Have you no boundaries?"

"My boundaries appear as flexible as yours. You got all Freudian asking me about my mother and the women in my life. For the record, Mom doesn't look like you or Lou. And she's nicer than either one of you."

"Happy to know that. Tell me, Jake, what happened between you and Lou?'

He set down his fork and appeared to have drifted off in a thought balloon.

"I ended up getting involved with her. Nearly deep-sixed the assignment by being overprotective of her. Turns out she didn't need my protection. We still terminated our target, a particularly nasty piece of work who trafficked Russian orphans as sex slaves with approval by the Russian government, which received a third of each sale of a child. Target was sipping a coffee outside King George V Café. On the Les Champs-Elysees. At exactly 10 am. After I blew off his head with the first round, I fired two more rounds into him. My way of making an example of this pig for a human being. Luckily, there was no collateral damage. Completing the mission saved my ass from a live burial at sea, compliments of my employer."

Reed cringed slightly at Jake's casual manner in telling his story.

"And what happened with you and Lou?" she asked.

"She broke it off once we finished the job. I mean, it was a brutally surgical break-up. I say without hesitation that Paris is a *lousy* place to recover from a crushed heart."

Reed placed her right hand on Jake's left hand.

"Bet it was rough for you."

"You mean for a stone-cold killer such as myself?" he asked sardonically.

"Stop it. Self-pity hangs poorly on those big shoulders. If I were in your situation and in the middle of Paris, I doubt even Monet *or* Manet would cheer me up."

"Sorry for playing the crying game. First time I've opened up so much. Don't know how to modulate here. I admit I spent most of three sulky afternoons in the Musee d'Orsay. Helped some, but I'll always associate that hit with the museum, because I used its rooftop to complete my mission, if you get my drift."

Reed tapped the table.

"All right, back to our friend Zorica, Queen of the Sonoran Desert."

Jake smirked. He cleared his throat.

Before he began, the server arrived to clear the table. Jake asked him for two bottles of Perrier. The server nodded, then walked away while balancing plates and flatware.

"I have to ask, Reed, are *you* going to share about your previous romances?"

"Maybe later, Jake."

"I think I'll hear those two words from time to time, as we go forward with this 'thing' of ours."

"You're a bright man."

"On to Zorica, then."

"Oh goody," Reed said approvingly.

"Tucson was home base for two years. An ideal location. Most of my assignments were in California, Mexico, Central America and Carib west. My sidekick Sergio and I lived in an old stone cabin up in the Rincon Mountains. No power. We used kerosene lamps and solar-powered radios, laptops and flashlights. There's plenty of sunshine for storing power out in the Sonoran Desert. Had a fireplace, bunks, wood-burning stove, big jugs of spring water, comfortable chairs and a table for checkers, chess and chow."

"Were you and Sergio *Sonoran* a lot?"

"As in snoring?" Jake deadpanned, "Yeah, we sawed enough logs in our sleep to keep fireplace *and* stove lit an entire winter, plus our snoring kept away both kinds of coyotes."

"Both kinds?"

"Human and furry four-legged ones."

"I get it now," Reed said.

"*All right, all right, all right.* One night I strolled into the Shelter Cocktail Lounge, out on the Death Metal tattooed fringe of Tucson's city center."

"There you go, evocative details. Continue, please."

"The bar was just bare concrete block walls. Resembled a psychedelic bomb shelter from the sixties. AC blasting so cold, it'd make a penguin shiver out ice cubes. The place was neon green lit. It had these sparkly red vinyl chairs and bar stools. Music continuously looped Buddy Holly and Jerry Lee Lewis and Little Richard and Roy Orbison, with some Dick Dale and the Del-Tones thrown in to keep things gnarly."

"I can see the bar clearly. Do go on."

Jake plunged forward with his tale of an affair in the torrid desert sands of Arizona.

"Like Fritz the Cat, I ambled up to the bar. There was Zorica bartending in the eerie green shadows. She had long black hair, was six-feet tall, had a figure to stump any mathematician. Truly, a stunning Balkan beauty."

"Balkan, not Baltic?" Reed inquired.

"Yes."

"Tall. Dark hair. Decent body?"

"Yes."

Reed appeared annoyed.

"*Humpf.* Going counter-profile, I see," she said. "Let's hear more about your rendezvous with Balkan romance."

Hell, what am I supposed to do, make Zorica out to be a fugly Amazonian freak? Jake wondered to himself.

Asked and answered, I guess.

"I was in a playful mood. I requested a non-alcohol martini. Neither shaken nor stirred. With a twist of lemon. Zorica smiled, then said, 'No problem, Double-A Bond.' Zorica popped a lemon twist into an empty martini glass, then slid it across to me while saying, 'Careful, don't spill it.' She charged me eight bucks."

"Then what happened?" Reed asked eagerly.

"I sipped from my Air Martini. Told her it was perfect. Put a twenty on the bar counter. Told her to keep the change. Realized right then and there, Zorica was a woman I wanted to get to know."

"And did you, get to know her?"

"We hit it off immediately. Within two weeks, she got comfortable staying with me a couple nights at a time at our mountain cabin. Sergio was a great sport. With an Excalibur assault rifle slung over his shoulder, he always took a walk when, you know."

"When y'all made like the beast with two backs?"

"Yes, Iago, but it wasn't Othello and Desdemona playing the old-black-ram-tupping-a-white-ewe. More like a young ram doing the tupping."

"Tupping, eh?"

"Sure."

"I take it you and Zorica no longer see each other?"

Best not be, she smoldered, silent as a sunset on the moon.

"No, I'm free and single now. Same as you, no?"

"Same as me, yes. What happened with Zorica?"

Jake raised his cup to get the last few drops of cappuccino.

"It didn't end well, sad to say. While completing an assignment a few miles east of Nogales, Mexico, Sergio was killed. I got re-assigned to Cartagena, Columbia. Went solo for the rest of my hitch with the Company. It was my call. Because really, who could replace Sergio? Jesus, I miss that guy. Also had to say goodbye to Zorica. Call of duty trumped romance. She was brave about it, because she understood. I miss her, but I won't stop by to see her in Tucson. Time passed. Things changed."

"Yeah, probably wouldn't be the same. I am so sorry about Sergio. Was he quite a sidekick?"

"He was the best *partner* any field op could want."

Jake signaled their server for two more cappuccinos.

Within two minutes, the server brought two foamy cappuccinos to their table.

Reed whisper-blew on her coffee. Took two sips. Took two more in rapid succession.

"In a hurry?" Jake asked as he drank his cappuccino at a more leisurely pace.

"Yes, because we have a situation brewing and I think we should get going."

Reed drank more of her cappuccino.

"You intrigue me right now," he said.

"When you have another drink of your coffee, casually scan the dining room," Reed said.

He did as Reed instructed.

"What did you see, Jake?"

"I noticed the front desk clerk."

"Her name's Cherish, by the way," Reed added.

"I noticed Cherish facing us, at a table that included a woman and two men with their backs to us. All locals, most likely."

"Anything concern you?" Reed asked.

"Yes. Locals kept looking over at us, while Cherish talked to them. Aren't exactly trained professionals. They're giving away their position."

"Are we in danger?" she asked.

Jake finished his coffee.

"Possibly. We'll exit slowly and casually, without acknowledging them," Jake said. "Roger that, partner?"

Reed Mona Lisa smiled.

"Roger that, partner."

CHAPTER 19

IT HAD BEGUN, the twenty-minute countdown to Jake rousting neo-Nazi bikers from white-noise dreams, ghoulish nightmares and cos-play fantasies.

Jake drove on Tampa's elegiac Bayshore Boulevard, heading due south to the Bavarians Motorcycle Club headquarters in South Tampa.

He ignored Tampa General's mega-campus on Davis Islands, the faux *Jose Gaspar* pirate ship docked harborside, the shiny new luxury condominium skyscrapers and the magnificently preserved mansions lining the historied boulevard.

Jake didn't bother to remind himself that Bayshore Boulevard's walkway was the longest contiguous sidewalk in the world.

He was too lost in thought to savor the alluring local color before him.

Jake's first thought was to automatically connect the Bavarians with Alicia Serrano's murder.

But he knew better than to leapfrog to a conclusion without sufficient intel.

Therefore, he stayed open minded as he electro-glided in a '71 Buick Riviera GS. The copper mist paint job was buffer polished to showroom glow. Bucket seats were reupholstered in original black vinyl. V-8 engine corralled three-hundred-thirty horses, making the Riviera GS less a muscle car, and more a Detroit-born freeway cruiser. The inimitable body style included tapered tails and elegant pontoon fenders, along with long flowing side views and a signature boat tail.

Jake was proud of his Riviera's VIN, "67," indicating the two-and-a-half-ton beast was a first-day production car. His own crankshaft pistons popped when he learned there were 38,810 Rivieras manufactured in '71; of that total, only 3,175 had Buick Riviera GS badging.

A special car for a special guy, Reed enjoyed telling him. Quite often, in fact.

Jake found a working eight-track tape deck, then installed it in the Riviera. He connected the throwback seventies tape player to a new Alpine audio system, a serious infraction in the eyes of Buick Club of America purists, but one Jake couldn't resist.

A refurbished aluminum case, filled with eight-track tapes he bought on eBay, reclined on the immense back seat.

With the sun shining brightly and a strong breeze tickling tall canary island date palms standing equidistant apart on Bayshore Boulevard, Jake felt cheerful enough to play an eight-track tape of KC and the Sunshine Band's take on Miami funk meets NYC disco, "Get Down Tonight":

> *Baby-baby, Let's get together*
> *Honey-honey, me and you*
> *And do the things, ah, do the things*
> *That we like to do*
>
> *Oh, do a little dance, make a little love*
> *Get down tonight, get down tonight*
> *Do a little dance, make a little dance*
> *Get down tonight, get down tonight*

Jake's cheerfulness dissipated when he thought of his blow out with Reed.

Get down tonight? he thought. Fat chance, good buddy, fat chance.

Jake needed to take his mind off marital strife. He was a professional. He couldn't allow distractions, no matter the importance to his marriage, to prevent him from carrying out his mission.

Once a government-certified assassin, always a paranoid, obsessive, cold-blooded bastard, he admitted to himself.

Jake turned right on Bay-to-Bay Boulevard to enter South Tampa, which nudged right smartly below the Kennedy Boulevard boundary line, blocking the more economically challenged and culturally diverse West Tampa.

Wealthy residents of South Tampa had an unabashedly upper-class way of doing things. That included showcasing architecturally diverse, though culturally exclusive, great houses, tastefully complimented by bougie stores & shops and even bougier bars & restaurants. That included the gastronomic crown jewel Bern's Steakhouse, known internationally for a wine list twice the thickness, three times heavier than, four times the appeal of any of the remaining twenty-three complete Gutenberg Bibles.

The exclusive urban enclave was home to Midas-touch attorneys, loquacious litigators and transcendent transactionalists all; home to glass & steel towered corporate CEO's tightly clutching the robber-baron brass ring; home as well to metaphysically talented physicians of OR-ER legend; even home to wispy martini-soaked rumors of a convivial crime figure channeling F. Scott Fitzgerald's Jay Gatsby in the rarefied cash green mist of this Deep South Neo Gilded Age splendor.

So how did the Bavarians manage to locate their headquarters within the gold-leafed boundaries of South Tampa?

Two words: automobile condominiums.

A complex opened recently on Bay-to-Bay Boulevard in South Tampa that offered auto condos. Well-off South Tampeños could safely garage a Jaguar XE SV or a Porsche Taycan Turbo S or even a Special Edition Sasso GL Mercedes-Maybach S 680, in separate "condos" with spacious bays, loft bedrooms, martini closets, kitchenettes, a brick-paved courtyard, iron gates and a sophisticated surveillance system that included two Great Danes named Odie and Hera.

The auto condos went for a million dollars each.

The Bavarians promptly bid six million in cash for the entire complex consisting of eight garage bays.

Real estate developer Marvin Lebowski summarily rejected the Bavarians' discounted bid for the entire complex. He believed individual buyers would pay a premium to keep their lux auto mistresses out of sight, yet cozily near, their high-octane sugar daddies.

Lebowski got it big that South Tampa faithfully followed the template of classic old money. These salty dog buccaneers of business and industry didn't need to do drive-by donuts on their own turf. But they couldn't resist razzie straz-zing their whips in front of the rest of Tampa Bay.

After playing several rounds at Palma Ceia Golf & Country Club, the hunter greenest grapevine of South Tampa insider gossip day trading, Lebowski was convinced he could sell all eight auto condos, one at a time. With each successive sale, he'd goose the asking price, incrementally widening his profit margin.

Unfortunately for Lebowski, he misjudged the Bavarians' pleasant demeanor and courteous ways. He sneeringly dismissed them as little more than Lowenbrau rubes in sweaty leather jackets and Oakley sunglasses worn indoors.

It was that arrogant attitude that got Lebowski in a serious jam with the Bavarians.

"Dear God, keep away from me, why have you kidnapped me, why?" Lebowski screamed from inside a tin-roof-rusting shack, most certainly not located in South Tampa.

"Carpetbagger, yell all you want," an unidentified Bavarian biker said. "We got you in a shack way down the Alafia River, hey, weren't that a song a ways ago?"

"No, 'Old Folks at Home' is also called 'Way Down Upon the Suwannee River,' that's what you might be thinking of," a second unidentified biker commented, as he set down a large blue cooler in front of Lebowski.

"Close enough for government work," First Biker decided. "Let's introduce this greedy carpetbagger to our little frens."

"I'm from Boca Raton, for fuck's sake!" Labowski yelled. "I'm a real estate developer, not a carpetbagger."

First Biker snorted, "Same difference, now, as I was a sayin' before Dude here interrupted me, let's show him to our little shrimp friends."

Labowski was bound naked in a steel tub filled with the Alafia River's finest fertilizer-nourished brackish water. He resembled a goliath grouper thrashing about in a confining makeshift aquarium.

Good enough for the manatees, good enough for the Dude, Second Biker thought.

"Know anything about mantis shrimp, Dude?" he asked.

"No, and my name's Marvin Lebowski," Dude said as he squinted at his captors.

"Mantis shrimp could care less about your name," First Biker decreed.

"*Couldn't* care less," Dude said, as he shook his head disapprovingly.

Second Biker grinned like a feral cat who never lost an alley fight.

"Dude, you have any idea how much trouble you're in? Then ya go and correct my generally accepted variation of a popular expression? Tsk, tsk."

"I'm sorry, I couldn't let it go by. I was a Business English major at Columbia."

First Biker laughed, checked Dude's restraints, then said to him, "Allow me to educate you about stomatopods, they's carnivorous marine crustaceans commonly known as mantis shrimp."

He kicked the blue cooler with his muddy black boot, causing calamitous crustacean commotion inside the container.

"Testy little fucks, mantis shrimps are. Most, only four inches long. Some can be fifteen inches, tip to tail. Usually brown colored, though some got these pretty colors. Bright red, that's my favorite, claws down."

Dude shook his head in annoyance.

"You've got me tied up and squatting naked in bilge water, now you're going to feed me shrimp?"

First Biker grinned ghoulishly while raising his tumbleweed eyebrows.

"Shall I enlighten Dude about the shrimp?" he asked of the Second Biker.

"Yeah, let's get the good times a rollin'," Second Biker answered excitedly.

"All righty then!" First Biker exclaimed.

He carefully plucked a foot-long blood red shrimp out of the blue cooler.

"This is a peacock mantis shrimp. Packs the strongest punch of any critter in the animal kingdom."

Dude *pfft!* disdainfully at the shrimp impersonating a Florida Keys rock lobster.

"I'm not eating that, that *thing*," he declared all Boca Ratonian.

"This ain't no Bubba Gump shrimp au gratin, Dude," First Biker said. "This peacock mantis is gonna punch the living shit out of you."

"Let me go and we'll call it a day, no harm, no foul," Dude Lebowski pleaded.

"Ha!" First Biker retorted. "No, I'll brief you on the peacock mantis' skill set, then let it go all Poseidon on your ass. Don't forget, this fella swings its front claw at nearly fifty-miles-an-hour, same acceleration as a 22-caliber bullet."

"But!" Dude exclaimed.

"No more interruptions! When Mr. Peacock Mantis punches you, your flesh will come clean off. Our crustacean friend can atomize a bone, I tell you."

"Dear God!"

"No deity gonna help you out, Dude. Agree to lower your asking price for the whole shebang to five-million and we'll call it a day. No harm, no foul, as you say."

Dude tugged vainly at the ropes, wildly thrashing water out of the tub.

"You offered six million yesterday!" he screamed.

"Your obstinance cost you a million dollars," Second Biker explained.

First biker held the angry peacock mantis against Dude's left knee cap. The bad-to-the-exoskeleton shrimp punched Dude's kneecap with such ferocity, the man's skin shredded like ropas viajas, while his patella exploded into so much paella.

Blood darkened the water to a deep septic tank brown.

Dude howled.

"Are you gonna lower your price to five-mil?" Second Biker yelled.

"No, I can't, I won't," Dude whimpered.

"All right, Dude, *this time right between the eyes*," First Biker drawled with Liberty Valance menace most genuine.

He slowly raised the peacock mantis to the bridge of Dude's nose.

"Wait, wait," Dude cried out. "All right, you win, five million in cash, it's all yours."

The two Bavarians high-fived one another.

The Dude abides, after all, First Biker thought.

"That wasn't so hard, was it, Marvin?" inquiring minded Second Biker wanted to know.

"Just take me home," Marvin whimpered.

"Why of course we will, soon as we get ya patched up 'n dropped off at the ER. Marvin, pleasure doing business with ya."

Jake pulled up in front of the closed gate to the Bavarians' compound. With the Riviera GS measuring twenty-feet long, the auto's boat tail protuded a foot into Bay-to-Bay Boulevard.

Great Danes Odie and Hera stood as quiet as a silent auction. They didn't bark. They simply stared at Jake. Stared very hard at him, in fact.

Shit, forgot my bag of bacon, he thought.

He peered between the iron bars. He saw a black '68 Lincoln Continental parked in the courtyard under a broad Florida live oak.

Den's here all right, he thought.

Jake gazed up at the iron gate. There was a message crowning the gate.

He halfway expected the Bavarians to have used the insidiously cruel proclamation, "Arbeit macht frei."

He was relieved the WWII Nazi death camp slogan, "Work Will Set You Free," wasn't employed.

Bavarians went in an altogether different direction by identifying their headquarters as "Salon des Refuses" or "Salon of the Rejected," referring to the 1863 Salon des Refuses art exhibition in Paris. The official Paris Salon, sponsored by the French government and the Academy of Fine Arts, insisted on idealized realism in paintings. The Paris Salon rejected avant-garde paintings by Edouard Manet, Camille Pissarro, Johan Jongkind, even James McNeil Whistler and his *Symphony in White, No. 1: The White Girl.*

Thanks to Napoleon III's intervention, the rejected, though not dejected, artists were granted their own salon to exhibit their paintings.

Mulraney's a clever bastard, Jake conceded. Wonder how many Bavarians get the gist of that sign, without Den having to explain it to them.

Before he hopped out of the Riviera to press the gate's speaker button, Jake double-checked that his matching Browning 45-caliber pistols, which he named "Wyatt" and "Doc," much to Reed's eternal chagrin, were safely out of sight under the driver's bucket seat.

No need for gun play just yet, Jake reassured himself.

CHAPTER 20

BONAIRE

SOUTHERN CARIBBEAN · 2014

"WHO KNEW avocado toast came with a side of danger," Reed exclaimed. "This spy stuff is kinda fun."

Jake smirked like the seasoned foxhole veteran that he was.

"Yeah, 'spy stuff,' as you so adorably call it, is fun until it's not, like when it gets deadly."

"Wise words from Spymaster Siddhartha, I suppose."

This time, Jake's smirk came with a snicker.

"I think you're sincere even when you're being a wise ass. But if you and I stay together, you'll need to learn some of my craft, because I come with a lot of baggage, some of which will adversely affect you."

Jake held her.

"Am I worth the risk, Reed?"

"Strictly on a preliminary basis? I'd say yes, but I'll get back to you with a final answer. Soon come. I promise."

She gave Jake a slow-ride-take-it-easy kiss.

"Time to snorkel, I want to see you in that little blue number," she said.

"And ye shall gaze most wondrously," Jake said with Old Testament vigor.

"Tempted as I am to yell 'OMG,' I'll just say it's great to see you loosen up, and not be such a wet blanket, a stick in the mud, a ..."

"Say 'limp noodle' and I'm leaving on my board shorts."

"Why? 'Limp noodle' doesn't really fit with the other expressions. But do you?"

"Do I what?"

"Have a limp noodle?"

"No, I do not."

"Just checking. After all, a woman needs to know certain stuff about a guy."

The couple strolled to the marina after breakfast.

It was a Monday. Eastern sun steadfastly took its noon pole position.

Reed carried a black nylon bag containing an O'Neill snorkel mask and deep-sea swim fins. Jake had a pair of beat-up swim goggles hooked around the index finger of his left hand.

"That's all you're going to use, a pair of swim goggles?" Reed asked incredulously.

He smiled.

"It's all I need. I have excellent lung capacity, since I stay in shape and don't use tobacco of any sort. How about you?"

"How about me, what?"

"Do you use tobacco?"

"Me? Nah. Never. No *tobacco* products. Never ever. Scout's honor."

"So, cannabis, huh?"

"Nunya, bub."

"You're right, it's none of my business." Jake said. "But now I have this image in my head of you topless and wearing a tiny green, black and yellow Speedo, holding a lit spliff in one hand and an ice-cold 'Hooray for beer!' Red Stripe in the other, while dancing to Marley on Seven-Mile Beach."

Reed laughed.

"Always glad to perk up your fantasies, dear boy."

They stood at the entrance to the marina, whose slips were occupied by ocean-going yachts, twin-hulled grand catamarans, all depth and breadth of single-hulled sailboats and a bright yellow cigarette boat that goes round & round.

"Where's our boat, Jake?"

"I think it's over there tied up at the end of the pier," he replied, while pointing to an eighteen-foot white skiff bearing the trademark flat-bottom with a sharp bow and square stern.

"That's definitely the hotel's guest boat, but I don't see anyone in it or even around it," Reed said.

They walked to the end of the pier. They saw a man sprawled out in the skiff. He employed four bright orange life jackets as his makeshift bed.

The man looked up at Reed and Jake.

"Good afternoon, the gentleman and his lady!"

Jake gave him the hairy eyeball.

"Watcha doing down there?" he asked.

The man smiled with Great White chompers.

"Letting my tan dry."

"*Humpf*," Jake said. "Any chance you're watching the boat until the captain shows up?"

The barefoot man, bearing Caribbean Black skin, graying disheveled hair and an unkempt beard, stood up on the boat. He wore a grimy white t-shirt and even grimier pants. He weaved slightly, though the harbor was dead calm.

"I *am* dee captain, sir!" the man said with a Jamaican accent. "I won't tolerate your American boorishness onboard this fine vessel, don't make me chum you for dee barracuda."

Jake rumbled, "Look, pal ..."

"I am not your pal, sir, I am your captain, and while I'm aboard my boat, I shall speak to you in any manner I see fit. Get onboard or piss off."

Disagreeable sort, Reed thought.

Fella has got a point, I guess, Jake conceded.

"Captain, my apologies," Jake said. "I'm Jake and my friend here is Reed, may we come aboard?"

The man immediately transformed into a benevolent boat captain of Ocho Rios lineage, not at all the recalcitrant pirate chum-master of Mo' Bay.

"Yes, yes, come aboard. I am Alfred, Alfred Newman of Jamaica way, mon. And that's Newman, N-e-w-m-a-n. You may address me as 'Captain Al.'"

He helped Reed into the skiff. Jake required no assistance, scampering onto the boat like a great river otter.

"Captain, what's your middle name?" Reed inquired as she sat down, tossing her snorkel gear bag to one side

"Edsel, why?"

"Just curious, thank you."

Alfred E. Newman? Fuck's sake, he's gotta be messing with us, she thought.

Jake leaned over to examine the boat's starboard side.

"Whatcha looking for, my friend?" Captain Al asked suspiciously.

"Oh nothing, I thought maybe you named your skiff, '*What, Me Worry?*'"

"Not my boat, but that'd be a fine name for her if she were mine. Her actual name is *It's a Gas*, tru dat."

Reed whispered to Jake, "Is he doing a *Mad Magazine* bit?"

Jake shrugged his shoulders.

"What is this *Mad Magazine*, mi lady?" Captain Al inquired.

Guy's got great hearing, she thought.

"Oh, no worries, Captain, no ting at all."

Captain Alfred E. Newman laughed with nary a worry.

"Every ting irie, then let's cast off and head out to dee *Hilma!*"

"One other thing, Captain," Jake said.

"Weh yuh dehpon, fass mon?" Captain Al asked.

"I'm not up to anything, and don't call me nosy," Jake spliffed back to the Jamaican. "I'd like to know why there isn't a HIN anywhere to be seen on this skiff, not on the transom or forward starboard side."

"What you mean, 'him'?" the captain replied.

"No, Captain, it's 'HIN' as in 'Hull Identification Number.'"

"Oh, dat. Boat just got painted. We haven't dee time to paint those numbers back on."

Such complete bullshit, Jake thought. Seems to me, he painted over the HIN, and not necessarily for a good reason.

Jake decided to let this one go, an impulsive decision that he'd repeat eight years later, costing the life of a beautiful Cuban dancer.

Captain Al deftly untied *It's a Gas*, tossed lines haphazardly on its deck, cranked the Merc outboard, then took off fast, completely ignoring "No-Wake Zone" signs posted prominently on barnacled pylons.

"No wake, you fuckwit!" a white-silk robed man yelled in an Aussie accent from the top deck of the yacht *Priscilla, Queen of the Desert*.

Captain Al cold-shouldered the man with a backwards victory sign.

"Why'd the captain flash him the victory sign?" Reed asked Jake.

"Not a victory sign, mi lady," Captain Al interjected. "It's a Jamaican's way of saying, 'Up your ass.'"

The boat skiffed across the smooth Caribbean Sea like a sandpiper av-gassed on double blasts of Cuban espresso.

Several miles offshore of Kralencijk, Captain Al brought the boat near, but not too near, a gathering of bright orange diving buoys. Close by, there were two other larger vessels, apparently transports for the divers below. Captain Al shut down the outboard. The three of them drifted slowly across Swarovski crystal clear water.

"Perfect day for snorkeling, Miss Reed and Mr. Jake," Captain Al exclaimed as he popped the cap of a Red Stripe with his shark's teeth. "Divers, dey be here a'fore us, but pay'em no mind a 'tall, dey bother you, do what I do 'n cut dere air lines."

"Really?" Reed asked.

"Truly, mi lady. Here, I'll give you a diver's knife. Strap dee sheath around your ... you right-handed?"

Reed nodded yes.

"Good, strap it on your right leg. Make it easy to get to. Knife's good for poking pesky divers, 'n peskier nurse sharks and dee great barracuda."

He handed her the sheathed knife. She stretched the Velcro strap around her right thigh, then attached it securely.

"Captain, I thought nurse sharks and great barracuda hang in deep water further out from the reefs," Jake interjected.

"Mon, not dee time for dee swinging dick contest," Captain Al answered. "Ya mon, the nurse and the great 'cuda, dey likes deep black waters, but sometimes, just sometimes, dey cruise dee sand flat between dee two coral reefs we're floating over, irie?"

"Irie, and thanks for the clarification."

"No problem, Mr. Jake. Now let me tell you about the shipwreck you're gonna explore."

"Oh goody, a lecture at sea!" Reed said with eagerness in her voice.

"Just like dee fancy cruise ships do, mi lady," the captain boasted, as he polished off his Red Stripe.

He belched and farted in one synchronized movement.

"Excuse me, please, I lose my manners at sea," he said. "Ready to learn all about *Hilma*?"

"The shipwreck below us?"

"Yes, mi lady. *Hilma* launched in '51. She's 235-feet long with a 36-foot beam. She's passed through several hands over der years: first dee Dutch, then dee Panamanians, Bahamians and Columbians."

"A cargo ship, right?" Jake asked rhetorically.

Captain Al, a sinewy man no more than five-feet, six-inches tall, snorted annoyance at the much larger Jake, then the captain used his ivories to pop the cap of another Red Stripe. He gulped half the beer.

"Yes, Mr. Tarzan of dee jungle," the captain answered with a slight slur. "*Hilma* was a cargo ship, which is why she got into trouble back in '84. She had engine problems. Got towed to Kralendijk Harbor. Port authorities, dey suspected *Hilma* was carrying dee drugs."

"Really?" Reed asked, enthralled with the captain's tale.

"Yes, mi lady. They discovered a false bulkhead. It had 11,000 kilos of ganja."

"Or twenty-five thousand pounds of cannabis," Jake proffered.

"Watch out for dat tree, George, George, George of the Jungle," Captain Al answered. "Yah mon, twelve-and-a-half tons of dee glorious ganja that'll get you in dee a couch for dee rest of ya life."

"What happened next, Captain?" Reed said.

"Miss Reed, *Hilma's* crew was detained while dee authorities searched for her owner. Never found him, they surely did not. But *Hilma* was a rust bucket taking on water. Was grave concern she'd sink and block up dee harbor, so the old lady, she was towed to anchorage right here. Real quick, *Hilma* listed. She took on water through her portholes. On September 7, 1984, *Hilma* rolled over starboard side. She sank in two minutes. Now she rests thirty-meters, or one-hundred-feet below us, *Mr. Jake,* nestled right peaceful like on a sand bar between dee two coral reefs."

Captain Al tossed the glass bottle over the side of the skiff.

Reed started to criticize him for littering at sea, then she backed off.

Out in open waters, way offshore in a small boat with a drunk captain, Reed reminded herself. I mean, what could go wrong?

The captain's toothy grin opened another Red Stripe.

"Are you going to be okay for, what the hell, never mind, Captain," Jake said in a tone singed by laissez-faire flames.

Captain Al pointed a bony Black index finger at Jake, then pretended to shoot him, all the while chugging his beer.

Fucker's lucky I'm in a good mood, Jake thought.

"Time for you two to get your white asses in dee water," Captain Al exclaimed. "I gotta take a stream over dee side, an' I don't want Miss Reed to read dee tattoo on my Jamaican steel."

"Really?" Reed asked too quickly. "At least tell me what your tattoo says on, you know, your appendage."

"Welcome to beautiful Jamaica, mon, have a blessed day every day on our happy island," the captain said proud & cocky as a red-billed Streamertail.

"All one *looong* sentence?" Reed inquired without even a hint of incredulity.

"Yes, mi lady, all one very long sentence."

"Oh my," she replied.

The three of them together broke out in laughter.

"Last time I say dis, get to your snorkeling, I got a date with a Caribbean queen," Captain Al said.

"Relax, Billy Ocean, we're jumping in now," Jake said.

Reed doffed her t-shirt and shorts. She wore a deep purple *thong-thong-THONG!* bikini adorned with a dare-you-not-to-look tiny pink bowtie on the t-backside.

"SMOKIN'!" Jake exclaimed.

"On *dee water*, mon," Captain Al exclaimed as well.

The men fist bumped.

"Respect," the captain said.

"Respect," Jake answered.

Reed decided against swim fins. She removed the snorkel from her mask, then put on the mask.

"Thought I'd try it your way, Jake."

He nodded his approval, then took off his t-shirt and board shorts, leaving him wearing only his royal blue Speedo.

"Nice swim trunks, Mr. Big Bamboo," Captain Al said, as he quaffed Red Stripe.

"Totally agree with our captain," Reed said to Jake.

Holding tight her mask, she jumped into clear blue water.

Jake placed swim goggles around his neck and followed her into the sea. He adjusted the goggles while treading water.

"Reed, let's swim for a while to loosen up. And I'm more interested in exploring the coral reefs, than checking out the wreck. Agree?"

Even while wearing a mask, Reed's crystal blue eyes shimmered, aided by high-noon sunlight reflecting off the calm water.

"Totally onboard with that," she answered.

They free-styled around the dive buoys, swimming in near perfect synchronicity, though each swimmer subtly maneuvered to take the lead. They finished together at the same spot where they started. It marked a trend in the making, for swimming and for other acts of physical pleasure.

"Wadda ya say we go below the deep blue sea?" Jake asked Reed.

"Let's do it," she answered enthusiastically.

They descended together. In less than a minute, they found themselves in an awe-inspiring world.

The reef resembled the immense diorama aquariums of Atlantis Paradise Island. But this was a living underwater ecosystem populated by reef-building corals. The two reefs served as aquatic digs for sea turtles, Caribbean reef squid, white-spotted eagle ray, horse-eye jack, sergeant major fish, blue tang, queen angelfish and, unfortunately, an overabundance of lionfish.

Reed and Jake carefully, respectfully, approached the coral reef.

They admired, but didn't touch, elkhorn coral with its flat broad branches resembling elk antlers, grooved brain coral diploria, achingly beautiful honeycomb coral and acropora coral boasting branches covered with blue and yellow bubble polyps.

Every few minutes, Reed and Jake would slowly ascend to the surface for more air.

"Can you believe I got to be in the middle of a sergeant major fish ball?" Reed asked Jake. "It was like being in a yellow-black underwater spout."

"So very cool," Jake said. "Any idea why they form those fish balls?"

She grinned slyly as she treaded water.

"You know very well why the fish do that, Jake Dupree. Makes them appear to be a much larger fish, but dolphins aren't fooled. They love ploughing through fish balls. It's like a whirling buffet for Flipper and co. No need to throw me a bonefish out here, little buddy. Saltwater practically runs through my veins, okay?"

"Roger that, Skipper," Jake responded. "Speaking of Flipper, did you know five female dolphins played the role of Flipper in the TV show?"

Reed sputtered salt water, then said, "Yuppers, and what were the girlfins' names, Mr. Smarty Speedo Man?"

"That's easy, let's see, Patty, Scotty, Kathy, Susie and Squirt."

"Very good, Jake. There was a sixth dolphin brought in to perform the famous tail walk. What was the lad's name?"

Jake let out a "Hooah!"

"Why, none other than Clown."

About to dive underwater again, Jake and Reed noticed Captain Al standing up in the skiff. He stared at them. He held a Red Stripe in his right hand. He held a handgun in his left.

Swaying pronouncedly, again on pronouncedly calm water, the captain began singing, "Hotel California:"

> *On a dark desert highway*
> *Cool wind in my hair*
> *Warm smell of colitas*
> *Rising up through the air*

"What the hell are colitas?" Reed asked. "And yes, I'm aware the man is brandishing what looks like a 9mm semi-automatic pistol."

"Glad you noticed the handgun," Jake said calmly. "And colitas are potent little buds at the top of a cannabis plant, much prized especially by Mexicans."

Captain Al drank more beer, then continued singing:

> *Welcome to the Hotel California*
> *Such a lovely place (such a lovely place)*
> *Such a lovely face*

"Always hated that song," Reed said. "Sure as fuck hate it more now."

The drunken captain drained his Red Stripe. He threw the bottle overboard. He fired a shot in the air.

"Das just a warning shot, batty boy Jake. My aim will be true next shot. But first, time for another beer."

Still holding the pistol, he zig zagged over to his cooler and got out a Red Stripe. Once more, he used his chompers to pop the top.

"Reed, start treading backwards. Slowly. Don't take your eyes off that asshole."

"All right."

She treaded away from the boat.

"Wah gwaan, Miss Reed, don't wan to play?" Captain Al called out.

She stopped treading.

"I'll play with you, Captain, if you get rid of the handgun."

"Ha!" the captain yelled, then poured beer into his mouth, while holding the bottle above his head. He missed wide right, then wide left, getting his scraggly beard all beer sudsy. He threw the empty beer bottle in Reed's general direction. The bottle plunked in the water a good ten feet, or three meters, from Reed.

"Okay, safe to say this guy means us harm, keep treading backwards," Jake said to Reed.

She again treaded.

"Shit, damn, fuck almighty," she suddenly blurted out.

"What?"

"Asshole welded my knife to its sheath, that's what," Reed answered.

Captain Al sang as he waved his handgun in the air like he just didn't care:

So I called up the Captain,
"Please bring me my wine"
He said, "We haven't had that spirit here
since 1969"

"Hey, Captain, come on, take a shot at me, if you got the balls," Jake teased Captain Al.

Reed whispered, "Jake, what are you doing?"

He whispered back, "My bet is he has twelve rounds in that clip. I doubt the turd blossom has an extra clip. He's down one round, eleven to go. I'm going to force him to empty his clip."

As if on cue, Captain Al fired three rounds at Jake. He missed wildly all three times.

"Captain Al, sweetheart, is your Jamaican steel all rusted out?" Reed asked.

Jake whispered, "Reed, don't."

She answered, "Hey, you don't get to have all of the fun."

"If my steel's rusty, bitch, it's cause I did ah dooks wid chew," Captain Al slurred.

He fired three rounds in rapid succession at Reed. First two rounds missed her. The third slightly grazed her upper right arm.

Guffawing at the captain's poor marksmanship, Reed wiped blood from the minor wound then tasted it, making loud smacking sounds while still treading in place.

"That's all you got in your tiny pistol, fuckface?" she said tauntingly. "Yuh a crassis."

Seven down, five to go, Reed counted. Hope Jake's right.

But Jake was nowhere to be seen.

Reed was the lone gunman's sole target.

"Time for you to go bye-bye, Little Miss Mosquito Net," the captain announced to her.

"Just a chaka-chaka bad bread ass, you are," Reed answered.

This time he fired four rounds at her. All of them missed.

"Goddamn mermaid, you are," Captain Al muttered. "Stop wiggling around soze I can finish you off and find Mr. Big Bamboo."

Said Mr. Big Bamboo rose up on the skiff's portside gunwale and yelled "Boo!" to Captain Al, who had his back to Jake.

The captain spun round, then fell on the boat deck as he fired a round in the air. Laying on his back, he repeatedly pulled the trigger from an empty pistol. He threw the pistol at Jake, missing him, of course.

Having swam underwater to get behind the skiff, Jake gambled Captain Al was too drunk and too focused on Reed for him to notice Mr. Big Bamboo coming aboard without permission.

Time to shut down this shit show, Jake thought.

He pulled himself up and rolled into the skiff, then ja-rocked Captain Al with an elbow strike to the Jamaican's jaw, sending the man off to a world beyond the sea.

CHAPTER 21

TAMPA, FLORIDA · 2022

"WELCOME to the Salon des Refuses. Fuck ya want?"

A porcine carrot-topped young man stood defiantly behind the iron gate to the Bavarians' headquarters in South Tampa. He wore a sleeveless blue denim jacket over a grimy white t-shirt bearing the band Judas Iscariot's logo.

He exuded the je ne sais quoi charm of Police Nationale officers on Paris' Les Champs-Elysée exuberantly skull-crushing des hooligans du foot celebrating France's entry to a FIFA World Cup Final.

Jake spotted the large-caliber revolver hardly concealed in the waistband of the young man's black jeans.

Jake knew he had to answer in the same coarse parlance as his new biker buddy.

"Fuck you, shitheel. Whadda I want? Talk to Denizen. Simple as that. Call him. Tell him Jake Dupree's here for parlay not gunplay. Move it, Mildred."

"Mildred" promptly called the boss. Thirty seconds later, the gate slowly rolled open, allowing Jake to motor into the complex's expansive courtyard. He intentionally parked crinkle close to Denizen's '68 Continental. As he climbed out of the Riviera, he tapped the Continental's right suicide door with the long side door of his fifty-year-old sports sedan.

"Hey, take it easy on boss' ride," portly young Mildred admonished.

Jake glared at him.

"You're annoying me, chub boy. Now stop blocking the sun and go find Denizen."

"Big talk coming from a broken-down CIA operative, and your fat shaming was quite insensitive on your part, Dupree, because Zeke has feelings, too, don't you know."

The voice called out from a bay farthest to the right of the complex.

It was Denizen Mulraney. All six-feet-six inches, 250 pounds of muscle, grizzle and Vlad the Impaler bad attitude.

Denizen. Den. *Never* Denny.

Here was a man notorious for knife play and for dressing his departed in Mexican Neckties.

A man who savored the apocryphal story of his eating a victim's liver.

"Just so I can get the necessary RDI in iron, riboflavin, vitamin B12 and copper," he told gullible listeners.

A man who partnered with Jake a dozen times for lethal black ops. Twelve targets. Twelve hits. Twelve dead men and women. Only one dead Cuban bull.

A man who called his partnership with Jake the "Death Squad," though he pronounced it as "Deeth Squid," due to his heavy Dublin accent heavily seasoned by too many pints of Guinness (est. 1759) stouts and Carroll's (est. 1824) cigarettes.

A man who crafted sociopathy into an artform worthy of D.C.'s National Gallery Art's performance art exhibit.

A man Jake trusted without hesitation.

Denizen Mulraney: former U.S. government-trained killer, former French Foreign Legionnaire, now president of the Bavarians Motorcycle Club, Tampa chapter, USA.

The big man walked out of the bay and into the unsparing Florida light. He wore a bright white t-shirt stretched taut with rippling muscles and skinny black jeans with black engineer boots. He was B&W noir Nazi from his bald head down to his nine toes.

At thirty, Denizen had straight blond hair. At sixty, he was completely bald. However, he sported a silver-blonde goatee that, coupled with his blue eyes, lent him the air of a Dubliner Doc Holliday.

Forming a triangle in the courtyard, Jake, Denizen and Zeke stood twenty-feet apart from one another.

"Jake, you need to apologize to Zeke for fat-shaming him," Denizen demanded. "He was just doing his job, and you have cop written all over your ugly mush, why, there's still powdered sugar on your chin from eating Boston crème donuts."

"Are you asking or telling me to apologize, Den?"

"Never ask. Ever. You know that."

Jake raised his hands in mock surrender.

"All right, Denizen, I'll apologize."

He looked at Zeke.

"Zeke, I'm sorry for suggesting you're a stanky leg fat ass named Mildred.

Zeke side-eyed his boss.

"Best you're gonna get from him, son. That's not a man to tangle with over a fatty insult. Back to your post, Zeke."

Zeke nodded. He returned to his post at the front gate.

"Interesting, Den. Our Namaste performer Alicia Serrano was shot and killed by a Smith & Wesson Magnum 500 revolver. Same type of handgun young Zeke is getting belly sweat all over."

Denizen laughed while keeping his distance from Jake, a blade man's signal he was relaxed. For now.

"Never were one to beat-off around the woman's bush, were you? Is there a question somewhere in that turd pile of words, words, words?"

"Yes. Did the Bavarians have anything to do with Alicia's murder?"

"Bold, aggressive talk on your part. But you're off target, my old friend. We might be a while unloading your question's implications. Longer we're out in this bloody sun, better the chances are that we'll lose our tempers."

"What're you suggesting?" Jake asked.

"We slowly take ten steps toward one another. Shake hands. Compliment one another as to how fit and handsome we are. Sorry about the 'ugly mush' jest, by the by. Then we repair to my abode for good cappuccinos and even better conversation."

Neither man said a word as Jake and Denizen slowly Sergio Leoned toward one another. They stopped. Shook hands. Hugged. Back slapped.

"See, lad, this is what we ought to have done from the start," Denizen lectured. "Gentlemen's mannerly foreplay is better than anything that follows."

Jake guffawed.

"Exactly what Reed says to me about our foreplay, though not sure how to take it."

"Take it as a compliment, man! Make a woman cum with your mouth, you'll never be alone, and you'll never go to bed hungry. Speaking of our Irish lass, how is Reed? Does she know I'm your neighbor of sorts?"

"She's doing well, though she's dangerously angry over Alicia's death. Since there appears some sort of connection between the Bavarians and Alicia's murder, I'll have to tell her the Grand White swims in our shallows."

Denizen grinned like a tippled parish priest conducting altar boy auditions in the rear of the church bingo hall.

"'The Grand White,' I like it. Say, that reminds me, whatever became of our formidable Irish operative, Lou?"

"Wouldn't know, but I have it from reliable sources you've seen her without her clothes on."

"Lad, I waited a polite twenty-four hours before serenading her, and she was most distraught and vulnerable over her sacking you," Denizen waxed puckishly.

"Funny man. I also learned through the Cote des Blancs grape vine you used that old chestnut of yours when you approached Lou in Paris. After your abbreviated waiting period, your being the Irish gentleman that you are."

Denizen face palmed.

"Did I not teach you how to tell a tale? It was winter in Paris. There she sat all by her blonde-hair, Emerald-Isle-eyes, small-in-stature, but big-in-bust self, outside at King George V Café on ..."

"Les Champs-Elysee, yes," Jake said pointedly.

"Cut me off again and there'll be fresh tri-cep sashimi for my mermaids, compliments of one Jacob Jordan Dupree."

"Wasabi always threatening me with that sashimi shit?" Jake asked.

"Clever, not funny," Denizen said. "I happened to be casing Di Giorgio's on the, well, you know, when I saw Lou drinking a Kronenbourg (est. 1664) in minus one-point-one-degree Celsius weather. A grand woman after my own heart, she was."

"You said it, didn't you?

"What?"

"The line, Den."

"All I said was, 'Excusez-mois, mademoiselle, but you must be Oirish because my cock sure is a Dublin!'"

"What was Lou's reaction?" Jake inquired.

"She jumped up and laid a big wet pug on me. Her diabhalta tongue liked to stick to my luscious lips, it was so cold out. Had to employ a mug of hot mulled wine to separate us. Rest of the day we smelled like clove, anise and cardamom pods. Told Lou it's best she get to my apartment, doff her clothes and slip into a hot dubbly bubbly bath. She agreed. Without hesitation. The rest of the story is epic and, I must tell ya, most privateer."

Jake laughed.

"Can we talk about Alicia Serrano?"

"Of course! Let's go in my ADU. It's the one farthest from the street."

"ADU?"

"Accessory Dwelling Unit," Denizen explained.

"'Granny flat over the garage' wouldn't cut it?"

"Hardly."

The two men walked to the newly constructed auto condo complex. They entered Denizen's ADU.

It consisted of a large garage where his Harley-Davidson CVO Tri Glide leaned on its jiffy stand atop a twelve-by-twelve-foot painting of a skull missing its mandible and buttressed by two crossed femur bones. The floor was glittery black and the walls a deep scarlet.

The back area of the ADU boasted a billiards table, a professional arm-wrestling table and a mahogany bar with taps that poured Pilsner, Schwarzbier and Guinness beers. Nary a drop of Bud Lite or Coors Light or Yuengling was to be seen.

A loft held an office, a bedroom and a bathroom.

"I have a hot shower and a heated turlette, though no bidet, sad to say," Denizen opined.

"Yeah, looks like you're roughing it in the untamed wilderness of South Tampa," Jake answered good naturedly. "Really nice touch with the Schutzstaffel skull and crossbones."

"No need for sarcasm, lad. The Totenkopf is more than an SS symbol. Also represents defiance of danger and death. Nazis didn't hold the rights on the Totenkopf or the Swastika. That symbology is ancient and worldwide. It belongs to everyone."

Jake gently shook his head, then said, "Thanks for the lecture."

"Lad, did we really wait so long to see each other to talk politics and history, while all the time risking heartburn and indigestion?"

"Take a couple Tums if I upset your delicate constitution," Jake suggested.

Denizen smiled. Predatorily. The smile exposed perfect white teeth and rose gold canines.

"I tolerate your wise assery for three reasons. I love you like a brother. We go *waaay* back to dark and bloody chapters that we carry 'round our necks like a fecking dead *albertruss*. Most importantly, you and Sergio, may he rest in peace, saved my miserable excuse for a life after that Juarez feck-up of all feck-ups."

"Good to know my credit's still good here," Jake said.

He looked out at the brick courtyard.

"It's quiet here. Where is everyone?"

"The lads and their lassies are sleeping it off. We made a late night of it yesterday."

"Seem to remember you mentioned something about a cappuccino," Jake said.

"That I did, Jake. Give me five minutes and I'll have our cappuccinos hot, frothy and delicious."

"Deal. I'll just sit at this tall table, all right?"

"Fine and dandy," Denizen replied.

He walked briskly to the bar. On the counter behind the bar was a Dalla Corte Mina espresso machine. He made two cappuccinos in less than four minutes, first pouring rich brown espresso followed by foamy steamed milk.

Denizen set down on the elevated square table two insulated stainless-steel mugs. Jake sipped his coffee.

"Bravo, Den. Tastes great. Hey, doesn't a Dalla Corte go for about ten grand?"

Denizen took an ambitious drink of his coffee, then said, "Retail? Probably."

"You get it wholesale?" Jake inquired.

"Not exactly."

"Fell out of an Amazon van?"

"Perhaps, but you still have that terrible habit of asking too many dangerous questions, my brother," Denizen warned.

"Price for my inquisitiveness, I guess," Jake replied.

"More the price for talking too much," Denizen said straight faced.

The veteran warriors laughed. Loudly.

They finished their coffees at the same time.

Denizen paused. Pondered. Weighed options. Decided.

"Ready to talk, Den?"

"Long as you're not wired."

"Gimme a break," Jake said. "I'm wired only by espresso."

"Had to say it. Believe you, though. I can see honesty in your eyes. Besides, you're not a man who wire-rats an old friend."

"No, I'm not. Enough of this. Were the Bavarians involved with Alicia Serrano's murder?"

They sat in silence for nearly a minute.

"The reason I don't kick your ass out of here is that I owe you. But you're asking a lot. Too much."

Silence again.

"I'm asking for the truth, Den."

Denizen paused. Pondered. Weighed options. Decided.

"Truth is just like trust, Jake. You gotta earn it."

"How do I go about doing that?"

"We're sitting at a top-of-the-line arm wrestling table."

"Yeah, elbow pads and grip handles tipped me off," Jake said.

"Well, good. This is my only offer. We'll arm wrestle. You win, I'll be as honest as I can without incriminating my brother Bavarians. My debt to you is paid. In full. Plus, we'll no longer be friends, sad as that surely will be. I win, which is likely, I get your Riviera and then I ghost you. Your decision. Smok'em if you got'em, lad."

Jake spoke almost immediately.

"Don't think you've thrown me on the horns of a dilemma here, Den. I'll gladly arm wrestle you. I'll whip your ass, too."

Denizen dropped all pretense of civility.

"Words, Jake Dupree, you're nothing but feckin' words, as always. Same as my arse for a father would say about me, until I grew up by shutting the feck up."

"Enough of your blather, Denizen Mulraney. Let's do this."

They squared off. Left forearms on the pads. Table handles gripped. Forearms raised on elbows. Right hands clenched.

"At three, shithead," Denizen said.

Denizen winked at Jake, then rapidly counted off, "One-two-three!"

He got a jump on Jake. Denizen strained mightily for a quick win over a younger opponent.

Jake grinned.

"Never good to rabbit, Mulraney, no matter the competition."

"Damn your mother to ifreann, Dupree. Do you commentate while you're feckin' your Oirish whore?"

Jake sensed Denizen's stamina slipping, his will to victory flagging. It was time to rainbow arc the man older than Jake by twenty years. Jake realized this Denizen wasn't the same man who arm wrestled, then defeated, six men in a row in Juarez, all the while he diddled a beautiful Mexican woman he nicknamed "Mescal," who in turn nicknamed him "El Gran Gusano."

Jake slammed a hard left.

Done and done, Jake won.

Denizen grabbed a black hand towel from a hook beneath the table. He wiped his bald head and face, then blew his nose into the towel.

"Haven't lost a match in ten years," he groaned.

"Same amount of time it took Odysseus to come home from the

Trojan War," Jake commented. "Ah well, all epic road trips and winning streaks have to end at some point."

They laughed raucously.

"You know, lad, that's the last time we'll laugh together. Strictly business from here on out."

Jake lost his smile.

"Yeah, I get that. Helluva price we're paying, but I gotta know about Alicia."

"My moral compass you'll always be, Jake. But it won't affect my aim. Ask your questions before I change my mind."

"Did you know Alicia was a BarraCuba?" Jake asked.

"Yes, but only recently. Before she got shot up, she wasn't on our radar. Was Paz Iberra on our radar? Feck yeah. Alicia Serrano? No way. Just a minnow. Meant nothing to us 'cept to my mermaids."

"How long did you know Alicia was a BarraCuba before she was murdered? Be precise, Denizen."

Denizzen grumped and growled.

"Three months, all right?" he admitted.

"Kind of stretches 'recently' doesn't it? She was, in fact, on your radar."

"All relative, lad."

"Enough with the 'lad' bullshit. You're getting hinky. Did you use Alicia as some sort of willing or unwilling mole to get intel on the BarraCubas?"

"Fine conjecture, lad, er, Dupree. No, not directly. Never met the poor girl."

"But she did provide you intel?" Jake inquired.

"Yes."

"Who was the cutout?"

"Dupree ..."

"Deal's a deal."

"You ask too much of me."

"You gotta give me a name. No backsliding, Mulraney."

Denizen pulled out a balisong knife, then whipped it open and gestured all Ronco Chop-O-Matic toward Jake.

Picking up the black hand towel, Jake lassoed Denizen's knife-wielding hand. He twisted tight the towel, then slammed Denizen's hand on the steel table handle. The balisong fell harmlessly on the floor.

"Let's play nice, shall we?" Jake demanded.

"I wasn't going to cut you! Holding Lucille helps me think. You know, you hurt my goddamn hand, Dupree."

"Lucky to get off that lightly. Now who's the cutout? Sooner you tell me, sooner I'm gone."

"I got a good gig here," Denizen said under his breath, while rubbing his bruised right hand. "My Bavarian brothers look to me for leadership, guidance and coordination of certain under-the-radar activities."

Jake shook his head.

"You've always been a mercenary, Mulraney, even when we worked for the Company. But I'm not here to blow your cover with the Bavarians, long as I get what I want. Give me a name."

"Ernie."

"Ernie?"

"Yeah, Ernie Friekorps."

"Who's he?" Jake asked.

"Detective. Narcotics. Tampa PD."

"On your payroll?"

"Yeah. For a while now. Ernie tips us about raids and investigations."

"How'd Friekorps know Alicia?" Jake demanded.

Denizen exhaled the remaining fight in him.

"Ernie found out Serrano was a dancer at your nightclub."

"It's 'performer,' but go on."

"He also discovered she was a BarraCuba, which is uncool from your standpoint, right?"

"Right. Tell me about Friekorps."

"He forced the bitch to snitch. Otherwise, he'd turn her in to you and Reed. Once he got his CI up and running, Friekorps threatened to give her to the BarraCubas if she wanted to stop snitching."

"Guy's a piece of work," Jake said.

"Yeah, Friekorps lube tubes all the angles. When Serrano tried to get out, he lied. Said it was okay to leave. Then he came to me and wanted twenty-five grand for her name. Had to admit, I was kind of curious. Gave him five G's for 'Alicia Serrano.'"

"Did you kill Alicia?" Jake demanded.

Silence descended on the men. Jake could hear Bavarians noisily stumbling awake from nacht Schlafen.

"We had nothing to do with that murder, nothing whatsoever," Denizen declared.

"How about a rogue Bavarian?"

"An oxymoron if there ever were one," Denizen said.

"That's a negative, then?"

"Extremely unlikely a brother would unilaterally orchestrate a hit. That's a death sentence around here."

"I'll accept that for now. Did Friekorps murder Alicia?"

"He was gonna lose her. He'd made serious scratch off the lass. Punk put a high price on the intel she provided. But no, killing her isn't his style. He's an invertebrate. Hasn't the courage of a Sassenach, even. I'd heard he sold her name to the BarraCubas as well. Got a hundred grand from them, least what I heard, probably less, but not a whole lot less."

"You're suggesting the BarraCubas killed her?"

"Follow the money trail, you'll find your killer. If Paz Iberra paid that many Benjamins, she'd want the straight shit on the traitor."

"Probably would, but a few too many 'ifs' involved here."

"Telling you everything I know, Dupree. We didn't kill Serrano. Friekorps hasn't got the appetite for a hit. BarraCubas are your best bet. Nothing more I can offer you."

Jake rubbed his chin.

"This it for us, Den?"

"Like you said to me, Dupree, no backsliding on our deal. Neither of us is a welcher hiding out in feckin' Cardiff."

"No, we're not. This is goodbye, my brother in arms. We meet up again, I may be much more unpleasant than I was today."

"I'd expect nothing less from you, Jake Dupree."

Denizen spit into his right hand. Jake did the same with his right hand. The two seasoned warriors shook hands.

Jake turned and walked away.

Denizen began singing:

When Irish eyes are smiling
Sure, 'tis like the morn in spring
In the lilt of Irish laughter
You can hear the angels sing
When Irish hearts are happy
All the world seems bright and gay
And when Irish eyes are smiling
Sure, they steal your heart away

Jake wouldn't let Denizen see him smiling. But smile, he did.

As he walked to his Riviera parked in the courtyard, he noticed two women sunbathing nude, while sitting on green and orange webbed lawn chairs in front of an auto condo. The women rested their feet in small plastic wading pools. They kept their cool by fanning themselves with bamboo & mulberry hand fans. It was a scene only Gauguin could've captured on canvas.

Jake smiled at one of the women. She wagged her index finger at him. The other woman made a shooing motion with her fan. Both women hissed at him.

As Jake politely stepped away from the women, he noticed what looked like the tip of a fishtail in one of the wading pools.

He climbed into the Riviera, then motored toward Zeke, who slowly opened the gate while making certain Jake saw his howitzer for a revolver.

Jake waved a thank you to him.

Zeke made a middle finger return-to-sender gesture.

Them Bavarians sure is a prickly bunch of coconuts, Jake thought.

CHAPTER 22

BONAIRE

Southern Caribbean · 2014

"You nuttin' but a batty boy," Captain Alfred E. Newman yelled at Jake, as the would-be assassin folded like a rickety aluminum lawn chair into a subcompact police cruiser in front of the Village Beach Resort lobby.

"Batty boy?" Reed inquired.

"Jamaican for homosexual," Jake answered.

He and Reed waved goodbye to Red Stripe Man who couldn't shoot straight.

Front desk manager Cherish approached Reed and Jake.

"I am sorry for what happened to you darlings! Why, the actual captain showed up in the lobby not ten minutes after you left the dock."

"Do you know Captain Al?" Reed asked.

"*Captain Al!* What a joke that man is, Miss O'Hara. He's a drunk Jamaican fool, always be a griftin' tourists and a driftin' around town and a siftin' through our garbage cans. Alfred doesn't belong on our island, he certainly doesn't."

Didn't answer my question, Reed noticed.

"Somebody put him up to this," Jake surmised. "Who would've hired him to take us out?"

"Are you asking *me*, sir?"

Jake stared at Cherish.

"I'm asking you, yes."

Cherish frowned.

"Why, sir? Do you think I was involved in this incident? Do you?"

Reed intervened.

"Jake doesn't suspect you; we don't suspect you. We're hoping you've heard something."

Cherish smiled crookedly.

"Only thing I've heard is you've a couple's massage in thirty minutes."

"Yes, well, I thought I'd check out of the resort right now," Reed said.

"Why, Miss O'Hara?"

"Our morning out on the water didn't engender my confidence in the Village," Reed answered.

Cherish became sad.

"Yes, I see your point. How about this. I'll check you out later today. Refund the remaining three nights of your stay with us. Couple's massage is compliments of management. This way, you might think of returning to this beautiful resort."

Reed smiled warmly.

"That's very generous of you. I accept. Thank you, Cherish."

"Yes, thank you, ma'am, you are a lady and a scholar," Jake added.

Cherish giggled.

"A handsome man's good manners always gets mi puddin' all a shaking!"

"I know what you mean," Reed said.

"Y'all making me blush." Jake said. "Should Reed and I start over to the spa, Cherish?"

"Yes, Mr. Dupree."

"Very good," he answered.

Cherish walked away in the direction of the resort lobby.

When she was a good fifty feet from Jake and Reed, he said, "That's odd."

"What?" Reed asked.

"I never told Cherish my name, and I don't think you did either."

"I made a point of not saying your name."

"Yet she addressed me as 'Mr. Dupree.'"

"That *is* odd."

"I recommend we file that away for future examination," Jake suggested.

"Roger that," Reed answered confidently.

Jake smiled at the woman with whom he was Acapulco-cliff-diving enraptured.

"Anyone else like you, Reed?"

"Not possible, Aquaman."

She got on the balls of her feet to kiss him.

They found the spa and strolled into its bright white lobby scented with fragipani blooms conjuring Caribbean daydreams of Bonaire, Martinique, Antigua and St. Lucia.

No one was at the long mahogany front desk, allowing Jake to ask his question in relative privacy.

"Were you really going to check out today?"

"God no, if I did, I'd have lost over a thousand dollars for the three nights remaining," Reed answered.

"You were negotiating for a full three-night refund *and* a complimentary couple's massage?"

"Yuppers," Reed replied casually.

"Why not try to get a refund for your entire stay?"

"Because that would be greedy on my part. The resort held up its end of the contract by providing seven lovely days here."

"Is that how you practice the law?" Jake asked.

"Absolutely. Never pad my billables. Never take advantage of my clients. Never get reimbursed for suspect business expenses. No matter how much money is involved or how it will affect my making partner, I navigate through the straight and narrow. Can I get an amen?"

"Preaching to the choir, the Most Reverend O'Hara," Jake said.

A tall attractive Black woman parted a white sea of drapes, providing her a cine-dramatic entrance.

"Let my people go!" Jake demanded in a jocular tone.

"Pardon me?" the woman asked.

She wore a sheer linen ensemble, wearing white boyshort panties under white cotton slacks and a white bra under a white top.

"Oh nothing, just made a Moses reference when I saw you part the curtains," Jake replied.

"Moses? As in Grandma Moses?"

"Well played, mademoiselle. In truth, I was referring to the bombastic Biblical Moses portrayed by Charlton Heston in ..."

"*The Ten Commandments*, yes I know," the woman interjected. "Awful film, not fit for Easter feast nor famine."

Time to intervene before Jake gets too smitten, Reed thought.

"Are you my masseuse, Miss?"

"I'm Lucia, and no, I belong to Jake today. Your masseur, Miss O'Hara, is *Daveed*. He'll join us once shortly. Don't worry, madame, Daveed is totally gay."

Reed looked at Jake. She raised her right eyebrow.

"It's 'mademoiselle,' and I pity the fool masseur *or* masseuse who tries something on me," Reed said.

Michelangelo's Black Daveed burst through the white curtains. He gave Lucia a headshake and a bow to Reed.

"Mademoiselle," Daveed said to Reed, "you've nothing to worry about, you are in safe hands."

Daveed's six-foot-eight inches of matching white linen ensemble loomed over Reed, Lucia, even Jake.

"Good to know, David," Jake said.

"It's *Daveed*," he snapped at Jake.

Ten seconds passed in slow-motion silence.

Then Reed spoke.

"Lucia and *Daveed*, let's shorten the couple's massage from ninety minutes to one hour, allowing Jake and me those last thirty minutes to meditate on today's events."

"Very well, mademoiselle, I trust you're aware our gratuity is based on ninety minutes of treatment," Lucia said.

"Management comped us, Lucia. Take up your gratuity with Cherish," Reed said, as she already was disliking Lucia.

Jake whispered to Reed, "I don't know how to meditate."

She reassured him, "No worries, Jakester, I'll teach you how to do it."

She reached up and pinched his left nipple. He pretended not to enjoy the tweak.

Lucia announced, "Let's repair to the couple's treatment room, shall we?"

The four musketeers, all for one and one for all, cavaliered down a hallway into a large treatment room. There were two side-by-side massage tables; a countertop displaying various potions, notions and lotions; four dimmed light sconces; and two chairs that'd seen better days. A diffuser misted the room with ethereal eucalyptus scent. A three-foot waterfall feature was centered on the countertop, producing a calming sound of cascading water.

Suddenly need to take a leak, Jake thought.

"All right, let's get out of your clothes, which you can place on these chairs," Lucia said. "We'll step out, of course, and please lay on your tummy with your face in the headset face cushion at the end of the massage table."

Lucia and Daveed left the treatment room.

Two fluffy white spa robes hung on hooks above the lunchroom chairs.

"Reed, should I grab one of these robes and change in a bathroom?"

"Normally, we change out of our street clothes into robes and slides in separate men's and women's locker rooms. I get the feeling this spa doesn't have locker rooms. So no, don't go to a bathroom. We'll undress here."

"Really?" Jake asked.

"Truly."

She went first, shushing her sandals under a chair, doffing her t-shirt and shorts, then her bikini.

She stood completely naked before Jake. Her light pink nipples were erect. Her full cream-colored breasts swayed ever so sensually. Her la foufoune flashed a comely victory sign to Jake.

Reed placed her hands on her hips.

"Your turn, Jake."

He stayed clothed.

"This is embarrassing. I'm kinda aroused right now."

She Mona Lisa smiled.

"Stop trippin' and get strippin'."

"Yes, ma'am."

Jake took off his Teva sports sandals, t-shirt and board shorts. There was a noticeable *boing!* sound when he freed his erection from the tight constraints of his blue Speedo.

He stood straight, vertically and horizontally, and looked at Reed.

"What do you think, Reed?"

Jake's chest, abdomen, arms and legs were cut to Merriam-Webster's very definition of sculpted muscularity. Scars on his right shoulder, on the left side of his chest and just above his left hip conjured forth Achilles returning from battling Penthesilea, minus Achilles' armor and loin cloth, of course.

"What do *I* think? Little old Moi? Hmm. First, I appreciate the manscaping. Makes your grand package look that much grander. Second, seems you've been shot and stabbed probably as often as you've shot and stabbed other people. Third, all I can say is, *hot damn.*"

"Excuse me, ma'am, but my eyes are up here."

Reed didn't look up.

"Oh, I know, I know. Let me take in every inch of this delicious manscape just a minute. Or two."

A knock on the door broke Reed's libidinous concentration.

Reed and Jake climbed on their massage tables, backside up. They kneaded their faces into terry-cloth face cushions that did, in fact, resemble more Dunkin' than Krispy Kreme doughnuts.

Jake lifted his hips and pushed his erection between his legs, as Lucia and Daveed walked into the treatment room.

"All right, you two, time to decide what kind of massage you'd like," Daveed said. "Shall we go deep tissue or Swedish relaxation?"

"What do you *think* I want?" Jake asked.

Lucia jumped in, "You're a massage newbie, Jake, so let's go Swedish, shall we?"

"Yes, please," Jake said.

"Okay, try to relax, dear."

"I'm trying, Lucia."

She gently patted his buttocks.

"There, there, you'll be so calm and mellow once I'm done with you."

Reed lifted her head from the face cushion.

She said to Lucia, "Not if you keep playing with his ass, he won't."

Lucia drew away her hand.

"Yes, mademoiselle, message received. Sorry, I tend to be very hands-on in my work, if you'll permit the pun."

"More like handsy," Reed said. "And Daveed, I prefer deep tissue."

"Yes, mademoiselle, deep tissue it is."

"Sounds painful," Jake groaned through the donut hole.

As she returned her head to the face cushion, Reed muffled a reply, "Oh it's painful, all right, yet so wonderful."

Yeah, no fucking way, Jake thought. Why go looking for pain?

Daveed slowly turned up the music emanating from four ceiling speakers.

Catalan guitarist Laura Almerich skillfully played her Spanish guitar over the treatment room speakers. She employed all six strings to draw sketches of Spain; of Don Quixote jousting with windmill dragons; of Fernando the bull preferring to sniff wild flowers in a pasture to fighting in a bloody, deadly bull ring; of ancient cedars comforting the departed in hillside cemeteries; and of great rolling fields of golden sunflowers undulating in the Andalucian plains' merciless sun.

In a word, the music was perfect.

Lucia applied honeydew massage oil over Jake's body. She started at his neck, rounded off his broad shoulders, moved down his back, got jiggly with his glutes, elbow massaged each leg, then thumbed the soles of his feet.

Reed's masseur performed a similar massage on her, except he employed considerably more pressure and deployed avocado massage oil.

Both the massaged and the masseur syncopated deep breathing.

Is Reed moaning over there? Jake thought. Am I getting jealous? And is my boner ever gonna chill?

For the next twenty minutes, Lucia and Daveed zeroed in on their clients' stress points: the base of the neck, beneath the shoulder blades, hip flexors, sacroiliac joints and the semitendinosus, semimembranosus and biceps femoris muscles, all commonly known as hamstrings.

"Am I applying too much pressure, mademoiselle?" Daveed asked Reed.

"No, it's not enough," Reed moaned through the donut hole.

"All right, then," Daveed said gleefully, as he applied enhanced interrogative pressure to Reed's tiny dancer body.

"Yes, that's *purrfect*," Reed uttered, as if in a trance.

She moaning again? Jake thought.

It was time to flip the burghers.

Again, Daveed shook his head vehemently at Lucia, while they held up sheets for modesty's sake and had Jake and Reed turn onto their backs. Daveed covered Reed with the sheet, leaving exposed her arms, legs, shoulders, neck and head. Lucia covered only Jake's waist. She noticed his early-on satisfaction with her massage, as his erection was in full bloom in love and rhythmically pulse-poking under the sheet.

"That reminds me, Daveed," Lucia said. "Still want to go camping with me this weekend?"

Daveed, Reed and Lucia laughed.

Jake didn't join the revelry.

"Very funny, guys," Jake said. "I'm just pointing to the North Star, so I don't get lost."

Everyone laughed this time.

Daveed quietly walked to the end of the massage table, partially separated Reed's legs, softly karate-chopped the sheet between her thighs, then folded back the sheet enough to expose her hips, legs and feet.

"Lovely tan lines, Miss Reed," he said.

She gave him her version of the Hispanola voodoo eye.

"Last man who said that to me was my primary care physician. I fired him right there in the examining room."

Daveed was properly chagrined.

"My error, mademoiselle. Please pardon my being overly familiar with you."

"Won't pardon you, but I'll at least commute your sentence."

"Merci beaucoup, mademoiselle," he replied.

"De rien, monsieur."

Daveed massaged Reed's hips and legs, then her petits pieds parfaits.

Using Jake's phallic compass, Daveed migrated due north to massage Reed's hands, arms, shoulders and neck.

The piece de resistance was his massaging her scalp, running his long, oiled Black fingers through her golden locks.

"*And that concludes the massage, my dear,*" the masseur said in a whisper.

Reed smiled dreamily.

"Thank you, Daveed, you've got me in the proper mindset for some serious meditation."

She winked at him.

He returned the wink.

What are those two up to? Jake wondered.

Lucia performed the same routine with Jake as her partner did with Reed.

Though it was a massage therapy no-no, she couldn't resist slowly counting with all ten fingers the prominent abdominals on his washboard stomach. Her breathing went deeper as she pivoted on each abdominal muscle.

"Gonna rub my scalp, too?" Jake asked in a husky voice.

"Yes, love, right now."

Lucia ran her talons through his light brown curls.

"That's follicle surfing," she said excitedly. "You've a gorgeous head of hair, Jake."

"Thank you, Lucia. That was wonderful."

"Hold on, not done yet."

She finished by gently rubbing his ears between her thumb and forefinger.

"Say, Jake?"

"Uh, yeah?"

"How does a Caribbean woman hold her liquor?"

"Ida know, Lucia, how does she?"

"By his ears."

"Wrong on so many levels," Reed said, while she kept her eyes wide shut.

Lucia cupped Jake's face with her right hand.

"Is there a cuter derp in the whole world?" she asked.

"I seriously doubt it," Reed answered on Jake's behalf.

Lucia joined Reed and Jake's hands while they remained on the massage tables.

"Namaste, my friends."

"What does 'namaste' mean?" Jake asked casually, comfortable now with his pitched big top tent on full display.

Reed explained, "'The light in me honors the light in you' is what it means, Jake. Such a beautiful Hindu sentiment, and I've had in mind a unique and ambitious project that I might call 'Namaste.'"

"How wonderful, mademoiselle, but it's time for me and Daveed to step out and let you two meditate."

As Lucia walked by the supine Jake, she daubed the tip of his erect penis as if she were snuffing a lit candle.

"Such a lucky lady," she said wistfully.

Once the massage therapists left the treatment room, Jake let go of Reed's hand, then sat up on the table. The sheet covered his lap.

He said, "What's up with Lucia talking about your being a lucky lady?"

Reed smirked, "I'll let you figure that out, my leprechaun gigantis."

And on the third try, Reed rose from the bed to take her seat directly facing Jake.

She cast aside the sheet. Her naked body gave off a lustrous sheen from the avocado massage oil. All the while staring at Jake, she slid her small hands around her large breasts, flat stomach and muscular inner thighs.

Perhaps to make certain oil was applied evenly on her body? Perhaps. More likely not.

"How about you ditch the sheet, Jake, then come over here and kiss me?"

Reed barely finished her sentence before Jake threw the sheet across the room, disrobing the spa robes from hooks on the wall.

He slipped between her parted legs. He hugged her. Their oiled bodies enjoined as if an erotic Roman bas-relief come alive.

They kissed. Slowly. Tongues darted between moist smacking lips.

Their breaths grew deeper.

Reed reached down to stroke Jake's erection.

"Understand now why Lucia thinks I'm a lucky lady?" she asked Jake.

He replied in a throaty whisper, "*Yes, I do.*"

Jake held Reed's breasts, squeezing them carefully while kissing and licking each pink nipple.

Reed groaned. Passionately. Lustfully.

She placed her left hand firmly around his right buttock.

She guided him inside her.

For a minute, they remained still as the moon's Sea of Tranquility.

Reed placed her hands on his hips. She pushed him out of her. Then she grabbed his glutes to pull him back inside her. Push out, pull in. Push, pull. It was Soul Train locomotion gathering steam.

"Think you got the gist of this meditating?" she asked, barely able to speak.

He exhaled blissfully.

"Yeah, babe, I got this."

Jake gathered Reed's legs. She in turn locked her ankles around his waist.

He wrapped his thick muscular arms around her. He lifted her above the massage table.

Jake's breathing became heavier than a rolling thunder revue. He braced for lightning to strike fast and furiously.

But Reed orgasmed first. Her small lithe body arched repeatedly with spasms born of the purest pleasure on earth.

Jake orgasmed shortly thereafter.

I love you, Reed O'Hara, he thought.

Fallen completely in love with you, Jake Dupree, she said to herself.

Cherish was on her phone. She stood outside of the spa where Reed and Jake were now catching their breath. Cherish gazed at the resort's lavish grounds that boasted of blooming flame of the forest trees and waxy corkscrew crotons the size of a horse jockey and as colorful as his racing silks.

Her shift had ended. She spoke with a guest. A very special guest. Who paid well.

It was Olivia, of Stanley and Olivia renown.

Cherish almost shouted into her phone, "Don't blame me for Alfred, Olivia. He was the best I could find on such short notice."

She woodpeckered nods as she listened to Olivia's response.

"No. No. No. There was no way I'd risk a second hit during their massage. Are you trying to get me arrested?"

This time, Cherish shook her head in disgust as she heard Olivia's answer.

"Whatever, bitch, I expect you to pay me in full, even if it didn't go as planned. You don't, the po-po gonna know-know aforeo the midnight hour," Cherish threatened.

She listened attentively.

"Well, all right. Just what I wanted to hear. See you down at your room at eleven sharp."

Turns out, Cherish was a few minutes early arriving at Olivia and Stanley's suite.

They would be the last people with whom she spoke.

Cherish's body was found at dawn by the captain of *Priscilla, Queen of the Desert*. She was floating under the marina's first pier. Her throat was slit. Crabs feasted on her overnight. A stiff morning breeze rolled an empty Red Stripe bottle across the pier deck. The bottle rolled off the pier. There would be no "Hooray for beer!" celebration that morning.

CHAPTER 23

TAMPA, FLORIDA · 2022

"Babysitting Ravel, are we?"

Reed and Ravel were snuggling on the living room sofa when Jake walked into their penthouse apartment at seven a.m.

Reed wrapped her arms tighter around Ravel, whose head nestled on Reed's shoulder.

They wore matching French silk pajamas, only Reed's were a deep John-Lee-Hooker-a-boom-boom blue, and Ravel's a pitch black Nine-Inch-Nails nihilism.

"Yes I am, Jake. Ravel was concerned about you. In the sixteen hours you were livin' it up at the Hotel California, both Ravel and I hoped nothing bad had happened to you."

Ravel stopped nuzzling Reed's neck long enough to say, "Actually I was hoping something bad *had* happened to the big lugnut. You know, not something as boring as flat tire. *Yeah!* A carjacking in Ybor at closing time would've been so cool. I can see Jake now, as he blasts carjackers with his trusty sidekick sidearms Wyatt and Doc."

Jake squinted his bloodshot baby-sings-the-blues at her.

"Look, nothing bad happened. Sorry to disappoint. And, Reed, if that 'Hotel California' jab were a veiled accusation that I've been hanging out at a brothel or a strip club or the Surefire Lounge at the 'Dan, then that's incredibly insulting."

Ravel whispered to Reed, "Are there brothels in Tampa?"

"Yes. They operate out of old mansions on Bayshore Boulevard. One of them is called 'Chateau Noir," an obvious nod to Cezanne."

"Really, Reed?"

"No. Now hush."

"Fine." Ravel gruffed.

Reed noticed Ravel undid three buttons on her pajama top, displaying significant cleavage.

Little snit, Reed thought. Musta done that one button at a time, all Sly and the Family Stone like.

"Button up right now, Ravel. We don't need to see your girls this early in the morning."

As Ravel buttoned her top, she said, "Yeah well, you weren't complaining last night."

Jake interjected, "That's so lame, Ravel. And such a lie. You're trying to stir up trouble while Reed and I are at odds with one another."

Ravel looked at Reed, who replied, "What my man said, snookums."

Ravel and Jake knew Reed would ask The Question.

"Where've you been, Jake?" Reed asked.

Jake was rumpled as crumpled aluminum foil. He hadn't shaved. His body odor was nauseatingly noxious. Truefitt & Hill of St. James's London (est.1805) could've gone cockeyed counterintuitive by bottling Jake's stench, then labeling it, "Stinking Bishop's Twiddle-Diddles."

Jake took off his brown Mephisto leather sandals. The pricey French footwear was saltwater stained and caked with white sand. If it were a serious domestic lapse on his part to track sand, dirt or dead floaters into their impeccably maintained home, all Jake needed this morning was a beached corpse to win the trifecta of scorn.

"After I met with the medical examiner regarding Alicia, I went to see Denizen Mulraney at the Bavarians compound in South Tampa. Grabbed dinner at Frenchy's, and walked all night long on Clearwater Beach. I even crossed over at the north point and walked Caladesi Island. I saw impressive casts of hermit crabs, which I haven't spotted in years."

"Denizen Mulraney, that bastard's here in Tampa?" Reed demanded.

"Yes, he is. Been here a couple years."

"Why haven't you told me before that Mulraney's skulking around in our backyard?" Reed asked with acidity in her voice.

"Didn't think you needed to know until now," Jake replied.

Ravel whispered in Reed's ear, "Oooo, this just gets better and better. Tell me, should we consider a courthouse ceremony or go for a destination wedding?"

Reed snapped back, "Hush, you rabble rousing Jacobin."

"If your meeting with Mulraney yielded a promising lead, Jake, I probably can overlook your holding out on me regarding that Oirish asal."

"Reed, I did get a substantial lead from the man you so insultingly called an Irish donkey. Had to arm wrestle Den for the intel."

"Ha!" Ravel chortled. "Talk about steel cage homo-eroticococo." Jake ignored her.

"It cost me his friendship, because I won the match. May not seem a big deal, Reed, but it is. Now that Mulraney and I severed ties, he can come after me without restraint, if that's how he wants to play it."

"I'm taking this seriously, *Jake*," Reed *oh, snapped!* "How will you handle him?"

Jake smirked, squinted his eyes, then turned toward the living room picture window's panoramic view of downtown Tampa's skyline.

Whatta ya know, it's the Man with No Name, Ravel noted. All he needs now is a cheroot and an alpaca poncho.

"Don't know how I'll deal with Mulraney, may have to kill him," Jake replied.

Damn, sometimes he scares even tough little old moi, Ravel said to herself.

Reed sat up and nearly pushed Ravel off the sofa. Ravel took the less than subtle hint. She got up and plopped down upon the other sofa.

She said in jest to Reed, "You have your way with me, then I get boot-scooted down the road, such a typical bi-curious chick move."

Three-way laughter ensued, which eased some tension in the room.

"First, Jake, *we* will handle Mulraney," Reed said. "Second, tell us about this substantial lead."

He went to sit on the sofa with Reed, when she ordered, "Oh no you don't, beachcomber, go wash off those feet first."

She ran her hand across the Reya curved sectional.

"Do you recall how much this sofa cost?" she admonished.

"Why is it your questions come off as criticisms?" Jake asked.

"Go on, Jake," Ravel ordered. "Get those insane clown posse feet to the bathtub, because you're such a *dirty dirty boy*."

Jake dutifully marched into the master bedroom.

In under ten minutes, he returned shaved, showered and shined. He wore a gray V-neck t-shirt with black loungewear pants and navy-blue faux crocodile moccasins.

"Have to say, you're looking caz cool," Ravel proffered.

"I owe it all to my dresser," Jake replied, as he winked at Reed, who returned his wink.

Isn't that just so adorable, Ravel thought sarcastically.

"May I now sit down next to you?" he asked Reed.

"Sit, boy, sit," Ravel mock ordered.

"One of these days, Alice," Jake said in jest to her.

"Yeah, do that, Jackie Gleason, and Reed and I'll end up honeymooners," Ravel warned.

Reed patted the sofa seat.

"C'mon, sit down and tell me all about your day at work, *hon*."

He promptly sat down.

"Who's a good boy!" Ravel nearly shouted.

"Not gonna acknowledge your existence for at least the next millennium," Jake teased.

"Good luck with that, *hon*," Ravel said.

"I'll probably need it, Little Miss Sunshine. So. I met first with Dr. Arland Hutchinson, the Chief Medical Examiner over at the county morgue. Good guy. Kinda odd. Clearly spent too much time around dead bodies."

Talk about the pot calling the kettle ganja, Ravel thought.

"Did you identify Alicia?" Reed asked impatiently.

"Yes, but only from a photo. That was bad enough."

"Thank you, love, for doing that."

"You're welcome. I used to see dead people quite often. One can grow inured with a view to a kill."

Ravel's eye sparkled. She started to speak.

"Do not say it, M. Night," Reed said.

Ravel *harumphed!* then sulked in her silks on the sofa.

"Was Dr. Hutchinson helpful?" Reed asked.

"Sort of. He mostly talked about himself. Typical of lonely people, right?"

"Right, but did you come away with anything useful to your investigation?"

Our investigation, he thought.

"Yes, he confirmed what I suspected. Bavarians were involved. Dr. Hutchinson warned me that the BarraCubas are every bit as dangerous as those neo-Nazi shitheads. He knows this from bullshitting with city cops and county deputies."

"Dr. Strangeglove is a whacker?" Ravel asked, having left her pouty party.

"Yeah, probably is a cop groupie. Again, the old guy spent too much time slicing and dicing and icing over how these stiffs got snuffed."

"Jake, please don't be coarse," Reed pleaded.

"You call that coarse?" Ravel injected. "Fuck's sake, coarse would be claiming this Doctor to the Dead sometimes Dahmer Del Monico's a cadaver or two."

"Oh my god," Reed said.

"Sorry, Reed, for what I said," Jake quickly added. "Dr. Hutchinson has done so many autopsies, he's become obsessed with how cadavers became victims, better?"

"Better. Thank you."

"You're welcome. Arland and I hit it off well enough that he promised to share Alicia's autopsy results and to pass on any relevant police scuttlebutt."

"Excellent," Reed said.

Ravel sat up on the sofa. The new day's sunlight from the grand picture window illuminated the black silk of her pajamas. She shined bright and beautiful, like a sleek Burmese black panther lounging across a thick limb from a rain forest titan arum tree.

She managed once more to undo three buttons on her pajama top.

Neither Reed nor Jake seemed to mind this time.

Ravel said to Reed, "I sometimes forget how good Jake is making friends with complete strangers, then getting them to open up, something I'll never master."

She smooched a kisslet at Jake.

"Thanks, Ravel, sometimes you're all right in my book," Jake said.

"Aww, that just makes me all moishe down there."

"*Really d*on't know how to respond to that," Jake said uncomfortably.

"Tell us about your arm-wrestling match with Mulraney," Reed said.

"Denizen wouldn't cooperate at first. He worried Bavarians might get implicated in Alicia's murder. So, he came up with the arm-wrestling contest."

Ravel snorted.

"Men and their big dick contests," she said, almost enviously.

Reed smiled lovingly at Ravel, then inquired of Jake, "I take it there was a wager connected to the arm wrasslin'."

"Naturally. If he won, I could never again ask him about Alicia, and we no longer will be brothers in arms."

"That's it?" Reed asked.

"I also would've had to give him my Riviera."

"No!" Ravel exclaimed. "Not your funkadelic pimper's paradise ride!"

"Afraid so."

"I'm impressed you'd risk losing your car," Reed said.

"I wasn't worried. I knew I'd whip his ass. Old guys, they've a hard time accepting their limitations."

"You won easily, I got it, but what did you get out of this Héctor Macho Camacho contest?" Reed asked.

Reed's just showing off now, Ravel thought.

"Quite a bit. Denizen divulged a solid prospect, TPD Narcotics Detective Ernie Friekorps."

Ravel threw her hands in the air.

"Sierra and I know that guy! Prick used to slither around Namaste at closing time. Andre told us he saw Friekorps and Alicia arguing out in the parking lot after Namaste closed. Alicia persuaded Andre she was talking with an ex-boyfriend. Such bullshit. I've seen Friekorps. Dude smells nasty as durian and sweats like a virgin 'bout to get tossed in Volcán Tajumulco. No way that turd blossom was ever Alicia's boyfriend."

"You're exactly right, Friekorps wasn't romantically involved with Alicia," Jake said. "She was his CI."

Ravel was almost speechless.

"Holy Sierra Madre de Chiapas, was she spying on us?" Ravel asked.

Look who's showing off now, Reed countered thoughtfully.

Ravel inadvertently, or advertently, flashed her right nipple to Jake. He noticed. Once more, he didn't object.

"Um, to answer your question, no, Alicia wasn't informing on us," Jake said. She was ratting out her sister BarraCubas to Friekorps, who turned around and sold her intel to the Bavarians."

"Alicia was a BarraCuba?" Reed asked incredulously.

"Yeah, babe, and I'm sorry for letting that one get by me."

"I missed it as well, Jake. We're busy people juggling too many balls in the air."

"Juggling too many balls," Ravel exclaimed. "That's so wickedly rich."

"Hush, you juvenile. And get that nip back undercover. I think Jake and I have enjoyed it long enough."

Ravel blushed, then diddled the spirited nipple back inside the pajama top.

"Apparently, Alicia couldn't handle the stress of being a CI, which added to her guilt over being a BarraCuba informant," Jake said.

"What happened?" Reed asked.

"She told Friekorps she couldn't live with a snitch jacket. He asked for a few more weeks. She agreed. But he lied. Of course. He angled to get one last pile of cash by exposing Alicia. The BarraCubas' president Paz Iberra paid Friekorps a lot of money for that intel. Bavarians paid only a few grand."

"Christ, what do we have now, about a hundred suspects?" Ravel asked.

"Maybe, but I'm not sure Bavarians were involved in the hit. What would be the point? Knowing Den, he'd kidnap her, then sell her to the BarraCubas."

"And Friekorps?" Reed asked.

"Den doesn't size him up as a killer. Anyway, the detective doesn't need any scrutiny by Internal Affairs."

"Did the BarraCubas murder Alicia?" Ravel asked.

"Yeah, it's likely Iberra killed Alicia out of revenge."

"With the BarraCubas looking good for this murder, how should we approach them?" Reed asked.

Jake paused to formulate a game plan in his mind.

"I think you and Ravel should approach Paz Iberra together. She and her crew live at the Floridan. If she won't meet in a neutral area, meet in her grand suite on top of the hotel. I guarantee you and Ravel won't be in danger."

Reed smiled warmly at her husband.

"I get what you're saying, love, but I want Ravel to understand as well."

Jake obliged by saying, "I'll have my sniper's rifle atop the office building behind the Floridan. We'll use hand signals. Things go south, I'll blow Iberra's head clean off her shoulders."

"That's my Watermelon Man," Reed said in a sultry voice.

"Watermelon Man?" Ravel wondered aloud.

"Tell you later, *hon*," Reed replied.

Chapter 24

Bonaire

Southern Caribbean · 2014

"Sonuva ceviche, that's great jerk," Reed exclaimed, as she and Jake feasted on grilled marinated chicken at a roadside jerk hut on Bonaire.

They had taken off on foot once Reed checked out of the resort.

Just hours prior to her horrific demise, Cherish comped the couple's massage and refunded Reed nearly one-thousand dollars for the three remaining nights.

"I just *know* you'll return one day to our beautiful resort, Miss Reed," Cherish said.

"I probably will, might even have this big guy with me," Reed answered.

Jake gave a thumbs-up to Reed.

"My, you darlings look so content," Cherish said. "Was it the massage, please tell me it was, even if you have to lie."

"No need to lie, Cherish, the massage totally relaxed us. The meditation session afterwards popped a cherry atop a perfect spa treatment."

The couple grinned at one another.

Humpf, horny goats best notta done the duggu duggu in my spa, Cherish thought.

"I hope you two come back real soon. Our island, after all, is made for lovers."

Jake cleared his throat.

"That obvious, Cherish?"

"Ya mon. You got dee scent of a man who been a cocoa strokin' Miss Reed's pretty pum pum with your big doggie."

Jake raised his eyebrows.

"Pure poetry that was, but I haven't the faintest idea what you're talking about, mi lady."

"I'm sure you don't, sir," Cherish replied.

"Jamaican aren't you?" he asked.

"Yes, I am. Proud of it. Why do you ask, sir?"

"Just curious."

"Well sir, the curious, dey can s'pose themselves to all sorts of danger, so beware, my friend."

"Thank you, Cherish, I'll keep that in mind," Jake said, having no idea that Cherish wouldn't live past midnight.

The pair walked for nearly thirty minutes before coming upon a jerk hut, though they could smell the grilled chicken well before they arrived.

Like a ravenous red-tailed hawk, Reed used her small razor talons to rip roasted flesh from a chicken breast. She popped the steamy white meat into her mouth. She luxuriated in carnivorous ecstasy.

Could get into off-the-grid living, she thought. *Long as I got Jake & the Jerk Huts to keep me entertained.*

"What'd you make of Cherish when we were checking out of the resort?" she asked between bites. "Seemed completely unprofessional talking about my pretty pum pum and your big doggie."

After every bite of chicken, Jake gulped down cold water.

"Nothing wimpy about Scotch Bonnet sauce," he said breathily. "At least Cherish was spot on about your pretty pum pum."

"Okay, but what's your assessment of her?" Reed asked.

"Was it coincidence she and Caption Al are from Jamaica? Maybe not. Captain Al and Cherish *might* be friends or family. Was Cherish the cutout for whomever ordered the hit? Pretty good chance of that. Remember, this shitstorm began at the resort."

"Or it began at the pub," she said.

"Go on Reed, you've got this."

"Olivia and Stanley," she declared somberly.

"What about them?" Jake asked, while impolitely licking his fingers.

"They ordered the hit. They're probably staying at the resort, but I bet they checked out too."

Jake stared at her.

"That is fucking brilliant," he exclaimed.

"Thank you, but were you thinking it as well?" Reed inquired.

"Yes."

"So how am I doing with employing paranoia as spy craft?" she asked.

"You're doing well. If I may say so, I'm damn proud of you."

"Of course you're allowed to be damn proud of me," she said.

"How about we jitney over to my humble beach abode on the windward side of the island? I'll fix hot chocolate, then show you my Kamasutra etchings."

"A delightful proposal, kind sir. Very Mr. Knightley of you. Can I expect those tiny marshmallows in my hot chocolate?"

Jake laughed.

"Of course, Miss Wodehouse. Hydrated mini 'mellows come with every packet of Caribbean Dreams hot chocolate mix."

Jake picked up Reed's large green canvas backpack and hoisted it upon his broad shoulders. He waved down a jitney.

They rode through neighborhoods of modest, well-kept homes, where there abounded brazilwood, mesquite, acacia and calabash trees, as well as all manner of cactus and blooming bougainvillea, hibiscus and oleander.

The jitney arrived at Jake's beach pad, which appeared desolate and abandoned.

His describing it as a "humble beach abode" was generous at best, deceptive at a minimum.

The beach shack was humbled long ago by the passing of time, along with an occasional tropical storm. There were four large windows, two in the front and two in the back that framed an uproarious Atlantic Ocean. There wasn't a single pane of glass in the windows. Ragtag drapes provided some privacy, though privacy wasn't much of an issue in this isolated area of Bonaire.

The roof consisted of irregular-sized sheets of rusted corrugated steel. An unfounded, yet persistent, rumor circulated that industrious beachcombers salvaged from a beached WWII German U-boat to construct the shack.

The salty dog structure made like Yo-Yo Ma's mournful cello when trade winds buffeted it. Which was often. Little wonder, then, locals ghost-toasted the shack, "Jacob Marley's Shanty."

The lawn was a yawn of scrawny weeds and scrawnier vinca scattered haphazardly across a bed of coral rubble and crushed limestone.

There were not one, not two, but three goats deforesting the lawn of its blooming periwinkle, as stands of prickly pear cactus observed with indifference.

Reed was first out of the jitney.

She studied Jake's love shack, then exclaimed joyfully, "Tin roof rusting!"

"You approve?" Jake asked eagerly.

"It's beautiful! I don't even care there isn't running water or electricity."

"What tells you that?"

"Really, Jake? Maybe it was the cistern on the left side of the house. The absence of a power hook-up. That'd explain the kerosene lamps I see inside. Perhaps it was the folksy outhouse over on the right side."

"All right, I get it. But do you like it? Will you stay the night?"

"Yes! The place is Henry David Thoreauly charming," Reed decided.

"Excellent. Shall we go inside?"

"Let's."

Reed made crunchy sounds with the world's smallest, most adorable hiking boots, as she walked across the hardscrabble lawn.

She unlatched the front door and stepped onto the set of *Gilligan's Island.*

There was a decent-sized great room.

To the left was a wood-burning stove and a tiny-house kitchenette equipped with a small sink, a water amphora and a propane hot plate.

Several hands of bananas, in various stages of golden yellow ripeness, were hooked on a rope hanging in a corner of the kitchenette.

In the center of the room was a small, dilapidated table with two mismatched chairs, one gray, the other pink. To the right, a hammock was hung with care next to a rear window. A thick mattress with relatively clean sheets and two pillows laid on a large textile mat perhaps three feet from the hammock. An upturned crate served as a night table next to the mattress. A kerosene lamp with Diamond strike-on-box matches rested atop the nightstand.

"Puts the Ritz-Carlton to shame, Jake."

"Yeah, I know, right?"

"I need to wash up and change, love. Where's the shower?" she asked.

"Outside by the cistern. There's bar soap, shampoo and a towel the size of a clipper ship's sail. It's showering in the great outdoors, okay? There's no one within three klicks of us."

"Perfect."

Reed took off her clothes. She dropped them in a pile. She walked naked out to the shower area where a makeshift sign read, "Welcome to Al Fresco's Shower Emporium (first one's free)."

Jake gathered Reed's clothes and placed them in a straw basket already half-filled with dirty laundry.

He called out, "I'll chill in the hammock 'til it's my turn."

"Okee, artichokee," Reed replied, as she massaged her scalp into a full head of shampoo lather.

"Got any conditioner?" she asked.

Jake answered, "Remember when they used to call it 'cream rinse'?"

"What?"

"Conditioner."

"Not really, but I believe you, " she answered. "Do you have any cream rinse conditioner?"

"Sorry, don't use the stuff."

After rinsing out shampoo lather, she used a bar of what might be Irish Spring soap to lather her body. She chuckled over the bar soap having been carved into a small handgun small enough for a leprechaun.

Hammock-Time Dupree happened to look out the window as Reed covered her breasts with soapy foam.

My oh my, Jake thought. She's like straight out of a Marcel Duchamp painting, man.

She rinsed away soap suds. She turned off the gravity rain shower. She practically disappeared into the over-sized blue bath towel.

Never been happier to feel normal again, she said to herself.

She wrapped the towel around her head, leaving enough of the towel to form a dragon's tail reaching down to her dimples of Venus.

Still naked, Reed returned to the love shack. Her full breasts bounced tautingly with each step. She was a naturist in motion, a nude ascending a driftwood staircase.

"You're up, buckaroo," she said. "And stop pretending to be asleep."

Jake opened his right eye.

"Eyelids fluttering?"

"Yup."

"Damn, skill set's atrophying," he said.

Reed sat crosswise to Jake on the hammock, then titled back across his lap.

"Give me your hand. Feel how soft my skin is."

She took his left hand and placed it on her left breast, then on her right breast.

Jake smiled dreamily.

"Yes, your breasts, they're very soft, sweetheart."

Mona Lisa smiled.

"Something's sticking in my back," she complained.

"That's Big Junior, he's saying hello to you," Jake said.

Reed shook her head in mock disapproval.

She reached over to play gently with his lower lip.

She breathed in Jake's scent.

"How about we get this hammock a swayin' before you shower?" she asked.

"Before?"

"Mm uh. It's not that you smell all nice & spicy. Believe me, you don't. It's just, I haven't been around stinky boy odor for a while. I rather enjoy it."

Reed freed Jake's erection from his shorts, then lowered herself on him, conjuring a comical coital image of a naked Reed standing on either side of the hammock, while performing reverse cowgirl, rocking the hammock with each thrust.

Jake uttered, "Oh my god, this is incredible."

Reed responded, "Jake, all I need is three minutes of silence, but please, enjoy the view."

Jake silently mouthed, "*Yes, ma'am.*"

Chapter 25

TAMPA, FLORIDA · 2022

"WE'RE THIRTY MINUTES EARLY, my little chickadee, let's recon."

Reed and Ravel entered the lobby of a restored Floridan Palace Hotel in downtown Tampa. They had a noon appointment with Barra-Cubas president Paz Iberra, who lived in a penthouse suite on the hotel's top floor.

"Done much recon, have you?" Ravel asked Reed.

There was a low-voltage undercurrent of skepticism in Ravel's voice.

"Yes, of course," Reed snapped back, "Most of it with Jake, but some on my own, why do you ask?"

"Because it's fucking important you're good at it. You're letting me partner with you on the case. You're teaching me how to recon. Like my Auntie Mae told me back in the old Zurich days, 'A dame that knows the ropes ain't likely to get tied up.'"

"Zurich!" Reed exclaimed.

"Yes, Zurich."

"I'd rather be in Philadelphia."

"I thought you felt fondly of fondue," Ravel wondered aloud.

"I do, but Philly's such a fun town. As Grandpapa William C. Dukenfield told me, 'I once spent a week in Philadelphia, I think it was on a Sunday.'"

"Didn't you tell me old W.C. invented the water closet."

"No, I certainly did not."

"Was it Thomas Crapper, then?"

"Complete folklore."

"Then who, god damn it!"

"Rudimentary toilets date back 5000 years to Mesopotamia."

"For god's sake, Reed!"

"Fine. Englishman Sir John Harington invented the flush toilet in 1756."

Ravel smiled a thank you.

"I'm flushed counterclockwise over your knowledge of shitters."

"Yes well, let's go grab some drinks in the Sapphire Room and observe the comings and goings of this beautiful hotel."

"Okay, but please, no more historical discourse," Ravel pleaded.

"Did you know this bar was known as the 'Surefire Room' during World War II?"

Ravel rubbed her eyes in disbelief.

Reed allowed Ravel to hold her hand as the two women, resembling figures from Seurat's *Sunday on Island of La Grande Jatte*, strolled into the Sapphire Room.

Reed was dressed for business. She wore an open-collar white oxford dress shirt under a meticulously tailored lapis lazuli blue suit. She completed the boardroom badass ensemble with Claude Black calfskin ankle boots. Her holstered Sig Sauer 9mm pistol was clipped to the right side of her waistband and out of sight.

Ravel surprised Reed by foregoing her standard "uniform" of black t-shirt, blue denim jeans and scuffed Doc Martens. She wore an LBD with Prada black suede boots.

"You look sharp," Reed said.

"Thanks," Ravel answered. "Keep in mind I'm not wearing panties, just in case you get a yen for some love in an elevator."

Reed laughed.

"Yeah, not happening, at least not today."

Ravel *tsked*.

"Such a tease."

"You betcha, gotta keep you wondering," Reed said playfully.

"And I gotta keep you wandering," Ravel shot back.

Reed led her to the bar. The tall high-back chairs were a smoky dark oak with gold leather seats. The darkened lounge was parsimoniously illuminated by a constellation of tiny menthol blue lights recessed in the ceiling.

Even approaching noon, the Sapphire Room cast shadowy suggestions of discreetly indiscreet possibilities.

Several tables were unoccupied, yet Reed opted for sitting at the bar.

Ravel whispered, "I thought we were going to recon the grand lobby, and if we sit at the bar, our backs will be to all the action."

"Relax, Nancy Drew. We can see everything in the mirror behind the bar. We'll look like a couple of chicks burning time with the lunch-hour special, before our next 'Time Shares with Jesus' presentation."

"Nancy Drew hell, we're more the Hardy Boys," Ravel whispered. "And did you make up that time-share shit?"

"Nope. Jake taught me to look around the second I enter a room. If you'd done that, you would've seen a 'Time Shares with Jesus' placard on the easel next to the front desk."

The bartender crab walked over to the two women.

"Almost high noon, ladies, how about I get you two 'Beneath the Sheets'?"

"If you're talking about the cocktail, I'll have one," Ravel said. "Otherwise, piss off, punter."

Reed cleared her throat.

"I apologize for my friend's coarseness. And your name is?"

Before the bartender could speak, Ravel jumped in: "Lloyd, his name is Lloyd, you know, from *The Shining*."

The bartender's smile was as chilly as a Rocky Mountain high up in the sky.

"My name is Earl Monroe. My friends and associates call me 'Pearl' though I don't know why. You may call me 'Earl,' young lady."

"Okay, but you look like Lloyd, all the same," Ravel responded.

Earl exhaled dramatically.

"Yes, yes, others have noticed that, but all I can say is that Stanley Kubrick had to be drunk when he directed *The Shining*."

"Sacrilege, sir, visigothic sacrilege!" Ravel cried out. "I hope you're a better mixologist than film critic, *Lloyd*."

Earl plucked an evil grin from the mason jar filled with various grins he kept under the bar.

"I am a mixologist to stars of the past, present and future, and to the BarraCubas in particular."

Reed had been studying people in the lobby reflected in the bar's mirror.

"Wait, did you say 'BarraCubas,' Earl?" she asked carefully.

"Yes, I did."

"Do they come in here often?" Reed asked.

"I should say so. Many of them live in the Floridan. I don't think I'm too out of line to mention Ms. Iberra, the club president, resides upstairs in our Santo Trafficante Senior Suite."

"Why 'Senior Suite'?" Reed asked.

"It's the larger of the two penthouses. The smaller one is called the 'Santo Trafficante Junior Suite.'"

"Clever, Lloyd," Ravel said.

"*Soooo*, how about a couple of 'Beneath the Sheets,' ladies?"

Reed smiled.

"Sure, but hold the rum, brandy and triple sec."

"*Reed*," Ravel whined.

"What you really want is a glass of orange juice with a spritz of lemon and an orange wedge garnish," Earl said.

"Exactly. Think of it as two 'Virgins Beneath the Sheets.'"

"Very good, mademoiselle."

"Thank you, and it's 'madame.'"

Earl nodded in acknowledgement of his puckered-up cheekiness.

"Back in the day, what did you used to drink?" Ravel asked Reed.

"Oh, let's see, strictly beer such as Heineken and Red Stripe. Plus, Jake turned me on to Bonaire Blond pale ale back when we first met."

"He doesn't drink, right?"

"Never has," Reed answered. "By the way, if you hadn't been jousting with Earl the Pearl, you would've noticed the six BarraCubas marching two at a time into the lobby."

"You saw them from the mirror?"

"Yes," Reed said.

"How do you know they're BarraCubas?"

"Weren't wearing colors, just black leather jackets with engineer boots. They'd been out riding, for sure."

"If they live here, why wouldn't they park their motorcycles in the garage, then use the service elevator?"

Reed tapped the tip of Ravel's tiny nose.

"Bravissimo, Bella. You're catching on fast. My hunch is they parked their Harleys out front because they don't live here."

"They're her security detail for our meeting, aren't they?"

"As Jake once said, 'Right as Queen Lizzie's reign.'"

"Did he really say that?" Ravel asked.

"Such a goof," Ravel said. "I really do kind of love the big guy."

"I'll let him know," Reed teased Ravel.

"Don't you dare!" Ravel exclaimed, catching Earl's attention.

"I'm kidding you, Ravel. It's time to interrogate a certain president of a kick-ass motorcycle gang."

Just as they were about to leave, Earl brought them their drinks.

Reed slapped a fifty-dollar bill on the bar.

"No time for those drinks, Earl. Pleasure chatting with you."

"Dug diddle dawdling with you, too, Lloyd," Ravel said. "Try to recast your view of *The Shining*, because it's great film."

"I shall try my best, mademoiselle."

"Hey, Lloyd, wanna know something?"

"You're not wearing panties, young lady?"

"How did you know?"

"Caught your zezette winking at me," Lloyd said off-handedly, as he checked the state of his manicure on his right hand.

As they walked out into the lobby, Reed asked Ravel, "Zezette?"

"French slang. He was talking about my pussy."

"Did you flash him?"

"Perhaps."

"What am I going to do with you, Ravel?"

"Oh, I got a couple suggestions in mind."

"Bet you do."

As they strolled into the hotel's palatial grand lobby, Ravel stopped suddenly.

"I don't notice things, huh?" she asked defiantly. "Check out the hottie sitting across the way."

"All right, I will," Reed said.

Reed studied the young woman sitting by herself, reading a paperback and sipping a rum runner.

She wore a rosa Versace jumper over a blanco Dries Van Noten dress shirt, whose tails peaked out from under the jumper's hemline.

Jimmy Choo fuchsia satin platform sandals complimented her blouse and jumper combo.

The woman's bone-straight blonde hair cascaded down her front, likely camouflaging a modest bustline.

Her full lips, lipsticked in fuck ya! red, were lo and behold Lolita lovely.

She wore a pair of Dolce & Gabbana sunglasses, despite her being indoors and reading from a book propped on the exposed right thigh of her tan crossed legs.

As she read, her right leg moved up and down with metronomic precision.

"Definitely a ten, right?" Ravel asked eagerly.

"More like a seven," Reed answered. "Is that what you wanted me to do, give her a chica caliente rating?"

"You mean you don't see her tell?" Ravel asked.

"Nope."

"She's reading her book upside down."

"Ravel, you may not be correct."

"No! Let me handle this. Woman's probably tailing us."

"In *that* outfit?"

"Sure, she fits in perfectly with this bougie hotel."

"Did you just use 'bougie'?"

"Yes."

"Roots and wings, love, I've given you roots and wings."

"I'm gonna confront her. Care to join me?"

"No thanks."

"You could play good cop."

"I'll hang back. I wouldn't miss this for the world."

"Why, Reed?"

"I just think your hoo-ha is blurring your vision."

"'Hoo-ha'? Jesus, why can't you just say 'pussy'?"

"Because it's vulgar."

Ravel stealthily slinked across the lobby and stood a foot or two in front of the woman.

Fuck, fuck, fuck, she's reading the book right side up, she realized.

"Whatcha reading?" Ravel jovially asked her.

The woman smiled, slid her shades down the bridge of a cosmetically refined nose, then gave Ravel a thorough once over.

She held up the front cover of the paperback.

"*Everything's Jake.*"

"How's the book?" Ravel asked.

"Odd & fascinating & kinda freaky, and I totally dig on the freaky bits. It's all about how this hunky boy becomes a hitman."

"Good stuff?"

"Totally flashing on this guy's novel," the woman answered. "I guess he lives around here, might look him up, but I heard he's got this gorgeous hottie of a wife who isn't to be fucked with."

"Cool."

"So, what the hell's on your mind," the woman inquired.

"First things first, I'm Ravel."

"I'm Tiffany, and you're sexy as shit, Ravel," the woman said. "I could be gay for a day with you, I think."

"Never hurts to spread your wings, sometimes."

"I've spread my wings plenty, thank you very much," Tiffany replied.

"Well, I'm pleased to meet you, Tiffany. I came over because I was wondering who a gal's gotta blow to get a pair of those Jimmy Choos."

"Do what I did yesterday. Go to Surstromming's shoe department over at IP. Ask for Stephen Dedalus. He'll hook you up with these very Choos, once you've hooked up with him in what Stevie Boy calls the 'Burt Backarack Room.'"

"Is there a password?"

"Yeah, two lips on an organ."

Ravel snort laughed.

"Easy to remember."

Tiffany closed her paperback.

"How else may I serve you, Ravel? I gotta go and pitch 'Timeshares With Jesus' in a min."

"Thought it'd be cool to chat you up, chica. It was. I'll be on my way."

Tiffany made annoying slurping sounds with her strawberry edible straw as she polished off the rumrunner.

"Catch ya later, girlfriend," she said, just before she chomped on her candy straw as if it were a to-scale replica of salesman Dedalus' pencil-thin phallus.

Ravel walked back to Reed, who was laughing demurely.

"Ready for an eye exam?" she asked her understudy.

"Yeah, whatever, I guess so," Ravel said. "So much for my farsightedness."

"That's okay, it was never one of your strengths," Reed said in Mommy Dearest manner.

"Uh fuck you, Joan Crawford, and I still use wire hangars," Ravel retorted.

"No accounting for taste sometimes, Ms. ..."

Ravel stomped a Prada as if she were Dublin's Lord of the Dance.

"Don't you say it in public."

"Robespierre," Reed said defiantly.

Ravel's face flushed red as fresh blood drippings from the French Revolution's overworked guillotine blade.

"Just for that, Reed O'Hara, you can do your own bikini waxing!"

Reed smirked.

"Yeah, like you'd miss that."

Ravel muttered, "Probably right."

"All right, Dolce Doble *Rrrrrrr*."

"Nice trillo Italiano," Ravel commented. "But that sounds like a gay dude ranch."

"Very funny. Let's catch an elevator."

Again, the women held hands. As they strolled together, Ravel Robespierre sang in a low voice, "Love in an elevator, livin' it up when I'm goin' down."

Chapter 26

Bonaire

Southern California · 2014

"Call it a blindfold all you want, Jake, but it's still a pair of your tied-up stanky socks. No way in hell am I putting that on my head. I just washed my hair, for god's sake."

Reed and Jake weren't engaged in a parlor game, perhaps called "Don Henley's Dirty Laundry."

Rather, Jake had Reed disassemble a Browning 9mm pistol, placing the slide, barrel, recoil spring, firing pin, magazine and gun frame on the bed in Jake's beach shack on the remote side of Bonaire.

He next wanted her to re-assemble the Browning while blindfolded.

Reed would have none of Jake's filthy socks.

They made love earlier in the day. It was slow, gentle sex, enhanced by trade winds sweeping through the shack's windows and caressing Reed and Jake's glowing bodies. They fell asleep holding one another, as the hammock swung in a trade wind inspired rhythm.

Once they awakened from post-coital slumber, it was all business. It was a very serious business at that, with both their lives at stake.

"What are your instincts telling you about Olivia and Stanley?" Reed asked.

She sat lotus positioned in the bed. She was still naked. She made no move to cover herself.

Jake was naked as well.

Reed became distracted by his bite et coulles.

"How's Mr. Bo Dangles doing?"

Jake was unfazed by her question.

"He's resting now. As far as Olivia and Stanley, they're usually free-lance, yet Cuba is their biggest client. Cuban intelligence assigned them to take me out."

"Why're you so certain?"

"Because I triggered a Cuban general and his prize bull. He oversaw intelligence gathering outside Cuba."

"The cow was in charge?" Reed inquired.

"No, smartass, the general was head of foreign intelligence."

"I'm udderly aghast you killed a cow. Care to explain?"

"The general was staying at his hacienda outside Havana. He was fussing over his bull. I couldn't get a clear shot. I put a single round through both their brain pans. Sweetbreads of a shot."

He scares me and excites me all at once, Reed thought.

"I take it some entity of the United States government wanted them dead. Well, the general, not necessarily the cow."

"Let's stipulate the CIA ordered the hit on the general. They didn't have a beef with Fernando the bull. Poor animal was collateral damage, no matter how you filet it."

"You call me a smartass," Reed said. "Why did the general have to leave this veil of tears?"

"Causing too much damage stateside. Guy built a network of spies, informants, traitors and useful idiots sympathetic to La Causa."

"He had to go?"

"He did."

"Olivia and Stanley are in charge of payback?"

"Yes."

"Are we both targets?"

"Yes. I'm sorry, but it is what it is. Once you step into the covert world, that world is always with you."

"No regrets on my part, Jake. Tell you what, instead of a blind-fold, how about I re-assemble while keeping my eyes tightly closed?"

"Yeah, I guess so," Jake said, obviously disappointed he couldn't deploy his murder-most-foul pair of socks.

"And don't peek at my hoo-ha," Reed admonished.

"Yes, ma'am."

Reed closed her eyes, then re-assembled the pistol in less than a minute.

Jake clapped his approval.

"Well done. The more familiar you are with your handgun, the safer you'll be. Now, if the Browning jams, you can dis-assemble, find the problem and re-assemble quickly, even in pitch-black darkness."

"But what will you do about a weapon, other than your blunt-force-trauma witticisms?"

Jake leaned way over to retrieve a backpack resting at the foot of the mattress.

"I see your butthole, darling," Reed said. "It may have just winked at me."

With backpack in hand, Jake righted himself lotus style.

"So very juvenile. Be honest with me, Reed, do you get bawdy to counteract nerves?"

"First time I've ever thought about it. Guess I do. Also, I tend to laugh when someone, say an octogenarian from Grosse Pointe, Michigan, gets attacked by a ten-foot gator on a beautiful spring day in March on the twelfth fairway at the old timey executive golf course in Dunedin, Florida."

"Wow, talk about painting a dramatic *and detailed* Florida landscape."

"I'm not laughing *at* the person. I did that only once, when my sister Debbie got baptized in a creek in West Virginia. She claimed she saw Jesus underwater. Am I making sense? About the laughing part, not the water sprite Jesus."

"You are, though I could see the old duffer pissed at you for laughing at a gator chewing on his one good leg."

"Nice detail. I'll add it to my story. But really, Jake, I'd giggle only a little bit, then I'd politely ask the geezer and his new buddy if I may play through."

They laughed together.

"So whatcha got in that knapsack besides more dirty laundry?"

"Let's take a look see," Jake answered.

First, he pulled out his travel wardrobe: two t-shirts, a pair of khaki shorts, three pairs of camo-green underwear, a soft blue casual dress shirt and a pair of white slacks that were more wrinkled than a Shar Pei from the Zhou dynasty.

"Like your green skivvies," Reed commented.

"Government-issued, guaranteed to outlast me. Sometimes, I kinda miss tighty-whities, though."

Reed snort laughed.

My last boyfriend wore tighty-whities. Went great with his race-car bed and glow-in-the-dark posters of Hooter's chicks on Harleys."

"Geesh. Was Timmy still living with his parents?"

"Yup. Sleepovers at his place were problematic, to say the least."

Jake reached into the backpack and brought out a handgun wrapped in flannel. He laid it carefully on the mattress. He slowly unwrapped the gun as if it were Vermeer's new-found thirty-fifth painting, *Maria: A Self Portrait.*

He held the revolver reverentially.

"My local guy had no idea this is a British Bull Dog revolver," he said, almost in a whisper. "In this mint condition, it's worth at least three-hundred dollars. He asked for fifty. I gave him a hundred."

"A win-win for both of you then," Reed said.

Jake grinned near maniacally.

"For this beauty? Better believe it!"

"What kind of revolver is it?"

"A brief historical lesson, if I may?" Jake asked.

"Sure Prof, let's hear it." Reed answered.

"Phillip Webley & Son started making the Bull Dog revolver in 1872 in Birmingham, England. It got so popular, gunmakers in the United States and Continental Europe copied it. Bull Dog has a two-point-five-inch barrel and an effective firing range of fifteen yards. It'd be great if I had .44 Bull Dog cartridges, but it doesn't matter, because Bull Dogs can use .45 Adams, and I have two full boxes of those."

"Your Bull Dog is most impressive, though I hope you won't have to use both boxes of cartridges."

"Not likely. This revolver is for close-up encounters. I'm going to need to get close enough ..."

"To see the whites of their eyes?"

"Hardly. That's a suicide mission. No, give me ten, twelve feet and I'll put two rounds in the head and chest of both those sociopaths."

"Does this mean they're coming for us here?"

Jake put both hands on Reed's knees.

"As long as we're here, yes."

"Can you handle them?"

"No, but *we* can."

"So, what kind of odds do you give us?"

"They're both stone-cold killers. I'm one as well. You aren't. They can approach here from all sides. Might split up to hit us from two sides at once. They'll use rifles, likely automatics, and semi-automatic pistols, possibly employ tear gas and grenades. We have a Browning and a Bull Dog. This is a deadly game for them to play. We don't consider it a game at all, because our lives are on the line. Motivation? We own it. Therefore, I give our situation a seventy-thirty split."

Reed held his hands.

"In our favor?"

Jake kissed her hand.

"Afraid not, my love."

She kissed his hand, then held it against her cheek.

"I am in love with you, Jake, and I'll go once more into the breach. If our best strategy is waiting for them to come to us, that's fine with me. I've never shot a person, much less killed someone. But if I had had a handgun when Captain Ablab was shooting at us, I would've parted his dreadlocks."

Jake stretched out on the mattress, then drew Reed into his arms. He kissed her passionately, as he caressed her breasts.

"I love you as well, Reed."

She stopped his foreplay when he placed his hand between her legs.

"Not before you give me something to eat. I'm starving!"

He smiled bah-bah-black sheepishly.

"Sorry, I was trained to go forty-eight hours without food or water."

"I *wasn't*. Watcha got in terms of repast?"

"How about bananas and warmed up pork and beans?"

"Hey, turns out beans and bananas is my last meal, so fucking be it. Now get into that shoebox of a kitchen and fix me something to eat!"

Chapter 27

***

Tampa, Florida · 2022

"Remember, security will frisk us," Reed said. "They definitely will commandeer my Sig, and are you strapping?"

Ravel giggled.

"Strapping, as in what?"

"A handgun, you ninny."

Reed and Ravel rode the elevator alone to Paz Iberra's penthouse suite at the Floridan Palace Hotel in downtown Tampa.

"Oh right, a handgun," Ravel said cheekily. "I have one hidden in my right boot."

"Don't foam at the mouth when they take it away from you."

"Foam at the mouth, that's just too rich."

"Will you cooperate?"

"Absolutely. I promise not to non-expanding recreational foam at the mouth."

"What?"

"You'll get it later."

"Oh god."

There were two BarraCubas, each one sitting in a Contessa Baroque throne chair and playing video poker on her phone, guarding the door to the Santo Trafficante Senior Suite.

"Sup, noobs?" Ravel asked.

Neither BarraCuba looked up from her phone.

"Got an appointment there, lil' nugget?" one of the women asked Ravel.

"You know we do, sabrosa empanada," Ravel answered.

The BarraCuba did a double-take when she looked up at the Swiss beauty.

"Ay mi madre," she exclaimed in a sultry voice. "I get to frisk *her*."

The other BarraCuba checked out Reed, then said, "You can have her, I'll take la rubia."

Both BarraCubas rose with a groan from their thrones.

"Time to get frisky, bitches," the short one said.

Reed raised her arms. She allowed the woman to pat her down head to feet. Her bra received special attention.

When the BarraCuba found Reed's pistol, she calmy unclipped the holster and dropped it on the throne chair.

"Get that back when you leave," she said indifferently.

"Take good care of my Sig," Reed said. "I counted the bullets before I came here."

"Count all you want, chica, I don't need to ... yeah, that's a good one ... you got me, taco pequeno."

The other BarraCuba ordered Ravel to raise her arms.

Ravel refused. She balled her fists. She rested her balled fists on her hips.

"You gonna cooperate?" the biker asked.

A good foot taller and at least forty pounds heavier than Ravel, the BarraCuba loomed like a caracara falcon prepped for pouncing prey.

"This is all the cooperation you get, bub," Ravel shot back.

"Whateva, still gonna get searched."

The woman stood behind Ravel. She first ran her fingers through Ravel's bobbed black hair.

Ravel giggled.

"Do I still have lice?" she asked the biker.

"No lice, no razor blades, no Cheese Whiz, just a beautiful head of hair. You should let me shampoo you sometime."

"Maybe later."

Learned that one from Reed, Ravel thought.

"Your loss, mine too," the BarraCuba said sadly.

The BarraCuba reached around to hold Ravel's breasts.

"Gorgeous, just gorgeous, pequeñita. Such big titties, and no bra."

Ravel smiled.

"The girls are well trained."

The woman laughed boisterously.

"Good one! You funny little shit, you know that?"

"Si, amiga, I'm well aware of my fulsome sense of humor."

The biker still held Ravel's breasts.

"Hey, how about we release the boobs on their own recognizance?" Ravel requested.

The BarraCuba laughed again, then knelt down to frisk the rest of Ravel's body.

When she ran her hands up Ravel's left leg, all the way to her derriere, the woman exclaimed, "No panties, no bra, la dee da!"

She paused at the shaft of Ravel's boot on her right leg.

"What do we have here?"

The BarraCubas extracted a small handgun from Ravel's boot.

"What the hell?" she asked loudly.

It was a handgun all right. More precisely, it was a NERF gun.

Ravel said to Reed, "Know what NERF means now?"

"Sonuva ceviche, non-expanding recreational foam ... I can't believe I missed that one," Reed said.

Ravel's BarraCuba aimed the NERF gun at the other biker, then fired the lone foam dart. She hit her square in the forehead. The two women began wrestling. Their grunts and growls seemed more cane corso than human.

They crashed into a throne chair. Bikers and chair toppled over. Reed took her cue to grab her holstered handgun and Ravel's hand, then walk into the suite.

She whispered to Ravel, "You know, that isn't what NERF stands for."

"Christ, feels like Jake stalking me," Ravel commented.

"I'll keep the pistol, Señora O'Hara, you can have the fucking holster," a voice called out at the end of the suite's darkened hallway.

It was Eden, Paz Iberra's right hand woman in matters of love, lust and war.

She pointed a large revolver at Reed, who stared at Eden, while saying, "Shoot, shovel and shut up, or get the fuck out of my way."

"You tell her, Reed," Ravel added.

The woman gripped and ungripped the revolver. Her instincts told her to blow away Reed and Ravel, let Paz first, and God second, sort it out later.

No gringa talks to me like that, Eden thought.

Paz intervened: "Eden! Put down that cannon and let those white chicks come into our home. Right now!"

Eden immediately lowered the revolver, then used it as a traffic baton to wave through Reed and Ravel.

Crossing guard from hell, Ravel thought.

They entered an elegant living room that even Daisy Buchanan would've admired. Sofas, accent chairs, end tables, lamps, coffee tables, Persian rugs, all were curated antiques arranged in feng shui perfection.

However, the air-conditioner certainly was not antique. The HVAC system engorged the penthouse with artic air cold enough to force a Swede into a spruce-goose-down parka.

Cold as a witch's tit, *now* I get it, Reed thought.

My nipples are frost bitten, Ravel moaned to herself. And what the hell, I'm either 'shroomin' or I really did see a frozen thought bubble floating by me.

Unfortunately, forest green, floor-to-ceiling living room drapes were closed.

Reed couldn't spot Jake atop the building across the way.

Paz reclined on a sofa. A young woman sat in an accent chair next to her. Both women listened to opera emanating from recessed speakers.

"Is that Cervantes?" Reed exclaimed.

Paz sat straight up. She clapped politely.

"First of all, welcome to my humble abode, Reed O' Hara and your little hottie Ravel Robespierre," Paz said pleasantly.

Ravel thought, how in fuck does she know my last name?

"Thank you for having us, Ms. Iberra," Reed hurriedly said.

"You're welcome, Reed, and yes, that's the opera *Meledetto* by

Ignacio Cervantes. A great composer, who happened to be Cuban born."

"Isn't Maria Cervantes his daughter?" Ravel asked.

Reed raised an eyebrow to her.

"What? I hang around Jake, too, ya know," Ravel said.

Paz laughed.

"You scamps are delightful," Paz said. "Y si, Señorita Ravel, Maria was Cervantes' daughter. As accomplished a musician and composer as her father was. Es la verdad."

The woman sitting next to Paz studiously cleaned a pistol, its parts spread out on a towel covering an antique coffee table in front of her. Also on the towel were plastic bottles of cleaner solvent and gun oil, along with flannel patches and a cleaning rod.

Even sitting down, she appeared over six feet tall.

Her long auburn-streaked hair was in a French braid ponytail that looped around her right shoulder and snaked down her chest.

The woman had petite breasts. Narrow waist. Legs long enough to require the better part of a morning to shave properly.

The woman wore a black t-shirt festooned with white roses garlanded around a smiling skull, black moto jeans and black Alpine SMX riding boots.

The woman kept staring at Ravel.

"What's on your mind, lanky?" Ravel asked. "Keep lasering me with those gorgeous eyes, I might just blow up."

The woman lowered her eyes.

"Du ar sa vacker," she said in a silky voice. "Det ar darfor."

Ravel grinned like a horny hobgoblin from Sheboygan.

"You think I'm beautiful. Works for me. Stare to your heart's content."

The woman sprang out of the chair. She put her arms around Ravel.

"You know Swedish, ja?"

"Ja och nej. I have an FWB from Stockholm who's teaching me the lingus bilingus."

The woman was confused.

"FWB?" she asked Ravel.

"Yeah, a Friend With Benefits."

"Ja, Ja, en van med formaner."

"Um huh, that's how Sierra puts it."

"Sierra?"

"Min vab med formaner."

"Ah, gillar du hennes fordelar?"

"Do I enjoy her benefits? Sure, some of the time."

"Are you and Sierra attached?" the woman asked.

"Not at the hip, right now."

"Pardon, I do not understand."

"Sorry, no, we are not a couple, except for some of the time."

"Underbar!"

Paz interjected.

"I should introduce you two before you run off and get married," she said. "Marika, meet Ravel; Ravel, meet Marika."

Marika and Ravel hugged, then bussed each other's cheeks.

"Our Marika is an ambassador of good will and sisterhood," Paz explained. "She comes from Gothenburg, Sweden, and is a member of the Hell's Belles Motorcycle Club."

"Didn't Hell's Belles start in the UK?" Reed asked.

"Ja, I mean, yes, our chapter in Gothenburg is quite new," Marika said. "The BarraCubas were kind enough to have me visit, so to learn all I can about the amazing motorcycle club."

"Hell's Belles is that rare women's biker club *not* sponsored by a men's club, right?" Reed asked and answered.

"Yes, they are, Reed," Paz replied. "BarraCubas Motorcycle Club also is free of any cock-and-balls attachment."

Cock-and-balls attachment ... this day just gets better and better, Ravel thought.

Paz eyed Ravel up one side, down the other and lingered in between.

"Is that Armani, Ravel?" she asked.

"Yuppers."

"You look sharp in it."

"Yeah, I keep hearing that, gracias."

Eden hovered nearby like a hangry javelina circling a cottonwood campfire in the Sonoran Desert.

"Las Damas, please have a seat," Eden said officiously. "Reed, join Paz on the sofa. Marika and Ravel, sit on the chairs opposite each other," she announced. "Reed, you may keep your pistol as long as it stays holstered, but, Ravel, I'm afraid my security detail took possession of your toy gun."

Brains, brawn and big balls, one potent-ass combo, Ravel said to herself.

Can't tell if Ravel's totally flashing on Eden, or is totally repulsed by her, Reed wondered.

"The NERF of them to take my trusty sidearm," Ravel said. "Guess I'm okay with that, long as you tell the pit bull out front that it has a twitchy finger."

Eden smiled malevolently at her.

"Thank you, Eden love," Paz said. "Por favor, join us."

Eden shone like a Champagne supernova when Paz spoke to her.

"No, no, I'll just hang around and keep an eye on that little one over there."

"Which one?" Marika asked, as she pushed the cleaning rod through the gun barrel.

"Ravel," Eden answered.

"Then there will be two sets of eyes upon her." Marika said.

"Ladies, please, I don't deserve all this attention," Ravel exhorted.

Eden's smile vaporized.

"Actually, you do, Ravel."

"Enough!" Paz yelled.

Eden lowered her head.

"Si, mi presidente."

Paz was in a loungewear state of mind, as evidenced by her blood-red silk pajamas and soft padded Prada slides. The first two buttons to her pajama top were undone.

Woman sneezes, those tits'll pop out like a runaway Slinkie, Reed observed.

For sure, Ravel thought, possibly drawing on her Swiss-infused telepathy to Reed's big brain.

What are Slinkies? Marika wondered, who also might have mental telepathy, only more of a Swedish origin.

"A donde van mis maneras?" Paz wondered aloud. "Chicas, would you like a coffee or a sparkling water, as I know you and your Namaste tribe don't partake of alcohol."

"A cappuccino perhaps?" Reed asked.

Paz's laugh was more like a war cry.

"Cappuccino? We drink café con leche solamente."

While studying Marika reassemble the pistol, Ravel asked, "I assume you think café con leche is like, muy macho bueno?"

Paz grinned at Ravel.

"If by 'muy macho bueno' you mean 'tan fuerte' or …"

"Very strong, yes, I know," Ravel said.

"Then of course a café con leche is better than some greasy Guido's cappuccino."

"We'll have two, please," Reed requested of Paz.

"May I have one as well?" Marika asked.

"Yes, after you join Eden in the kitchen to make four café con leches," Paz said.

"With pleasure," Marika answered. "Ravel, please join me."

Ravel looked at Reed, who nodded yes.

"And away we go!" Ravel exclaimed.

She and Marika and Eden went into the kitchen. Marika sneakily patted Ravel's bottom. Ravel returned the favor.

Paz micro-nibbled from a slice of carambola lanced on her infamous abalone handle switchblade.

"You gringas call this 'starfruit,' correct?"

Reed nodded yes.

"Want some carambola?"

Reed again nodded yes.

Paz flicked the carambola slice off the steel tip of her switchblade in the direction of Reed, who sat at the far end of a chartreuse Glabman Paramount couch.

She caught the slice of bright yellow fruit without looking.

Just like Sanne did in Bonaire, only she caught a beer glass, Reed thought.

Reed bit into the tangy sweet starfruit.

"Ready to get down to business, Reed? Something tells me you don't want to join the BarraCubas. You're too vanilla anyways, but we might make an exception for that Ravel."

Eden heard Paz from the kitchen. She scowled at Ravel.

"It's business only today," Reed said. "And, Paz?"

"Si?"

"Let's keep it real, esta de acuerdo?"

"Always do," Paz answered, as she fussed over her cuticles with the switchblade.

"Did you have anything to do with Alicia's murder?" Reed inquired forcefully.

Eden dropped a ceramic coffee mug on the kitchen tiled floor.

"Let me help you with that, Eden," Ravel said in the kitchen.

"Don't you fucking touch it!" Eden screamed.

Marika put her arm around Ravel's waist and guided her away from Eden.

"Best not to tangle with her," Marika said soothingly.

Eden was speechless.

Paz wasn't.

"I invite you into our home and you ask if I had something to do with my baby girl's murder? What the fuck, O'Hara?"

Reed looked directly into Paz's dark molasses eyes.

"All that bluster doesn't deny your involvement, Ms. Iberra."

Eden entered the living room carrying a wooden tray with four mugs of café con leche on it. Her hands shook with such jealous anger, some of the coffee high-tided over the edge of the cups.

"Eden, stop shaking," Paz ordered.

Eden lowered her eyes in acquiescence. Yet her bodybuilder figure remained carotid-pulsing tense.

Marika held Ravel's hand as the new besties returned to their chairs.

Eden first offered coffee to Paz, who said, "Gracias, mi Cubanita bonita. Now offer coffee to our guests."

Eden *pfttt,* but she obeyed.

Reed took a cup from the tray. Marika followed. Eden almost skipped Ravel. She thought better of it. She offered her the last café con leche.

Eden paused to admire Ravel's beautiful violet eyes, her raven black hair, her full breasts, her slim diminutive figure.

She gonna star in my next snuff vid, Eden declared to herself.

Reed drank her café con leche.

"It's delicious, Eden," she exclaimed. "Heat the milk instead of steaming it, and use dark-roasted robusta, is that about right?"

Eden nodded curtly. She was one pissed-off BarraCuba barista.

"Why you think we kill Serrano?" she exclaimed. "Mi jeffa, she never let that happen because Paz loved that girl."

Paz retracted her switchblade, then set it in on the coffee table.

It remained within easy reach for Reed.

Paz didn't notice Reed surreptitiously palm the knife when she set down her coffee cup next to it.

"I love all my chicas, including Alicia. But I play favorites only with Eden. She's right, we did not harm Alicia."

"Honest to God, Paz?" Reed asked.

"Honest to God, to Siddhartha, to Haile Selassie, to mi abuela and her enchiladas."

Starting to believe this woman, Reed thought.

"How can I doubt you, Paz, when you include your grandmother's stuffed tortillas?"

Paz high-fived Reed, holding her hand until Reed disengaged.

"Got a helluva grip," Reed said. "Reminds me of my husband's."

Paz frowned.

"Now why did you bring Jake into our hot bitches drum circle? Hmm? I know you're struggling with bi-curiosity, Reed, but don't overcompensate by swinging Jake's dick in my face."

Hopped up on espresso, Ravel jive jumped into the conversation.

"'Don't go throwin' your Big Johnson in my tear-stained face," she said. "Now *that's* a great country song, if there ever were one."

"Ja! Ja! I get that one! Bra en, min lilla loganberry!"

First time I got compared to a loganberry, Ravel thought. Totally groovin' on this Scandinavian string bean right now.

"I brought Jake up because he and I are skilled investigators. We're going to find Alicia's killer. Together."

"Dupree still shooting livestock?" Paz inquired.

"That was *one* Cuban cow caught in a crossfire," Reed said defensively. "No, he doesn't shoot anyone these days, unless he gets shitty service at Bern's, which isn't likely."

"I happen to know Dupree still has his Barrett M82. I also know he and his elephant gun are on the rooftop of the office building to our east."

Reed was taken aback. Nonplussed. Rendered silent.

"Would you like to see your husband, Miss Honey Trap?" Paz asked.

"Yes. Yes, I would. Right now."

Eden muttered as she opened the drapes, "Perra sucia, me cago en su leche."

Why is she shitting in our milk? Ravel wondered.

Reed couldn't believe the scene before her.

She could make out Jake's head in the background. He wore a white Tampa Bay Rays ball cap. Backwards. He had covered his Barrett M82 in white gauze, as the office building serving as his perch was itself a dingy shade of pale white.

The foreground alarmed Reed. There was a large, uncovered patio. A table with four chairs and two chaise lounges were pushed to the side.

Four BarraCubas were on the patio.

They weren't soaking up rays and sipping Margarita Coronitas.

Teams of two BarraCubas each were on their knees and faced Jake on the office building rooftop. One BarraCuba aimed a Karabiner 98 sniper rifle in his direction. Another used high-powered Skyway 25 binoculars to spot for her partner. It was two sniper teams pitted against a lone shooter. Bad optics. Bad odds. Bad juju.

Paz grinned like a wet gremlin eating at a midnight chocolate buffet aboard a cruise ship.

"Did you really think we wouldn't outflank you and Dupree, Reed?" she asked smugly. "You shits assume Cuban biker chicks are all about our rides and our bitches and nothing else. How you like us now, puta?"

"I like you even less now, if that were possible," Reed answered.

Paz guffawed dismissively.

"Aww, lil' whitey don't like the BarraCubas. Such a shame. Least recognize we triangulated Dupree. He could get one of our shooters, but not both, before we 'splode his big old watermelon head."

Reed raised an eyebrow.

"That's right. We did our recon on you and Shootin' Blanks Dupree."

Reed pulled out Paz's switchblade and clicked it open lickity split. She made certain to be-bop bounce sunlight off the long steel blade directly into Paz's eyes.

"Go ahead, asshat, insult my man again," Reed said threateningly. "You do, I'll cut your throat and laugh while you bleed out."

Eden aimed a Smith & Wesson revolver at Reed.

"Drop mi presidente's cuchile," she said in a steady voice.

Reed smiled.

"Standoff seems unbalanced, and not in my favor," she said.

Paz laughed ever so slightly.

"Quite a woman, O'Hara," she said. "I sure as fuck would tap your ass."

Ravel and Marika stood at the entranceway to the patio.

"Fuckin' crowded out here," Ravel said. "Forget tapping *anything* of Reed's, because if you try it, you'll get a bloody Swiss bowtie."

Whateva da fuck dat is, she thought.

Eden turned and aimed her handgun at Ravel. She went back and forth, pointing first at Ravel, then at Reed.

"What do I do, Paz?"

Paz didn't move. She was ever so relaxed, as if this scene were but a trifle annoyance.

"Put the gun away, baby," she said to Eden. "If you don't, everybody out here dies, entiendes?"

"Si, si, si," Eden answered, as she reluctantly lowered the Smith & Wesson.

"Put the safety on," Paz ordered.

Eden obeyed.

"Thank you," Paz said. "Reed, I apologize for insulting your man, please lower my knife."

Reed retracted the blade, yet still held Paz's knife.

"I apologize for losing my temper, Paz, it was unprofessional, but I won't tolerate criticism of Jake."

"Understood," Paz said in a soothing voice. "How about you call off Jake and I'll stand down my teams?"

"Deal."

Reed waved her left arm three times to Jake, then placed her right fist over her heart.

She could just make out Jake turning around his Rays ballcap, then slowly disappearing with the stealthiness of a space alien abducting a Taos new ager.

She tossed the closed switchblade to its owner.

Paz caught the knife while staring unblinkingly into Reed's mesmerizing blue eyes.

"Nice catch," Reed said.

"Yes, you are," Paz answered.

Eden got angry again.

"Bitches got any more questions before we throw your asses over the side?" she said disdainfully.

"I have a question, Paz" Reed said. "Why did you let Alicia perform at Namaste, knowing I'd fire her if I discovered she was a BarraCuba?"

Tears welled in Paz's eyes.

"Because dancing made my little girl happy," she said, choked up. "She knew the risks, I knew the risks, we figured you Anglos wouldn't figure it out, and Namaste general manager Jake didn't figure it out, did he?"

Reed clenched and released both hands. Clench. Release. Clench. Release.

"Jake and I *both* missed it. And you can forget dividing the two of us, Paz. Isn't ever happening."

Ravel still held Marika's hand.

"You go, Reed, set that bitch straight," Ravel said. "Good thing, Paz, I don't have my NERF gun, otherwise I'd dart you right between those wicked black-as-ass eyes."

Eden rushed Ravel.

"That's it, right over the balcony you go," she yelled.

Ravel stepped back into a fighting stance.

Before Eden could grapple with Ravel, Marika stuck out her boot and tripped Eden, who sprawled across the patio, her revolver *chunka chunk chunkin'* on the tiled floor and resting at Reed's feet.

Reed picked up the handgun. She took off the safety. She aimed the revolver at Eden and at Paz. She pulled out her Sig Sauer pistol and tossed it to Ravel.

Marika drew her pistol from behind her back waistband and aimed it at Eden.

"I have Eden, Ravel, you watch those BarraCubas, and Reed can cover Paz, ja?"

When the BarraCubas went to pick up their rifles, Ravel waved them off with the Sig Sauer.

"*They tried to make me go to rehab,*" she sang. "*But I said no, no, no.*"

The four BarraCubas moved away from the rifles.

Paz maintained her composure. She left her switchblade in the front pocket of her pajama top. She considered all available angles.

Outmaneuvered in my own fucking casa, she said to herself. Ay tu madre.

"Enough, Reed," she said. "Time for you to leave."

Reed lowered the revolver. Ravel and Marika followed suit.

"I believe you didn't have a hand in Alicia's murder, so I'm asking you to guess who did, Paz."

Eden got back on her feet and brushed herself off.

She scowled at Ravel and Marika, then said, "Ernic Friekorps, he did it."

"Friekorps, he's your best bet," Paz said.

"I know the backstory about you and Alicia and Friekorps," Reed said. "I guess it's possible."

"Fine, now give me back my piece," Eden demanded.

Reed shook her head no.

"I'll hold on to it for now. Don't worry, you'll get it back. Oh yeah, give me the firing pins to the Karabiners."

Eden looked for help from Paz.

"Chill, my baby," Paz mourning doved Eden. "Now go get the firing pins and give them to that lesbo Ravel."

Marika whispered to Ravel, "Is that true?"

"What?"

"That you're a lesbian?"

"Thought you'd figured that out, with the way you've been playing with my ass, but yeah, I'm like super gay. You?"

"Oh ja, *very* super gay."

"Good to know, Maid Marika."

"Do as I say," Paz commanded Eden.

Eden's broad shoulders slumped. She extracted the sniper rifles' firing pins and gave them to Ravel.

"Enjoy your last days, Ravel," she said menacingly.

Ravel giggled.

"Big old tub of lard, you don't scare me for a nanosecond."

"A what?" Eden asked.

"Never mind, la gorda."

Sensing another blow-out, Reed forcefully interceded.

"Ravel, let's leave, we got what we wanted," she counseled.

Ravel nodded yes.

Eden stood next to Paz.

"Reed, return the handgun and firing pins by tomorrow, or Eden will come looking for them. And for you three."

"Three?" Reed asked, though she understood what Paz meant.

"You, Ravel and that fucking traitor Marika makes three, bumble bee," Paz rhymed, in English, no less.

Marika raised her hands WTF style.

"Why do I have to leave, Paz?"

"You sided with Ravel and Reed. Get out. Or you'll be Eden's new chew toy."

"Can I at least pack?"

"No! Take your skinny white Scandi-candy ass outta here," Paz yelled.

"Okej. Skit och faller tilbaka i det, Paz Iberra."

While watching Paz and her switchblade, the three women backed out of the patio and into the living room, then left the Santo Trafficante Senior Suite.

They stood in the hallway and waited for an elevator.

Barry Manilow belted out "Mandy" over the hallway speakers, "*I remember all my life, raining down cold as ice.*"

The two BarraCubas sentries sat in their throne chairs. They paid no attention to the three women. The bigger one, playing with Ravel's NERF gun, accidentally shot herself in the face with a yellow foam dart. The smaller BarraCuba laughed and snorted uncontrollably. The larger BarraCuba punched the smaller one in her arm.

"You know you're coming with us, right?" Ravel asked Marika.

"Oh, thank you, Ravel," Marika said. "Reed, is it okay with you?"

"Of course. Jake and I have two guest bedrooms. Ravel has one. You may stay in the other."

Humpf, Marika won't be staying in her bedroom for long, Ravel promised herself.

Marika smiled her thank-you, then chimed in with Barry Manilow, "*Oh Mandy, you came and you gave without taking.*"

Reed rock 'n rolled her soulful blues.

Let's see, I have one registered handgun and one unregistered, a partner who leads with her hoo-hah and a Swedish biker chick who digs Barry Manilow and is coming home with us, Reed thought. Really, just another day at the office.

"Did you really tell Paz to shit and fall back in it?" Ravel asked the Swede.

Marika's face blushed.

"Was I too gross?" she asked.

"Nope, Marika, I'd say you were right on the mark."

"ABBA."

"What?"

"ABBA."

"ABBA what?"

"ABBA wanting to say, Jag vill knulla dig."

Ravel was saved from responding by the elevator bell dinging them aboard.

Yeah, I want to fuck you, too, she thought.

Chapter 28

Bonaire

Southern Caribbean · 2014

Midnight at the beach shack. Jake caught zzz's. Reed kept watch with eyes wide open. Her sonar echolocated like a horseshoe bat's. She was vigilance personified.

Jake's dreams inevitably morphed into nightmares. Allegories all. It was Orwell's *Animal Farm* levitating from a dose of psychotropic fungi psilocybin.

His most horrific fearscape was of the poisonous blue-ringed octopus and her court jesters, the cone snails. They liked to tag team a naked Jake trapped in an aluminum cage beneath the blue Pacific Ocean off Bimini.

It was for him a three-strip Technicolor hell, where ungodly pain was delivered without hesitation.

On this ominous Bonaire night, his nightmare happened to be set at the Plaza de Toros Mexico, the world's largest bull ring. A collaterally damaged bull stomped dusty circles around Jake. The bull's head bore a left temple egress/right temple exit wound, which oozed candy-apple red blood and glutinous viscera.

There was no bullshit given or taken. Senor Toro sought revenge.

Fortunately, Jake jump-jerked awake just as the bull was about to trample him in the bullring.

"Tough one, lover?" Reed asked in a soothing voice.

Jake ran both hands through his light brown curls. His exhale resembled an orca's lament over the paucity of puffins, puffins who's got the puffins.

"Yeah, guess so. Happens every time I sleep."

"Least you got some rest. We need you alert, right?"

"Sure. How about you? Want some sack time?"

She chuckled quietly.

"Nah, fucking twice in one day is about my limit."

"Not *sack* time, *sleepy* time."

"I get it, Jake."

He raised his eyebrows and grinned at Reed.

Even in slim shady darkness, she saw that his smile could smelt iron ore.

"Careful, that smile's going to give away our position," Reed cautioned playfully.

"We stay down, we'll be okay. I made a low barrier around the shack's four sides with sections of gnarly steel sheets I took from the roof."

"Explains the abundance of skylights above us."

"It does, indeed. All about ambience I am. Look up through the roof. See Jupiter cozying up to a full moon."

"I do."

Jake kissed her forehead.

"I hope one day you'll say that to me before a judge in her court room."

"Whoa there, good buddy, need to slow down. That's sweet as hell, but you might be succumbing to love in an elevator."

He didn't respond. He began re-packing the rucksack with spare ammo clips and a cartridge box, then a sheathed trench knife and high-powered compact binoculars.

"Are you pouting?" she asked.

"Maybe a little."

"Suck it up, nunchuck. Isn't the time for planning your destination wedding in the Poconos."

"You're so goddamned level-headed. 'Love in an elevator.' Didn't even think of that. Thought you'd say, 'love in a foxhole.' All right, I'll chill out, but I'm going to insist that if we emerge from this situation relatively unscathed, then I want a heart-shaped tub in our honeymoon suite."

"Deal, but only if you stop pouting."

"Fine."

"Thank you. Now what're you doing with your backpack?"

"Making a bugout bag."

"And that is?"

He slid protein bars and a filled canteen into the backpack, along with cash and a medical kit.

"We need to put our passports in the ruck as well. A bugout bag is for an emergency. If we must bug out, we have absolute essentials in hand. But don't forget your toothbrush. Mung mouth on a mission is murder."

Reed held Jake's hand.

"You obviously know what you're doing. Makes me feel secure."

"Good. Worst case prepping is meant to keep us safe and alive."

"Don't varnish things, do you?"

"Afraid not."

Reed was about to speak when an object *plunked*! on the roof.

"What the fuck!" she exclaimed.

"Stay calm. Think I know what's happening."

Seconds later, they heard a *swoosh*! An orange glow-in-the-dark golf ball fell through a skylight and *ploofed*! on the mattress.

"Who the hell is playing midnight golf at the oasis?" Reed asked in a near whisper.

Jake smiled.

"You'll be my belly dancer and I'll be your sheik?" he asked.

"Maybe later, and quit showing off."

"You started it, Ms. Muldaur."

"And he keeps going."

Two golf balls *bonked* on the steel roof.

"When avocation meets vocation," Jake said wryly.

Reed exhaled sharply.

"Please explain, and should I put a bucket on my head?"

"As much as I'd like to see that, you don't have to be a buckethead," he answered jocularly. "Just don't get underneath a skylight."

"And avocation meets vocation?" Reed inquired.

"Olivia and Stanley are out there. They're as fanatical about golf as they are about killing people. They're probably fifty yards out in the Carib's biggest sand trap. The arc trajectory tells me they're using nine irons. Doubt I could nail 'em that far out. But let's take a look."

Using military grade night vision binoculars, Jake made out two figures moving about in the darkness.

"It's them," Jake said. "Clever fuckers, they're gambling we have only sidearms, so we'd have to go outside and get close up to blow their heads off. Won't be easy."

"Putting on your game face, *hon*?"

"Yeah, only this isn't a game."

Plunk! *Plunk*! Two more balls bounced off the roof.

A male voice called out, "Hey, Duty-Free, what'd you once call a preacher riding a horse?"

Jake answered, "Sermon on the Mount, Stanley."

"That's you all right. Easy to I.D. a fucker with his own lame jokes. Wouldn't want to blitz kill a pair of tourons, you know?"

"Very sensitive of you, Stanley. Looks as if Olivia lets you show your nurturing fem side on occasion. How is your dear partner, anyway?"

Whoosh! *Whoosh*!

Donk! *Donk*!

Two glowing blue balls fell through the skylights. One ball bounced off the wood floor and shot straight out a rear window. The other blue ball tea-bagged Reed's forehead.

"Goddamn that hurts!" she exclaimed.

"Rub some dirt on it."

"Uh really? Fuck you, Duty-Free."

They laughed.

Woo-whoosh! *Woo-whoosh*!

Wonka! *Wonka*!

Golf balls slammed against the front of the shack.

"Jesus, they're using drivers now," Jake said.

Woo-whoosh! *Woo-whoosh*!

Wonka! Wonka!

Two yellow glo-balls *whiffed* through a front window. The makeshift drapes *poofed* inward, snaring the golf balls and rendering them harmless.

"If you force us to, we'll sand wedge M67's right through your roof," Olivia warned.

"M67's, I don't like the sound of that," Reed said.

Jake scanned the terrain with his night vision binoculars.

Reed asked, "Do I want to know what an M67 is?"

"Of course. Fragmentation grenades, slightly smaller than a baseball. Nasty little shits."

"Can they really drop those grenade thingys into our humble abode?"

"Absolutely."

Olivia called out, "Jakie Poo, give yourself up and we'll let the little bitch go free."

Jake paused.

He waited, waited, then answered, "Swear to God you won't harm her?"

"Our contract is on you," Stanley said. "We'll let her skedaddle to Seattle, or wherever the fuck she's from."

"Let me think about it," Jake said.

"You got thirty seconds, 'cause the M67's are all teed up," Olivia warned.

Reed grabbed Jake's shoulder.

"No, I'm not walking away from you," she declared.

"That's sweet, but unnecessary," Jake said. "You wouldn't get ten feet before they put six rounds in you."

"Charming. Remind me to approve your wedding vows."

"Hey, I'm giving it to you straight."

Olivia or Stanley dropped another golf ball, this one an iridescent pink, through one of the skylights.

"Got fifteen seconds, friends!" Stanley yelled.

"What're we gonna do, Jake?" Reed asked.

"It's a simple plan. When I say go, empty a magazine in their direction. Then you grab the bugout bag and wait long enough for me to fire my Bulldog. We both get the fuck out of here, and I hope Stanley and Olivia will hunker down long enough for us to get to the shoreline."

"Then what?" Reed asked with growing panic.

"One stage at a time, my love. I've done this before. Please notice I'm still breathing. Just as incentive for you, you'll probably get a chance for your first kill."

"Geez, a vacay of a lifetime. What do I win with my first kill?"

Jake slid over to the window on the left.

"You get to keep breathing."

Chapter 29

Tampa, Florida · 2022

"Another mystery solved, the magnificent derriere of Botticelli's Venus finally is revealed."

Jake and Reed barely communicated of late. Jake wasn't aware Marika was staying with them in their penthouse.

"Venus" was naked in the living room. She stood with her back to Jake. She gazed out the grand picture window at the expanding sunrise.

It was *Nascita di Venere* in the flesh.

Upon hearing Jake's remark about her bum, Marika turned to face him. She stared at him. Her right hand covered her right breast. Her left hand covered her bella figa.

"Vackte jag dig?" she inquired politely, quietly.

"No, you didn't awaken me," Jake replied.

His garnet robe was open. A morning erection tented his white briefs.

He immediately closed his robe.

Did I just Anthony Weiner her? he thought.

"I'm Jake Dupree, Reed O'Hara's husband."

"Oh yes, you are the Jake. I have heard many positive objections about you. I am Marika, from Sweden."

Of course you are, Jake thought. Are the Norse gods testing me?

"May I get you a robe, Marika?"

Before she could respond, Ravel appeared from her bedroom. She wore only an oversized t-shirt bearing an image of Florence Welch in a Pre-Raphaelite fluid crimson gown.

Ravel held a plush white terry cloth bathrobe.

"Thanks, Jake, I got this," she said.

She helped Marika into the robe.

Ravel put her arms around the Swede and gave her a gentle morning kiss.

"How are you, lover?" Ravel asked.

"Daffodils and dandelions, min heta lilla nisse."

"Hot little pixie. I dig it."

"Let me tell you something, Ravel."

"Sure, my lovely."

"The Jake, he wears the tightly whitelys under his robe," Marika whispered.

"Tightly whitelys, yeah, you meant 'tighty whiteys.' Please forgive him. Jake is something of a man-child."

"Ja? Hmm, ar han galen i huvedet?"

"Well, he *was* dropped on his head several times as an infant, as an adolescent *and* as a teenager," Ravel answered. "It's sad really, just talk to him slowly and loudly."

Marika yelled at Jake, "I ... AM ... SORRY ... YOUR ... BRAIN ... IS ... BROKEN!

The master bedroom doors swooped open. Reed emerged furious as Alecto, Megaera and Tisiphone combined.

She angrily cinched her robe.

"Can't a woman catch some fucking zzz's in her own fucking home! And goddamn it, Ravel, Jake isn't slow in the huvudet!"

"Everyone speak fucking Swedish here, ja?" Marika asked.

Ensemble laughter ensued.

"We learned Swedish from Sierra," Jake said.

"Ja, ja, Sierra," Marika opined. "Always the Sierra, blah blah blooey."

Ravel smirked, "Jealous much?"

"Ja!" Marika exclaimed. "You're my sugar baby."

"Jesus, one night of fantastic sex and now you're my sugar mama?"

The two women hugged tightly. Breathily. Passionately.

"All right, y'all, let's sit down and talk," Reed declared.

Jake placed his arm around her, then said, "Good idea, love. How about I fix coffee?"

Reed less than subtly shifted away from him.

"Ladies, let's repair to the dining room." she announced. "Ravel, you're not wearing panties again, so sashay your bare booty into the bedroom and put some on, maybe even a pajama bottom, too."

Ravel pouted. But she dutifully went in her bedroom. A minute later, she returned wearing green pajama bottoms emblazoned with tiny pink flamingos.

"Thank you, Rave," Reed said.

"You're welcome, Mommy Dearest."

Marika frowned.

"You are Ravel's mother, Reed?"

The Wild Irish Rose flushed red as Saint Brigid's hair.

"Not unless I was ten years old when I had her," Reed replied testily. "Ravel's being a wiseacre."

Marika frowned again.

"Let's see, a 'smarty,' a 'wisenheimer,' a 'pisser'?" Reed offered. "No? How about 'smartskalle'?"

Marika sunbeamed, "Ja, a 'smartass' then, oh she is one, last night she said in the bed, 'Rock, paper, scissors, choose one,' I did not understand, so she explained."

"Which did you choose?" Reed asked.

"Scissors, of course," Marika answered proudly.

Jake carried a tray that held an unplunged coffee Bodum and a plate of Sucré Table Bakery croissants.

Jake plunged the Bodum. He poured coffee for the women. He offered croissants to them. Only Reed didn't take one.

"Jake, please sit down with us," she said.

"Are you sure you want me to?" he asked like a sulky child.

Reed tapped an Italian-manicured fingernail on the fossilized wood dining room table. She sipped her coffee.

Tap. Sip. Tap. Sip.

She'll stop that shit when she needs to pee, Ravel thought, as she touch-counted the flamboyances of pink flamingos on her pajama bottoms.

"Ravel, please let me help you count the flamingos."

Marika ran her index finger along Ravel's inseam.

"Are you moistened yet?" she asked Ravel.

Marika smiled.

Ravel smiled.

Reed frowned.

She banged her hand on the table. She uttered official U.S. Navy-sanctioned obscenities.

Jake remained as quiet a Silent Bob on valerian root.

"Damn it all, Ravel and Marika, keep this fucking professional," Reed said. "As for you, Jake, quit being such a silly-ass chick and sit the fuck down!"

Jake's face was expressionless. He swayed slightly. He clenched his fists.

He sat down. He surrendered. For now.

"Thank you, my big beautiful sulkster of a husband."

Jake tipped his imaginary Stetson.

Having won that battle, Reed reported to Jake everything significant that had happened with Paz and the BarraCubas.

Ravel and Marika weighed in twice, adding useful details and insight.

Jake poured himself a cuppa joe. He listened. He nodded affirmatively. He appeared engaged.

He recounted his encounter with Mulraney and the Bavarians. He left out the Weeki Wachee mermaid women sunbathing nude on lawn chairs at the auto moto condo.

"These two motorcycle clubs are locked in a death match." Reed commented, as she finished her coffee. "Poor Alicia simply got caught in the middle."

Jake scratched his shaven chin in search of wisdom and the errant whisker stubble.

"It's all about holding territory for selling drugs, pulling off burglaries, running escort services, extorting businesses and murdering for hire," he said with authority.

"Make 'em unstoppable if the two clubs ever joined forces," Ravel said.

Marika shook her head.

"Would not happen, Ravel. Bavarians and BarraCubas, they hate each other too much."

Jake continued to rub his chin.

"Funny how Eden's name keeps popping up," Jake said.

"She's Iberra's right-hand sociopath," Reed declared.

"Eden's totally dedicated to Iberra?" he asked.

"Totally dedicated, totally psycho jealous," Ravel answered.

"Totally," Marika added.

"*Totally*," Reed said with Regina George mean-girl archness.

The women laughed.

Then Marika said, "Eden murdered Alicia."

"*Fuuuuuuuck*," Ravel uttered.

"How do you know this?" Reed asked Marika.

"Such a jealous woman, Eden. She hated Alicia. She thought Paz was going to replace her with Alicia, which never would have happened, because Paz needs Eden for the sex, for the love, for the killings."

A single tear cascaded down Marika's left cheek. The tear splashed on the dining room table.

She quickly gathered herself.

"I heard Eden on her phone outside on the balcony. She either didn't know or didn't care I was out there. She knew if I said anything, she'd kill me."

"Eden didn't figure on your leaving with Reed and Ravel, did she?" Jake asked.

Marika shook her head no.

"What did you hear Eden say out on the balcony?" Reed inquired.

Marika gulped.

She exhaled.

She stared at her hands on her lap.

Then she looked Reed straight into her eyes.

"She was talking to a man. Using a sexy voice on him. So sweet, you know?"

"So weird!" Ravel added.

"Ja, ja, you bet. Eden talked this man into killing Alicia."

"Because Eden was jealous over Paz paying attention to Alicia?" Jake asked incredulously.

"Ja, but more than that. When that disgusting police detective ..."

"Friekorps?" Reed and Jake said simultaneously.

"Ja! Friekorps. Very bad hygiene. Smelled worse than surstromming. Paz gave him many thousands to betray Alicia. She was Friekorps' informer, I guess."

Jake asked Reed, "Ever had that fermented Baltic herring?"

Reed sensed Jake was showing off to Marika. Reed ignored him.

"Did Paz want Alicia dead as well?" Reed asked.

"No, she ordered Eden *not* to kill her," Marika snapped. "Paz said she needed the time to come up with a plan for dealing with Alicia."

"Why did Eden disobey Paz and murder Alicia?" Reed said.

Marika frowned lost in thought, then said, "Eden thought she could eventually convince Paz that Alicia had to die, and I did nothing to stop it."

She wept in her hands.

Ravel tried to console Marika.

"Come on now, we need you to keep it together, okay?" she said to her.

Marika tremored yes.

Good thing, because my sympathy department just closed for the day, Ravel thought. I am Swiss, for fuck's sake.

A mindful minute of silence ensued.

Marika dabbed her eyes with a fawn cloth napkin.

Two more minutes of silence.

Marika blew her Scar Jo nose into the napkin.

"I am better now. Thank you for the waiting."

Reed held Marika's hand.

"You thought you could've done something to save Alicia," Reed said to her. "All of us at this table feel the same way."

Marika said, "No more pity pottery, I promise."

Stifling laughter, Ravel asked, "Who did Eden talk with on the phone?"

"Zeke, from the Bavarians," Jake announced. "Two days ago, I saw him strapping a Smith & Wesson revolver over at the biker compound in South Tampa."

"Yeah, so what?" Ravel said.

"So what? The chances are good the revolver Zeke showed off to me is the same one Eden waved around."

"It's one and the same gun?" Ravel asked. "And it's the murder weapon?"

Jake flashed all smug like.

"Yup. On both counts."

Marika rubbed Ravel's back in soothing sensual circles.

"Jake is correct, Ravel. Eden gave Zeke $25,000 and the big gun. When he killed Alicia, he did not return the gun until the morning you and Ravel visited the hotel."

Jake clapped in Marika's honor.

"*There* is a prime example of observe, analyze, disseminate. Great job, Marika," he announced.

Reed looked at Jake.

"Good to be back on the team?" she asked him.

"Goddamn good," he answered in a gravel choked voice.

"Excellent," she said. "Like another piece of good news, hubby o' hubby o' mine?"

"Of course, love."

"You know the revolver I absconded with from the Floridan?"

"Yes, and I like where you're going with this."

"My intuition told me to have our new associate, Mike Langdon, take the revolver over to TPD and have it checked out in the ballistics lab." Reed said. "Figured with Mike being a former Sheriff's homicide detective, he'd get his TPD counterparts to cooperate."

"What'd you learn?" Ravel asked eager beaverly.

"Won't get the results until tomorrow," Reed said. "I'd bet my Mustang GT that that's the weapon used to kill Alicia."

"What's the plan, Reed?" Jake asked convivially.

"Mike will bring us the ballistics test results early tomorrow morning. If it's a match, we all set out at smiling 10:10 a.m. Ravel, Marika and I will try to bring in Eden for questioning at Tampa PD. Jake, you bring in Zeke for questioning as well."

"Smart," he said. "We hit 'em both at the same time."

"Exactly, and let's hope this ends peacefully, but if it doesn't, all of us are to stay locked, cocked and ready to rock," Reed said.

"Roger that," Jake said.

Ravel and Marika were too occupied with tallying every pink flamingo on Ravel's pajamas, front and back, to respond properly to Reed's plan.

CHAPTER 30

BONAIRE

SOUTHERN CARIBBEAN · 2014

"Your Browning holds a rare place in history," Jake lectured by the light of the silvery moon.

"Even if I were to ignore you, as in *completely totally* ignore you, you'd still tell me about the Browning's rare place in history, wouldn't you?" Reed asked.

She and Jake were about to fire their sidearms in the direction of Olivia and Stanley.

"I certainly would proceed with my commentary," Jake said. "U.S. military and Waffen SS and Fallschirmjagers prized the Browning in World War II. It was the only production firearm to see common issue among Allied and Axis forces."

Pause.

"Jake, that bit of history will true my aim with this Browning. Thank you."

"You're welcome." Jake answered, doubtful of Reed's sincerity.

"You know, lover, there's nothing wrong with moments of silence," Reed said.

"Yeah, you're right," Jake conceded. "Guess that's why the Company made me go solo on missions after Sergio was killed."

"Did you still talk to yourself when you were alone on an assignment?"

"A little."

"Perfectly normal, perfectly normal," Reed said.

"Thanks."

"C'mon, me and my girlfriend, we're itching to trigger some rounds at Olivia and Stanley."

"Now!"

Reed chambered a round and took aim.

"Spread your fire along the top of the dunes. Keep it frenetic, haphazard. Make 'em think it's not ground cover."

Doesn't ever stop talking, does he, Reed thought.

"Roger that," she replied, as she *popped-boomed popped-boomed* rounds into the Caribbean night.

"Fuck, this is fun!" Reed exclaimed. "Take that and that, bad guys!"

Won't think this is fun once she gets close and comfy with her first kill, Jake thought.

The Browning was empty. She continued to pull the trigger. "Wanna give me another clip?" she asked.

Jake chuckled softly.

Out of habit, because he knew his British Bulldog held five cartridges, he spun the revolver's chamber, creating a seductive clickety-whir. He barned the chamber with a snap of his wrist.

He fired the Bull Dog in a random pattern.

Suddenly, an object larger than a golf ball *thwacked* on the wood floor.

"Fore!" Stanley yelled. "See what a mess you've got yourself into, you didn't fool me with your bullshit fire pattern, Duty Free."

The object cozied into the mattress.

"Is that a grenade?" Reed asked.

"Yeah, but it's a dummy. They're demonstrating they can high-iron an M67 into our home."

Reed picked up the grenade.

"Can I keep it?"

"Sure, it'll be more weight in the ruck, but you deserve a souvenir."

He uncased his binoculars. He scanned the sandy ridgeline where Olivia and Stanley likely were hiding.

"I make out movement over there, definitely not giant sand crabs."

"How about atomic-radiated red ants the size of a VW Bug?" she asked.

"Colorful image, but they're more like a pair of sand weasels in need of exterminating."

"So, what do we do next?" she inquired.

"Like I said earlier, we grab the rucksack and fuck off outta here," Jake said. "The real M67's will be dropping like iguanas in a winter freeze."

"Where are we going?" Reed asked.

"Like I said earlier, we'll zig-zag down to the beach. Thought we'd catch some submarine races."

"Seriously, dude, you need to update your playa lines."

Whoosh! Plink! Whoosh! Plink!

"I'll make a note of that. Meantime, *we gotta go*," Jake said.

Go they did. With deliberate speed.

They weren't ten zig-zagged feet from the beach shack, when two explosions erupted inside the dilapidated structure.

The blast from the M67 grenades torpedoed the rusty metal shingles on the roof, causing rusty steel sheeting to buoy up like flaming cherry Pop-Tarts catapulting from a Haden Heritage four slicer.

Two more explosions followed.

The beach shack shattered all to hell, then caught fire.

Two more explosions reduced Jake and Reed's love shack to a fire and brimstone mini-cyclone.

Reed and Jake laid together on the wet-sand shoreline.

They stayed low and quiet as Egyptian cobras in a tomb raider's tent.

Reed whispered, "I think some sand got up in my panties."

Jake whispered back, "You'll be okay, long as a hermit crab didn't skittle up in there."

"Merci, Jacques Cousteau, now you got me worried."

Jake grinned.

"Don't abandon the *Calypso* just yet. We're safe down here. Safe from Olivia and Stanley, that is. Hermit crabs and sand fleas, whole different story."

It was Reed's turn to smile.

"Nervous, aren't you?"

"More anxious than nervous." Jake replied. "Don't want anything to happen to you."

Reed placed a sandy hand on Jake's shoulder.

"Listen, you screwed up when you got your head turned in Paris by that Irish operative ... what was her name?"

"Kennedy, Louise ... Lou Kennedy," Jake answered. "Won't make that mistake with you."

"Because you think I have sand enough for this mission?"

"Yeah, you have sand enough, and not just in your shorts," Jake said.

"Thanks, I actually believe you," Reed said. "Something tells me you've got a super-secret plan to get us out of this nasty predicament."

"You're right, I got a plan."

"Oh goody," Reed whispered back.

At only a few decibels above complete silence, Jake laid out the plan.

"Fucking-a, my man, I like it," Reed said. "It's risky, but doable."

A red-and-yellow-kills-a-fellow explosion erupted over what remained of Reed and Jake's charred maison de batons.

For just a minute or so longer, they stretched out alongside one another on the beach. They both knew they might not make it out alive.

A wave rushed up alongside them.

Jake gathered Reed into his muscular arms.

He kissed her with a passion that could've lasted from here to eternity.

Reed exhaled languorously.

"Just in case, love?" she asked.

"Yeah, babe, just in case."

CHAPTER 31

TAMPA, FLORIDA · 2022

"WE'RE NOT HERE to lick Green Stamps, Jake. Nothing that fruitless. Why, used to take filling five hundred Green Stamps books to get an egg timer. No, my friend, we're here on this beautiful day to confab, to enjoy each other's company and maybe settle a score."

"Sounds interesting, Doctor," Jake said.

He wore a red guayabera shirt with black slacks and black Mephisto sandals.

Dr. Hutchinson had on a dark tailored vest suit with a white shirt and high winged collars and a burgundy Victorian ascot scarf. He wore a charcoal Callahan frock coat over his suit.

Victorian steampunk? Jake wondered. Dig those crazy threads.

"You bet, Arland. Say, I'm really enjoying that suit and long coat."

"Do I look like an undertaker?"

"No."

"A butler."

"Not at all."

"Prince Albert in the can?"

"There you go."

"I was in the mood for wearing popular gentleman's attire from the mid-to late-eighteenth century. These are clothes much like Whistler wore. Does this getup suggest I'm more than just an enthusiast of Whistler's? Guilty as charged."

"Works for me," Jake said.

"And how about you, I love the guayabera. You look like Carlos Marcello's hitman in Havana, say around 1958."

"Or maybe 1959, when my assignment would've been to clip the Beard."

"Delightful retort," Arland exclaimed. "On to the work at hand."

Jake and Arland met in the sprawling Al Lopez Park on Himes Avenue in West Tampa. It was three p.m. on a Wednesday. The two men had the municipal park almost entirely to themselves. They sat at a picnic table under a shelter painted deep green and roofed in brown asphalt shingles. A broad tree canopy of live oak, sweetgum, hickory and red maple kept the men cool, while providing a degree of privacy.

Arland reached into his Brunello Cucinelli calfskin briefcase and extracted brightly colored plastic files.

He saw Jake eye spy his briefcase.

"You are an astute private inquiry agent," Arland said. "While it may look like some kind of a bribe, since it's a $5000 Italian leather briefcase, it was in reality a gift from parents whose son was murdered, and I played a small hand in finding the killer."

"Arland, I wasn't implying anything."

"Your eyes were, Jake."

"My apologies, then."

A mockingbird landed on Jake and Arland's picnic table. Known for its uncanny impressions of other bird calls, the moxie Mimus polyglottos appeared to extend a middle-feather salute to the men. It then took off to improve on its impression of a passerine songbird's rendition of the Ink Spots' "When the Swallows Come Back to Capistrano."

"On to Ms. Serrano's autopsy."

A thunderstorm, powerful and electroluxed, rapidly moved east from the Gulf of Mexico. The dark clouds possessed a terrorific beauty.

"What do we have, twenty minutes before we get doused?" Jake asked.

"Perfectly safe under this pavilion. Besides, I have a special surprise for you. I've asked an individual to join us."

"Is it in connection with Alicia?" Jake asked.

"Yes," Arland answered.

"Autopsy results, then the surprise?"

"Yes."

"Let's green-light this," Jake said as he kept watch on the fast-approaching storm.

Arland handed him a red plastic file that contained Alicia's autopsy report.

"Nothing surprising there," Arland reassured him. "She appeared to subsist on tequila, cannabis and cocaine, with an occasional Cuban sandwich and Spanish tortilla thrown in the mix.

Jake read the report.

"She took three rounds up close, probably didn't suffer a lot of pain," he said. "You're the pro here, Arland, any red flags in this report?"

Arland gazed stage left, uncertain of to how to respond.

"No red flags. Just an interesting discovery. Ms. Serrano was a virgin, a twenty-one-year-old virgin. Extraordinary for this day and age."

They sat in silence.

"Talk about dedication," Jake then said. "Alicia told me she hadn't time for romance, only for dance."

"For dance, for the BarraCubas, for Detective Friekorps," Arland added.

Jake raised his thick eyebrows.

Arland chuckled.

"Been talking with my contacts at TPD," he said. "Friekorps kept a snitch jacket on Ms. Serrano, and he was prone to brag about how he's getting wealthy from playing the Bavarians and the BarraCubas off one another, a dangerous game to play for someone with a big mouth and no self-control."

Jake shook his head in disgust.

"Prick also sold out Alicia to both biker gangs. He's responsible for her murder. What I would give to strangle him, very slowly."

Arland smiled like the wise sage that he was.

"You'll have your opportunity in just minutes. But remember, Friekorps is gold shielded. Hurt him, yes, kill him, absolutely not."

"Well, all right," Jake said exuberantly.

"Jake, do you promise not to kill him?" Arland asked somberly.

Jake shrugged, "Sure."

"Good, because he's walking up right now," Arland said, as he pointed a bony index finger over Jake's right shoulder.

Rain started when Friekorps was about 100 feet from their pavilion.

Ferocious winds whipped the trees, animating even the enormous grand live oaks.

Engulfing storm clouds, sponged full of fury and moisture, turned the sky a gray black. Then the tempest burst from its titanic teapot.

Jake turned to watch the lone figure loping casually toward him and Arland.

"Talk about a goddamned Faustian entrance," Jake said. "Bet the sap isn't even aware of it."

Friekorps got under the pavilion without uttering a hail fellow and well met.

He shook rain off himself like a shaggy dog story.

He blew green and yellow snot from his nose.

"Wassup, Doc?" Friekorps said.

Arland pulled a white hand towel from his briefcase and gave it to the detective.

"Don't blow your nose in that," he said.

"Whatever, Doc. Hey, who's the palooka? You call me out here in the middle of a fucking monsoon to meet Man Mountain Mike?"

"Detective Ernst Friekorps, allow me to introduce you to Jake Dupree," Arland announced.

Friekorps gave Jake an indifferent sidewave.

"I know who you are, Dupree," he said. "You and your wife, you rescued some blonde twinkies from being sold as sex slaves in Mexico, right?"

Jake gave Friekorps an equally indifferent sidewave.

Friekorps tossed the damp hand towel to Arland. Jake's silence irritated the detective.

"Got a problem with me?" he asked Jake, as he opened his black pleather jacket to display his pistol and gold shield.

Jake lifted his shirttail to expose a British Bulldog revolver in his waistband.

He rose from the picnic table and faced the detective. He was at least six inches taller than Friekorps.

"Nothing would make me happier than to shoot it out with you, asshole," Jake said. "So yeah, I got a major beef with you."

Friekorps was agitated. Sweat, not raindrops, rolled down his forehead.

"What's your so-called beef, big man?"

Jake squared up with Friekorps.

Arland, who remained seated, interjected, "Jake, remember your promise."

"Fuck almighty, Doc, you look like Dr. Paul Bearer," Friekorps said with nervous laughter.

"Arland might be dressed for your funeral," Jake said.

"Fuck off, Dupree," Friekorps scoffed. "Ima gold fuckin' shield, you can't touch me, aight?"

Jake smiled demonically, his blood lust approaching 212 degrees Fahrenheit.

"You're responsible for the death of Alicia Serrano, because you set her murder in motion. You're gonna pay for that. Haven't decided how I'm gonna hurt you, but I aim to see you bleed."

Friekorps spat on the cement floor.

The thunderstorm continued to pummel the pavilion.

The two men stared at each other, cut off from the world outside the pavilion by a four-sided waterfall.

Friekorps went for his pistol.

Jake grabbed the gun from him first. He examined it. He wasn't impressed.

"Piece of shit Baretta. Old Pietro had too much Campari when he designed this temperamental piccolo bestia sexy," Jake said.

Neither Arland nor Friekorps responded.

Jake shrugged.

With quickness reminiscent of Satchel Paige throwing to home plate, Jake wound up and fastballed the Beretta *just a little more than outside* in the thunderstorm.

Friekorps jerked his head back and forth, incredulous over what he just witnessed.

"You fucking asshole!" he screamed.

Should I make those his last words? Jake wondered.

Nah, fuhgeddaboudit, Jake, Arland thought, after recognizing the expression on Jake's face.

Static, static, static went Friekorp's brain.

Friekorps lunged at Jake, who deftly sidestepped him, while lunar landing a ferocious RC Cola right cross to Friekorps' Moonpie face.

Thunder clapped apocalyptically. A lightning bolt struck a hickory tree, turning it into an exploding munitions depot of a show.

Friekorps fell to his knees. His broken nose fauceted twin streamlets of brilliant red blood. Saliva spooled from his mouth.

He feigned he was beaten.

Suddenly, he jumped up like a frightened feral cat.

He took off. Was he running scared?

He wasn't.

Friekorps was searching for his pistol.

Jake caught on quickly.

He warned loudly, "Don't make me blow a hole through your skull, Friekorps."

Arland counseled Jake, "Self-control, my friend, let nature take its course."

With his back to Arland, Jake begrudgingly nodded yes.

Friekorps thought he found his Beretta, but the weapon was a pitted chrome .357 Magnum revolver with three rounds left in the chamber.

"Never know what you're going to find in a City of Tampa park," Arland said, rather ghoulishly. "Before you know it, the fool will trip over an unfortunate."

Crack went the thunder, as if it were crushing bones and skulls into a fine powder.

A lightning bolt landed, this time closer to the pavilion.

Friekorps raised the XXXL revolver.

He aimed unsteadily at Jake in the pavilion.

He cocked back the hammer.

He saw Jake raise his revolver.

Then nature, in fact, took its course.

After a nasty thunderclap, a bolt of lightning currented 300 million volts of electricity atop the detective's head, which geysered like an over-ripe pumpkin. Shards of brain matter, flesh, hair, bone, teeth and, quite possibly, pieces of Van Gogh's missing right ear jettisoned from the headless Ernst Friekorps.

"Hope that was a lesson learned, Ernie," Arland called out puckishly.

The only parts left intact of Ernie's head were his eyeballs a pop pop popping out of their sockets like a pair of airborne dice. They *plopped plopped, fizzed fizzed* into a rain puddle.

The eyeballs floated on the surface of the murky water.

"Snake eyes!" Dr. Arland Hutchinson screamed with joy.

CHAPTER 32

BONAIRE

SOUTHERN CARIBBEAN · 2014

JAKE AND REED set in motion a two-prong beachhead counterattack by silently crawling away in opposite directions.

They left behind the bugout bag.

Reed had the Browning, Jake his Bull Dog revolver.

They maneuvered around the shack that resembled the Wicker Man in flames.

Olivia and Stanley continued golfing M67 grenades doom kabooming into the night.

Smoke from the fire swirled like mad sinning souls seeking salvation.

Consequently, Jake and Reed had decent cover to edge closer to the hit team's position.

"These people won't hesitate to kill you," Jake whispered to Reed, before they split off into the starry Van Gogh night. "You get your one and only chance, you take it, don't bail, you must put them down. Time for you to be totally uncivilized. It's your first kill, savor it."

Jesus, he's sexy, Reed thought. If it weren't for the sky dropping bomb balls, I'd fuck him right now.

Low sand berms kept them out of Olivia and Stanley's sight.

Tradewinds from the Atlantic bullied forward crashing waves, thereby muffling Reed's and Jake's movement as they crawled closer.

Both now could hear Olivia and Stanley arguing.

"I'm telling you, Liv, you hooked that last one."

"Fuck I did, Stan."

"The fuck you did is right. You blew up the cistern. That isn't very green of you."

"I'd like to be on a real green, maybe at Ponte Vedra, instead of this saber-toothed tiger's litter box."

Stanley pinged another grenade.

"Only two grenades left, Olivia."

Five, four three, two, one. The grenade went off in dramatic style.

Stanley placed the one-wood over his right shoulder. He silhouetted against red and orange and yellow flames.

"Look at that," Olivia said of Stanley. "It's John Daly in hell ... hmm, ladies and gentlemen, is he going to use a nine iron to get over that bonfire trap, when a wedge is the smarter choice?"

Stanley propped the one-wood in his lime green double-knit crotch. He removed his golf glove. He took off his white golf cleats and replaced them with black combat boots.

"You sound just like Jim Nance at Augusta, Ollie, except your voice is more virulent."

"Quel estrange compliment, mais je l'accepte," Olivia replied.

Stanley took Olivia into his arms.

"Tish, you spoke French!"

Olivia gave him un petit bisou sur la joue.

"Settle down, Gomez darling, we got two smoked barbecue stiffs to bag and dump in the deep."

Stanley lifted his nose into the wind.

"That's odd," he said.

"What is it?"

"I can't pick up the scent of smoked meat."

"Then let's mount up and go find the happy couple. Where is the AK-50?"

Known as the "Skunk Thumper," the AK-50 assault rifle was an American-made Kalashnikov rifle built to fire .50 Beowulf cartridges.

Tweren't nothing pink tea about this rifle, Stanley liked to say.

"Thumpers are over in their cases, dearest."

"Then snap to it, we got places to go and bodies to dunk." Olivia ordered.

Jake jumped out from behind a sand berm. He aimed the Bull Dog at the hit team.

"You chose the wrong pair of beach bums to fuck with," he said in a calm, even voice. "And I was just realizing my vision for the beachside abode."

"Where's Agent 99, Max?" Olivia asked.

"Over here, Olivia."

Reed emerged from the darkness.

She experienced a quaking adrenaline rush.

Is this blood lust? she wondered.

"Jacob, are you really going to kill us?" Olivia asked. "We aren't armed, for goodness sake."

"Olivia, I dare you to call me 'Jacob' again."

"Stop it right now," she admonished. "What would your mother say about murdering a defenseless older woman ... Jacob?"

Jacob kept the revolver pointed at Olivia, while Reed covered a nervous, perspiring Stanley.

"You know what my mom would say about this clusterfuck of yours, Olivia?" Jake asked.

"What?"

"Kill her before she kills you."

Mom sounds like a badass, Reed noted. Gotta be sure to wear that orange hunting vest when I'm around her in deer season.

"Please don't hurt me, Jake, I'm begging you," Olivia pleaded.

"Sorry, but Mom's always right. Been real, Olivia. Goodbye."

Jake fired three rounds into her. One in the forehead, a second in her neck, a third round in her chest.

Olivia's lifeless body crumpled undignifiedly upon sand and crushed shells.

Meanwhile, Stanley creepy creeped toward the two rifle case.

Witnessing Jake fire successive rounds into Olivia caused Reed to freeze just long enough for Stanley to desperately attempt to get to the assault rifles

With uncanny quickness for a big man, he leapt for the rifle cases, opened the case nearest him, then extracted an AK-50.

Reed got her bearings in time to warn Stanley, "Drop the rifle or I'll drop you."

"Not likely, rook," Stanley said.

He was about to put a full clip into the rifle, when Jake yelled, "Put him down, Reed, now!"

Reed kept her eyes on Stanley.

"Jake, will you please shut the hell up, I got this."

Jake shut the hell up.

Stanley popped the clip into the AK-50.

As he raised the rifle, Reed emptied her Browning into Stanley.

She didn't miss once.

Pop! Pop! Pop! Pop! Pop! Pop! Pop! Pop! Pop! Pop!

Stanley seized up like a Ford Pinto on a hot summer afternoon on an L.A. freeway.

He fell backwards onto a sand berm.

Reed stood over him.

She replaced the empty clip with a full one.

"You're only a girl," Stanley gurgled.

His eyes froze Stalingrad dead.

"Yeah, well, this girl just did a woman's job, motherfucker," Reed said in a deep, halting voice.

"Coming up behind you," Jake said.

He gently took the Browning from Reed.

"Overkill on my part, Jake?"

"No such thing, my love."

CHAPTER 33

TAMPA, FLORIDA · 2022

"LET's hit BarraCubas and Bavarians at the same time," Reed declared. "And we need to keep the body count to zero."

"Won't let me have any fun, will you?" Jake complained facetiously.

"C'mon now, ya big palooka," Ravel interjected. "We don't your PTSD flaring up."

The big palooka smiled at her.

"Do you actually care about me, Rave?"

"Can't believe I'm saying this, but I do care about you," Ravel answered.

Jake gently tapped the tip of her tiny Swiss chalet ski-slope nose.

Ravel responded by lightly kissing his left cheek.

Reed, Jake, Ravel and Marika sat in the penthouse living room to strategize how to best confront the BarraCubas and the Bavarians.

"I think your kissing Jake has made Marika jealous," Reed commented jocularly.

Ravel *tsked*.

"People get like that around me."

Ravel and Marika and Reed laughed together, though Marika didn't entirely understand why.

"I am not svartsjuk, liten pumpa," Marika said to Ravel. "Jake is a man-child, I have no worries, correct?"

Ravel paused.

"Yeah, you probably have no reason to get your panties all in a bunch."

Marika frowned.

"But I don't wear the panties."

"Jesus, do women wear underwear anymore?" Reed asked.

Ravel giggled.

"Well, Whistler's Mother, an awful lot of women have set free their vulvarines."

"Wolverines?" Marika asked.

Ravel kissed her.

"No, not 'wolverines,' you goose, I said 'vulvarines'!"

Marika remained puzzled, as usual.

"Vulvarines ... lurviga fittor," Ravel said.

Marika's face lit up.

"Ja, ja, 'hairy pussies,' now I get it," she said triumphantly.

Reed snickered, then said, "All right, enough talk of lurviga fittor — we don't want Jake feeling uncomfortable."

He was lost in thought.

"Huh? Oh, I'm not uncomfortable ... hey, is lurviga fitter' really 'hairy pussies' in Swedish?"

"Ja," Marika confirmed.

"Yup," Ravel said.

"Apparently," Reed added. "Now, let's finish up here."

Jake saluted her. Ravel and Marika followed suit.

"Jake, can you handle the Bavarians by yourself?" Reed asked.

"It shouldn't be a problem. I'm going unarmed as a sign of peace with Mulraney. I see my mission as convincing him Zeke was the shooter. I don't know how it'll play out."

Reed showed concern for her husband.

"Is it a good idea to be unarmed with those thugs?"

"Long as Mulraney's in charge, there'll be no need for gunplay, my love. Can you trust me on that?"

"Yes," Reed answered with certainty.

Ravel interjected, "So the women folk are going to shoot it out with Paz and the BarraCubas?"

"No, we're not looking for a shootout, though the three of us will be armed. I'll have my Browning and Marika will have her Sig Sauer."

"Can I bring another NERF gun?" Ravel asked facetiously.

"Absolutely not, "Reed said. "Bring that derringer of yours."

"And what *is* our mission?" Marika asked.

"TPD confirmed this morning that Eden's revolver was the weapon used to murder Alicia." Reed answered. "We're heading over to the Floridan to face Paz and Eden, maybe we can convince Paz to have Eden turn herself in to TPD."

"What about Eden's Smith & Wesson?" Jake asked.

"TPD's holding on to it, but we're coming in hot under false pretensess—Paz thinks we're returning Eden's revolver and picking up Marika's belongings."

"For what it's worth, I think it's a solid plan," Jake said. "Does all this go down in the hotel lobby?"

"We're definitely staying in the grand lobby," Reed said.

"Shall we engage our targets at 1200 hours?" Jake asked Reed.

"Gomez, darling, you spoke military jargon!" Reed exclaimed.

She gave Jake a light peck, then said, "Yes, we engage at noon ... you leave ahead of us, Jake, since it won't take long for us to walk to the Floridan."

Jake nodded affirmatively.

"Excellent, time to get in the shit," he said excitedly.

"Just be careful," Reed urged. "All goes well, I'll have a special surprise for you tonight."

Jake gulped.

"Thoroughly incentivized, I am."

———

"Whatcha' peddling today, old man?"

Zeke was feeling his Wheaties at high noon. It helped or hindered that he had avalanched the breakfast cereal in refined sugar and submerged it in chocolate milk.

Jake approached him at the iron gate of the Bavarians' compound.

"Not peddling anything, young man. But you remind me of a joke. Wanna hear it?"

Zeke fiddled with a long-barrel .38 handgun wedged tightly in the elastic band of his black underwear.

"Sure. Why not?"

"Traveling salesman was walkin' down a country road," Jake began.

"What's he selling?" Zeke asked.

"I dunno, maybe hair-growth tonic."

"Go on."

"Salesman needed to drop a deuce, but there wasn't a farmhouse anywhere nearby."

"So, what'd he do do?" Zeke asked, quite pleased with himself.

"He saw a pumpkin patch and ran to the biggest pumpkin on the ground."

"And then?"

"He cut open the top of the pumpkin and shit right into it."

"He have toilet paper?"

"No, and stop fucking interrupting."

"I bet he didn't," Zeke said.

"Three days later, farmer Cye was at the general store when he heard that same traveling salesman goof with the store owner about how the salesman took a dump in a pumpkin patch."

"Um huh."

"When the salesman left, Cye asked to use the store phone to call his wife."

"What'd he say to her?"

"He said, 'Vie, it's Cye, looks like there *was* shit in your pumpkin pie.'"

Zeke laughed like Friar Tuck on yet another bender.

"Damn, Dupree, that's a good 'un. Here's an even better one."

Jake smirked.

"Let's hear it, Zeke."

"How ya tell the difference between oral and rectal thermometers?"

Jake smirked again.

"The taste?"

"Fuck you, Dupree!"

"How about you call Den and tell him I want to smoke the proverbial peace pipe with him?"

"He knows you're here, Geronimo."

"Well then?"

Denizen Mulraney approached Zeke and Jake. He stood inside the gate.

"This better be good, Jake."

"It is, and I come unarmed."

"Smart man."

Jake looked over Mulraney's right shoulder to check out two women wearing only thong bikini bottoms ... one thong a hot pink, the other a bright purple ... while washing Mulraney's Continental.

"Any chance I can get my Riviera washed while I'm here?" Jake requested.

Mulraney laughed deprecatingly at his former m8's request.

"No way, Dupree, those are my old ladies," he said. "They serve only me."

"Excuse the fuck out of me, Den."

"What do you want to talk about?"

Jake grasped an iron bar, then said, "I'm here to hold Zeke accountable for the death of Alicia Serrano."

Zeke immediately went for his revolver.

Mulraney waved him off.

"What, Zeke, you gonna shoot an unarmed man?" Denizen said.

"Why not, Den?" Jake asked. "He's already shot and killed an unarmed twenty-one-year-old woman."

Zeke pulled the .38.

Mulraney slapped him to the ground.

"Don't you disrespect me," he yelled. "Get up off the ground."

Zeke held his reddened face.

"Give me that gun, boy, handle first," Mulraney ordered.

Zeke handed him the revolver.

"Dupree, what the hell?" Mulraney said.

"Do you know who Eden is?"

"Never met her, but I know *of* her. Paz has herself a first-class Abby Normal, she certainly does."

"Did you know Eden was jealous of Paz paying attention to Alicia?"

"Nope."

"Well, she was."

"So what?"

"Did you notice the Smith & Wesson Zeke carried around for a couple of days?"

"Of course. A heavy fucker. I figured Zeke got bored with lugging it around."

"Zeke's Smith & Wesson was the revolver used in Alicia's murder. TPD confirmed it this morning."

Mulraney squinted demonically at Zeke.

"Care to explain, boy, why your gun is in the possession of TPD ballistics?"

Zeke didn't hesitate.

"Swear to Jesus, that's not my gun."

"Then whose is it?" Mulraney gruffed.

"It belongs to Eden, Den," Jake said. "She gave it to Zeke, along with a few grand to kill Alicia."

"Bullshit!" Zeke yelled.

"Maybe not, young man," Mulraney said. "I heard you were hanging in Ybor City with a Hispanic broad that looked like a sumo cum lotta lesbo."

"That's not too bad, Den," Jake said.

"Thank you ... Jake."

"All right, I confess, that was Eden," Zeke said with deep resignation.

Mulraney put his hand on Zeke's left shoulder.

"Son, we could go 'round and 'round on the Emerald Park carousel all day long, and we'd end up right where we started, agree?"

"Yes, boss."

"Then tell me the truth."

"Gonna kill me?"

"Probably not."

Zeke toed the ground with his battle-scarred black engineer boots.

"Have to say it in front of him?" he said, pointing at Jake.

Mulraney grabbed Zeke's finger and snapped it like a piece of blackboard chalk.

Zeke immediately came down with a bad case of the screaming meemies.

"Isn't polite to point, boy," Mulraney said. "Yes, you must confess in Jake's presence."

"Boss, that Eden talked me into it. Flashed me a shitload of cash. Gave me the Smith & Wesson, but I returned it to her, swear I did."

"After you used it on Alicia?" Mulraney inquired.

"Yeah ... plus, she made me dress up like Johnny ... Johnny Strabler in *The Wild One*."

"Why?"

"Don't know. It's a shitty movie."

Mulraney kicked Zeke between his legs.

He punched Zeke's nose.

He pushed him to the ground.

He pulled handcuffs from a back pocket and cuffed Zeke behind his back.

"You think you're home free enough to give me a goddamn movie review?" Mulraney said.

"No, boss, please, please don't change your mind 'bout killin' me," Zeke cried out.

"If you don't stop cryin', I'll put you down with your own shitty cap gun."

"I'll stop cryin', boss."

"Good thing," Mulraney said.

Jake cleared his throat.

"Convinced, Den?"

Mulraney made as if he were washing his face sans water.

"Yes, Jake, I'm convinced."

"Want me to take him down to TPD headquarters?"

Mulraney emptied Zeke's revolver of its cartridges onto the ground.

"In case I get impulsive and shoot your sorry ass, Zeke ... or Jake's for that matter."

"Appreciate that, Den," Jake said

"And we're going to take care of this Zeke situation in-house," Mulraney added.

"Which means what?" Jake asked.

Mulraney turned to the two women washing his Continental and said, "Put on your goddamn t-shirts and get over cheer."

Zeke was on his knees.

"God no, boss, not them."

"Zeke, I said I probably wouldn't kill you, so I'll leave that to my mermaids."

"Your what?" Jake asked incredulously.

"Mermaids. Why, don't you believe in them?"

"No."

"Your loss," Mulraney retorted.

Wearing t-shirts now, the two women walked up and stood almost at attention in front of Mulraney.

"See those moonstone necklaces my old ladies are wearing?"

"Sure," Jake replied.

"That's how you can tell if a woman is a mermaid on land."

"Um huh."

"Still don't believe me?" Mulraney asked. "Corelia, Gemma, show this man your fangs."

One of the women was a blonde, the other a brunette. Their long hair was in matching braids. There was a wild sensuality about them.

They showed their fangs, or what could have been filed down incisors, then smiled into a snarl.

Corelia and Gemma both have Alexandrite crystal eyes, much like Ravel's, Jake noted.

Wonder if Ravel is a ... nah, cut it out, he thought. But I'll sure as hell ask her if she has moonstones.

"Ya'll are extraordinarily beautiful women," he said, as if in a trance.

Corelia and Gemma hissed viciously at him.

Mulraney raised his hand to silence the women.

They stopped hissing.

Hope they're current with their shots, Jake said to himself.

The tall one, is he free-range beefcake? Gemma wondered.

Pretty, pretty boy looks like a tasty chew toy, Corelia thought.

"Corelia and Gemma belong to me," Mulraney said with a chuckle. "Best be careful playin' with them, my man ... they're strong enough to shred your body through these iron bars."

Jake stepped back a foot or two.

"Thanks for the heads-up, but I meant no disrespect."

"No problem, Jake. A little-known fact is that mermaids are most attracted to pearls."

"Okay."

"Bet you don't have a single pearl on ya person," Mulraney postulated.

"Yeah, I forgot my mermaid treats."

Mulraney turned his attention back to Corelia and Gemma.

"Take Zeke inside. Put him in your water chamber. Feed him to the Irukandji."

Both women whistled like bottlenose dolphins.

"Boss, please, not the jellyfish," Zeke cried out.

"What, you'd prefer life without parole or death row, because you can't take a few hours of excruciating pain?"

"What are Irukandji?" Jake asked.

Mulraney flashed a devilish grin.

"Little tiny jellyfish, most are only a cubic centimeter big. Deadliest jellyfish in the world, they are."

"Oh God," Zeke moaned.

"Shut up, ya amadan," Mulraney shouted. "Now where was I, yes, we just got in a gross of the malo kingi species of Irukandji, and these children pack the most potent venoms in the world, while being no bigger than my thumbnail."

"Are they for aquariums?" Jake asked.

Coralia and Gemma gasped in horror.

"Jake, please don't use the 'A' word around them," Mulraney cautioned.

"You're kidding me," Jake deadpanned.

Mulraney frowned like a retiree who lost his fruit cup money by pitching pennies in the back alley of his nursing home.

"I never joke about my beautiful maidens of the sea."

Maidens of the sea smiled at Mulraney, in turn exposing their fangs.

"Gemma, help Zeke up," he ordered.

Using but one hand, Gemma lifted Zeke completely off the ground.

Impressive, Jake thought. Steroids, mermaid growth hormones or is Zeke made of balsa wood?

"Come along, butter sauce, our hungry babies are waiting for their chicken of the Zeke," Gemma said.

Geesh, all that and a bag of quips, Jake observed.

Mulraney reached into a front pocket and took out two pearl bracelets.

Corelia and Gemma hissed in delight.

He handed them the bracelets.

"Do ya a good job with this cryin' capon, you'll get more," he said.

The women fanged delight.

They led away Zeke as he called out from the last-gasp time zone, "I am so sorry, boss."

Mulraney shook his head in disgust. "It's high tide for you, Zeke."

"Boss, please!"

Displeased Boss turned his back on the dead man scuffling toward jellyfish doom.

"Satisfied, Jake?"

"Satisfied."

———

"Hot as fuck, right?" Ravel asked rhetorically.

"Um huh, the fuckiest hot," Marika said.

"Well, I love it!" Reed declared.

The three women walked from Reed and Jake's apartment to the Floridan in downtown Tampa.

It was suitably warm at 11:50 a.m.

Fortunately, Reed, Ravel and Marika wore matching Swedish-yellow linen tops and slacks, just as Jake had advised.

"Linen lets you flex, you've got room to move and best of all, you won't sweat your derriere off," he explained to Reed. "Try to think of the yellow linen outfits as high visibility safety vests."

As the women approached the hotel, Ravel whined, "Why do all of us have to look like Bananarama groupies?"

"We don't do anything haphazardly," Reed said.

"Please explain," Ravel asked.

"Things get helter skelter inside, we'll know not to shoot each other, all right?"

"Aight," Ravel answered.

"I understand, Reed," Marika said.

"Suck-up," Ravel countered.

"Suck-up?" Marika asked.

"Yeah, you know, ass kisser."

Marika giggled.

"I kiss only your little ass, Ravel," she said.

Ravel blushed ever so slightly.

"You're getting this down aren't you, love? The lingo, the double entendres."

"Ja, all … the … way down."

The women laughed.

"Isn't that so fucking cute," a woman said while walking behind them.

Reed stopped to see who had spoken.

It was Eden.

She wore a yellow ribbon 'round her bobbed black hair.

She wore a yellow t-shirt emblazoned with the Chiquita brand logo most prized among collectors, that of a naked blonde woman holding a banana while erupting from a giant peeled banana.

She wore a yellow scarf.

She wore yellow Crocs with yellow socks.

It was an ensemble befitting tonier Orlando rather than hipster Tampa.

A wardrobe coincidence? Something more nefarious?

"Like my outfit, O'Hara?" Eden asked.

She twirled gracefully.

"I do like your outfit, but how did you know?" Reed answered and asked.

Eden chuckled.

"Ernest T. Bass," she said.

"What about him?" Reed asked.

"No me preguntes y no te contare mentiras."

Reed appeared not to understand, even tossing in arched eyebrows for added effect.

Marika interjected, "Ask me no questions and I will tell you no lies."

"Impressive, Marika," Reed said.

"Tack, I watched a lot of the Andy Mayberry in Spanish with the BarraCubas. Wasn't anything else to do."

"It's time to go inside," Reed decreed. "Eden, care to join us?"

"More like you joining me, O'Hara."

"Fair enough."

Eden led Reed, Ravel and Marika into the hotel lobby.

There was Paz standing by herself, the center of attention in the center of the Floridan lobby.

She wore a Versace black velvet catsuit, with sheer striped panels revealing her nude bra and panties.

"Hello, Kitty," Ravel said. "Gettin' cat scratch fever over here."

The women approached Paz.

Eden joined Paz at her right side.

Reed faced Paz, with Ravel on her right side and Marika on her left.

The Art of War be damned, Paz thought.

"Marika, do you want to sit this one out?" Paz said. "It'd even the odds and keep you safe."

Marika scoffed.

"Why should I worry about safety, when all we're doing is getting my property and giving Eden hers?"

Eden scoffed.

"Careful, cutey, don't get caught in a crossfire."

"Why a crossfire?" Marika asked.

"We're not here to barter," Eden warned. "And you better have brought the firing pins and my revolver."

She followed with a full-fledged boisterous scoff.

"Eden's right." Paz said. "You're in over your head."

Suddenly, Timeshares for Jesus sales rep Tiffany approached Ravel. She wore a revealing soft pink romper with four-inch wedge sandals. She pulled a hot pink faux fur wheelie bag, which displayed Tom Brady as Jesus. TB12's fiery red eyes followed everyone in the lobby.

It was Barbie meets Barbarella.

"Ravel! How are you?"

Ravel whispered, "Isn't a good time, Tiff."

"Why not?" Tiff asked. "Can't we go to the bar, didn't we hit it off the other day?"

"We did hit it off, but I'm here on business, it's best you don't stick around."

"Oooo, sounds exciting, but I can't stay, really I can't," Tiff said. "I'm shipping up to Boston in a couple hours to see my boo Dimitris or Nikolas or Christos, one of those, they're all Greek to me."

"Tiff, I don't have time today."

Tiff narrowed-eye Ravel.

"I only wanted to give you my paperback. I'm done with it. Want it?"

Ravel took the book from Tiff.

"Thank you. C'mere, let me give you a kiss."

Ravel kissed her hard on the mouth. Tiffany's pink lip gloss smeared onto Ravel's lips.

"Woo, Ravel, best chicklet kiss ever," Tiff exclaimed.

"Nothing sweeter than a hetero girl's compliment, but you have to go, right now." Ravel said.

Pink Lady Tiffany roller strolled away outside into the brutal sunshine.

Paz and Eden annoyed Marika.

"Do not do the coddle with me, either one of you. You don't frighten me, Eden, and I'm going to tell the police everything about Alicia."

"Marika, don't say that," Reed said.

"Are you saying Eden was involved with Alicia's death?" Paz asked.

"First, Paz, that's a helluva outfit you've got on, far more revealing than anything I'd ever wear,' she said.

"Gracias, O'Hara, but don't sell yourself short. You got a sexy vibe. You're welcome to come over anytime and play dress up with me."

Eden scowled at Paz.

Wonder if the humidity makes you horny here? Marika thought. Should be the proper study done.

"Thanks, but no thanks, Paz. The real reason we're here is to bring Eden to justice for the death of Alicia Serrano."

Paz cut off Eden when she was about to speak.

"How did Eden have anything to do with that?" Paz said in a singularly calm voice.

Does this woman ever get flustered? Reed wondered.

"It's as simple as it is pathetic, Paz. Eden was jealous of your attraction to Alicia, so she hired a Bavarian named Zeke to gun her down last Saturday night."

"Mentiras! Mentiras!" Eden cried out.

People in the grand lobby, several of whom studied slick brochures of local attractions on display next to the concierge desk, pretended not to stare at Eden.

"Silencio, Eden, ahora," Paz commanded.

A restless silence set in, so the crowd returned to booking excursions to mermaids of Weekie Wachee or swamp things of Gatorland or tyrannosauruses, triceratops and stegosauruses of Dinosaur World.

Marika went from wingman to agitator in a Blink 182.

Low voiced, she countered to Eden, "Those are *not* lies. I know, Eden. I heard you on the phone with that Bavarian Zeke."

Using an even lower voice, Eden replied, "Novia, got some big mouth on you, needs some stitching up, con alambre de espino."

Marika was demonstrably annoyed.

"What is with you and barbed wire? Always the barbed wire. You need to chill out with some vodka in the sauna. Lakares order."

Eden looked to Ravel for help, as the Cuban didn't understand "Lakares order."

Reed nudged Ravel.

"What? Oh yeah. Marika said either 'doctor's orders' or 'dachshund's odors.' You pick'em."

Eden remained lost in translation.

"Que?"

"Enough of this SHIT!" Paz yelled.

Excursionists again looked up from their colorful touron brochures.

This time, they didn't pretend not to stare.

Even Lloyd the bartender abandoned his post in the "Surefire Room" to find out who dared raise a voice in the sacred palace of Old Florida opulence.

Paz regained her composure.

"It's all right, everyone. You know us Cubans, hard to tell when we're making love or making war. Lo siento, I'm sorry for the commotion. We shall be quiet as titty mice."

Betcha she's used that old chestnut a few times, Reed thought.

A few people giggled at Paz's remark. Most simply turned away.

Lloyd the bartender saluted Paz, then marched double-time back to his posting behind the bar.

"I take it, O'Hara, you're not going to return Eden's revolver," Paz said.

"No, we are not," Reed said, striking the stance of a battle-ready Hippolyta. "Tampa Police are keeping it, since it's the weapon used in the shooting death of Alicia Serrano, all of this just because Eden was jealous of the attention you paid to Alicia."

"Mas mentiras, mas mentiras," Eden said in a tone of desperation.

Paz held Eden's face with both her hands. She kissed Eden ever so sensually.

"You are my one and only passion, querida, my one and only. I never have bedded anyone else," Paz proffered.

That is a damn lie, Marika thought indignantly.

"And Alicia?" Eden asked.

"Nothing more than a little flirtation."

"Es la verdad?"

"Claro, but is O'Hara right? Did you have Alicia killed because you were jealous of her?"

Jesus, talk about a loaded question, Ravel thought.

"Yes ... I mean, no," Eden stuttered.

"So, there's another reason you killed her?" Paz asked.

"There is no reason, because I didn't mean for her to get killed. I just wanted to scare her away from you. That Zeke, he took it too far. On my mother's grave, I did not want Alicia to die."

Paz let out a black mamba's *hissss*.

"You don't even know where your mother's grave is, do you, Eden?"

"No, but that doesn't mean my mother, may she rest in peace, isn't in a grave."

"You ... never ... knew ... your ... mother," Paz fumed.

"I'm still telling the truth!"

Paz paused to exhale deeply.

"Si, a veces, la verdad es mas extrana que la ficcion," she allowed.

Eden's face brightened.

"So, you believe me?"

"No," Paz replied.

"Porque?"

"Dos razones. Primero, the police, they say your gun was used to kill our baby girl, right?"

"Yes, but ..."

"Numero dos, Marika says she was a witness to your scheme."

"Not a scheme, a prank that went bad. Una broma, mi Paz."

"A deadly joke, Eden," Paz countered. "And Marika right over there is going to put you in prison forever."

Goddamn it, Paz is tossing Marika to Eden, Reed thought.

"Paz, shall we go together to take Eden to the police station," Reed asked gently.

Before Paz could answer, Eden brandished a pistol.

"Not gonna get arrested, no way," she declared defiantly. "Take all of you to hell before I go back to prison."

Eden yanked the yellow ribbon from her black Cuban hair.

She threw the ribbon at Marika, then spat at her, with foamy droplets of spittle landing on the Swede's boots.

Marika looked at her violated boots. She recalled what she said to Ravel earlier in the day.

"If I die today during some Custer fuck at the hotel, I want everyone to know I died with my boots on."

Eden aimed her pistol at Marika.

It was too late for Marika to draw her Sig Sauer.

Eden fired at her.

The shot shattered full-on into Marika's chest. The Swede collapsed on the morgue-cold white Carrera lobby floor. Her blood made an expanding red ink spot on her yellow blouse.

Without hesitation, Ravel used her derringer to plunk Eden twice in the head. The .22 caliber rounds ping-ponged in Eden's cranium. Her brain most certainly imploded into a crockpot of washday mush.

Eden dropped dead.

Paz screamed. Her trademark poise vaporized completely.

"You killed my Eden!"

She rushed toward Ravel. She held in her left hand the opened abalone-handle switchblade.

Employing the same Browning 9mm pistol she used to kill Stanley in Bonaire, Reed calmly took aim. She fired a round that traveled at a velocity of 1200 feet per second or 853 miles per hour. It entered Paz's right temple and exited her left.

Paz Iberra died instantly, denied any memorable last words about her tough life or about how dreadful Reed looked in that plantana amarillo outfit.

However, Marika got in her two ores' worth before she died.

Ravel was on her knees and holding her paramour.

"You know what, my lover?" Marika gurgled.

"What baby?" Ravel asked, as tears riveleted down her face.

"Your scars make you more beautiful," Marika said. "Jag iskar dig."

While keeping her small hand over the gaping wound in Marika's chest, Ravel kissed Marika for the last time.

"My Ravel, I'm bleeding, I'm pleading ..."

Those were Marika's last words.

Within seconds, Ravel's beautiful Viking warrior was Valhalla bound for glory.

"I love you, too," Ravel uttered, too late for Marika to hear her.

Chapter 34

Bonaire

Her face and hands smeared with Stanley's blood, Reed struggled to see the positive side of killing a fellow human being.

"I rarely got to do this," Jake said of the blood ritual. "Usually had to get the hell out of there, might be why I'm so screwed up."

He instructed Reed to daub Stanley's blood on her forehead and cheeks.

"First time I took down a deer in Upstate New York, my father introduced me to the ritual."

"Feels sticky and gross," Reed said. "And good luck describing that smell."

"You're not putting on make-up. No need to be neat and precise, right? You're a blood warrior now. The ritual signifies your respect for the kill. You defeated the enemy. You saved your life. You saved mine. You owe no one an apology."

Reed nodded in agreement with Jake.

She daubed blood on both earlobes and on the tip of her nose.

Jake anointed himself with Olivia's blood. He resembled a Port-au-Prince voodoo papaloa seeking Bondye en ce au Bonaire macabre burlesque.

He smiled ghoulishly at Reed.

"You're very messy, Reed remarked. "Someone, preferably a woman, needs to teach you how to properly apply spilt blood to your face."

Jake ignored her.

"We can't take too long here, Reed. Even though we're far enough away from town, somebody might've heard the ruckus and called the police."

"Forget about the police, Jake, it's Chinatown," Reed said through her blood mask.

He laughed, then said, "Goddamn, I love you so much."

"And I you, Mr. Gittes."

The pair sat in lotus position near the bodies of Olivia and Stanley.

The smoldering beach shack resembled a mosh pit at a Napalm Death concert.

Jake proffered, "Did you know the Bible mis-translated the Commandment, 'Though shall not kill'?"

"*What?*" Reed asked.

She was annoyed with his loquaciousness. Again.

"Yeah, they mixed up the ancient Greek words for 'kill' and 'murder.'"

"*Humpf,*" Reed grunted.

"The Commandment should have warned, 'Thou shall not murder.'"

Reed uncrossed her legs, stood up, then said, "Cry me a swamii riva, that actually helps a little."

Jake stood as well.

"We need to go down to the water to wash off the blood, which'll conclude the ritual."

Before they left for the beach, Jake grabbed two M67 grenades.

"Why'd you take those?" Reed asked.

"Kidding me? These babies are hard to find. Besides, never know when you need to explode a noun or two in quick order."

"Exploding nouns, huh?" Reed asked.

"Yes."

"As in, blowing up a person, place or thing?" Reed wondered.

"You got it, mi lady."

"Hold on there. How're you going to get the grenades through Customs?"

Jake grinned.

"Who says I'm going through Customs?"

He and Reed trekked by moonlight down the shoreline.

They came to a gathering of cairns that were carefully stacked stones, some a few inches tall and others as much as two-feet high, erected to honor the departed or to declare love found or lost or found again.

"I feel like Gulliver hangin' with the Lilliputians," Reed said, as she walked among the cairns.

"I feel like the big kid on the beach 'bout to bully over rock towers and sandcastles and any Lilliputians who get in my way."

Reed chuckled.

"Mothra Leo or Godzilla?"

Jake didn't hesitate: "Definitely Mothra Leo."

"Tell me," Reed said. "Do you still enjoy breaking things and making people cry?"

"Of course, I still like to make people cry, but only if they're perfectly awful people," he said nonchalantly. "And I remain committed to breaking stuff, on or off the clock."

Two-foot waves kept a steady rhythm, ceaselessly reaching the shoreline, then summarily retreating. The waves reminded Reed and Jake that theirs was a small part of a larger world reluctantly hosting humanity's gross stupidity, unchecked greed and a taste for violence.

As they washed off the blood in brisk Atlantic saltwater, Reed did as Jake suggested. She performed the ritual reverentially, slowly releasing Stanley's congealed blood to the waves.

Jake did the same with Olivia's blood.

The ritual was complete.

After hand-toweling off, they stood arm-in-arm, gazing at a lonesome moon, an infinity of stars, an always agitated Atlantic Ocean and their charcoal-briquette love pad.

Reed hugged Jake.

"What are your plans, love, and does Reed O'Hara fit into them?"

"Reed O'Hara?" Jake asked facetiously.

"Yeah, that pesky broad you can't shake," she said.

"Oh right, the woman who slips into third-person sometimes. Yes, she fits into my plans."

They kissed.

"So, let's hear it," Reed demanded.

"We first need to walk on the shoreline until we get to my friendly local arms dealer's home. It's just a shack, but I don't think you'll complain about resting on a soft dry bed."

"Any sand fleas?" Reed inquired nervously.

"Sure, but they're housebroken," Jake answered jovially.

"He won't mind that we stay with him?"

Jake smiled.

"Not after I give him the M67's, just before we leave the island."

"Clever man," Reed said. "But what do we do in the morning?"

"We wash up, grab a banana, pack our gear, then part company."

She shook her head.

"Wait ... what?"

"Don't worry, Reed, at least we'll always have Bonaire," Jake said solemnly.

Pause. Another pause. Yet another. All syncopated with Reed's short breaths.

"Are you fucking with me?" she asked.

"A little. But we must go our separate ways. I'm leaving Bonaire in a smuggler's cove sort of way. You're getting out of here in the more conventional legal manner, all right?"

Reed parkoured up to Jake's left ear, darting her tongue all around his ear, then whisper sang, *"But I'm leaving on a jet plane, don't know when I'll be back again, oh babe, I hate to go."*

Jake slowly exhaled.

"Any chance, sweetheart?"

Reed giggled.

"Nope. Not until I see you again in Tampa Bay, on our wedding night."

"Not until our wedding night?" Jake practically screeched.

"Well, I could be talked into a rehearsal or two before the Big Signing Day."

Jake held her in his arms.

"Reed, will you marry me?"

"After what I've been through with you?"

"Yes, after all that," Jake said.

"I'll pass," Reed said.

"You'd pass on an epically exciting marriage, one filled with adventure and intrigue? And sex? Lots of sex?"

"Tell you what, my handsome buccaneer, I'll marry you if you keep the bloodletting to a minimum."

"Deal," Jake said triumphantly.

They kissed passionately, then held each other as the sun hinted at a blood orange sunrise.

They held hands as they walked along a shimmering shoreline.

CHAPTER 35

TAMPA, FLORIDA · 2022

ENTERING THEIR APARTMENT AT MIDNIGHT, Jake didn't notice the hand grenade sitting atop his bookcase full of *Harvard Classics* in the dining room.

Mars *and* Venus could attack, I still wouldn't be the dope to wake her up, he vowed.

The apartment's darkened great room was illuminated by a lone and lonely dining room floor lamp.

Jake finally spotted the hand grenade.

He walked to his bookcase, which was next to Reed's bookcase of her own *Harvard Classics* set.

He picked up the grenade and idly tossed it up and down in his hand.

The ordnance was Reed's souvenir from the Bonaire Affair. The dud M67 grenade kept in place a sandalwood-perfumed envelope marked with his name on it. The handwriting was in Reed's calligraphy.

Holding the envelope while basking in their home's peaceful milieu, he thought of somber events having occurred recently.

Jake, Reed and Ravel arranged for Marika's body to be flown to Sweden, where grieving parents awaited the return of their beloved daughter's body.

Ravel paid all expenses related to Marika's trip home.

She was devastated to lose her beautiful lanky lover.

Jake sat with Ravel on a saltwater-and sun-burnished wooden bench far out on Ballast Point pier on Bayshore Boulevard in Tampa.

"Could you use a hug?" he asked her.

Violet eyes still deluged in tears, Ravel smiled at Jake, then said, "Creepo fish guy over there asked me the same question, said no to him, but I'll say yes to you."

Diminutive Ravel disappeared into Jake's lumberjack arms.

They hugged as if neither wished to let go. Nothing less than a Miracle at Lourdes, Jake remained silent as Ravel cocooned in his body warmth.

Then she pressed her breasts against him while making massage circles with her hands on his back.

"That's your reward for not talking," she said.

Her eyes twinkled, as she lifted her head to lock into his frosty blues.

Jake understood.

He bent down, way down, to kiss Ravel.

He found her kiss sensual, soft, overpowering.

"Ever get a kissing lesson from Reed?" Jake asked her.

"I wish," she opined.

"You understand we'll have to discuss this tender moment with Reed?"

Ravel still held on to Jake.

"I kissed a boy, and I liked it," she whispered.

"I'll talk with Reed tonight," Jake said.

Ravel released him.

"No, I'll talk to her. It'll go better that way."

"As you wish, Rave."

She placed her hand on his chest.

"Don't get comfortable kissing me, but thank you, Jake. It took me a long time to realize you're a helluva good dude."

Still standing in the penthouse dining room, Jake started opening Reed's envelope, then stopped.

Is this the big kiss-off? he wondered. Probably deserve it, been such a shitty husband lately.

He set the envelope back down on the bookshelf.

He admired the two bookcases of *Harvard Classics*, his, a gift from his parents, hers, a gift from her former principal at Dupont Junior High School in West Virginia, who sent her one volume a month when she and her family moved to Florida. She received the last volume days before her graduation from Clearwater High School.

Then he thought of the burial at sea.

As the sun set like a Spanish gold doubloon frame by frame returning to its sunken galleon beneath the Gulf of Mexico, the group performed Alicia's scattering at the north end of the Clearwater Beach barrier island.

Denizen Mulraney and his female companions, Corelia and Gemma, stood alongside Jake, Reed and Ravel on the Carlouel Yacht Club boardwalk that led to the pristine white sand beach.

"Shall we make amends and return to being friends, my brother?" Denizen asked Jake.

"You bet, Den."

The men shook hands, then hugged the hug of bloodied brothers in arms not yet willing to give up the ghost.

Having received permission from Reed and Jake, Denizen instructed Gemma and Corelia to swim about a hundred feet out in the Gulf, taking with them the cremains of Alicia Serrano.

No one spoke as the mermaids freestyled out into the aquamarine water.

Gemma and Corelia swam until Denizen signaled them to stop.

Jake had his arms around Reed and Ravel, as the trio watched the women scatter Alicia's ashes.

"Ar dheis Dé go raibh a sí," Dennizen said in Irish Gaelic.

Ravel looked askance at him.

Denizen smiled at her.

"That's, 'May her soul be at God's right hand,' for you heathens."

"Thank you, biker guy," Ravel replied.

Corelia and Gemma swam back ashore.

Suddenly, Reed reached across and accidentally palmed Jake's crotch while trying to get his attention.

"Oh, sorry, Sparky, but did I just see two shiny fishtails?"

Denizen interjected, "Aye, lass, that you did, right Jake?"

"That's right, Den," Jake answered. "To borrow from Anais Nin, they must be mermaids, because they have no fear of depths and a great fear of shallow living."

The group let out a collective groan.

Even the mermaids rolled their eyes.

Reed took from her pocket two strands of Akoya pearls. She gave them to Corelia and Gemma, who were overjoyed with the gifts.

"Very nice of you, Reed," Denizen said. "Allow me someday to return the favor."

She gave him a stern look.

"Best favor you can give me is to not get my husband involved in any of your fuckwit schemes," she declared.

Denizen half nodded at her.

Jake couldn't take it any longer. He had to know what Reed wrote to him.

He tore open the envelope.

The note was in an elegant calligraphy that Reed only recently perfected:

Jake -

I am sorry for the ill feelings I held toward you. I understand better now. You are your own person, not some extension of myself. I shall endeavor to see you as my equal and I trust you will keep communicating with me.

I love you very much and plan on growing old and even crankier with you. As I told you, I have a very special gift for you. The gift will expire in the morning and do not expect to receive it ever again. Ravel and I are waiting for you in the master bedroom. You'll find us snuggling naked under the duvet. Please join us, lover.

-Reed

Jake carefully folded the note and returned it to its envelope. He returned the envelope to the top of his bookcase. He placed Reed's Bonaire souvenir on top of the envelope.

He walked quietly toward the master bedroom.

He noticed a full-Windsor rep tie hanging on the doorknob.

As he opened the door to the bedroom, where Reed and Ravel awaited his joining them in the king bed, he realized one amazing adventure concluded, as another even more wondrous adventure was about to begin.

And really, who doesn't like a happy ending?

About the Author

George Fleming is more than a former journalist and college writing instructor, more than a holder of two college degrees in English, more than the author of the Tampa Bay Tropics Thriller series, which includes BAD HABITS, DON COYOTE, NEVERMORE and now BONAIRE BLONDE.

Fleming also is a husband, father, grandfather & great grandfather. He & his wife Linda (L. Fleming Esq.) have been married for 45 years. They have two daughters, Margo & Jennifer, three granddaughters, Cloe, Mya & Macy, and, announcing the latest addition to the Fleming family, great grandson Bryson.

www.ingramcontent.com/pod-product-compliance
Lightning Source LLC
Chambersburg PA
CBHW071247300726
48975CB00002B/583